Divided Loyalties was r
indie novels by I

MW00879012

What Reviewers Are Saying

Divided Loyalties: Algiers 1941

Myers adroitly limns not only the perilousness of Algiers in 1941, but also the war as a whole. The author's command of the historical period is simply magisterial—the serpentine politics of a cleaved France is masterfully and vividly depicted.

A **riveting fictionalization** of an all-too-neglected, pivotal moment in Algiers in 1941.
—Kirkus Reviews

Featured in the March 2019 issue of Kirkus Reviews as one of *17 Great Indie Books Worth Discovering.*

Betrayal in Europe: Paris 1938

Explores Parisian politics on the eve of the Second World War…Myers has done his research and impeccably draws the month-to-month social and political situations. An intriguing, historically grounded imagining of behind-the-scenes machinations during a crucial moment in European history.
—Kirkus Reviews

Fast Money and French Ladies

The novel is fast-paced, with an intriguing plot, and Myers demonstrates that a financial story can be a thriller even without a single drawn gun or weapon of mass destruction. An enjoyable novel based on a piece of recent economic history.
—Kirkus Reviews

Greek Bonds and French Ladies

Love and money are both at risk in Myers' politically driven novel of intrigue and betrayal...told with humor and sophistication.
—Kirkus Reviews

A Farewell in Paris

Few places evoke nostalgia like the City of Light in the 1920s, and Myers doesn't skimp on the literary and historical details in his latest novel.
—Kirkus Reviews

In this lively novel, Myers clearly demonstrates his familiarity with the intellectual culture of Paris in the 1920s.
— Publishers Weekly

A Farewell in Paris explores a "lost generation" of American expatriates who converge on Paris after World War I in a maddening search for the meaning of life and love...Myers succeeds in displaying sophisticated and empathetic insight into the period's mindset, an era he captivatingly sketches.
— Blue Ink Review

Paris 1935: Destiny's Crossroads

Takes us into the back rooms of high-level officials, writers, and media stars in order to understand why events happened as they did...involved and intriguing, Myers' work definitely is worth reading.
—Historical Novel Society Online Review

Paris 1934: Victory in Retreat

Descriptive and thoroughly researched narrative feels true to the era; the "City of Light" shines through the page.
—Historical Novel Society Online Review

Vienna 1934: Betrayal at the Ballplatz

Myers' characters feel true to the era...an excellent job of making the story real due to his good research and fine storytelling. The interweaving of fact, fiction, real, and fictional people makes this book exciting and romantic.
—Historical Novel Society Online Review

Divided Loyalties

Algiers 1941—A Novel

Paul A. Myers

Volume 1 of the Fighting France series

Copyright

About the Author

Paul A. Myers has written six historical novels, two satirical novels, and a maritime history about the Spanish discovery of California. He lives with his wife in Corona del Mar, California.

The author on the terrasse at Café Les Deux Magots in Saint-Germain-des-Prés on Paris's Left Bank.

What books influenced me? The atmospheric thrillers of the 1930s and early 40s, the sense of place and feeling captivated me. Histories of the 1930s that capture the terrible uncertainty of events before one knew how it was all going to turn out.

Other influences? An interest in art history, which is the story of how people see themselves through the images and artifacts they create at the time. The art of an era is a mirror of the culture.

Follow author's history blog at https://myersbooks-history.com
Webpage: myersbooks.com.
Email: myersbooks@gmail.com.
Follow on **Facebook** at myersbooks and **Twitter** at @myersbooks

Also by Paul A. Myers

Novels

Betrayal in Europe: Paris 1938
A Farewell in Paris
Paris 1935: Destiny's Crossroads
Paris 1934: Victory in Retreat
Vienna 1934: Betrayal at the Ballplatz
Greek Bonds and French Ladies (a satire)
Fast Money and French Ladies (a satire)

Travel profiles

French Sketches: Cap d'Antibes and the Murphys
French Sketches: Cap Ferrat and Somerset Maugham
French Sketches: Monaco, Onassis, and Prince Rainier

Other

North to California: The Spanish Discovery of California 1533–1603

All titles available in e-book editions.

Contents

Cast of Characters

Fictional

Jacques Dubois—a young investment banker in New York working for international businessman Jean Monnet at the Anglo-French Purchasing Commission buying war munitions for the British and French governments.

Jacqueline Smith—a young journalist working as a researcher for renowned international affairs columnist Anne Hare at the *New York Times Tribune.*

Marie Rambert—a young secretary working for General Maxim Weygand at the French military headquarters in Algiers and wife of a diplomat assigned to the Franco-German Armistice Commission in Wiesbaden, Germany. Daughter of a prominent French colonial family in Algiers.

Elke von Koler—a midthirtyish German news and newsreel foreign correspondent based in Algiers.

L'inspecteur—a Vichy French counterespionage agent spying on German intelligence. L'inspecteur and his chief, le chef, are making their fourth fictional appearance in one of the author's historical novels.

Cosette—a French counterespionage agent working with l'inspecteur.

Hans—a Gestapo bodyguard.

Historical

Robert Murphy—counselor to the American embassy in Vichy and secret personal representative of President Franklin D. Roosevelt in French Africa.

Jean Monnet—French international businessman and head of the Anglo-French Purchasing Commission and later an architect of the US Victory Program that greatly expanded US war production to meet war needs.

Orray Taft, Jr.—a career US consular official in Algiers.

John Knox—a merchandise-control officer and US vice-consul in Algiers.

Joan Tuyl—a British-Dutch national living in Algiers and involved in underground resistance activities.

General Maxim Weygand—a French general who was an architect of the French Armistice with Germany in June 1940 and assigned to Africa as the delegate general (the top civilian and military official) by Maréchal Pétain in October 1940.

Theodor Auer—a German diplomat and chairman of the Italian-German Armistice Commission supervising French colonial possessions in Africa.

André Achiary—a police captain in charge of the political police in Algiers.

Jacques Lemaigre Dubreuil—a French businessman in Africa conspiring to create a breakaway government in North Africa that would rejoin the war on the Allies' side.

Epigraph

The atmosphere over there is not comparable to the confusion in Vichy. If France is going to fight again anywhere in this war, I believe North Africa will be the place.

> –Commander Roscoe Hillenkoetter in an attaché report to the State Department, August 1940. He was the US naval attaché in the American embassy at Vichy, France, and had just completed an inspection tour of North Africa.

These reports were brought to the attention of President Franklin D. Roosevelt by Undersecretary of State Sumner Welles, who reported that Roosevelt read them carefully.

Chapter 1: 1938

Paris. December 1938. Inside the well-chandeliered lobby of the Hotel Crillon, the quiet settled in. A man stood in somber black tie and black suit behind the concierge desk and let his eyes—always watchful—meander around the sumptuous room, empty of guests. They were all at the German embassy for a celebratory reception. The entire hotel was reserved for a German delegation from Berlin accompanying Foreign Minister Joachim von Ribbentrop on his state visit.

The German foreign minister, a former champagne salesman, was taking a personal victory lap for the Munich Pact concluded two months before by the German chancellor, Adolph Hitler. The pact dismembered Czechoslovakia, destroying France's alliance with the countries of eastern Europe. The goal of the alliance had been to box in Germany from the east. Ribbentrop had contributed nothing to the negotiation. Hitler had singlehandedly achieved the humiliation of the prime ministers of Great Britain and France. The foreign minister's superfluous trip was at the *führer's* indulgence.

Tonight, the junketing German delegation was at the embassy reception following a similar gala the night before at the Quai d'Orsay, home of the French foreign ministry. Tonight, the society of Paris—*Tout Paris*—was at the embassy—except various Jews and subversives not invited. The French guests were to remember the champagne as dreadful.

Earlier that day the man at the concierge desk, a French counterespionage agent, had stood at the outer edge of a small crowd and watched the German foreign minister, dressed in his black Nazi uniform with the silver trim, place a wreath at the eternal flame to France's Unknown Soldier. The ceremony was held at the Arc de Triomphe under the gaze of *Maréchal de France* Henri Pétain. The agent had been struck by the Nazi swastika on the black peaked cap. The black Nazi uniform was a startling contrast to the life-giving ideals of the French Republic symbolized by the Arc and its bas-relief sculptures celebrating past sacrifices by the French for a better future for all. A small, sullen crowd of French watched the ceremony. Insulting of course. But then that had been the object of the entire trip. The German führer had been amused to set loose his foreign minister's endless vanity on the now-cowed French.

The French agent looked around the vacant lobby. Soon the Germans would return from the reception, and there would be work to do later in the night. Surreptitious work. Another operative was hidden in a room with concealed cameras next to the suite where a ranking Gestapo diplomat was staying. Two boys from the back alleys of Montmartre were already in the suite. A family-photo night, thought the agent, a somewhat distasteful task in his job as a French counterespionage agent, but often necessary. The most sordid of weaknesses had the greatest leverage.

Across the room the man looked at the attractive blond woman in the dark-blue suit and chaste high-necked white blouse. She was in her late twenties and another operative. Her specialty was getting important men to say unguarded things during her slow-moving, carefully crafted seductions. She was fluent in German. While her fingers and lips removed barriers of prudence, her whisperings encouraged torrents of words to pour forth from unguarded thoughts deep in the minds of men who saw themselves strutting on the parade grounds of their self-importance. Germany in 1938 was like that. The woman knew what the fires of sexual passion did to men. She had learned the art while in her teens up in Montmartre with a succession of voluble French ministers, corruptible men from the revolving door ministries of the never-ending parade of cabinets that rose and fell during the Third Republic.

The man, known in the small elite bureau as *l'inspecteur*, walked across the room and spoke to the woman. "They'll soon be here. Our man is well concealed."

She looked at the clock on the wall and said thoughtfully, "I have a rendezvous in about an hour. At the other end of the hotel."

"High up in the foreign ministry?" the intelligence agent asked.

"No, Hervé. They know nothing at the Wilhelmstrasse," she said dismissively, mentioning the name of the headquarters of the German foreign ministry.

L'inspecteur took this in. His boss, *le chef*, had said Cosette knew the true power structure at the top of the Reich like the back of her hand, where the real influence was, and more importantly what it liked—deep down amid its darkest desires. And le chef had a nose for these things.

"Then where?"

"The Reich chancellery."

"Close to the top?"

"Very."

"I'll see you later."

"Yes."

The agent walked back to concierge station. He always had to contain a strangling sense of physical jealousy whenever Cosette left for an assignation. He was more than a secret admirer. He wondered if someday somewhere…possibly with her. He hoped it didn't cloud his professional judgment since distance is the first prerequisite of objectivity. He knew all that. Nevertheless, she was under his skin…

The doors opened and a rush of formally attired gentlemen in warm top coats, accompanied by women in lush evening dresses flowing out below the hems of thick fur coats, swept into the lobby chattering away in German. The agent's eyes were drawn to the slender blonde in the white silk evening gown and matching white fur coat, the famous German correspondent and newsreel personality Elke von Koler. This morning, he had watched her carefully film the laying of the wreath at the Arc de Triomphe, her still photographers and newsreel cameramen capturing the event for worldwide distribution. She was rumored to be close to Joseph Goebbels, the powerful German propaganda minister. He presumed the man with her was her husband, Gerhard von Koler, a high legal official in the foreign ministry. But where Koler was a transparent and glittering star, tonight's film agenda centered on the unseemly doings by a certain member from the German secret service operating in Paris under diplomatic cover.

Hervé watched as Cosette slipped away from the reception desk and mingled with the crowd of Germans. She took up station behind one gentleman in a dinner jacket, noticeable for its lack of medals, and followed him and several others into one of the elevators. She was smooth. Experienced. She had picked out the jewel with the sparkling inside knowledge from among the flock of strutting peacocks.

His eyes swept the remainder of the crowd, and he saw the German diplomat who was the target of tonight's surveillance heading for another elevator. The *bureau* had run into him during its surveillance of certain officials with the German embassy and their interactions with the archbishopric of Paris. Initially, the bureau thought it was monitoring a simple influence-buying scheme, but it had then found itself on the trail of a sordid sex scandal. L'inspecteur sighed at the memory and went into the inner office to catch some sleep.

Hours later, around dawn, l'inspecteur was awoken in the concierge office by a coworker, and he came out to take another shift. He looked across the room and saw the blond woman speaking with some other people at reception. She was back. She looked across the room, caught his eye, and made the slightest of nods. She started walking toward the doors; he came up and whispered to her. "Good information?" he asked.

"Yes. They'll take the rest of Czechoslovakia in the early spring, and then some sort of diplomatic initiative in the east to isolate Poland over the summer. Then an ultimatum on Danzig. These are new developments," she said, paused, and then continued, "of old fears."

Hervé noticed a hesitancy in Cosette's manner. "Anything else?"

She lifted her eyes upward. "There's something creepy here. The Germans…their security…I don't know."

A warning signal went off in his mind, and he mumbled, "I'll check in later."

"Be careful," she said.

He was struck by her concern. She turned and departed. He watched her go, those long legs moving her toward the door, the hips swaying ever so gently. Always understated, he thought. To devastating effect.

L'inspecteur returned to the concierge station and gazed out over the empty lobby. He looked at his watch; he'd meet Etienne upstairs in a maid's station in half an hour and get the film.

A few moments later, a French policeman, a *flic*, came through the front doors and walked up to the desk, his dark cape damp with snowflakes, his kepi completing the distinctive profile. "I believe you're the agent I am supposed to inform?"

"Inform?"

"Yes."

"What about?"

"Around back, monsieur. You better follow me." The policeman turned and started walking for the door. L'inspecteur followed. Outside they walked to the far side of the hotel and then down a small alleyway toward the rear behind the service areas.

"Here," said the policeman pointing down to a body near the trash cans. He lifted the body on its side to show the bloodstain on the chest and stomach. A knife wound up under the ribcage. Then he lowered the body back down the way he found it.

L'inspecteur looked around the crime scene but suspected there was nothing to be found. He said to the policeman, "Take the body to the police morgue. Let's keep this quiet. No one in authority will want to disturb the state visit. Write your report. I'll go tell le chef."

L'inspecteur walked back to the hotel lobby. Cosette had been one floor down. She had sensed the intrigue. With the Germans, the game was now deadly. He would not forget. Etienne had been his friend.

Chapter 2: 1940

May 15, 1940, New York. Jacques Dubois sat in his cramped office at the Anglo-French Purchasing Commission in Rockefeller Center as a secretary walked in and handed him a telegram. He opened it and read:

LONDON. SURPRISING GERMAN BREAKTHROUGH IN ARDENNES REGION IS SPLITTING THE BRITISH AND NORTHERN FRENCH ARMIES AWAY FROM MAIN FRENCH ARMY. BE PREPARED TO REROUTE WAR MATERIALS TO BRITISH PORTS. MONNET.

Jean Monnet was the French head of the commission and was shuttling between Paris and London coordinating the delivery of munitions to the two allied countries. He set the telegram aside and reached for a second message that had also just been delivered by messenger. He opened it and read:

Jacques. Anne is sending me to cover the Wilkie campaign and feed gossip and tidbits back to her from the campaign trail. See you in New York third week of June. Love, Jacqueline

Jacqueline Smith was his latest girlfriend, an American with a French mother and American father, just the opposite of his own cover story, which was a French father and an American mother. Anne worked as a researcher for renowned world-affairs columnist Anne Hare on the mighty *New York Times Tribune*. The redoubtable Miss Hare had asked Jacqueline in her job interview how many languages she spoke and Jacqueline had replied French, some German, and of course English. Miss Hare replied that was three more than the other applicants she had interviewed that morning and she got the job. Jacques laughed at the recollection.

Jacques sympathized with Jacqueline's inner belief that the coming war and America's potential involvement would catapult her into the ranks of foreign correspondents, her deeply held dream since working on the campus paper at Wellesley.

For himself, Jacques was just hoping that the coming war would eventually catapult him out of the dreary business of shepherding purchasing orders across the now-mobilizing American war economy. He would look forward to seeing Jacqueline in June. Spending a night with her was always a blazingly intense journey through youthful passion. To think of losing those American girlhood inhibitions while going to school in Boston! Maybe there was more to those Harvard guys than he thought. He smiled to himself.

Beirut, French Syria

May 17, 1940. The message from the prime minister recalling the general to Paris arrived in Beirut in French Syria in the morning. No reason for the recall was given. News reports about the German offensive in Belgium and northern France were ominous, but vague. The massive German armor, parachute, and infantry assault had begun the week before on May 10. Heeding the message from Paris, the general and his aide left for the aerodrome.

The general assumed that the French supreme commander had not been keeping him fully and accurately informed. The two generals were bitter rivals. Over the past week, the unwarranted optimism in the supreme commander's official reports forwarded to the general from Paris had contrasted with the dark tidings of the daily news reports in the papers and the ominous communiqués echoing out from the wireless.

Arriving near Paris, the bomber aircraft in which the two officers were riding set down on the runway. Suddenly, the undercarriage collapsed, and the plane spun around in an impromptu crash landing, sparks flying amid the screech of twisting metal. Possibly an ill omen. The general and his aide, shaken but undeterred, managed to pry and worm their way out through the wrecked fuselage. A waiting car sped them to the Hôtel Matignon, the seat of the French prime minister and head of government. The limousine was waved through the entrance gates and into the courtyard; the general alighted from the rear seat into the courtyard before twenty newsreel cameras.

The cameras saw a small, wiry man in his early seventies with high cheekbones and deep-set eyes that were never melancholy. Nervous energy seemed to vibrate off him. He bounded up the steps three at a time. Inside an usher guided him through thronging officials and army officers crowding the corridor to the office of the prime minister. The general was shown into the prime minister's office.

"General Weygand, I'm relieved that you are here," said the prime minister, Paul Reynaud. The prime minister was a small bantam rooster of a man, known to be peppery and quick. Now he was a nervous man caught up in a whirlpool of events as the French military situation collapsed by the hour under the relentless pounding of the German military offensive, an offensive of such power as to shock and stun the French army from top to bottom. The civilian government was taken aback by the rush of events, shaken by a growing lack of confidence in generals who could not master the crisis.

The prime minister had recalled Weygand from Beirut, heeding the famous dictum of Marshal Foch, the architect of the victory in 1918 over Germany. On his deathbed, the marshal had gasped, "If France should be in danger, call Weygand." Weygand had been Foch's chief of staff in those momentous months of 1918 when Germany was ground down and defeated. Reynaud acted on the famous dictum.

"Please go and visit General Gamelin at the supreme headquarters and General Georges at his army command post. Then the air-force headquarters. Report back to me this evening," said the prime minister. General Maurice Gamelin was the overall supreme Allied commander and French commander in chief. General Georges was the commander of the critically important northeastern sector of France, a region now under intense assault from fast-moving German spearheads.

"*Oui, Monsieur le Premier,*" replied the general. The two men spoke for several minutes and then the general and his aide departed. Outside a staff car awaited to take the two officers to the three headquarters on the itinerary. All the headquarters were within a short drive of Paris.

Arriving at General Gamelin's headquarters at Vincennes on the eastern outskirts of Paris, Weygand found Gamelin deeply discouraged by a flood of adverse events he neither foresaw nor understood. Weygand sat through a briefing, observing that Gamelin's discouragement had infected his staff.

The Germans had broken through in the Ardennes region rather than repeating the giant wheeling movement through Belgium that had characterized the opening weeks of World War I. Then, rather than wheeling their forces south toward Paris, the Germans drove west toward the French Channel coast, driving the British Expeditionary Force and the best divisions of the French northern army north toward the Channel coast. A brand-new strategy for a brand-new war. The Germans had completely split the allied force in two.

Weygand could see that Gamelin had never been able to adjust his thinking to the war that was now spreading across his maps like a stain. The war on the map was simply a different war from the one he had imagined he would fight. The war was not supposed to proceed that way. Weygand could see that Gamelin's mind was trapped and now defeated by its own preconceptions.

The next stop for Weygand and his aide, Captain Gasser, was the drive to Coulonniers east of Paris and the air-force headquarters of General Joseph Vuillermin. Weygand listened as staff officers explained that the Germans had 4,200 combat aircraft compared to 1,400 French and 416 British planes. Surprisingly, neither the French nor the British had any dive-bomber aircraft. The Germans had them in abundance and had sharpened their tactics and operation since the Polish campaign the year before, a lightning campaign that transfixed world audiences watching the newsreels with screaming Stuka dive bombers hitting targets in front of fast-moving tanks. Over the winter, the Germans had further improved the close coordination by radio of dive bombers and tanks, which gave the Germans a one-two punch at the front of their spearheads that devastated all before them. The French found that their forces could not stand their ground against the storm of a combined German air-tank attack. Weygand listened carefully, grasping that airplanes had become the decisive weapon. It wasn't theoretical anymore.

"And the new aircraft from America?" asked Weygand.

"Several hundred are on ships ready to sail for France," responded General Vuillermin. "But the battle will be over before the planes can be assembled and flown."

Weygand nodded in understanding. He recalled that then Premier Edouard Daladier had said in 1938 that if he had three thousand aircraft, there would have been no Munich. Shortly thereafter French businessman Jean Monnet had been dispatched to America to arrange for a massive purchase of aircraft. Monnet, meeting with President Franklin D. Roosevelt, had arranged for the purchase of a thousand planes by the end of 1938 for delivery in 1940. An additional order for a thousand planes was arranged in 1939. But factories had to be built and planes produced. The war had come too soon.

Weygand also recalled Daladier's impatience with Reynaud, then the finance minister, and Reynaud's shortsighted lack of cooperation on financing the aircraft purchase. Monnet, who had grasped the central fact of modern-war finance—you order the war material and figure out to pay for it later—had creatively worked around the wooden-headedness of Paris by structuring with the Americans an unprecedented and innovative financial maneuver, the pledging of French colonies in the Caribbean as collateral for the required war loans.

Weygand and Captain Gasser next drove to General Georges's headquarters and received more specific information about the westward drive of the German spearheads that had split the British-French front in northeastern France. The French and British divisions were being driven back on to Channel coast near the French-Belgium border at Dunkirk. South of the salient, the approaches to Paris from the north would soon be vulnerable once German units had defeated the British and French units crowded along the western Channel coast.

With evening approaching, Weygand and Gasser returned to Paris to meet with Prime Minister Reynaud. In the premier's office, they were surprised to find Henri Pétain, the last surviving Maréchal from World War I. Reynaud had just recalled Pétain in mid-May from his post as ambassador to Spain and had appointed him deputy prime minister to shore up his authority. After a brief discussion, Reynaud and Pétain offered the supreme command to Weygand, who accepted out of a deep sense of duty.

"Yes, I will assume the responsibility," said Weygand, "but do not be surprised if I am unable to deliver victory."

Reynaud and Pétain nodded in acknowledgment. Events were dire.

"There is a service of national prayer at Notre Dame. Would you please join us in attendance?" asked Reynaud.

"Yes," replied Weygand, a deeply religious Catholic. But Weygand was not praying for deliverance but rather for the spiritual resolve he felt he was sure to need to face the hard decisions ahead.

In the coming days, Weygand attempted to organize a counterattack on the German salient with pincer attacks from the north and from the south. In a meeting with Reynaud and Pétain, and joined by recently appointed British Prime Minister Winston Churchill, Weygand's plan was enthusiastically supported. Churchill promised full Royal Air Force support, a crucial step to counter the German advantage in the air.

But during the days of May 23 and 24, the pincer attacks on the German salient bogged down due to lack of mobility and strength. Weygand observed that the Royal Air Force had withdrawn its fighters to fields in the south of England, only launching fighter sweeps across the Channel to France. Most of the planes' fuel was consumed traveling, not fighting. Weygand also observed that for this war the British expeditionary forces only totaled nine divisions, a far cry from the sixty divisions the British had fielded on the Western Front in 1918. The British commitment simply was not there; the winter months of stalemate had been wasted, concluded Weygand sadly.

At a meeting of the War Council in Paris on the evening of May 25, Weygand reported on the retreat of British and French forces to Dunkirk and the evacuation of forces to England. Weygand described Dunkirk as a catastrophe averted. In his mind, other catastrophes now lurked in the future.

Thinking ahead, Weygand for the first time broached to the council the possibility that an armistice might become necessary. Reynaud's reaction was to fight on. Weygand also posed the question about what would happen if social disorder overtook the country, leading to a communist uprising in Paris. Might the complete destruction of the French army become possible? The collapse of the French state would follow. France would lay unprotected from pillage and ravishment.

A Not-So-Slow Defeat

Over the next several days, as May turned into June, Weygand tried to organize defenses along the approaches to Paris, but an absence of reserves led to French forces having to withdraw under pressure of German assault. One June 8, a tactical blunder by the French army on the Channel coast led to the Germans further dividing the force and compelling the surrender of British and French forces at several Channel ports.

In Paris, Reynaud appointed Charles de Gaulle to undersecretary of defense in the cabinet; Reynaud personally held the defense portfolio. De Gaulle had only recently been promoted to *général de brigade*, a two-star rank in the French army. The young general brought fresh ideas about resistance to the policy debate including the idea of forging a strategic redoubt on the Brittany peninsula. De Gaulle also agitated *sub rosa* for the appointment of another general to succeed Weygand.

With intrigue in his rear, Weygand at his headquarters tried to organize a strategic defense across central France, but no line could be made to hold. Effective defense was now beyond the capability of his forces. Weygand exclaimed to his staff, "Our last line of defense has fallen. The Battle for France is lost. Let the general retreat commence. I will go and ask the government to conclude an armistice."

As the army retreated, the government made plans to abandon Paris for Bordeaux with a halfway stop at Tours.

Weygand now formally broached the issue of asking for an armistice with the Supreme War Council at its meeting of June 13 at Tours. Weygand wanted to avoid a Dutch-style capitulation that would mean total surrender and collapse and, significantly, allow the Germans to go anywhere including North Africa. In contrast, an armistice would be a negotiated cease-fire leaving armies intact and in place. Millions of French soldiers might avoid prison camp.

In the ensuing days, there were members of the government, including Reynaud, who seemed to favor a capitulation by the army while the government abandoned the metropole for North Africa to fight on. But defeat and capitulation were two entirely separate states in Weygand's mind; one might be inevitable, but the other was always a choice that could be avoided.

In contrast, Reynaud talked about a Dutch-style government in exile after a capitulation. Weygand sharply retorted that three years in safety and comfort was a rather different fate from that of the soldiers who would be left behind in prison camp as a result of such a capitulation. Other members of the government increasingly seemed to support Weygand, stating that he was bravely facing facts. Weygand refused to consider leaving France, refused to preside over a capitulation, and refused to resign. He stormed out of the cabinet meeting and returned to general headquarters, now on the Loire River.

Outside the cabinet meeting, the general ran into former Prime Minister Pierre Laval, who was scheming his way back into power as the French government collapsed. Weygand snapped, "You wallow in defeat like a dog in filth."

But the government had collapsed because the army had buckled. In the cabinet meeting, Pétain now moved into the debate, arguing strongly for an armistice and for the government to remain in France. The eighty-four-year-old Maréchal walked over to a nearby window to capture the afternoon light and read his handwritten statement:

> *It is impossible for the government to emigrate, to desert, to abandon the territory of France. The duty of the government is to remain in the country. To deprive France of its natural defenders is to deliver it to the enemy.*
>
> *The renewal of France can only be obtained eventually by remaining where we are rather than by depending on a reconquest of our territory by Allied guns...*
>
> *I am against abandoning French soil. We must accept the sufferings that will be imposed on the country and on its sons...I shall refuse to leave the metropole. I shall rest among the French people to share its pains and miseries.*

The armistice is the necessary condition for the perpetuity of an eternal France.

The Maréchal returned to his chair and sat down. The cabinet now understood that it was past time when military action could alter the onrush of events.

Weygand's vehemence—he was always stiff backed in his rectitude—was driven by disgust for the corrupt lifestyle and promiscuous sexual behavior of many of the government ministers with their entourages and mistresses. At the apex of this emotion was Weygand's contempt for the comtesse de Portès, the malignly defeatist mistress of Reynaud. It was as if all the rottenness of the Third Republic were crowded into the caravan of vehicles taking the government on its path down the refugee-clogged roads toward Bordeaux.

Reaching the riverfront city, Pétain felt the issue of an armistice was coming to a head, and he called for Weygand to meet him in Bordeaux. The Maréchal explained that the council of ministers had delayed the decision on asking for an armistice until there was a response from President Roosevelt to Reynaud's telegram setting forth the dire circumstances of imminent defeat. A response was pending. Weygand reached the city from his headquarters at Briare located on the Loire River, the current front line of French resistance, on June 15 after a sixteen-hour train journey.

Paris—Rue de Miromesnil

Several blocks behind the ministry of the interior, in a small office on the top floor toward the rear of the deserted building, l'inspecteur entered the now-empty counterespionage office and found le chef standing by his desk. Two suitcases sat on the floor, large belts securely strapping the bulging contents inside. There was a perilous journey ahead.

"Where did all the files go?" asked l'inspecteur.

"They're on a barge on the river with the other ministry and police files. They're to be hidden in the south of France," said le chef.

"And these?" asked l'inspecteur nodding at the suitcases.

"The most sensitive files. They're going to Marseilles with us. Vivienne is already there."

"I have the big Citroën waiting downstairs. Extra petrol in the trunk."

"Good. We can get more in Lyon."

The men picked up the suitcases and walked out of the office and down the hallway to the elevator. Outside they came up to the long black Citroën coupe, its rear springs sagging under the weight of the petrol. They placed the suitcases in the backseat with some personal valises. They got in, and l'inspecteur pulled the heavily laden vehicle out onto the vacant boulevard. They motored through the deserted streets of Paris, past shuttered buildings.

"The traffic jams will start just south of Paris," said l'inspecteur.

"Yes, they're all flocking south. But they will eventually have to return."

"It will mean living under occupation."

"Yes, and that will be a hard boot," said le chef. "I'll relieve you in a few hours. We'll drive all night."

"Understand," said l'inspecteur.

Paris—the Diplomat

Saturday, June 15. In a cold, driving rain, Robert Murphy, the senior counselor at the American embassy, stood at the iron gates of the majestic building facing Avenue Gabriel, the broad tree-lined thoroughfare running in front of the embassy. The diplomat was accompanied by the naval attaché, Commander Roscoe Hillenkoetter, and the military attaché, Colonel Horace Fuller. Rain rolled off their umbrellas. They watched the sad drama unfold before their eyes.

Under German guard, French prisoners of war trudged by in dirty and worn uniforms, faces unshaven, eyes sunken in faces strained with fatigue. Many of the men carried long loaves of rain-soaked bread, meager sustenance in the despair of defeat.

As they shuffled along, some of the prisoners looked across the high stone fence to the American flag flying from the top of the building. With disgust they said to one another, "There, look at the American flag," a bitter rejoinder against the once-revered symbol of the ally who had not come to France's aid in its hour of need. "Worse than the Tommies," one remarked of the now-departed British? Had the British really made an effort? Many wondered.

Other prisoners looked with disgust at Murphy and the attachés. "Look at the Americans...they look well fed...why the hell didn't they help us?"

The question floated in the drizzle of the rain-sodden day as the German army, oh so correctly, established its grip on the defeated French capital.

Chapter 3: London

Saturday night, June 15, 1940. The tall French general with the awkward but imposing manner knocked on the white enameled door of the fashionable Mayfair apartment hard by St. James's Park. A maid in black dress and white apron opened the door and ushered the general and his aide-de-camp into the foyer. *"Bonjour, mon général,"* said the maid in her native French. "Madame is in the drawing room." The general removed his white gloves and the kepi with the two stars of a French brigadier general and handed them to the maid as did the general's aide, an army lieutenant.

"Merci, mademoiselle," said the polite general. He walked into the drawing room and held out both of his hands in warm greeting. "Madame Monnet, so pleased to see you. My aide, Lieutenant de Courcel."

"Pleased to meet you," said the woman as she shook the aide's hand. She turned to the general. "Jean will be along shortly."

The general stepped back and made a slow sweeping gaze around the drawing room taking in the vivid paintings on the walls, clearly French in their color and originality. "Impressive, madam. Like being in the best of the Parisian drawing rooms."

"Thank you, mon general." She took a seat, and the general and his aide seated themselves in the stiff-backed Louis Seizième chairs just across. "And how long do you think your mission to London will last, mon général."

"I am not here on a mission, Madame. I am here to save the honor of France."

Just then the door opened, and Jean Monnet walked in, a man of about fifty with thinning gray hair, a small moustache, and wearing a Saville Row suit. Accompanying him was his aide. He came into the room, and the general stood. "General de Gaulle, so nice to see you again," said Monnet. "You know my aide, René Pleven, I believe."

De Gaulle shook Pleven's hand as did Courcel. "Yes, a man of numbers," said the general. "Numbers are crucial in war; they get extinguished so fast."

Monnet nodded at the insight and continued, "We have much to talk about." Monnet was the chairman of the joint Anglo-French Coordinating Committee tasked with the joint management of purchases for the French and British war economies. The immediate task of the commission was the urgent need to purchase aircraft engines and aircraft.

Monnet had held a similar position in the First World War at a remarkably young age, proof of his unique abilities to combine long-range vision with pragmatic business practices. He broadened his wartime experience into a highly successful international business career between the wars. Years before, his family had been a major producer of cognac in France, and he had established a worldwide distribution network for the business in the years leading up to the First World War.

"Yes, we do," said the general.

"It's late. Let's go in and have dinner," said Monnet as he led his wife and guests into a dining room with a large table able to accommodate a dozen or so guests. The Monnets entertained frequently. Monnet seated his wife and then de Gaulle, and his aide took a seat as did Monnet and Pleven.

"You are here to organize the transportation of the government to North Africa to continue the fight?" said Monnet, making the question a statement. Keeping France in the fight was the overarching goal for Monnet.

"Yes, ostensibly so," said de Gaulle.

"Ostensibly?"

"Yes, I am of course pursuing that, but I fear the cabinet is being swamped in defeatism and will seek an armistice. If so, I shall stay in London and organize a resistance."

"That may be premature, General. Getting the current government to move to North Africa and organize the empire for resistance seems to be the immediate course," said Monnet with clear insistence. Keeping the French Empire in the fight was a crucial goal from the vantage point of London.

"Yes, that is true. Reynaud asked me yesterday to rejoin him in Algiers. But I have just come from Bordeaux, and the defeatism in the cabinet threatens to swamp Reynaud," said the general. Prime Minister Paul Reynaud was beset by defeatist voices led by Pétain, who was urging the cabinet to ask the Germans for an armistice.

"Why the pessimism?"

"First, I was not able to convince Reynaud of the need to replace General Weygand with a general who would fight."

"Weygand supports Pétain?" asked Monnet. He understood that Pétain wanted the government to surrender to the Germans via an armistice, not just surrender the armies in the field as the Dutch had done. That Weygand also supported an armistice was news to Monnet. Under the Pétain position, the government would stay in France, not leave for North Africa—and for sure never move to London and set up a government-in-exile.

"Completely. I failed in my mission as undersecretary of defense to rally the defense behind a general who would continue the fight." De Gaulle looked down at the tabletop, a rare display of discouragement by the proud general. He was a junior minister in the cabinet, second only to Reynaud in the defense ministry, a position far above his brigadier general's rank.

"And where is Weygand now?"

"Weygand has left in his private train for Vichy, the site of his newest headquarters," said de Gaulle with scorn in his voice.

"He will not be present to dominate the cabinet then?" asked Monnet, seeing an opening.

"He dominates Pétain. That is enough," said the general. "Mandel talked me out of resigning." Georges Mandel was the powerful and capable minister of the interior, a former aide to Georges Clemenceau, the famed Tiger who led France to its bitter victory in World War I. "He said it was not yet final that the government had decided against leaving for Algiers."

"Mandel is right. The issue is still open," said Monnet. "We have more cards to play."

De Gaulle looked sharply at Monnet, his interest peaked. "A card or a conjurer's trick?"

"A joint Anglo-French Unity Plan," said Monnet. "It was presented to the British prime minister this afternoon. It will be taken up by the cabinet tomorrow afternoon."

"A unity plan?"

"A merging of the sovereignties of the two countries. One cabinet, one parliament, one army, a total unity of resources and determination."

"The sweep of your plan has true grandeur," said the general thoughtfully. "A convincing manifestation of solidarity."

"We need one of Reynaud's ministers to present it to him in Bordeaux with clarity and force."

"Yes, it would give the premier confidence at the point of supreme crisis, an argument for tenacity."

"Will you help?"

"In any way I can," said the general firmly.

"Good. Tomorrow I'm meeting with Sir Robert Vansittart at the Foreign Office for a final polishing of the text. Could you join us?"

"Of course."

"Afterward, I believe, you will luncheon with Churchill at the Carlton Club. Then we'll all meet at Downing Street just prior to the cabinet meeting."

"Yes, I see. A serious effort."

"After cabinet approval, I believe you will be asked to telephone Reynaud in Bordeaux and give him the text."

"It will take more than my voice."

"Churchill will then speak on the telephone line."

"What then?"

"The British will fly you to Bordeaux immediately after, and you can meet General Spears and Ambassador Campbell. They will work with you to stiffen Reynaud's presentation to the French cabinet."

"It might work," said de Gaulle, deeply moved by the daring and commitment of the British effort conceived and pushed by Monnet. The French cabinet was closely divided; this show of political resolve might prove decisive.

The group continued talking about the situation in France during the meal. De Gaulle mentioned that as undersecretary of defense he had just diverted a large arms shipment to a British port for safe delivery.

"Yes, that is necessary," said Monnet. "Tomorrow I'm sending a telegram to Jacques, my assistant in New York, to tell him to start arranging the transfer of the aircraft orders to the British government."

"Strategically sound," said de Gaulle.

"We can't afford to lose the production capacity by canceling orders. The buildup of future industrial capacity is critical to eventual victory. Those orders will lead to something much bigger," said Monnet. "An American commitment to Germany's defeat."

De Gaulle, a successful armored general, nodded. Tanks without airplanes were like a one-armed man. The guests continued chatting during dinner, the surprising turn of events in the war dominating the conversation.

Bordeaux, Sunday, June 16

The British ambassador, Sir Ronald Campbell, and the British military liaison to the French government, Major General Edward Spears, walked in the twilight of Sunday evening to the entrance of the Quartier General on Rue Vital-Carles where the French government had set up its most recent headquarters.

"What do you think the French will do?" asked Campbell.

"I don't know," said Spears. "The telegram from Roosevelt this morning making it clear that the Americans are not going to intervene in France snuffed out Reynaud's last hope."

"The French are down to their own resources then?" asked Campbell.

"Yes. I'm afraid British assurances have run out of currency," replied Spears.

"That means the chances of the French going to North Africa to carry on the war are looking slim," said the ambassador.

"I'm afraid so," said Spears.

"Nevertheless, we must urge continued resistance," said the ambassador with renewed resolve. He understood his instructions.

The two British diplomats had been waiting at their hotel to be called to the French cabinet meeting to receive the results. The meeting had begun at five in the afternoon to discuss the issue: would the French cabinet accept the British proposal for a pooling of sovereignties, a necessary step to carry on the war from North Africa? By six-thirty, Spears had grown increasingly worried about the outcome. It was now seven as the two men walked up the street to the majestic government building.

Inside the marble building, Prime Minister Reynaud's *chef de cabinet,* Roland de Margerie, hurried up to greet them. "He is going to tell you that he is going to resign and that Maréchal Pétain will be called to form a new government."

"What's that, what did you say?" exclaimed Spears, taken aback by the sudden news and seeing the goal of continued resistance slip from the realm of possibility.

"The president of the council is going to tell you he is going to resign," said Margerie coldly.

"What about the British proposal to pool sovereignties?" asked the ambassador.

"The word circulating among the cabinet is that Pétain has said it would put France in a state of vassalage, like a British overseas dominion," explained the French official.

"And the military? Can it not fight on from North Africa?" asked the general.

"To what purpose? Weygand told the cabinet that in three weeks' time England will have its neck wrung like a chicken."

Spears gulped. Defeatism was winning the day.

"Here you go," said the chef de cabinet as he opened a door to an office. The men went inside and met Reynaud. Spears observed that Reynaud seemed immensely relieved to be freed from his frightening responsibilities as he recounted the details of the cabinet meeting.

The ambassador forcefully advanced his position to Reynaud: "You must postpone this irretrievable step until there has been time to consider all its implications." The ambassador and the general presented arguments to the premier for half an hour. Finally, the ambassador concluded: "Take some rest; speak with your colleagues. The cabinet must have time to consider its implications. We'll return at ten."

The two British officials stood up and shook hands with Reynaud. Both men left to meet various contacts in the confused halls of power in Bordeaux. They agreed to meet later for dinner.

Dinner

22

Campbell and Spears sat at a large round table in the center of the world-renowned restaurant Chapon Fin in the center of Bordeaux. Around them at their table was a rotating mix of harassed employees taking a break from the chaos of their duties in the crowded hotel rooms that now served as the British embassy.

"I spoke with Darlan's chief of staff," said Spears to Campbell. "I met him on the street just now, and he assures me the admiral has no intention of letting the fleet fall into the enemy's hands." Darlan was the commander in chief of the French navy.

"Yes, Darlan," said the ambassador. The question of the French fleet falling into the hands of the Germans was of life-or-death concern to the British war cabinet. Vital sea-lanes in the Mediterranean and the South Atlantic would be cut. Britain would starve. The ambassador got to the nub of the argument: "But would he be prepared to sail the fleet to British or neutral ports in case of a capitulation to Germany?"

"Darlan says that he did not create a fleet to offer it to the British," said Spears repeating the words of the chief of staff.

"But if the Germans insist on its surrender as a condition of an armistice?" asked the ambassador, getting at the essential point.

"Hard to tell," answered Spears equivocally.

"Well, what would he do as commander in chief. Scuttle or surrender?" asked the ambassador.

"If the new government orders its surrender…" Spears let the question hang in the air. Would the Pétain government trade the fleet for an armistice? Such a trade could condemn Britain to defeat.

"A paramount issue for sure," said the ambassador, "but the most important issue tonight is to get the French government to go to North Africa and stay in the war."

"Yes," said Spears. "That would keep the French fleet out of Germany's hands." He looked across the dining room and scowled. He nodded toward Pierre Laval, the former prime minister, and archenemy of the British. "The rumor is he wants to negotiate an alliance with Germany, not just an armistice."

"Yes," said the ambassador, adding with undiplomatic scorn. "He's picking his winner early." A mixture of disdain and disgust colored the ambassador's face as he looked at Laval, a man around whom swirled many dark conspiracies. "Indeed," pronounced the ambassador, "dark, bloated, and satisfied."

"The worst of the *capitulards*," added the general, mentioning the most craven advocates of capitulation.

Campbell looked back at the Spears. Time was getting near. "Well, it's just on ten o'clock." The two men stood and walked out of the restaurant back toward the Rue Vital-Carles and the waiting premier.

Final Meeting

Entering the Quartier General, the ambassador started walking toward the small office where they had previously spoken with Reynaud. Spears went looking for an aide. Suddenly, walking past one of the large stone columns, the general was startled by a surprising presence, a tall figure flat against the wall shrouded in shadow. It was General de Gaulle, who loudly whispered, "I must speak to you."

Spears walked over. "I can't now. The ambassador and I are meeting with Reynaud."

"It is extremely urgent. I have good reason to believe Weygand intends arresting me."

"I believe you," said Spears. He had heard rumors that Weygand was threatening the arrest of any cabinet members who opposed the government's plan to ask for an armistice. "But I must go now. Wait right here, and I'll be back shortly." Spears turned and headed toward the small office where the ambassador stood waiting. The two men went inside.

Reynaud stood and greeted the men. "The president of the Republic has asked Maréchal Pétain to form a government. The Maréchal had a list of his cabinet in his pocket when the request was made." The president of the Republic, Albert Lebrun, was the head of state; the premier was head of government. Reynaud started to describe the cabinet to the two British diplomats.

"Defeatists," said the ambassador dryly after a few names were spoken.

"Baudouin as foreign minister," added the general disappointedly. "So Italy has not made a bad investment." A long-heard rumor in Paris political circles was that Baudouin had been on Mussolini's payroll during the 1930s.

"And the defense ministries," asked the ambassador. Reynaud replied with the names.

"Weygand to be minister of defense?" asked Spears with astonishment on his face as he ground his teeth at the thought.

"Weygand buttonholes the defeatist ministers and says that the Nazis will defeat Britain next," said Reynaud. "He says in three weeks' time, England will have its neck wrung like a chicken."

The ambassador looked at Reynaud with a shocked expression at so blunt a prophecy. Spears observed this was the second occurrence of the wrung-chicken-neck quote; the metaphor was obviously gaining currency.

"There will be no allies to continue the war he assures them," said Reynaud. "Further resistance would be futile goes the defeatists' argument."

"The navy?" asked the ambassador, regaining his composure and getting to the core issue in his brief.

"Minister of marine goes to Admiral Darlan," said Reynaud.

"He would have to abide by any decision made by the cabinet to surrender the fleet in an armistice negotiation," said the ambassador, immediately summarizing the strategic peril to the British government.

"Or resign," added Spears, seeing the futility of this option as soon as he said it.

"I trust the admiral will settle the matter of the fleet to your government's satisfaction," said Reynaud in a voice falling away into vagueness, his eyes vacant.

The general looked at the deposed premier, and he saw that lassitude had overcome his mind as it sought escape from the pounding stresses of the past several days. Spears felt Reynaud was drifting off into a state of unreality, a spent force.

The ambassador nodded at the general signaling it was time to leave. The two men stood and shook hands with the broken Reynaud and departed.

Outside, Spears walked over to where he had left de Gaulle, who stepped forward. The ambassador joined them.

"Weygand plans to have me arrested. I must depart," said de Gaulle, furtively looking about him.

"I agree. We can't talk here," said Spears. "Can you meet us at the Hôtel Montré?"

"Yes. I'll get there shortly," said de Gaulle.

The two British officials walked out of the front gate; de Gaulle slipped out of a side entrance.

The two British diplomats returned to the ambassador's room at the hotel. De Gaulle joined them shortly.

"I must return to England," said de Gaulle. "The fate of the French Empire is at stake."

"The course of the new government has not been set," said the ambassador, making a glance around signifying all the confusion besetting Bordeaux. "Maybe it's premature?"

"It will be tomorrow morning," said the French general. "There is no one in France who can rally the government now that Pétain and the defeatists have taken over. With Reynaud gone, the Republic is threatened with demise."

"How about Mandel and some of the other ministers?" asked Spears. "They are to depart on the cruiser *Massiglia* for North Africa. To continue the fight."

"They have been outmaneuvered," said de Gaulle. "That was bait to buy time for the defeatists to complete their coup."

"Yes," said the ambassador, seeing the correctness of de Gaulle's remark. He nodded for de Gaulle to continue.

"The call for continued resistance must be made at once before an appeal for armistice can be made from Bordeaux," said de Gaulle, forcefully making his point.

The ambassador nodded in agreement.

"Time is of the essence," said de Gaulle to drive home the point. The ambassador grasped the point.

"If North Africa and the French Empire are to be saved," said de Gaulle, "this can only be done from England. A challenge to the defeatists can be sent out from London that will be certain to be heeded."

The ambassador nodded. For sure, such a call would be heard and repeated. Heeded? Not so sure.

"I will give that call myself," said de Gaulle. "I will ask all those who will resist to join me."

"Yes, an instant retort to Pétain's appeal for an armistice," said Spears. He liked the action implicit in de Gaulle's plan, which was appealing to Spears after days of lack of action and the nerve-wracking indecision of the French cabinet as it retreated across France.

De Gaulle nodded, relieved that his plan was being seconded.

"We'll use the plane you arrived in, General," said Spears. "It's under my orders. We'll take my official car to the aerodrome tomorrow morning."

"Good," said de Gaulle. A path of escape was set. Like a master conspirator, he could sense that unseen eyes were searching for him in Bordeaux, possibly closing in.

"I'll go make the arrangements with London," said Spears, and he departed. A few moments later, de Gaulle left the hotel to spend the remainder of the night hiding out in a backroom of a nondescript building, far from searching eyes.

Flight from Bordeaux

At seven-thirty in the morning in the alley at the rear of the hotel, General Spears stood by his staff car, now truly worried since de Gaulle was more than a half hour overdue. Suddenly, de Gaulle and his aide, Lieutenant de Courcel, arrived with a surprising amount of luggage. They stowed the luggage and a small trunk in the car and threw some overcoats on top. Spears and de Gaulle whispered out a little stratagem to throw off any suspicious eyes at the aerodrome. De Gaulle would make a pretense that he was at the aerodrome in an official capacity to say good-bye to Spears. The men got in the car and departed for the aerodrome through the congested streets of Bordeaux.

At the aerodrome, General Spears returned a nonchalant salute to the gate guard while hiding his acute anxiety. Confusion was his ally this morning. The staff car proceeded into the aerodrome that was chockablock with airplanes of all sizes and shapes in almost every available space. Maneuvering around, they found the small two-winged British Rapide near where de Gaulle had left it the previous evening. The pilot and the crew were alert and efficient. The crew quickly put the luggage in the plane while the pilot walked out and scouted a path through the parked airplanes. Walking further, he spotted a clear stretch of runway from which he could take off.

The pilot returned and started the airplane's engine. As he prepared to taxi, Spears and de Gaulle went through the motions of saying good-bye to one another. Then Spears got in the plane, and the pilot started to throttle it forward, and the plane inched ahead. Spears pushed his door wide open and waved his arm, and de Gaulle ran over and dove through the open door while Courcel shoved the legs of the ungainly general in behind him. Courcel piled in after, and Spears pulled the door closed. The pilot pushed the throttle forward and increased speed across the ground, weaving around the parked planes. Coming up to the clear space on the runway, the pilot put the roar to the engine, and the little plane raced at speed and was up in the air on one hop.

As the plane reached altitude, it turned north and flew up the coast, the passengers looking out. Suddenly Spears saw an overturned troop ship lying on its side with hundreds of tiny figures in the water. It was the British troopship *Champlain* with two thousand British soldiers aboard. Many were lost. The life-and-death consequences of defeat, made bitter by the enveloping chaos, were again driven home to the two generals.

Hours later, the plane arrived at an airport outside London, and General Spears delivered General de Gaulle to Number 10 Downing Street and a warm welcome from Winston Churchill.

De Gaulle broached his idea of a broadcast over the BBC to the people of France to the indomitable British prime minister. Churchill agreed but said they must first wait to see if the new government in Bordeaux was indeed going to ask the Germans for terms.

That afternoon Maréchal Pétain went on Bordeaux radio: "I give to France my person to assuage its misfortune. It is with a broken heart that I tell you today it is necessary to stop fighting." The personality cult surrounding the Maréchal had begun with those words.

It was decided that de Gaulle should prepare his broadcast. De Gaulle departed for a small apartment off Hyde Park belonging to a French banker and wrote out his address in longhand. Courcel got a family friend, a young woman working in London for one of the French missions, Élisabeth de Méribel, to come over and type it.

At Number 10 Downing Street, British officials observed that although the Maréchal had told French troops it was necessary to stop fighting—with potentially disastrous consequences for British troops still fighting side by side with the French in Brittany—Pétain had simply asked for terms but not called for an armistice. But one decision had been made by Pétain and his new defense minister, General Weygand: the politicians had not been allowed to capitulate. The French army was still in place in the field.

But the British officials asked themselves: if the soldiers quit fighting, could not an armistice be the inevitable result? Or was further resistance in North Africa still possible?

BBC Studios, June 18

General de Gaulle, General Spears, and Lieutenant de Courcel walked into the BBC studios shortly after five o'clock in the afternoon. They were greeted by Elisabeth Barker from the staff of the BBC Foreign Broadcasting Service. She had only just been informed of the broadcast, but she observed the icy containment and remarkable self-possession of the French general. No anxiety in his manner about the broadcast.

"You will go on at six o'clock from Studio B-two," said Barker pointing down the hall.

"Merci," replied the general. The three men followed the British woman down the hall and into the studio. The general arranged his papers on a small podium behind the large microphone and waited.

A large white light went on; the general cleared his voice and began.

"Alleging the defeat of our armies, this government has entered into negotiations with the enemy with a view toward bringing about a cessation of hostilities."

Spears listened intently and observed the words were a highly accurate statement as to the current state of events.

"But has the last word been said?...Is our defeat final and irremediable? To those questions I answer—No!

"France does not stand alone...it can make common cause with the British Empire...and draw unreservedly on the immense industrial resources of the United States.

"I, General de Gaulle, now in London, call on all French officers and men who are at present on British soil, or may be in the future…to get in touch with me.

"Whatever happens, the flame of French resistance must not and shall not die."

The general concluded and handed his papers to Courcel, and the three officers shook hands. The door opened, and Barker came in. De Gaulle went up and thanked her for her assistance. The three men departed.

The call had been made, what was to be known in France forever afterward as *L'Appel*. The disobedience had been made clear.

Bordeaux, Wednesday, June 19

Jean Monnet and his deputy René Pleven sat in the rear of the giant Sunderland flying boat named *Claire* that Prime Minister Churchill had made available to them. Across the passenger space was British Colonial Secretary Lord Lloyd, a member of the war cabinet.

The day before as de Gaulle prepared to give his radio address, Monnet had called Churchill and said there was one more card to play. He felt de Gaulle was premature in making his call to rally a resistance in exile. He asked for transportation to Bordeaux to try to bring out such members of the French government willing to continue a government in North Africa. Churchill had readily agreed. Salvaging something from the debacle at Bordeaux was imperative.

If Monnet's mission were successful, prominent members of the French government would depart on the flying boat for North Africa to organize a *résistant* government to carry on the fight.

Monnet was an international businessman with a broad horizon, a man not conditioned to look at international problems in terms of national sovereignty. Where national politicians saw limits, Monnet saw the dividends that flowed from cooperation among nations.

Approaching France, the giant seaplane put down in the Gironde estuary, and a launch came out and ferried the men up the Garonne River to the quay fronting the city of Bordeaux. Monnet and Pleven headed straight for the office of Foreign Minister Paul Baudouin, a longtime acquaintance of both Monnet and Pleven. Monnet understood that Baudouin enjoyed great influence over the aged Maréchal Pétain; therefore, Baudouin was key to Monnet's plan.

"I listened to your radio address of June seventeen," began Monnet to Baudouin, "and quite agree with your statement that there can be no question of accepting terms that would deny our honor or our national independence." Monnet hoped to find some common ground.

Baudouin nodded solemnly acknowledging that his words were accurately repeated.

"But the enemy is likely to impose just such terms," said Monnet, driving home his central point of unjust terms in a German-imposed armistice. "The men in authority of the government should withdraw beyond the reach of the enemy. The British government has provided me with a large seaplane to facilitate the evacuation."

"We have already taken this into account," said Baudouin with well-practiced ease. "The cabinet has already decided that the president of the Republic and the presidents of the Chamber and Senate, together with other members of the government, should withdraw to North Africa. The Maréchal and General Weygand along with myself will remain."

Monnet continued: "German policy is to divide France from Britain. That is the purpose of the unity proposal you received from the British cabinet."

"The offer has not been rejected," replied Baudouin with a wave of his cigarette. "We shall study it with care."

Monnet ignored the wave-off and continued with a series of arguments, the afternoon slowly wasting away. Finally, he and Pleven stood up and departed. Outside, Monnet said derisively, "The pawn is blocking the chessboard."

"Let's go see Herriot," said Pleven, referring to Édouard Herriot, the rotund president of the Chamber of Deputies and longtime man of the parliament.

The two men reached the building where Herriot had his quarters and walked up a large stairwell teeming with aides and favor seekers. In a dining room, they found Herriot seated at a dining table replete with a full meal spread out before him, a classic Third Republic politician renowned for his appetites for food and women. Former prime ministers and other ministers, the president of the Senate, and other politicos watched Herriot devour a leg of lamb. Herriot greeted Monnet warmly and pointed for him to take a seat.

"We have both a plan and an airplane for departing to North Africa," said Monnet, getting straight to the point. "You just have to say yes."

"I spoke to Admiral Darlan this afternoon about some ministers leaving," replied Herriot, "and that undoubtedly he was taking steps for their departure to North Africa."

"What did he say?"

"An emphatic no. A government that leaves never returns, he said." Herriot, jabbing the leg of lamb at them, added, "He has a point."

"The defeatists got to him," countered Monnet.

"The Maréchal for sure," replied Herriot. He took a bite from his leg of lamb and smiled, adding, "This is an admiral who knows how to swim."

Monnet took a breath and repeated his arguments on the importance of carrying on the resistance.

"You don't need to convince me," said Herriot. "I persuaded the cabinet to take the decision this morning. But we shall leave under the flag of France. It cannot be otherwise. The *Massiglia* is ready to sail."

"And what if it doesn't sail," asked Monnet, sensing the same trap that de Gaulle had foreseen two evenings before. Admiral Darlan would control the means of implementing any decision and thus could stymie it.

"Then my voice will be heard protesting against an unjust peace in the parliament," thundered Herriot. Monnet sensed that the great parliamentarian did not understand how futile his gesture would be in a government where there would be no parliament. The time for debate was over; the time for action had begun.

Monnet drummed his fingers impatiently on the tabletop; again, he saw the way forward blocked. He stood up along with his aide, and they departed. On the way out, they met Lord

Lloyd, who was working his way through a round of meetings with President Lebrun, Maréchal Pétain, and other officials. Monnet gave him his discouraging news. Lloyd sighed knowingly and continued with his rounds.

Outside, the two Frenchmen went to a park and sat on a bench and ate sandwiches as they discussed the next step. Returning to see Herriot one more time, they found the Chamber president worried because Admiral Darlan had postponed the embarkation aboard the *Massiglia* for that evening. Nevertheless, Herriot was adamant; he would not leave. The cabinet was to meet the next morning, he said. He was determined to attend.

Again, the three French emissaries left. On the streets heading back toward the quay, Pleven spied his wife and children in the teeming crowds. Utterly surprised and brimming with joy, he ran up to them and hugged them as tears of relief welled from the eyes of his family. They quickly got their luggage and met Monnet at the quay. Meanwhile Monnet had also encountered Henri Bonnet and his wife and added them to the entourage.

At the quay, Monnet turned around and made a wide sweeping gaze of the riverfront city. A setback had turned into withdrawal—for now. The launch took the now-enlarged party back to the Sunderland seaplane. Later in the evening, Lord Lloyd rejoined them, his mission no more successful than theirs. The seaplane remained anchored in the estuary, bobbing in the swell, for an uncomfortable night with its anxious passengers grabbing what rest they could. In the distance could be heard the drone of German planes, some dropping mines in the estuary.

London

In a small apartment off Hyde Park on Wednesday, June 19, General de Gaulle read intelligence reports that indicated General Auguste Noguès, the French governor general in Morocco, was prepared to fight on. Morocco, facing the Atlantic on the northwest African coast, was of the first importance since some of England's most important sea-lanes ran right past its front door. The French general wrote out in longhand a telegram for transmission to Rabat:

"Hold myself at your disposal, whether to fight under your orders, or for any step that might seem to you useful."

The general handed the paper to his aide, Lieutenant de Courcel, and told him, "Take this to the Foreign Office." It was the first of several telegrams de Gaulle dispatched to governors across the French Empire in the coming days as he strove to assemble a resistance in France's overseas empire. Few responded. Military men all, they looked to Maréchal Pétain for direction.

Bordeaux

On Thursday morning, June 20, with the sun just rising over the vineyards spread along the eastern banks of the estuary, the crew of the big Sunderland seaplane untethered it from its mooring, and the plane motored into middle of the Gironde estuary. Reaching a smooth patch of water, hopefully free of mines dropped by German aircraft, the plane made a slow turn, and the pilot pushed the throttles forward. The plane accelerated across the water, bounding in big flashes of spray, and then slowly rose from the water like a big goose taking off from a northern lake on migration. The passengers looked out of the windows as the dawn sky turned into a bright-morning sunshine. The plane headed far out to sea away from German interceptors and then set a course toward England. Monnet stared out of the window at the French coastline receding behind him and pondered his options.

Monnet was not ready to abandon so vital a project as a resistance government willing to carry on the struggle from French North Africa. For sure, future solutions had to go beyond mere cooperation with what was left of the French government. He knew that hard choices often ran into prolonged discussions that avoided taking decision. So it was with a government in retreat. Monnet felt that cooperative and collegial decision making was undertaken to improve decisions, not delay them. If the French Empire in North Africa held firm, then he believed Anglo-French union was still possible. Necessity would drive the decision. The stirring vision of one parliament, one cabinet, and one flag burned itself into Monnet's consciousness. Unified European government burned as a bright beacon on his mental horizon.

Monnet took his decision: he resolved to urge Churchill to try to seek support in French North Africa, estimating that the colonies had not yet submerged into the swamp of defeatism that had overwhelmed Bordeaux. For Monnet, the last card had not yet been played.

Chapter 4: Return to London

London. Thursday, June 20, 1940. Jean Monnet followed General Edward Spears into St. Stephen's House, a Victorian brick building in Westminster across from the towering spires of parliament. Upstairs, General de Gaulle was working to organize a résistant organization in London, a task undertaken while Monnet was in Bordeaux. Monnet had just returned from Bordeaux that morning.

Before meeting with de Gaulle, Monnet had stopped by the Foreign Office and spoken with Permanent Undersecretary Sir Alexander Cadogan, who had updated him on what had been going on while Monnet was in Bordeaux. He was told that de Gaulle had made a second radio address the previous evening over the BBC. The broadcast was a stirring call to arms: "I, General de Gaulle, a French soldier and military leader, realize that I now speak for France. In the name of France…I make the solemn declaration…to continue the struggle…soldiers of France, wherever you may be, arise!"

Monnet had read through a transcript of the speech at the Foreign Office and felt the effort was premature. He was concerned about the personification of a resistance movement around one personality, and that a personality ensconced in London would be seen as a pawn of British interests and not those of the French. Monet understood that Perfidious Albion had a well-deserved reputation among the French people. Lack of British airplanes in May being only the most recent instance. As to General de Gaulle broadcasting from London, the French people had a long mistrust of generals riding to their rescue on political horseback.

Then there were the telegrams de Gaulle was sending to French governors across the French Empire. Monnet found them presumptuous.

At St. Stephen's House, Monnet went upstairs and found de Gaulle in a small office with Spears. He entered and sat down.

"You were unable to get anyone from the government to go with you on the seaplane?" asked de Gaulle, using the question to make an assertion of fact. Like a lawyer at trial, he knew the answer to the question before asking it.

"Yes, but many important members are still waiting to board the *Massiglia* and sail for North Africa," replied Monnet. In his mind, a résistant government made up of leading members of the last government of the Third Republic was still possible.

"But Admiral Darlan has delayed the sailing of the *Massiglia*—again," said the well-informed general.

"Leading members wanted to attend the cabinet meeting. The voyage is delayed, not canceled."

"We will see," said de Gaulle.

"I have just come from speaking with Sir Alexander Cadogan at the Foreign Office," said Monnet. "He briefed me on what has been going on while I've been away."

"Yes?"

"The question of France's role in the war remains open," asserted Monnet. "Your actions here in London threaten to freeze a situation that is still fluid. It may still be possible to organize a resistance in North Africa under a legitimately appointed authority."

"I have offered my services to General Noguès," said de Gaulle, deflecting the criticism. Noguès was the French resident-general in Morocco who had indicated a willingness to carry on the fight.

"While you organize a committee in London?"

"There are French fighting forces here in Britain. They need a point to which they can rally."

"To what point?"

"To fight."

Monnet understood. Direct and simple. "Fine. Nevertheless, you must stop sending off telegrams. Those to whom they are addressed cannot help but think that with the help of the British prime minister you, a young French general, are arrogating to yourself the right to represent France. Are they, your seniors in age and service, to take orders from you issued in London on foreign soil?"

"Yours is an argument," said de Gaulle. "Mine is a course of action."

General Spears entered the conversation to smooth over the mounting disagreement between the two men. He explained that the British government wanted to organize resistance to Germany wherever it could be found, that for the British a decisive moment in the war was coming up. "England faces Germany alone," said the British general gravely. He stood up as did Monnet, and the men departed.

Armistice

Sunday, June 23. London. Generals de Gaulle and Spears listened to the radio broadcast from France. The Pétain government had accepted and signed the Armistice with the Germans. The worldwide news announcement came from correspondents gathered outside the old railway carriage at Compiegne where the Germans had signed their armistice with the Allies in November 1918.

General Spears then called the British cabinet office and had a brief discussion. He hung up the receiver and said to de Gaulle, "There, your proposal to set up a national committee has been approved by the war cabinet. It formally recognizes your Provisional French National Committee as the body fully representing independent French elements determined on prosecution of the war in fulfillment of the international obligations of France."

"Yes, we begin," said the French general.

"Yes, but it is understood, as you set forth in your proposal, that for your committee to have legitimacy it must account for its actions to the representatives of the French people when they can assemble in conditions compatible with liberty, dignity, and security. Most of the world and many of the French will continue to look at the Pétain government as the legal government."

"I understand," said de Gaulle, "my committee will not have the status of a government-in-exile."

"Yes, that's the diplomacy of it," said Spears.

"But it will present a clear choice to the French."

"Yes, it will impose hard choices on many of them," said Spears.

De Gaulle nodded in assent. "But it is for me to take the country's fate upon myself." He sat down at a desk and drafted an enlistment form for the soon-to-be Free French forces setting forth an oath of allegiance to serve General de Gaulle, *commandant-en-chef*, and not the French state, for the duration of the war with "honor, fidelity, and discipline." The French state was a prisoner of war in de Gaulle's view. He handed the draft to his aide, Lieutenant de Courcel.

De Gaulle turned to Spears and said, "Indeed, I now speak for France," echoing words he had said in his second BBC radio address the previous Thursday evening. Spears could see that de Gaulle had adopted the position that he was now France, and it was up to Frenchmen to choose between Pétain's France or de Gaulle's France. The choice would be clear and simple in the general's view.

An aide came into the room and delivered a letter to de Gaulle from Jean Monnet. De Gaulle read the letter out loud: "…it is wrong to try to set up in Britain an organization that would appear to the French as a movement under British protection, inspired by British interests and therefore condemned to failure that would make further efforts at recovery all the more difficult."

"That may become a problem in getting any independent elements left in the French Empire to rally to your committee, General," said Spears.

De Gaulle nodded, but overcoming difficulties was the nature of his enterprise. His course was set.

Courcel added, "Monnet is leaving Rene Pleven here in London to work with you, General."

"He is an able man," said de Gaulle. "There will be others."

"Churchill is eventually sending Monnet to Washington to work with the British Purchasing Mission," said Spears. "He is highly effective with the Americans."

De Gaulle nodded. He could see the benefits of having the pesky Frenchman in Washington. The three men left to get a meal.

A New Headquarters

Monday, June 24. General de Gaulle walked into his triangular office in St. Stephen's House on Victoria Embankment and looked out over the Thames River shimmering in the summer light. This is where it begins. He walked over to a wall and looked at the map of France and then the maps of Africa and the world. The French Empire was a globe-spanning enterprise with colonies and possessions in every ocean and on every continent. He glanced at the letter he had received from Jean Monnet and pondered the map. He went to his desk and started to write:

"My dear friend. At such a time as this, it would be absurd for us to cross one another because our fundamental aim is the same, and together perhaps we can do great things. Come and see me, whenever you choose. We shall agree."

The general took the draft out to Élisabeth de Méribel, now his secretary, who was ensconced in the outer office. "Please type this up. We have to get it off to Monsieur Monnet."

De Gaulle turned and went back into his office. He sat down and read news dispatches about the new government being formed in Vichy. General Weygand was to be overall minister of national defense. Although the terms of the Armistice were hazy at this distance, a large French army was being left in place in North Africa, undoubtedly to keep order over the native people and to keep the British out, thought de Gaulle.

He sat and pondered the new developments. He would need to rally dissident elements across the French Empire to his cause. He stood up and walked across the room and stared at the map pinned to the wall. He looked carefully at the French Empire in Africa and calculated.

But first, a new French fighting force had an urgent need of being organized among the French units stranded in Britain. Then Africa. The road back to Paris would begin in Africa. Would the French in Africa see it that way?

Morocco

Tuesday, June 25. In the late-afternoon twilight with a red sun setting on the western horizon, a lumbering Sunderland seaplane approached a long narrow waterway in Rabat, a beautiful white Moorish city set in a desert bordering the

Atlantic Ocean. Rabat was the capital of Morocco. On board were Duff Cooper, British minister of information and member of the war cabinet, his secretary, and Field Marshal Lord Gort, former commander of the British Expeditionary Force that had been heroically withdrawn from Europe at Dunkirk three weeks before. These top-level emissaries from Winston Churchill were to meet with the French ministers and other officials on the battle cruiser *Massiglia* that had conveyed them from Bordeaux. The vessel had belatedly left France on June 21 after Admiral Darlan had released the ship. These French statesmen were to make up a resistance government that would continue the fight from French North Africa, or so went the hope when they departed. But by the time the ship reached Casablanca three days later on June 24, the Armistice had been signed.

The seaplane set down in the narrow waterway and taxied up near a landing dock and anchored. There was no welcoming party. Eventually a launch came out, and the three British dignitaries got ashore and found British General Lord Dillon, the liaison officer to the French resident-general, General Noguès.

"I'm afraid your reception here will be cold," said Lord Dillon by way of introduction. "They tried to telegraph you not to come."

"Why?" asked Cooper.

"They don't want you to see any of the French ex-ministers."

"They're now 'ex'?"

"I'm afraid so."

"Where are they?"

"They're confined to the *Massiglia* moored out in the harbor at Casablanca, about an hour away from here."

"Well, let's get up to the consulate and see if the consul general can contact our consul in Casablanca. Maybe he can get a message out to the officials on the ship," said Cooper, resolving on a plan.

Lord Dillon's car took the party to the consulate, and the consul quickly got through by telephone to Casablanca and conveyed a message to be delivered to Mandel and the other officials out on the *Massiglia*. Several minutes later, another telephone in the office rang. The French deputy governor was calling to say, "I have instructions to prevent you from contacting the officials on the ship."

Unsurprised that the telephone line had been tapped, Cooper coolly asked, "Under whose authority?"

"From General Noguès who received his orders from the Maréchal directly."

"So the officials on the *Massiglia* are practically prisoners?" asked Cooper.

"Not exactly prisoners," temporized the Frenchman.

Cooper sized up the situation: the military governors in Africa had fallen in step with Maréchal Pétain and the new government. The old man had won the race of time. French North Africa and the powerful French fleet stationed there were under the Maréchal's control.

"Orders from General Noguès?"

"Yes, the orders given to me are most cruel," said the deputy governor, his voice quavering in a nervous and agitated state. "You must promise me you will not try to contact them."

Realizing there was nothing to be done, Cooper said, "Okay, I'll make no further efforts to contact the *Massiglia*."

"Good," said the deputy governor, greatly relieved.

"Can I speak with General Noguès?"

"Unfortunately, he has been called away?"

"Yes, I see," said Cooper. He hung up and turned to the generals and shrugged his shoulders. "Nothing to be done here. The promise of a resistant government is stillborn."

Lord Gort and Lord Dillon took their leave to go and dine together in the hotel and catch up on military tidings. The consul general invited Cooper to dine at the consulate with some of his friends. The consulate was a beautiful villa situated in a lovely garden. The dinner was held on the veranda under a black-satin evening sky. After dinner, the British emissaries returned to the flying boat and spent an uncomfortable night aboard. The seaplane took off at dawn and arrived at Gibraltar shortly after eight in the morning.

On the way up to Governor House for a shower and a good meal, Cooper remarked to Lord Gort, "It was a lovely evening at the consulate last night, but you did not miss much. The food was filthy. There was plenty of inferior wine, however."

"About the same as the hotel," replied the field marshal.

Chapter 5: New York

New York, Sunday, June 23, 1940. A sharply dressed man in his midtwenties walked up Broadway, his dark business suit seemingly more appropriate for Monday morning than this softly lit Sunday evening. For Jacques Dubois, the long-delayed dinner date with Jacqueline was on. He turned down a side street that led west away from Little Italy. Up ahead, he could see the silvery iridescence of the sky at the end of the street. The sun was now below the golden glow of the western horizon. It had been a glorious summer day.

In the next block, he glanced up at the side of a building along the deeply shadowed street and saw a neon sign in large green letters announcing "Mom's" and below it in dark red the word "Ristorante." The restaurant was a favorite of theirs, a rendezvous away from their regular haunts. Good food and discreet. Neither Mom nor any of the waiters understood French so there were no overheard discussions. But Mom and her extended family were effusively warm to fellow Latins.

The man pushed open the door to the restaurant taking off his snap-brim fedora as he entered the small foyer and approached the slender woman in a dark fashionable suit holding a black polished leather handbag trimmed with a gold buckle. She was standing to one side waiting for him.

"Jacques," she said and came up and kissed him on both cheeks. "You look haggard. Been working today?"

"Yes," he replied. "Supply issues." He had spent the day furiously rerouting cargoes destined for French ports to British ports, a matter of highest urgency. Jacques was indeed his name, but these days the last name Dubois on his passport was something borrowed. There were other, more legitimate names in his past, but this was now a time when having a short past was a tall advantage.

"Oh, those dull paper work problems," said Jacqueline.

"Yes, deadly dull," he deadpanned. He could never share with Jacqueline what he did, or it would wind up as a confidential nugget in her boss's newspaper column. "How are you, Jacqueline?"

"Fine," she said with a gleam in her eye. Friends had remarked on the similarity of their names and joked that they might share a destiny. But she felt no one knew where destiny might lead these days. Jacqueline Smith was sure her destiny would take her beyond being a research assistant into the glamorous world of foreign correspondents. She already knew the trench coat she wanted to buy. She'd seen it at Bloomingdale's.

"You're dressed for the office, too?" he remarked.

"I've been there all day reading the teletypes from Europe," she replied. Destiny clattered out at about twenty lines a minute downtown.

Jacques nodded in weary agreement. Troubling news from Europe was constant. Just then Mom came up, a big dark-blue billowy dress girthed by a wide cloth belt around her stout trunk, a small bouquet pinned above her left breast. "You two—again…for dinner?"

"Yes," replied Jacques.

"More plotting on the napkins?" asked Mom.

"No, just business," said Jacques. Jacques had been writing numbers on napkins at the last dinner as he explained production numbers to Jacqueline.

Mom looked at Jacqueline. "You must plot your wedding. Then can come the babies." She looked at Jacqueline with a faux look of disapproval. "No practicing before you see the priest."

Jacqueline laughed. "At least no babies before the priest."

Mom doubled down on her faux look of disapproval. She looked at Jacques with a frown. Yes, boys will be boys. "Oh, you children. Too modern."

Mom turned and led them down the candle-scented dining room to a small dark leather booth with a red checked tablecloth set against a brick wall cool to the touch. Strands of ivy hung down the side of the wall, cascading from wooden flower troughs hanging on small brass chains just below the ceiling.

Jacqueline slipped into one side of the booth and Jacques into the other. A waiter came and Jacques said, "A bottle of Chianti." The waiter walked away.

"So what was happening at fifteen Broad Street today?" asked Jacqueline, mentioning the office building just off Wall Street where the Anglo-French Purchasing Board was located and where Jacques worked.

"It's all about airplanes."

"Yes, you always say that."

"Well, it is. In 1938 after Munich, Daladier said that if France had had three thousand fighter planes, there would have been no Munich," said Jacques referring to then French Premier Édouard Daladier. Jacques's shoulders sagged as he thought about the lost opportunity. "Anyway, that's where it began—this time." European history had turned on a lack of airplanes, not a lack of will despite the odor that surrounded Neville Chamberlain's appeasement policies.

A waiter came up and put a basket of bread down on the table and dragged little bottles of olive oil and vinegar from the wall over next to the basket. Then he set a bottle of Chianti down and produced a corkscrew and withdrew the cork with a small pop. He poured a small amount into Jacques's glass and waited for the inevitable approval. Jacques tasted, smiled, and nodded. The waiter filled Jacqueline's glass and then topped off Jacques's.

"And?" asked the waiter solicitously.

"We'll have the spaghetti Bolognese," said Jack, looking at Jacqueline to confirm the order. Her eyes brightened, and she nodded in agreement. The waiter walked away.

"So, now where we?" asked Jacqueline. "Oh yeah, the three thousand planes?" She had never before gotten Jacques to be so forthcoming about what she knew to be his work, and now Jacqueline wanted to know all she could about the war for her own work. Up to the past couple of weeks much of the journalism commentary had focused on the failure of diplomacy as a cause leading to the war; now it looked as if lack of airplanes was the reason for the enveloping defeat occurring in France.

"In 1938 when Daladier sent Monnet to the US, Jean met with Roosevelt, and they got agreement on a thousand planes. They firmed up the order in February 1939 for five hundred aircraft for that year and a thousand to be delivered in 1940."

"What about the neutrality laws?" asked Jacqueline. Neutrality and its malicious parent isolationism were still dominant in American politics.

"The planes were built in Canadian factories," crisply replied Jacques. As a member of Jean Monnet's investment bank in New York, he had worked on the financing arrangements.

"Did the airplanes get delivered?"

"Some did. Of the 1940 order, a hundred planes left Halifax last week for England, and there are another hundred planes sitting on an aircraft carrier down in Martinique."

"Sounds like you missed your target," said Jacqueline.

"The Germans simply attacked first."

"I know Germany is the enemy," said Jacqueline sympathetically before moving to the knifepoint question, "but a lot of people in France think that Britain let France down when they didn't send enough fighter planes to France last month. The Germans marched across northern France unimpeded."

"Yeah, but there were simply not enough planes to stop all those German tanks. You also need tanks to stop tanks."

"France had a lot of tanks. General de Gaulle successfully counterattacked the Germans with tanks before he got yanked back to Paris to be undersecretary of defense."

"But he was the only one. The rest of the tanks were not in massed formations like the German tanks. Aircraft and tanks have to be massed and sent into the fight in one big fist."

She said sweetly, "You should have been a general."

"I'm a lieutenant. My regiment is up on the Maginot Line."

"And you're not there?" she said with a questioning but sympathetic eyebrow. She quickly added a merciful "Thank God."

Just then the waiter came up and put steaming plates of spaghetti on the table, the thick red sauce richly layered across the top. Mom came up and said, "The red is for romance. Forget your talk. The war is in the old country...here we still have peace." She smiled and walked away.

"Yes, the old country," said Jacques.

"You wouldn't have made any difference," said Jacqueline in an even tone.

"Yeah, Jean agrees with you. He said another lieutenant wouldn't make any difference and that I was needed here in New York. It seemed like the right decision at the time," said Jacques, a downcast look on his face as he thought about his regiment and its now troubled destiny.

"Maybe that decision still is," said Jacqueline with warmth in her eyes, and she reached across the table and put her hand on top of his.

"Thanks," said Jacques. He knew it was the correct decision even if it did not always feel right.

"Are airplanes that decisive?" asked Jacqueline turning back to the conversation.

"Yes, the British aircraft in France were chewed up at a furious rate in May and June. Simply astounding. The Royal Air Force would have been destroyed by the end of June at that rate. That's why they felt they had to hold some back for the defense of their own islands."

"And the planes from America?"

"They're getting produced, but they didn't arrive soon enough."

"Too little, too late."

"That's about right."

"What's going to happen to the French orders?"

"We're now routing the planes for delivery to England since we don't know if there's a French government still in the fight."

"And the planes in Martinique?"

"Who knows?"

"Was this the wrong plan?"

"No, the French orders resulted in an immediate ramp-up of American aircraft production by a factor of four. Munich did have one dividend. From Munich on, Jean always saw that a big ramp-up in aircraft production was the strategic goal."

"He saw the future better than the generals?"

"Yes, certainly."

"And now?"

"Jean talks about fifty thousand planes a year." He looked at her not quite believing the number himself.

"And the Germans?"

"No one—not the French, not the English, not the Americans—can hope to stop German military might without aircraft."

"What happened to the rumor that France will continue the fight from North Africa?" asked Jacqueline.

"You know the news as well as I do. The government is going to stay in metropolitan France. No running off to North Africa."

"Who decided that?"

"Marshal Pétain insists."

"And his authority?"

"He's now the head of the government. Reynaud buckled and was forced to resign. Pétain insists that it is duty of the government to stay in the country. He says it cannot abandon French soil. Many in the cabinet agree. General Weygand supported Pétain on military grounds."

"That's a powerful argument."

"Yes, it is. Powerful men. The Maréchal said no matter what he would remain among the French people to share its tribulations and misery," said Jacques, using the now ubiquitous Maréchal to describe Pétain as the cult of the Maréchal began to take hold in public discussion among the French.

"That makes the others sound like deserters."

"Exactly. He also says that the armistice is a necessary condition for the survival of eternal France. It's an argument that has its merits." Jacques deeply felt the frustrations of the people living in France, people who had seen their once vaunted army routed in a matter of days. It had almost seemed like a conjurer's trick.

"Where does it all go?" asked Jacqueline.

"You tell me. You're the one reading the latest teletypes coming in from Europe," said Jacques referring to Jacqueline's job as an editorial assistant to famed international columnist Anne Hare at the mighty *New York Times Tribune*.

"I think Anne's column today described some of the dilemmas of the future," said Jacqueline.

"Yeah, I read it. She described the armistice at Compiegne as the French surrender," said Jacques with a downcast look. "She said this opens up the third and worst act of the tragedy."

"Yes, she said France and the other occupied countries will be put under blockade by the British."

"So begins the hideous dilemma of letting France starve," said Jacques dejectedly. "So that Britain can keep fighting. What a choice."

Jacqueline moved to change the conversation before Jacques fell into a funk. "Did you read what she wrote about the wonders of American organization and its potential for unlimited production?"

"Yes."

"That's what you've been telling me Monnet believes in to his core. Won't you be part of that?"

"Yes, I think so. I'll probably hear more in the days and weeks ahead."

"Isn't that what the work you do at Purchasing Commission is all about?"

"Yes, it is. Just that we thought France—our country—would be an ally standing shoulder to shoulder with the British against the Nazis. Now that's off the table."

"Maybe not," said Jacqueline. "General de Gaulle made another radio address from London last night calling on French soldiers and sailors to rally to him, that he was going to continue the fight from London. That's his second address in a week."

"There's still a legitimate government in Bordeaux...de Gaulle may be premature...I don't know."

"Nevertheless, events will march forward," insisted Jacqueline.

"Yeah," said Jacques, uncertainty in his voice, "but where?"

"What do you hear from Monnet?"

"Jean is in London, and he'll surely send word. We'll do something."

"You said he was the great business diplomat of our time."

"He has been. I'm not sure what his new role will be. Jean gets on well with the British; he's tight with the Americans."

"I'm sure you'll be part of it," said Jacqueline reassuringly.

"Yes, whatever it is." Jacques took a sip of wine and looked at Jacqueline. "How about you? Are you going to remain Miss Hare's errand girl?"

"For now, yes. I hope to be able to go with her on her next foreign assignment."

"That could be dangerous."

"These are dangerous times." She moved her head into a glamorous pose like she saw in the British war moves. And cracked a wicked smile.

Jacques laughed. "What will you do overseas?"

"Between running my girl errands"—she made a playful frown at him—"I'll be cabling news accounts back home while Anne provides the big-name commentary. That's my opening. Get some bylines."

"Glad someone has it all figured out."

"I've also got this week figured out. The Republican convention starts tomorrow," said Jacqueline. Her expression said she was leaving another thought hanging.

"You're telling me what?"

"I have to be at the office tomorrow morning at six."

Jacques's face fell. "At six?"

"The teletypes start coming in from Europe," she explained, "and Anne wants a briefing from me before she goes over to the convention hall." She looked at him and added, "But you could come over to my place—*chez moi*—tomorrow night. I'll make dinner."

His smile brightened. "*Chez nous?*"

"We can sleep in Tuesday morning." She smiled. "To seven maybe. Ensemble."

"And *la patronne*, the redoubtable Miss Harc?"

"She'll be hobnobbing with the bigwigs in Philadelphia late into Monday night. I don't expect to hear from her until at least noon."

"She has a life, too?"

"A career at least."

"And you, a life or a career?"

"*Peut-etre*," she said fetchingly. Perhaps.

"Well, yes," said Jacques. "An enigmatic future. Tell me, what's the key issue at the convention?"

"She says the Republican convention is meeting in the shadow of the defeat of France."

"What does that mean?"

"She thinks that hard facts must be faced," said Jacqueline. "Isolationism is no longer the answer. The Republican internationalists understand that."

Jacques nodded in agreement with a sentiment he had long shared. "Yes, events are coming fast."

"At a gallop."

"Who does she think is going to win the opportunity to get crushed by Roosevelt?"

"She thinks Wendell Willkie will float on a rising tide, that the times demand new men and a new approach."

"Yes, Dewey probably sunk his chances with his isolationism."

"He's also quite young—not yet forty—when people are looking for judgment that comes with age."

"So, it'll be the barefoot boy from Wall Street?" asked Jacques with a laugh referring to Willkie, a prominent New York corporate lawyer.

"And tomorrow night it'll be the barefoot boy from the Anglo-French Purchasing Commission."

"I look forward to it. Getting barefoot."

Chapter 6: Algiers

Algiers. Wednesday, July 3, 1940. A fetchingly pretty woman wearing a gray summer frock walked down the road toward the British consulate in downtown Algiers carrying a packet of papers, her blond hair shimmering in the sunlight. Events were moving fast. Seven weeks earlier, on May 15—it had been her birthday—she attended luncheon with the British consul, Captain Gatlow, and his wife. France and Great Britain were steadfast allies at the time. Now with the defeat of France, the relationship was in precarious jeopardy after Maréchal Pétain's address to the nation ten days before announcing the Armistice with Nazi Germany. Relations between France and Britain were in a state of daily flux. No one knew where new loyalties might lie, and the British were deeply concerned where the French fleet might find its political anchorage.

The woman, Joan Tuyl, was the daughter of an English couple who had lived in Algiers for many years. Her late father had been Church of England rector in Algiers; her widowed mother was an artist living in a large studio up the hill behind the Government House. Earlier that day Joan had heard the news that Holland had been completely overrun by the German army in its shattering offensive against the Allied armies. Her husband, a reserve officer in the Dutch army, had returned to Holland when war broke out. She had no idea what had become of him. She and Gerry Tuyl had diary farmed out in an oasis south of Algiers in the years before the war; they had two small boys, one age four and one just two. Now she was living with her mother and the two rambunctious boys.

At luncheon that beautiful day in May when the dark tidings about the allied armies starting to crack was broadcast on the wireless, Captain Gatlow had asked if she would work for the British Military Mission. She eagerly agreed as she needed money. She remembered Captain Gatlow's words: "We have good reason to believe that North Africa is going to be an important seat of operations. We need people like you who have been here several years and know both the language and the inhabitants."

She was momentarily taken aback. This might get serious.

"Well, what about it?" pressed the captain.

"Yes, a thousand times, yes. If you really think I will be useful." She remembered the enthusiasm of that day; she had found a way to share in the common struggle with her absent husband.

So it had begun. She worked as a receptionist and telephone operator in the office but more importantly circulated among the teaming masses of people flocking into Algiers from defeated Europe. As the defeat of France set in, she was one of the first to pick up murmurings of discontent among the French about perfidious Albion, a centuries old staple in the long and stormy Anglo-French relationship. She briefed General Lord Dillon, the head of the Military Mission, on the changing currents of public opinion in Algiers.

But Lord Dillon had personal experience with changing French opinion in the last bitter days of June as the defeat and then the Armistice settled in. She knew that Lord Dillon had been in contact with General August Noguès as the defeat unfolded and had broached the possibility of a French resistant government becoming established in North Africa. General Noguès had initially shown an inclination to fight on in North Africa.

Later when Lord Dillon traveled to Morocco, he found that General Noguès had experienced a change of heart. Always a soldier, Noguès had telegraphed Maréchal Pétain for instructions, and General Maximilian Weygand, the French commander in chief in Vichy, had responded with an order to Noguès to give up any idea of continuing the fight. The French Empire must remain faithful to Maréchal Pétain; that is where duty lay. The French generals and admirals commanding in Africa fell into line.

Lord Dillon had returned to Algiers empty handed. Nevertheless, during the interval while international diplomacy was failing, Joan and others had helped six hundred Polish pilots who had escaped across the Mediterranean from France reach Gibraltar. The Poles were tough men looking for the opportunity to fight again with the Royal Air Force. Later other Poles came to Algiers and stayed, exceptional men good at espionage, under the direction of a man named Rygor. Eventually, months later, Rygor established a radio link in Algiers with the British.

Behind the scenes, Joan worked every night with French air-force intelligence sergeant Jean Castet in copying codes and delivering the nightly work in a rolled-up packet of papers each day to the consulate.

On this Wednesday morning, walking down the road toward the consulate, she turned and saw Captain Gatlow driving at speed down the street. He braked instantly when he saw her and leaned out of the car window and said, "Burn everything, and lie low." He put the car back in gear and raced down the road to the consulate. The world had changed in an instant.

British Consulate

At the consulate, Gatlow quickly entered and started to burn papers. He kept at his work as he saw French policemen take up station at the entrance. In a few minutes, he was interrupted by a Frenchman, one he knew well. He had watched the man approach out of the corner of his eye. The French police guarding the entrance threw salutes and addressed the man: "*Monsieur le capitaine.*" Authority had arrived.

Gatlow looked at the man, who was of average height but had a bull-like presence, and asked apprehensively, "Yes, Chief?"

"I just heard about the ultimatum at Oran. I thought you'd be here. I wanted to inquire about our mutual friends," said the man, dressed in a nice summer suit as befitting his position.

Gatlow thought for a moment and responded, "Undoubtedly, our friends in London will be in contact with you."

The Frenchman nodded in understanding; the answer seemed to satisfy him. He said, "*Au revoir*" and turned and left as silently as he had entered. Gatlow returned to burning his papers.

Joan Tuyl

Up on the hill, Joan turned around and walked back to her mother's studio and burned all the papers she had. She wondered what new and unexpected development had rocked the world she now found herself living in. She stirred the ashes of the papers to dust and then departed. She crossed Algiers going through back alleys and unlocked gates to the apartment building where Sergeant Castet's father lived. She left a message to cancel further meetings. Already she could sense the enveloping presence around her of Vichy surveillance.

In the afternoon Joan met a French air-force officer named Roger with whom she had worked on getting the Polish pilots to Gibraltar. He wanted to escort her to the bar at the Hotel Aletti for drinks. As they walked, he explained that the British had delivered a stiff ultimatum to the French fleet at Mers-el-Kébir outside Oran to either join the British fleet or sail to a neutral or British port with reduced crews.

Joan grasped the situation. If the British ships opened fire on the moored French ships, the uneasy truce between Britain and France would be over. Undoubtedly, with hostilities imminent, it had been the ultimatum that sent the British consul scurrying to the consulate earlier in the day to burn his secret papers.

As Joan and Roger walked down to the Hotel Aletti, Roger said, "Joan, as I promised, I will introduce you to Saint-Exupéry. But I also want you to tell him about the telegram you saw at the consulate from Admiral Darlan to the French fleet. The admiral at Mers-el-Kébir may have a way out if he follows the spirit of the telegram."

"Fine, I'll explain it if you think it will do any good."

"I'm sure it will."

Entering the swank Hotel Aletti, Joan and Roger found a group of French air-force and naval officers sitting around a large table at the corner of the spacious bar trying to sort out the day's events. The group broke up, and Roger introduced her to Antoine de Saint-Exupéry, the famed French author and airman.

Joan explained the telegram that she had seen and added her thought: "I think the ultimatum is a vast piece of acting—a display of force majeure—a ploy to allow the French to sail to a British port or neutral port without violating the terms of the Armistice."

"No, this is no game," said the big, heavyset forty-year-old Frenchman with the startling dark eyes.

"The enemy is Germany," protested Joan.

"Agreed."

"It's not possible," she asserted. "The British will fire to one side. The British could never fire on the French."

"The French will not fire first," agreed the aviator.

Joan nodded. Worry came over her face. What if the British fired directly at the ships?

Saint-Exupéry took a sip from his whiskey and concluded, "People who were most friendly to the British are now keyed up in the opposite direction. That was not the way to do it. Churchill miscalculated."

Joan gulped. She finished her drink and asked Roger to escort her home. She stood up, bowed to Saint-Exupéry, who stood and returned the bow. Then she and Roger departed.

Later that night, listening on the radio with her mother, Joan heard the electrifying news: at Mers-el-Kébir, the French admiral had refused the British ultimatum, and the British had opened fire, disabling and destroying the French warships and killing twelve hundred French sailors. The famed entente cordiale died with the deaths of French sailors under British guns.

Joan sensed that relations between partisans of the British cause of continuing the fight and French fatalism arising from feelings of betrayal and defeat would grow bitter. The amiability between nationalities—neighbors for decades—in Algiers would fracture.

Espionage—an Opener

A few days after news from Mers-el-Kébir upended politics in Algiers, Joan met again with Castet, the air-force intelligence sergeant.

"I have an important piece of information, Joan, another telegram," the sergeant said. "But how do we get it out?"

"The British consulate is closed and under guard," said Joan in acknowledging that their existing communications channel was shut down. "I have some contact with the American vice-consul, Orray Taft. We could try him?"

"Here, I have the original copy of a telegram signed by General Weygand to the French air force containing a plan to bomb Gibraltar in case of any future aggression by the British," said Castet. "Look, here is the original stamp proving its authenticity. I have to get the original back into the files by this evening."

Joan scanned the telegram: it listed the French bases from which an attack would be launched and other details. "This could be gold. I'll take it to Taft now. Meet me at my house in three hours' time," said Joan. She slipped the telegram inside the waistband of her skirt and took off.

Arriving at the American consulate, Joan got right in to see Taft. He scanned the telegram and asked, "Who would believe anything like that?"

"See the stamp. This is original. It's authentic," protested Joan. "Please copy it."

"I don't need to copy the message. I can remember it," said the vice-consul with a wave of dismissal.

"Remember all the details?" she asked incredulously.

Taft made a blank look.

"But the British need to know about a plan to attack Gibraltar in case they ever launch an attack on Africa," protested Joan.

Taft didn't make a move.

Joan stood motionless, internal anger freezing her like a statue. She turned on her hell and left to return the telegram back to Castet. Such enormous risks undertaken for such a stupid response, thought Joan. The Americans, at least that one, simply were not in the game. One got tired of hearing about the Americans.

Le Club

The following day after a day of work, Joan walked out from the American consulate late in the afternoon on Rue Michelet, the beautiful boulevard that wound its way up from the waterfront and through the graceful commercial section of the European section of Algiers. Further on, the road curved up through the foothills overlooking Algiers. A handsome boulevard in one of the most beautiful cities in the French colonial empire, she thought. She again met the French air-force officer Roger outside a sidewalk café. Her hope was that by widening her net she would find a communications channel out of Algiers to the British—somehow, somewhere.

"Ready for some chess?" asked Roger.

"After a good drink first," replied Joan. "Then chess."

They walked down the wide street past the government offices toward the Hotel Aletti and turned up a side street and went into a large, well-appointed bar called Le Club full of French officers and government functionaries. An interesting selection of handsome and suave young Germans and Italians from the recently arrived Armistice Commission rounded out the clientele.

Roger guided Joan over to a vacant table with a chessboard and pieces sitting on it.

"A whiskey and soda?" asked Roger.

"Excellent," said Joan.

"Be right back." Roger went over to the bar and ordered two drinks and returned. He sat down. "What's neat about these seats is you can watch what is going on throughout the bar while pretending to concentrate on your game."

"What is our game?"

"Watching."

"For what?"

"Well, that handsome Italian with the Rudolph Valentino looks is Prince Chigi, a prominent member of the Italian Commission."

"Does he spy or seduce?"

"Mostly the latter, a little of the former."

"Is he any good?"

"To the one I can't say, as to the other I don't know."

"Well, there certainly are a lot of attractive young women in here to practice upon," said Joan looking at the many smart young French women on the arms of French officers or sitting at the bar waiting for the right Italian. A few others were hanging on the arms of the flashy young Germans. "But would the prince even know what he was trying to spy on—once under the covers?"

Roger laughed. "Good question. Does anyone?"

"For us, even if we do learn something, how do we get the information to Gibraltar or London?" asked Joan, summarizing her current dilemma. She and Castet were developing information but had no way of sharing it with the allies.

"You're close to the Americans."

"Yes, but they're not Gibraltar or London. They're a longer play, if ever."

"The Free French?" asked Roger.

"Too risky, too reckless," said Joan rather firmly.

"Yes, too obvious," said Roger.

Joan looked around the bar again. "And the others at the bar?"

"Undoubtedly the political police, they're everywhere."

"Yes, but none of the ones that follow me. Maybe I'll pick up a less clumsy one here tonight?"

"Only if they think you're on to something."

"Unfortunately, there's little in Algiers but endless rumor."

"Have you heard from Holland?"

"I got a short letter from Gerry. He says he's been demobilized and well. But that's all."

"It's a terrible war," said Roger.

"Yes, it is. That's why we must resist," said Joan with firm conviction. She hoped her husband in Holland shared that feeling, but she wasn't sure. An unsettling doubt in what had once been a solid relationship gnawed at her.

"Your move," said Roger pointing to the chessboard.

She moved a chess piece. She thought about confiding in Roger and then thought better of it. She had heard that after the British ultimatum to the French at Mers-el-Kébir, the French had rounded up their sailors in Oran and put them back on the anchored ships in the harbor, lambs tethered to stakes waiting for a coming slaughter. Twelve hundred had been killed when the British opened fire. She clenched her jaw as she understood: the French admirals were playing a hard and cynical game.

As she moved her chess pieces, she pondered and understood that the French army had failed on the battlefield; it was discredited. In the shadows, in her mind, the navy had failed on the field of honor. Nevertheless, she could see that the navy was poised to come out on top in the power struggles racking the new collaborationist regime in Vichy.

Meanwhile, the out-of-work French officers in Algiers were beset by lassitude, their own version of *le cafard*, the madness and despair of loneliness that hits those long stationed in the vast spaces of Africa.

Chapter 7: Marseilles

Marseilles, August 1940. The heavyset man known as l'inspecteur wore a loose shirt and baggy trousers as he walked up the sidewalk in the sultry summer heat toward a small bistro a couple of blocks back from the harbor. He looked like a lot of the other swarthy, heavyset men on the streets of Marseilles, always a crossroads of the Mediterranean. He walked inside and nodded at the attractive woman behind the bar. "Vivienne, how are you? Haven't seen you since Paris."

"It goes well, Hervé," said the woman. "Would you like a drink? He'll be back in half an hour."

"Fine," he said. "How's Cosette?" he asked casually, not betraying any concern, although Vivienne read him like a book and had for some time. He would be good for Cosette, she thought. Someday.

"She's in Morocco. Running a few girls, keeping tabs on the very top."

"Yes, le chef won't miss a trick," said Hervé. But it sounded like Cosette herself had given up the most intimate aspects of the trade. He picked up a glass of wine and walked over and sat down near a window looking out over the harbor, alone with his thoughts. He first saw Vivienne—and he meant saw—with le chef about ten years back at *La Boheme* up on the hill of Montmartre. All the waitresses wore cute little white aprons like maids but without another stitch of clothing. Nothing much left to anyone's imagination. Not surprising, it was a great hangout for French politicians and others of the governing elite. Vivienne quietly organized some of the girls into a lucrative after-hours business handling only the most select of customers. Cosette had been one of her stars. Sort of a ministers' only property.

Le chef saw the game and offered Vivienne top-level protection for topnotch information. Le chef kept the vice squad away from Vivienne; in turn, he became the best-informed young intelligence inspector in Paris. Le chef knew more about the government than the government. The game put him in his own office two blocks back from Place Beauvau, home of the all-powerful ministry of the interior. Then his relationship with Vivienne deepened to one of enduring commitment, two realists in world of illusion.

Transferring into counterintelligence had been good for Hervé, too. Got him out of the seamy world of undercover work for the *brigade criminelle* and the back-alley knife fights with Corsicans. After a half hour of looking back, Hervé stood and walked over to the stairs. On the second floor, he turned toward the rear of the building where he opened a door onto a landing. He took another set of stairs to the third floor. He walked over to a door and knocked.

"*Entrez*" came a voice from inside. The heavyset man opened the door and went in.

"Ah, l'inspecteur," said the man with the thinning brown hair behind the desk, a cigarette burning in the ashtray on the paper-strewn tabletop.

"Chef," said the heavyset man in acknowledgment as he sat down. They were an inside-outside duo. Le chef was continuing the small counterespionage operation that had formerly been part of the ministry of the interior in Paris. They were now provisionally attached to a Vichy counterespionage agency.

"The German divisions?" asked le chef.

"I was in Toulouse. There were six divisions along the Pyrenees at the beginning of July after the Armistice. Rumors abounded that the Germans were going to cross Spain and take Gibraltar and then cross the strait and conquer Morocco. Some said they'd go all the way to Dakar," mentioning the big colonial city in Senegal sitting on the West African coast.

"Very audacious."

"Who or what could stop them?"

"Good point," said le chef. He drew on his cigarette and blew a plume of smoke toward the ceiling. "Where are they now?"

"Gone."

"Gone?" said le chef with astonishment, sitting bolt upright. "Where?"

"To the north of France."

"For the invasion of England?"

"That's what everyone believes."

"But first the Germans have to destroy the Royal Air Force."

"The *Boche* pretty much destroyed the RAF in France in about three weeks last May. Shouldn't take them long to polish off the remainder."

"Possibly. But the English are tricky that way. They held the best squadrons back from France," said le chef as he took another long drag on his cigarette.

"Yes, that's why we lost so quickly," said l'inspecteur with weary resignation, reflecting the deeply felt pessimism of the French at the suddenness of the defeat and a gnawing sense that the British had contributed to it by not playing fair. *La perfide Albion.*

"Nevertheless," said le chef, "we have work to do."

"Just who are we?" asked l'inspecteur.

"Good question. We are now part of the *Travaux Ruraux*—the Rural Works. Our identification gives us justification to travel all over France and North Africa."

"Where did it come from?"

"The *Cinquième Bureau* was shut down after the Armistice. Our old friend Commandant Paul Paillole gathered together some of the best and set this up last month. He grew up in Marseille."

"And the ministry of the interior? We're not with them anymore?"

"I wanted to get away from them. Compromised. They're up in Vichy. Too close to Laval," he said mentioning Pierre Laval, the former premier and the eminence grise behind Maréchal Pétain. Laval was believed to be the architect behind the Armistice.

"And Travaux Ruraux. Safe?"

"Very. The headquarters is a couple of blocks away, code name Cambronne," said le chef. The code name came from a French general famous for telling the British *merde* during the Napoleonic wars. Telling the British *shit* felt good these days.

L'inspecteur smiled approvingly; the British were a bitter aftertaste in the summer of 1940.

"And the Germans? Are they in Marseille?"

"A few watching the port. During daylight. They walk carefully."

"Our cover?"

"Solid and official. Here's your new identification. Authentic." Le chef pushed the ID card and papers across the desk.

"Hervé Alphonse?" said l'inspecteur. "Close to the real thing. And you?"

"Bernard Roche. *Un commissaire.*" A superintendent.

"What's our mission? There's not much happening down south with the Germans headed north."

"Nevertheless, the Germans. We want to keep an eye on the Germans in North Africa."

"In North Africa?" asked l'inspecteur, astonished. "They're there?"

"Not many. Right now, about a hundred. Just an armistice commission."

"Anyone we know?"

"Interesting you should ask. Remember Theodor Auer, the German counselor in the Paris embassy?"

"Before the war. Of course. Worse than a priest."

"Yes," said le chef thoughtfully.

"Do you still have the photos?"

"Yes, they're in records cache. The cache is hidden in the sewer running underneath this building. I'll show it to you later, or at least the trap door leading down to it. Same with the files on the Paris priests. But we're years away from any government cleaning up that mess. The cardinal is safe for now."

"So what do you want me to do?"

"Go to Algiers and then Morocco. Scout it out. For now, just sniff."

"Will do."

"Cosette is there."

"Yes?"

"She's in Rabat and Casablanca. She has a small circle of girls, very select, just for the top. She can help you with boys if the need arises. We're going to get to Auer—eventually."

"Yes, an unfortunate business," said l'inspecteur. "But with Auer..." He let the words hang.

"Exactly," said le chef.

"I saw Vivienne downstairs," said l'inspecteur. "What's she up to?"

"She's mostly just doing this bistro. It was always her dream during those years up in Paris. Move to the south of France. Have her own *boîte.*"

"Yeah, you're lucky to have her," said l'inspecteur with a wistful air, a man now approaching middle age alone.

"As you can imagine, Vichy is a hot bed of sexual intrigue," continued le chef.

L'inspecteur nodded in understanding. The darkened bedroom was always an open door to the intelligence agencies. The Germans knew that, too. It might get crowded around the keyhole.

"Eventually Vivienne will get something going there. But we can't let it lead back to Marseille. Our cover here is too good," said le chef with evident satisfaction.

"When do I leave?"

"When you feel like it. There're ships heading for Algiers every day. And almost every day for Barcelona."

L'inspecteur stood up.

"Oh yes, Vivienne wants you to keep an eye on Cosette. She wants her back here as a partner when we wind this up," said le chef.

"Will do," said l'inspecteur as he turned and left. Two things to settle in North Africa, he thought.

Bermuda

At the end of August, Jean Monnet and his wife Silvia stood among passengers just debarked from the Pan American Airways Clipper in the customs shed next to the harbor at Darrell's Island in Bermuda, the mid-Atlantic stop on the way to New York. The British customs officer in crisp khakis and an even crispier mustache looked suspiciously at Monnet's French passport. In Monnet's pocket was a British passport signed by Winston Churchill himself in case he needed it. The customs officer knew the Clipper was for important people, not refugees no matter how well connected they might be. Monnet pulled out of his pocket the letter signed by Churchill sending him to Washington to work with the British Purchasing Commission. The customs officer read it with open-eyed amazement.

"It just doesn't make sense for a Frenchman to hold a British job at this point," said the puzzled customs officer. How can you trust a Frenchman? French rancor toward the British after the June defeat and the July attack at Mers-el-Kébir was well known.

"My mission is to seek additional American support," said Monnet. "I've lived in America for many years."

"Yes, sir," said the customs officer. "Support is much needed, I daresay." The German air assault on England had begun; the world was watching with hypnotic dread. The customs officer pointed them toward the luxurious passenger lounge.

Later the Clipper lifted off from the harbor and flew north to New York, landing at the La Guardia Marine Terminal. Along the way, Monnet took stock. He was going to Washington to lead an effort for increased solidarity between Britain and a still-neutral America at a time when isolationism was strong in America, particularly its Congress, thoroughly rooted in the heartland. The pivotal presidential election was coming up in two months.

"What are you thinking, dear?" his wife asked as the big flying boat droned through the skies.

"The Battle of Britain is coming up. The British will surely win. That will effectively defeat any invasion attempt."

"My goodness, that bad? You really think the Germans could invade?"

"No, but the more difficult challenge will be the coming Battle of the Atlantic. That almost turned the trick against the British in the last war. The U-boats are a mortal threat to British shipping."

"But you're not a sailor?"

"This war, like the last, will be a matter of supply."

"And the Germans?"

"We'll surely defeat them."

"How?"

"The US has an immense economy. It needs to be organized into a huge undertaking, a victory program."

"That would make a nice name. The Americans like slogans."

"Yes, it would," said Monnet. He leaned back in his seat and smiled. At the end of the day, the biggest ideas would carry the day. The well-traveled international businessman knew that was the key to understanding the modern world. Only America offered a big enough space to give the big ideas the big play.

Chapter 8: Washington

White House, September 1940. The president's secretary escorted Jean Monnet into the Oval Room. Behind a large wooden desk sat Franklin D. Roosevelt in a billowy white shirt with loose sleeves coming down to French cuffs, a cigarette burning in the long black cigarette holder stuck between the teeth and jutting outward at a jaunty angle—a classic pose of the president.

"Welcome," said the president waving to a vacant chair. "Nice to see you again, Mr. Monnet." The president was referring to the previous meeting in 1938 at Hyde Park when Monnet had discussed placing large French orders for airplanes with American aircraft companies.

The president leaned forward. "You've seen Churchill?"

"Yes, just before I left," replied Monnet.

"How are the Brits doing?" asked Roosevelt, anxiety deepening the lines on his face.

"I can testify to their bulldog determination," said Monnet.

The president seemingly waved away Monnet's assurance with his cigarette holder; the president's eyes darted this way and that. He was worried. "How soon will there be fog in Britain?" A possible German invasion was clearly on the president's mind.

"Britain can withstand any invading force," replied Monnet firmly.

"Good," said the president as he leaned back and relaxed. The complete defeat of France so quickly had been a large shock. Britain stood frighteningly alone.

"I understand Britain's needs," continued Monnet.

"Needs? We've done the fifty destroyers for the Caribbean bases. We can do more…but only later…after the election."

Monnet took it in and then shifted direction. "I'm certain that the Nazis can no longer win the war," said Monnet in his most determined manner. The president looked at him intently. "The question is how to defeat them," said Monnet with characteristic bluntness.

"Yes, defeat them," said the president, repeating the strategic dilemma that faced him in a way unprecedented in American history. How to defeat an enemy that you were not at war with.

"We must mount an effort commensurate with the size of the United States," continued Monnet.

"What is your strategy?"

"Allied orders are the key to increasing American production. We must add the requirements of Britain and America together and begin letting contracts to bring forth the production."

"Add the requirements all together," said Roosevelt, pondering the wisdom of Monnet's approach. "Not letting the priorities of one block the priorities of the other?"

"Exactly. One set of priorities."

"I understand," said Roosevelt. The president had been assistant secretary of the navy in the First World War and was intimately familiar with mobilizing and organizing the vast American economy for war. He and Monnet were on the same page. The president listened to this with practiced acceptance. His thinking was evolving along these lines. "Well, you and your associates can work on this," said the president.

"We're getting a combined estimate of needs in place as we talk, Mr. President," said Monnet.

"Yes, and while you're working on that I have to bring public opinion along," said the president with deep reflection. He was not going to lead a divided country into war. The president clenched his teeth, and the cigarette holder bolted to its jaunty, upthrust position. The infectious smile widened and the teeth flashed as he said, "And an election to win."

"I better not keep you from that election," said Monnet as he arose. "This meeting is a strong start. We're refreshingly clear on the objectives."

The president made a farewell wave with his cigarette holder as Monnet headed for the door.

Foxhall Road

"Welcome, gentlemen, to my new home," said Jean Monnet to the two men entering the spacious house he had rented on Foxhall Road in a fashionable tree-lined neighborhood just west of Georgetown. The visitor with the scholarly air took a long revolving look at the original French art hanging on the walls with obvious interest.

"Nice," the man murmured.

"The selection of the art is Silvia's doing."

"Serious French paintings. I'm impressed," said the man with a hint of a German accent. He was Felix Frankfurter, the Supreme Court justice, who had been born in Austria. "So often you see Whistler's *Mother* or something more appropriate from a cover of the *Saturday Evening Post* hanging in most American homes." The justice had always been impressed with the exceptional in America, never its averageness.

"Thank you, Felix," said Silvia Monnet.

"Felix, let me introduce you to my aide, Jacques Dubois," said Jean, who turned to his aide. "Jacques, this is Justice Frankfurter of the Supreme Court."

Jacques stuck out his hand and said, "Pleased to meet you."

"And this is Jack McCloy," said Jean, introducing the stocky, businesslike other man. "He's working for Secretary of War Stimson," and added impishly, "part time, a couple of days a week."

McCloy made an ironical laugh. "My partners go weeks without seeing me," said the Wall Street lawyer.

"Pleased to meet you," said Jacques as he shook McCloy's hand.

"Let's go into the dining room and get to dinner," said Jean.

"Gladly," said McCloy. "A glass of Silvia's good wine will be appreciated."

The group went into the dining room, and Jean took his seat at the head of the table and Silvia at the other end.

"Jean, just where does Britain fit into our plans here in Washington," asked McCloy, quick off the mark.

"The defense of Britain and the United States are indissolubly linked. It's not a question of either or, but rather the needs must be added together," responded Monnet.

"How?" asked McCloy. Stimson had asked McCloy to look into how war production could be increased. Frankfurter, a large behind-the-scenes presence in Roosevelt's inner circle, had put McCloy, the man with the question, in touch with Monnet, the man with the answers. Frankfurter had quickly grasped that Monnet had the best answers to the big questions around. Frankfurter thought Monnet was so concise that he could write a Supreme Court decision in a short paragraph.

"Allied orders for war munitions are the key," said Monnet with deeply felt insistence. "Hard purchasing orders must be released. Otherwise the manufacturers will not build the capacity that we need."

"Just whose purchasing orders?" asked McCloy.

"Right now, the British orders. We've calculated our requirements, and we're preparing three billion in new orders."

McCloy was taken aback by the size of the dollar figure. "Can Britain afford that?"

"That's not the question. That is what is needed. First we state what is needed."

"And?" said a still skeptical McCloy.

"We will figure out how to finance it later," said Jean. "Better to have ten thousand tanks too many than be one tank short at the moment of crisis."

"I see," said McCloy, struck by the originality of Monnet's solution. "And American production?"

"We need to do what we did in the First World War. We came up with one combined balance sheet showing total needs on one side of the ledger and how to get there on the other side. My staff at the British Purchasing Commission are working on it right now with American experts."

"Yes, we could orchestrate that from Washington and get industries across the country to meet the production targets," said McCloy. "Stimson will like it."

"Stimson will like any well-presented plan you put in front of him," said Monnet. "That's why you're here. I know that."

"And Stimson's job is to sell a plan to Roosevelt on how to win the war," said Frankfurter. He smiled deeply and winked at Jacques. One of Frankfurter's roles was to get the right men with the right thinking into the president's office. It was all coming together. Stimson and McCloy at the War Department, Acheson over at State. The New Deal at its best—talent on task.

"Okay, we'll all work together on this project," said McCloy. "Where are you at now?"

"We're working on the detailed needs to outfit ten British divisions. All new, all better. The new divisions have to be able to beat the Germans one-on-one."

"How?"

"We're going to have to out-firepower them."

"We're not going to outfight them?"

"You're not going to outfight the Germans," said Monnet. "That's what the May-June offense in northern France was all about. A new kind of war."

"Makes sense," said McCloy. "The German divisions walked all over the British and French divisions last May. There are arguments raging all over the War Department on what the new US divisions should look like. The German use of dive bombers and tanks in both Poland and France has overturned army thinking completely."

"General Marshall is bringing in new weapons and retiring old generals every day, probably a winning combination," added Frankfurter.

"Do you have a detailed list of what is required?" asked McCoy.

"Yes, Jacques is working on it now, a plan for outfitting ten new British divisions. I'll have him deliver a document to you next week."

"Be ready for a detailed cross-examination," said Frankfurter with a smile toward Jacques. "McCloy is nothing if not always well prepared with the best brief in Washington."

"Yes, sir," said Jacques.

The guests continued eating dinner.

"We need to pull all this into one overall program," said Monnet, "so the president can present it to Congress and the public at the right time."

"You said 'victory program,' dear, when we were flying over on the Clipper," interjected Silvia.

"Yes, I did," said Monnet.

"Let's keep that phrase 'victory program' to ourselves," said Frankfurter. "It has a nice ring. Bob Sherwood might want to use it." Pulitzer Prize-winning playwright Robert Sherwood was the president's speechwriter.

"Yes, it would fit nicely in a Fireside Chat," said McCloy. "The president has a sure ear for this type of thing."

Chapter 9: Algiers

Joan Tuyl crossed Rue Michelet, glanced behind her, and then walked down a narrow passageway behind the hospital. Because of her work for the American consulate, she was often followed by French plainclothes political police. She had a sixth sense about being followed and how to evade it. She had learned the backstreets as a girl growing up in Algiers. After passing the hospital, she opened a gate and entered a walled garden, took a brick path between small lemon and orange trees. The fragrance of the blossoms was a tonic to her spirits this Sunday morning. At the far end of the garden, she opened a gate and stepped out onto a crowded street in the mixed European and Arab neighborhood of Belfort. She made a crazy quilt path through the pedestrians toward the university, coming out on Rue de Lyon near a small square across from the university gardens.

Up ahead, she saw the young man she was to meet sitting at a table at an outdoor café, a thin waspish student with black tousled hair. Her mother had invited the young man over for tea earlier in the week. After a brief talk, she had decided to chance this meeting. A few customers were sitting in the shade enjoying a morning aperitif and conversation with their friends. She walked up as the young man stood smiling in recognition; she kissed him on the cheek before sitting down at the table. Just a couple of meetings.

"Hello, Thomas," she said. "So?"

"He'll be here shortly," said Thomas cryptically. He had wanted Joan to meet someone.

Soon a man in his forties, sturdy with blue eyes and curly hair, approached and sat down at the table.

"Hi, my name is Curly," he said. He looked at her with understanding eyes. "That's enough name for now."

"Understand," said Joan.

"I hear you've been developing information separate from your work with the Americans," said Curly.

"Yes."

"What are you going to do with it?" asked Curly.

"That's the problem. How to get it to the British," said Joan, identifying the choke point affecting information she collected with her underground contacts.

"Yes, ever since Dakar." The French security services had clamped down on communications after the unsuccessful attack.

Joan looked at Curly. "Do you know how the French reacted to the Dakar attack?"

"Yes, some French aircraft attacked Gibraltar."

"Any damage?"

"Not really. The attacks were ineffective. A lot of the pilots dropped their bombs in the sea."

"I see," said Joan, deciding not to confide any additional information. But yes, Sergeant Castet's information had been good; the American consulate's lack of assistance discouraging.

Curly looked at her and wondered what she wasn't telling him. Well, fine. You didn't want to associate with talkative people in this line of work. Soon several other serious-looking middle-aged men came up and sat down. Again, one-name introductions were quietly whispered around the table. Curly looked at Joan and said by way of warning, "No politics."

"Understand. Too dangerous," she replied. She looked at Thomas with mild reproach. He had been too indiscreet with her mother when he had introduced himself to her at the English Library.

A desultory conversation flowed around the table and slowly a plan came together. Curly summarized: "Most of you are going to work on the propaganda side. Print the newspaper, mimeograph the information, spread the word." Heads around the table nodded. "But the other work, the intelligence, that must be kept separate."

Joan simply nodded in agreement. She could not keep any secret information in her mother's studio. The political police all but ransacked the place whenever she and her mother both went out. A stray pamphlet would lead to arrest. But her relationship with the American consulate was also a shield; the political police hoped to glean something from their constant surveillance of her. But she also knew that the well-watched bird would have her opportunities, too. The surveillance was also an alibi.

Curly put an end to the meeting, saying, "Cafés are too dangerous. From now on, we'll meet in apartments. Out of the way. Be careful about being followed." Heads nodded in agreement.

Joan stood up and shook hands with Curly. "Good," she said firmly. "Finally, an organization."

"Yes," said Curly. "I'll work with you on the communications angle later."

She turned and started the walk back to her mother's studio. The men stood as one watching her go, the bright blond hair iridescent in the morning sunlight, the stunningly beautiful figure bringing her dress and their imaginations alive.

Chapter 10: Lisbon

September 4, 1940. The cablegram from Washington had caught the diplomat unawares several days before. Forty-six-year-old Robert Murphy had been summoned back to Washington without explanation. As the chargé d'affaires of the American embassy at Vichy, he presumed the State Department wanted a first-person account of the defeat of France and its aftermath. The American government had made plain its support for Britain and was completing a transfer of fifty old destroyers in return for bases in the Caribbean. The deal was being completed as Murphy traveled toward New York.

But Murphy thought to himself as he sat in the departure lounge: "The odds against the allies winning are overwhelming." He shook his head at his own diplomatic pessimism; he was not a stormy petrel, but his characteristic optimism had been dented by the defeat he had witnessed. German power was immense and seemingly unstoppable.

Escorted into the Pan Am flying boat, the Yankee Clipper, by a svelte stewardess dressed in a stunningly crisp white cotton uniform, Murphy took his comfortable seat in the big flying boat, an aerial incarnation of first-class luxury travel worthy of an ocean liner. After idling away from the dock, the flying boat accelerated down the Taugus River and lifted off into the sky. Over the Bay of Lisbon, the Yankee Clipper turned west toward Horta in the Azores, its first refueling stop.

The following afternoon the big Clipper gracefully pulled up to the LaGuardia rotunda at the Marine Air Terminal in New York. On the dock, a *New York Times Tribune* reporter peppered the diplomat with questions. He breezily responded with short answers. A waiting aide hurried him out to a taxicab. He was in Washington the following day.

But a thought nagged at him. Who would want to see him in person in Washington? Normally his reports answered all the questions stateside officials asked and then some. In his experience, most of the men in the State Department were not the type to ask a lot of questions. The State Department in Washington was an insular club full of men from good families who were not quite good enough to be investment bankers. So just who wanted to know something now?

Chapter 11: The White House

Undersecretary of State Sumner Welles guided Robert Murphy toward the office of the president's trusted secretary, Missy LeHand. The tall immaculately dressed Welles, his cane swinging nonchalantly from his right hand, said in a low voice to Murphy, "Missy's the real boss in these corridors."

Entering LeHand's office, Welles said, "I believe the president's expecting us?"

"He sure is," said LeHand. "He has his maps spread out all over his desk."

Murphy's eyebrows shot up at the mention of maps. Maps? What was this all about?

"Missy, let me introduce you to Bob Murphy."

She stood up and shook Murphy's hand. "Pleased to meet you." She turned to Welles and said, "Let me see if he's ready for you." She reappeared in a few moments and said, "This way." She guided the two men into the Oval Room.

The president was seated behind his desk in his shirt sleeves. He looked up with expectation as the two men entered. "Sumner," said the president. He turned to Murphy and said, "Pleased to meet you, Mr. Murphy. I've read your dispatches with interest." The president tapped a pile of papers sitting on top of one of the maps while pointing the two men to chairs. He looked at LeHand and said, "We'll be a while, Missy."

"I'll keep the calendar clear," she replied and departed.

Murphy looked at Welles. A long meeting? With maps? What was all this about?

"I've been reading Commander Hillenkoetter's reports of his inspection of French North Africa," said Roosevelt. Hillenkoetter was the American naval attaché at Vichy. "These reports interest me a great deal." He ran his cigarette holder, minus a cigarette, over the map of the Mediterranean and Africa spread out on his desk.

"Yes, Commander Hillenkoetter told us the atmosphere in North Africa is not comparable to the confusion in Vichy," said Murphy. "If France is going to fight again anywhere in this war, Hillenkoetter thinks North Africa will be the place."

"Exactly," said Roosevelt. "For now, we want to help the French officers there maintain their independence. Keep the Germans out. General Weygand has just been appointed to the top job there."

"Yes, Delegate General," responded Murphy. "He's just taking up his duties."

"Weygand was an aide to Marshal Foch in the First World War. I met Foch in Paris in 1919," said the president. "I believe Weygand will want to preserve French independence."

"Undoubtedly," agreed Murphy, though keeping his reservations about Weygand to himself. Weygand had been an architect of the Armistice.

Roosevelt ran his hand over the coastline of North Africa. "For sure, we want to help the French keep their fleet out of German hands." The president discussed this with Murphy for several more minutes showing his deep knowledge of the subject. Roosevelt had been assistant secretary of the navy during the First World War, then the number-two job in the Navy Department. People joked about the president's stamp collection, but he had an encyclopedic knowledge of world geography. The president then shifted the conversation while tapping his finger on Gibraltar, a small peninsula jutting out of the south coast of Spain. "Spain? Why didn't the Germans go on to Gibraltar?"

"Yes, you are quite right to ask, Mr. President. There were ten German divisions on the Spanish frontier at the time of the Armistice," said Murphy. "Then we saw them melt away, withdrawn to the north."

"Why?" asked the president. "The Germans had the Mediterranean in the cup of their hand."

"Yes, an intriguing question. Later at Vichy, I spoke with the Spanish ambassador, Senor Lequerica, about what happened."

"The Spanish ambassador? What was his role?" asked Roosevelt, deeply intrigued.

"Lequerica was Franco's emissary to the Franco-German armistice talks. He told me Franco wanted to keep the Germans out, but that Spain would not be able to resist if the Germans moved. Lequerica said, 'We told the Germans what they wanted to hear on everything else, but ultimately we used diplomacy to keep the Germans out.'"

Roosevelt was impressed. Diplomacy had so rarely stopped the Germans before. Reading the president's thoughts, Murphy said, "The ambassador told me that Hitler had a blind spot regarding the Mediterranean."

Roosevelt leaned back and soaked up this bit of wisdom. Murphy could see that Roosevelt did not have a blind spot about the Mediterranean and that Roosevelt's instinct that Africa presented a strategic opportunity was correct. "Well, we want you to go back to Vichy and get, unostentatiously as possible, permission to make a thorough inspection of French Africa. Then report your findings back to me."

"Yes, sir," replied Murphy. "Are you concerned with me being seen with the Vichy generals?"

"I understand the cruel fate that overtook the French last June," said the president. "I would like you to make friends with General Weygand. He seems to me to be the key to any plans we might develop for French Africa."

"Yes, sir. I know him well," said Murphy.

"In fact, I believe you're a Catholic, too," said Roosevelt, leaning forward as if he were sharing a confidence.

"Yes, sir, Mr. President."

"Good, you might even attend mass with him." Roosevelt sat back up and beamed with appreciation at this minor point of guidance. Roosevelt was a great practitioner of the politics of the personal.

"Yes, sir."

"Make a thorough inspection, Bob," said the president, lapsing into the familiar. He tapped the map down at the bulge of West Africa at Dakar.

"Yes, we reopened the consulate at Dakar, just before the attack," said Murphy.

"Well, bad judgment on the part of de Gaulle. The effort was way too premature," said the president of the combined British-Free French assault on Dakar in the third week of September.

"Yes, sir," responded Murphy. Clearly the president had no intent of repeating that mistake. Timing the masterstroke was one of the gifts of the president's strategic mind.

"Something of a mountebank, I would say," added the president. Murphy carefully registered the president's negative assessment of de Gaulle.

"If you learn anything in Africa of special interest, send it to me. Don't bother going through State Department channels," said the president, concluding the meeting.

Welles and Murphy stood up and took their leave.

Outside the White House, the two men walked back to Old State just up the street.

"Does the president really want me to communication directly with the White House?" asked Murphy.

"Yes," replied Welles. "That's the way he often operates. Send it encoded and headed 'for Welles's eyes only.'"

"Got it."

"You're now one of his personal representatives, but that of course is the holiest of secrets."

"I see he wants it all under the hat."

"Yes, this is a card the president will turn over when he judges the time right. Not before," said Welles. "That was de Gaulle's mistake."

"How so?"

"Every tailor shop in London knew the Free French were sailing to attack Dakar. The French officers blabbed about it while they were buying their desert kit."

"Not very discreet."

"The president notices things like that. Therefore, the personal channel with you."

"Well, the Germans will know I'm an American diplomat and that I'm in Africa."

"But they will not know you have the president's interest; that must be kept secret."

"Understand. Just inspecting consulates."

"Remember, some day when the Americans come to North Africa, the president wants the French traffic cop on the waterfront in Algiers to be surprised as hell at the American troops rushing off the assault boats landing at the quay."

"Got it," said Murphy. Diplomacy was taking a fascinating turn.

Chapter 12: Winter Palace

Algiers. October 1940. The ornate reception hall of the Winter Palace—an immense Moorish palace just down the hill from the Casbah—housed the administrative office, the *Délégation Générale*, of the supreme civil and military authority of French Africa. At one end of the space, stairs led up to the magisterial office of the newly designated delegate general himself, five-star General Maxim Weygand. Weygand had been edged out of Maréchal Pétain's cabinet by a combination of German insistence and backroom maneuvering by Pierre Laval, who was aiming to consolidate his power under the Maréchal's broad authority.

Marie Rambert stood in front of a half-height wooden railing demarcating the secretarial area from the wider reception area and watched the general approach. In her midtwenties, she was dark haired and slender and wore a well-tailored, lightweight white suit, almost a uniform for French women in tropical Algiers. She presented a restrained and professional appearance befitting the daughter of a prominent merchant family.

General Weygand worked his way down the central aisle nodding his greetings to the staff and shaking hands. He had just arrived in Algiers having been delayed in taking up this new appointment due to recovering from injuries sustained in an airplane crash the previous month. As delegate general, he was the top-governing authority for Algeria, Tunisia, and Morocco, and also military commander in chief of all forces in the region. These forces represented the bulk of military power left to France by the Armistice.

Around the base of the stairs were some of the general's senior staff, military and civilian. Over coffee, one of the military aides had said approvingly of Weygand to Marie, "During the retreat to Bordeaux, he told Laval that he rolled in defeat like a dog in filth." Pierre Laval had adroitly moved into the number-two slot at Vichy, a faded spa town now trying to masquerade as a capital city, a place from which originated the bleakest of news and the faintest of hopes. For many, Laval symbolized the rottenness of the governance now operating in Vichy.

This afternoon, Marie's highest hope was that the new general would keep the war away from North Africa where her family was prominently established in business. Her husband Henri was now a French diplomat at the Armistice Commission in Wiesbaden, Germany, representing Vichy, France. Before the war he had been a banker. He had made a brief trip to Algiers the previous week in the aftermath of the Dakar attack. He had told her that his German contacts had told him about an incredible plan: the German air-force chief, Reichsmarschall Göring, did not want a direct attack on England but rather argued that an indirect attack on Africa would allow the Germans to take both Dakar and Cairo. From these bases, the Germans could strangle British trade in the South Atlantic and in the Middle East, its lifelines from the far-flung colonies. Britain would have to sue for peace or starve. No invasion would be required. Now waiting for brief remarks from General Weygand, she wanted to hear what the new delegate general would say.

Standing unobtrusively behind the other officials were two general staff officers whose offices were separately guarded by security personnel sitting outside. Marie could feel their importance; she had been firmly instructed that all coded communications were to be taken to these officers. Individuals who presented themselves at reception with a need to speak with "someone" were to be directed to the one of them.

Most of the civilian staff had followed the now-supplanted Admiral Abrial over to the Hotel St. Georges, site of naval headquarters, where he exercised the now-diminished functions of governor general of Algeria. The admiral had taken great umbrage at the appointment of General Weygand. But the secretary-general of the Délégation Générale, Admiral Raymond Fenard, had quickly assembled a new staff; he had personally interviewed and selected Marie. Being of a good family was an important consideration. Loyalty and discretion were greatly prized in the Winter Palace. Admiral Fenard was close to Admiral Darlan, the overall commander in chief of all military forces in Vichy. He would keep an eye on General Weygand.

Reaching Marie and the other two secretaries, Weygand stopped and smiled warmly at them and said, "*Mesdames.*" He dipped his head politely and turned and walked back to the stairs. He mounted two steps and turned around to address the two-dozen staff:

We must hold French Africa intact free from all foreign encroachment. Maintaining our legal control is of central importance. We must be on constant guard against meddling by foreign officials from whatever quarter.

Marie understood. No German attack from Spain. As for daily routine, Marie saw that the new German and Italian officials of the Armistice Commission were meddlesome in the extreme. They walked into the Winter Palace as if they owned the place, or soon would.

"We are not here just to defend North Africa but to prepare to clear the enemy out of France." The general paused to let the words sink in.

Marie felt the sentence was contradictory. She understood the need to protect French Africa ever since the aborted attack by British and Free French forces on Dakar two weeks before. The military staff had made it clear that such provocations would invite a possible German invasion. Why Germany had not occupied North Africa right after the Armistice was something of a mystery except the belief that the Germans had turned toward a possible invasion of Great Britain. As her husband had explained to her, even the Germans were divided on the question.

The general had said they were to prepare to clear the enemy out of France? What did that mean? Were the Germans the enemy to be cleared out? If so, how? France had been thoroughly defeated. Her husband was in fact administering the defeat as a member of the French Armistice Commission at Wiesbaden, Germany.

"We must remember our duties and train hard and keep fit for the challenges ahead." The general looked around the reception hall and concluded, "Thank you." He turned and walked up the stairs.

Marie watched the general ascend to his office. She also knew that the general's wife Renée was taking over the local Red Cross, a charity in which her mother and sister were active. The Red Cross was meeting later that week.

Hotel St. Georges

The limousine drove up Rue Michelet climbing the hill overlooking Algiers. The car turned into the entranceway between stone pillars as armed sentries swung open the big-black iron gates. The limousine halted at the sentry box. A sailor wearing a pistol and a rifle slung over his shoulder stepped forward, asking, "Monsieur?" The hotel was French naval headquarters for North Africa.

The chauffeur handed across an engraved invitation, and the sailor glanced at it and handed it back. He peered into the rear passenger compartment at the three well-dressed ladies. Satisfied, he stood back and said, "*Allez.*" Go.

The limousine turned into a parking area and pulled up among a group of other touring cars where ladies were getting out, straightening dresses with the palms of their hands, and looking into the little round mirrors in compact cases and dabbing a final touch of powder to rosy cheeks. All sorted out, the ladies walked over to the front steps of the hotel.

The chauffeur parked the limousine and quickly went around and opened the rear door. The three women slid out and stood on the pavement, straightening their dresses with the palms of their hands, centering their hats while looking at their reflections in the vehicle's windows, and finally pulling on gloves. The older woman said, "Thank you, Pierre." The chauffeur tipped his hand to his cap brim and then turned and walked over to a table in the shade of a tree where other chauffeurs had gathered.

The three women followed the groups of other women up the steps and into the building. At the top of the steps, a woman came forward and said, "Ernestine."

"Yes," replied Madame Sauveterre with a bright smile of friendship. "How are you, Hélène?"

"Fine."

"You know my daughters, Madeleine and Marie."

"Of course," said Hélène. "Have you heard Madame Weygand has been appointed to head the Algiers Red Cross."

"Yes, we're all here to hear her speech this afternoon." The four women chatted for a moment and then went into the lobby of the hotel where they were directed to a large reception room where tea was being served. They took seats and waved and spoke with their many friends among the women gathered to hear Renée Weygand make her opening speech to the ladies of the Red Cross.

At the head of room, the current head of the Red Cross took to the podium and after a brief introduction said, "Here is Madame Renée Weygand." There was polite applause as the older women, now in her early seventies, came up to the podium.

"I would like to say how pleased I and my husband, the general, are at being in Algiers. The wonderful climate, the warm people." Applause rippled across the room.

"I would like to say that we have much work to do. Everyone's help will be needed. The French state has to carry heavy burdens under the Armistice." Gloom fell across the room. No ray of good news here.

"The empire will have to come to the assistance of the mother country in its hour of need." The women in the audience listened intently.

"In particular, we must get tinned milk to the children in the Metropole for the winter," said Madame Weygand, and she looked out across the room portentously, "for it will be a hard winter."

The women looked at one another and understood. The rumors about the severity of the coming food shortages in the Metropole were real.

"Thank you. I look forward to working with all of you."

Applause spread across the room. Several women stood up and applauded. Most remained seated, struck by the starkness of Madame Weygand's tone.

Madame Sauveterre turned to her daughters and asked, "What do you think?"

Marie answered, "It is consistent with what General Weygand told the staff at the Winter Palace earlier this week."

"The navy officers"—Madeleine nodded to the other parts of the hotel—"seem to feel they're still the guardians of France, that it was the army that failed. Admiral Abrial has set up his headquarters here," she said, referring to Admiral Jean-Marie Charles Abrial, the governor general for Algeria. The admirals did not like a general placed between them and Admiral Darlan in Vichy. Madeleine listened to all the corridor gossip while working part time as a secretary at the navy headquarters.

"What will we do?" asked Madame Sauveterre.

"What we are asked to do," replied Marie.

"No more?" asked Madame Sauveterre.

"I am going to take nursing training three afternoons a week from the Red Cross," said Marie. "We are encouraged to do so at work."

"And be?"

"An *infirmière bénévole*," said Marie. A volunteer nurse.

"Me, too," added Madeleine. "The piano can wait." She had been studying piano in Paris before the war. "Except I also want to become an ambulance driver."

"Why?" asked her mother.

"See the action."

"I'm not sure I approve."

The three women stood up and departed, Madeleine's plans not quite agreed to.

Chapter 13: Algiers

Algiers. November 1940. On a wet, rainy night, Joan Tuyl and her mother listened to the BBC from Gibraltar. They were trying to sort out just where the war stood. Contradictory information flooded Algiers. What was clear was that the Germans seemed to be winning—everywhere. Increasingly, the people in Algiers felt isolated as German power spread across the Mediterranean like one of the black stains spreading across the map that you saw in the Allied newsreels.

There was a knock on the door. The two women froze. A knock was not always a pleasant thought considering Joan's many surreptitious activities. On the other hand, the political police already had her under near-constant surveillance. Her mother's face eased its startled look. "Who could it be?" she asked.

"Let me find out," replied Joan, and she went to the door and asked, "Who's there?"

"Orray,"

"Okay," replied Joan, and she unbolted the door and ushered Orray Taft in.

"Joan, two British officers came to Consul General Cole's villa tonight," said the diplomat.

"So?"

"What are we going to do with them?"

"Do?" asked Joan.

"Yes, the British officers have escaped from the Germans after Dunkirk. They've come from France. Someone in Marseilles gave them the consul general's address, and they made it up the hill tonight after dark. We've fed them dinner, but they can't stay. They'll be seen, and it violates our diplomatic status as a consulate representing a neutral power here in Algiers."

"Yes, I understand," said Joan. "But"—she nodded out of the window—"I'm under surveillance, too, by the political police."

"You've got to come up with an idea, Joan," said Taft.

"Do you have your car?" asked Joan.

"Yes, it's outside—with the British officers in it," replied Taft, adding that last startling piece of information.

"Outside?" said Joan, momentarily stunned. She thought for a moment. "Let's take them out to May Egan at the Golf Course. It's just five miles up the road. She's Irish and will be more than willing to help the lads out."

"Let's go," said Taft, relieved that someone had solved his conundrum for him. Joan was always so inventive. All this stuff was way outside the book. Uncomfortable.

The two of them went out to the street and got into Taft's consulate car, a gray Studebaker, and drove off.

"Where are they?" asked Joan.

A blanket in the back seat rustled and a voice whispered. "We're here."

"Got it," said Joan. The Studebaker came up to the main highway and turned and followed the road up the heights behind Joan's flat. Beyond the crest, Taft drove the car down into the valley behind the city. They came up to the golf course and drove over to a little cottage near the small shack that was the clubhouse. Joan got out and went up and knocked on the door.

The porch light came on, and the door opened; a middle-aged woman opened it. Joan spoke for several minutes, and the woman smiled and waved her arm indicating the way through her door was open. Joan walked back to the car and whispered into the back seat. A dark blanket moved, and two men crawled out from under it and squeezed out the rear door.

"Where are we?" asked one of the officers in a British accent.

"At an old golf course outside of Algiers. My friend will put you up," answered Joan. They followed Joan up to the cottage.

"This is May Egan," said Joan introducing her friend. "She'll put you up and feed you until we can figure out how to set you on your way to Gibraltar."

"Pleased to meet you," said May in an Irish brogue.

"Yes, ma'am," chimed the two officers politely.

"Remember," warned Joan. "Stay well hidden. Algiers is crawling with informers."

"We will," said one.

Paul A. Myers

Joan turned and returned to the car.

Café de Paris

Captain André Beaufre asked his driver to drop him off at the intersection of Avenue Pasteur and Boulevard Lafferriere not far from the American consulate. The staff car pulled over, and the captain got out and said to the driver, "That'll be all for today." The car drove off, and Captain Beaufre turned and entered the Café de Paris and walked up to the maître d' and said, "I believe a gentleman is waiting for me."

"Yes, this way, Captain," said the maître d' and led Beaufre across the dining room to a booth in a rear corner. A man in a dark pinstripe suit stood up and held out his hand. He was Jacques Lemaigre Debreuil, the prosperous head of a large vegetable-oil producer and distributor.

"Nice to see you again," said the businessman. "I believe the last time was in Paris in May."

"Yes," said the officer. "Your reports to the government on advancing the Weygand project in Romania were well received. If the events of May had not intervened, Reynaud would have made the changes to the French command in the Balkans," said Beaufre, describing the plan to assign overall responsibility for Romania to the commander in chief in the Levant.

"Yes," said the businessman. "I'm afraid the Romanian oil industry fell into the Germans' hands without a fight."

"Did you rejoin your regiment?" asked Beaufre, shifting subjects.

"Yes, I led two squadrons of the First Armored Regiment into battle at Troyes. We were ambushed by a German panzer division, and our vehicles destroyed and all of us captured."

"Captured?"

"Yes, I escaped at Chateau Thierry in mid-June and made my way to Paris and then to my brother's home in central France."

"How did you come to your present position?"

"I went to Vichy and met with officials including General Weygand. I stressed that we must organize our commerce to at least meet the needs of France where we could. We should not abandon the field to the Germans."

89

"So that's how you went back into business?"

"Yes, I returned to the family firm Georges Lesieur et ses Fils. We were the largest vegetable-oil producer in France before the war, but unfortunately, our business was centered in Northern France and Eastern France, regions under harsh German control or English guns."

"So what brings you to Africa?"

"We got permission to open a large processing plant in Dakar for peanuts and rights to distribute product across Africa and in Unoccupied France. We're building additional plants in Casablanca and Algiers."

"Amazing. In such a short period of time."

"Necessity drives an insistent schedule."

"So what is your thinking?" asked Beaufre.

"I, and my circle of friends, which is quite extensive, believe that we should build up strength in Africa and at an opportune time declare an independent French state in North Africa. Then we could rejoin the fight against Germany and liberate the fatherland."

"Without outside support?"

"I've had discussions with a colonel from the American army. He is encouraging. Getting the right political and military support from America is key to the plan."

"Yes, but that may be further off than you think. Right now, I am working with other officers to build up our support in Africa. For now, we support General Weygand's 'against all comers' policy of resisting all outside military forces who try to enter Africa," said Beaufre. "American intervention is far from certain at this time. I would not get too optimistic."

"There is hope that General Weygand will support our effort," said Dubreuil.

"I would be careful there also," said Beaufre, "as we all are. After you left Paris for the front, Weygand was the architect of the Armistice and convinced Pétain of its necessity. Weygand is quite committed to the Armistice, and his loyalty to the Maréchal is unquestioning...at this point, anyway."

"Will he interfere if we go ahead independently?" asked Dubreuil.

"I'm afraid so. We expect there will be a purge. Weygand expects obedience."

"Yes, he's a five-star general," said Dubreuil. "Well, I never thought it would be easy."

"It won't," said Beaufre.

"Remember," said Dubreuil. "I have excellent contacts across France and Africa and in Vichy. I've contacts close to the top. My business allows me to travel back forth between Africa and France."

Beaufre took this in. A good person to know. He firmly concluded, "We must meet again and coordinate our plans."

"Yes," said Dubreuil. "I'll be back in early December. I'm bringing my family to Algiers."

Beaufre stood up. "We'll get together then." The two men departed separately.

Chapter 14: Georgetown

Washington. Mid-November 1940. The government limousine pulled up in front of Jean Monnet's house on Foxhall Road in west Georgetown. Undersecretary of State Sumner Welles got out and walked up to the front door where Jean Monnet was waiting for him. They shook hands and went inside. Jacques Dubois was standing in the drawing room.

"Mr. Secretary, I would like to introduce my aide, Jacques Dubois," said Monnet. Welles had inquired about Jacques this morning on the telephone.

"Pleased to meet you, Mr. Secretary," said Jacques as he shook hands with the tall, patrician Brahmin standing before him. The three men took a seat.

"I didn't quite catch what was on your mind," said Monnet, looking at the undersecretary.

"Yes, well I've come to discuss a mission of which I cannot talk a great deal about," said Welles.

"And it involves Jacques?" asked Monnet. Something was going on.

"Most certainly," replied Welles. "We have a mission we would like Jacques to undertake. McCloy speaks highly of him. Says he has detailed knowledge about the organization and equipment needs of the new divisions."

"Yes, that's true," said Monnet. Jacques had delivered several detailed briefings to John McCloy over the past several weeks on the equipment needs for ten new British divisions. "Just which new divisions?"

"Can't really say," said Welles.

"If they were Free French, we could say, couldn't we?" said Monnet.

"Yes, we probably could."

"Just where do you plan to send Jacques?"

"Robert Murphy has been back here in Washington for consultations with State…and others."

"Well, that rules out the Free French, doesn't it?"

"Most certainly."

"You want Jacques to give Murphy a briefing like the one he's given McCloy?"

"No, we want Jacques to meet Murphy at the La Guardia Marine Terminal next week and accompany him to Lisbon. Jacques will go as a third secretary."

"For an embassy?"

"No, for a consulate."

"Consulate? Can I remind you, Jacques has important work here, much more important than stamping visas in some damn consulate."

"You can remind me, but I'm afraid this is the way it has to be."

"Just like that? So they send the undersecretary of state over to snatch my assistant to be a third secretary at a consulate?"

"Murphy is returning to Europe as the personal representative of the president…this is ultra-hush-hush." Welles turned to Jacques. "You can't say a word about this to anyone. Hear?"

"Yes, sir," replied Jacques.

"And Jacques goes with him?"

"To Lisbon. Then Jacques goes on to Algiers."

"Why Algiers?"

"The Germans aren't there. 'We'"—Welles emphasized the breadth of the word—"want to keep it that way."

"Why Jacques?"

"At the right time in the future, if the French in Africa join us, they will need to be reequipped. If we know what they need, we'll have it on ships ready to sail."

"That sounds farfetched."

"Farfetched? We made good the British army's losses of equipment at Dunkirk in seven weeks. Remember?"

"Yes," said Monnet.

Jacques nodded. Thirty ships had been dispatched from Canadian ports stuffed with "surplus" American army material right after Dunkirk. Almost no one knew about it. He had worked on the project.

"Someone is thinking long term here," said Monnet, catching the strategic goal of a rather audacious undertaking.

"Very," agreed Welles. "Jean, you'll have your man on hand at the center of American policy concerning France."

"Toward North Africa?"

"All of France. Some skillful maneuvering will be undertaken to separate the French in North Africa from their oaths of obedience to the Maréchal in Vichy."

"And de Gaulle?"

"We'll have to maneuver around him for now. The French in Africa and Syria despise him."

"Yes, that's true," conceded Monnet. He remembered the abrasiveness of the haughty general.

Welles turned to Jacques and said, "We have your application for US citizenship almost completed."

"I set that aside when the war started," said Jacques, surprised anyone remembered.

Welles moved on as if he hadn't heard. "My aide will come by and collect you in the morning. Take you to the District Court and a magistrate will administer the oath. In the afternoon you can process your diplomatic passport at the State Department. It's all arranged. Then the briefings will start."

Jacques looked at Monnet and shrugged. He turned back to Welles. "My girlfriend is in New York?"

"You can see her before you leave."

"What if she wants to see me off?"

Welles sighed and heaved. "Okay, how romantic. But you can only tell her you're going to Lisbon. Nothing about Algiers."

"Yes. She may pry around, though. She's a researcher for Anne Hare."

"Oh my God," exclaimed Welles, truly astonished. "We'll read all about it in the *TeeTee*." The undersecretary thought about this for a moment. "Oh, well, it can't be helped. The reporters watch the Clipper like hawks anyway. Just say you're an assistant."

"Where can she write me?"

"Overseas diplomatic section, State Department, here in Washington. You'll get the mail…eventually."

"Fine."

"When you get to Algiers. You can send her a letter," said Welles. "Be sure to complain about the dull routine and the standoffish, chaperoned young women."

"Will they be standoffish?" asked Jacques with a smile. "Should I be standoffish?"

"They'll be French. You be American." Welles raised an arched eyebrow over a faint smile. Monnet laughed.

Welles stood up, and he looked at both men. "This is one of our earliest moves." Then he turned and departed for the waiting limousine.

Monnet watched Welles depart and turned to Jacques and said, "Maybe the president's thinking is further ahead than I thought."

Jacques nodded. "I wanted to do something more active. I guess it's coming."

Rainbow Room

New York. Saturday night, late November. Jacques and Jacqueline got out of the elevator at the Top of the Rock, the nickname for the Rainbow Room, the large supper club on the top of Rockefeller Center. Jacqueline was radiant in a sleek dinner dress flaring to midcalf and made for "cutting a rug," although the dance floor of the Rainbow Room was polished tile. Jacques wore black tie, dinner jacket, and a blazingly white shirtfront.

The maître d' checked off his name and said, "This way." He led them across the room and up to a small table on a terrace overlooking the dance floor. The maître d' seated Jacqueline and left menus for them. Jacques mumbled a request to him, and he nodded and walked over to a waiter. Soon a waiter returned with a bottle of champagne in an ice bucket, popped the cork, and poured the bubbly golden liquid into champagne flutes.

"You're surprisingly dashing tonight, Jacques," said Jacqueline playfully as she took a sip. "Maybe you'll make diplomat yet."

"I've just been detailed as an assistant because I speak French."

"You know, Jacques, I don't entirely believe that."

"Well, until I get there I won't know either."

"Where is there?"

"Lisbon to start."

"Surely you're going beyond there?"

"I'll write you when I get there."

"Promise?"

"Promise."

"I spoke to Anne. She thinks you're going to London. She said to mark her words—de Gaulle is going to be the big thing. Has Churchill's backing."

"She may be right."

"Monnet was in London all summer, and you're close to Monnet."

"I can see you've got it all figured out."

"She wants me to stay in touch with you. She said the future of Europe will pivot on London. She's eventually planning to go there," said Jacqueline. Then her whole manner became convulsed with enthusiasm and excitement, and she blurted out, "She said she'd send me ahead to London to scout it out."

"That'll make you a correspondent," said Jacques. "Then the byline."

"Just one step away," said Jacqueline, simply bubbling with expectation. "So maybe it should be two bottles of champagne for us tonight?"

"To start, for sure," said Jacques, and he looked at her with deep affection. Nights with her were a swirling whirlwind of enthusiasm. He smiled at the upcoming evening.

La Guardia Rotunda of the Marine Air Terminal

Sunday morning. Jacques and Jacqueline walked into the spacious Marine Terminal and went to the white Formica-topped ticket counter where Jacques gave his name and pushed across his passport. The pert young woman behind the counter swopped up the passport and walked over to another desk and had a whispered conference with an older man. The man pushed across a ticket envelope; the woman put the passport inside and came back and handed the packet to Jacques. "All set," she said. "The customer lounge is just over there. You can leave your luggage with me."

"Thanks," said Jacques. He turned around and walked with Jacqueline over to the lounge.

"That was a diplomatic passport. I saw it," said Jacqueline in a whisper. "When did you become an American?"

"It's been in the works for years," said Jacques casually.

"The citizenship or the passport?"

He looked at her quizzically.

"Oh," said Jacqueline, backing away from the prying question. She looked around and exclaimed excitedly, "There's Robert Murphy." She leaned over and whispered in his ear. "He's an important diplomat. I read about his arrival here in this very terminal in September. The paper had a short news item on the diplomat back from the war zone." She looked at Jacques. "If I could just ask him a couple of questions maybe…"

"I'm supposed to travel with him."

"You are?" said Jacqueline incredulously. "How far?"

Jacques let the question hang. Robert Murphy walked over, a tall man with a slight stoop in a black suit. He had a dark fedora on his head and a bright smile on his face. "Jacques, you're here. Good. We'll be traveling together."

"May I present my good friend Jacqueline Smith. She's come to wish me farewell."

"Pleased to meet you," said Murphy and stuck out his hand.

"Jacqueline works as a researcher for Anne Hare," added Jacques.

"She does?" said Murphy not betraying the least surprise. "Well, all of us overseas love to read Anne Hare when the papers finally arrive from the States. Her columns used to be printed overnight in the Paris dailies, but those days are all gone." Murphy had not missed a beat, noticed Jacques.

"Just where is Jacques going, Mr. Murphy?" asked Jacqueline.

"If I were to say, they'd take away my diplomatic merit badge, now wouldn't they, Miss Smith?"

"And if I don't pick up some good tidbits, Miss Hare might not take me to London. She'd just think I was extra luggage," said Jacqueline.

"Well, we're both going to Lisbon, and there we will get our instructions for the next leg of the trip."

"So you don't know?"

"Not exactly."

"How diplomatic."

"Can I take that as a compliment."

"Of course."

"What were you doing in Washington?"

"Just the normal briefings, getting an update on Stateside thinking."

"Do you know who the new American ambassador to France will be?"

"I'm not sure the previous ambassador is quite yet gone." Murphy knew the rumors were circulating in Washington that Roosevelt had grown displeased with William Bullitt. The president felt he should not have stayed in Paris when the Germans came—something of a grandstand stunt, thought Roosevelt. Instead, Roosevelt felt Bullitt should have gone with the French government in its flight to Bordeaux. That's where the big decisions were going to be made. Possibly the ambassador could have stiffened the French government's will to resist. Roosevelt wanted big men for the coming fight, not petty jealousies.

"That's the rumor," said Jackie.

"That's why we all read Anne Hare. To keep abreast of the rumors about what is going on above us."

"Not just one teeny-weeny tidbit?"

"Keep your eye on London."

"We are."

"That's where the big news will come from."

"Tell me something I don't know."

"You're too well informed for me to be able to do that, Miss Smith."

"One more thing, Mr. Murphy. Was there any criticism in Washington of you being filmed on the reviewing stand next to the German general when the German troops marched across the Place de Concorde last June?"

"Relief that it wasn't the ambassador."

"And the ambassador…"

"You'll have to ask him."

A blue-suited cabin steward announced that passenger would now start boarding for Bermuda. Murphy turned to Jacques and said, "I'll leave you to an affectionate farewell from your charming girlfriend." He turned and walked over toward the gangway leading up to the massive flying boat floating on the water.

"Maybe I'll see you in London," said Jacqueline, a longingness in her voice.

"Or somewhere," said Jacques.

"It's a big world."

"It will be a big war."

Chapter 15: Algiers

Businessman Jacques Lemaigre Debreuil sat at a corner table in the darkened dining room of the Taverne Alsacienne impatiently staring across the room toward the entrance. He needed to put the pieces together for his plan to move forward.

Soon a gentleman in a three-piece suit and homburg hat came through the door with a stylish woman in a black dress, black high heels, and a wide-brimmed hat rakishly slanted over the right side of her face. The woman pulled off her gloves and put them in her handbag. She looked around while the man inquired of the maître d', who pointed with his arm toward where Debreuil was sitting. Debreuil stood up to welcome his guests.

"So nice to see you again, Henri," Debreuil said, and he turned to the woman. "Marie." The three sat down.

"Yes, I think we last met in May in Paris upon your return from Romania," said Henri Rambert. At the time he had been a diplomat specializing in commercial affairs. "Your work untangling France's interest in Romanian oil from various private interests was superbly done but unfortunately came too late in the struggle."

"I understand," said Debreuil.

"General Weygand recommended your report highly," said Rambert. Weygand had been the plenipotentiary stationed in Beirut who was responsible for Romania. But before anything could be untangled, the Germans interrupted everyone's plans with the May invasion. "The favorable impression with Weygand should do you much good with your current project."

Debreuil answered, "Yes, in fact I saw Marie just last week at the Winter Palace." He nodded graciously at Marie. "They have approved my business plans."

"Yes, Marie told me," said Rambert.

A waiter came up, and Debreuil ordered a bottle of wine and listened as the waiter recited the daily specials. The three all agreed on the fish dish, sure to be fresh.

"What do you need from me?" asked Rambert, getting back to business.

"Approval from the Germans to dismantle the vegetable-oil processing plant in Dunkirk and ship it to Africa."

"What do you have in mind?"

"Processing plants in Dakar, Casablanca, and here in Algiers."

"Where will the product go?"

"Vichy has agreed to the duty-free export of the vegetable oil to metropolitan France."

"Yes, you're well connected in Vichy, I see."

"A necessity in today's world."

"Well, I see no problem getting German permission for this transfer. It furthers their interests in increasing the food supply in France."

"So you'll help?"

"I'll get the approvals in place as soon as I return to Wiesbaden."

"Good."

The waiter approached and set down three plates each with a steaming fillet of fish. The remainder of the plates were piled high with succulent vegetables.

"So much better than the food on the mainland. Even Germany is on meager rations," said Rambert.

The three tucked into the meal. Debreuil politely asked, "Marie, are you pleased your husband is back for a visit? Getting away from Germany is never easy."

"Yes," she said, and she slid her hand across the table and grasped her husband's hand. He looked at her and smiled weakly and then looked away. She withdrew her hand back across the tablecloth. He had always been distant, more interested in business trips to Paris before the war than life in Algiers. She felt there had been too much family arrangement and not enough romance in their marriage. Debreuil noted Marie's reaction and filed it away.

"My wife and her sister are joining me here in Algiers in December," said Debreuil. "I'm sure they would enjoy meeting you, Marie."

"I will be pleased to introduce them to life in Algiers," said Marie. "There is much that is pleasant here."

"Yes, we're all a long way from the high life of Paris before the war," said Debreuil.

"I visited Paris only occasionally," said Marie, "when I was invited." She looked at her husband with an arched eyebrow.

The three continued to chat during dinner.

The following morning Marie's family limousine drove her and Henri down to the Air France quay by the harbor. A large seaplane sat on the water like a fat duck. The two got out and walked over to the small office where Henri checked in. Then the two stood on the dock next to the gangway to say their good-byes.

"Marie, after the war…"

"Yes, the war…will it ever end?"

"Someday. We'll be able to resume our marriage, I can return to the bank. The future of Africa will be bright."

"I'd like that."

"Maybe start a family?"

"Yes, time is getting on, isn't it," she said with a touch of melancholy. She often ruminated upon that. She made a sigh. That was the trouble with marriage in a good French family; you wound up more as a brood mare, desired as a mother to have children destined as heirs to the family estates. Not even the briefest of illusions that you were a princess living in a castle with a handsome prince. When the beautiful wedding dress came off so did the illusion of romance. The fairy tales never prepared a girl for real life, she thought. Returning to the present, she said, mustering what affection she could, "I wish you good luck in your duties at Wiesbaden."

"We must all do our part for France in these difficult times. So many have it much worse than we," said Henri. He reached out and pulled his wife into an embrace and kissed her good-bye.

"Au revoir, Henri," she said as he turned and walked down the gangplank and ducked his head through the little door and entered the plane. She watched the seaplane pull away from the dock and move across the water. She waved as it receded into the distance. Then she returned to the limousine and got in the rear seat as the driver held the door open. It was all a little sad, she reflected.

Chapter 16: Marseilles

November 1940. L'inspecteur walked up the hill from the old port; he had just arrived on an overnight steamer from Algiers having received an urgent message from le chef. At the bistro, he entered and looked at Vivienne standing behind the zinc bar polishing a glass. She made a nod and said, "They're upstairs waiting."

They? L'inspecteur grasped the significance. Something was up. He climbed the stairs of the ancient building to le chef's office. He made a short knock and entered. L'inspecteur nodded at le chef while quickly inspecting the second man, who stood up from his chair and held out his hand. This new man was dressed in nondescript clothes but of immaculate bearing as if he had just walked off the parade ground from a smart regiment. He was blond, about six feet, and quite handsome. A movie-star German. L'inspecteur looked at le chef.

"Captain Brinckman is of the British army, but of German background."

"Yes, I see," said l'inspecteur.

"He was wounded at Dunkirk and later escaped from a Belgium hospital."

"Intriguing," said l'inspecteur taking a chair. There were escaped prisoners, shot-down pilots, and missing soldiers everywhere in the wake of the stunning German victory the previous spring. "Are we now doing escaped prisoners?" he asked.

"This case is different," replied le chef.

"I have information," said the British officer as he sat down.

"Information?" said l'inspecteur, a mild look of perplexity coming over his face. Everyone had information.

"Yes, Captain Brinckman was given a complete set of plans for the German invasion of Britain, from barges to invasion beaches," explained le chef.

"But the Germans never invaded," said l'inspecteur. "Out-of-date information."

"But they might mount the invasion in the late spring or summer of 1941," said Captain Brinckman, leaning forward and entering the conversation.

"That would mean no invasion of North Africa in 1941," said le chef.

"Yes," said l'inspecteur. "And we want to help the British?" he asked skeptically.

"We're in this together," said Captain Brinckman.

"Not very together last June," said l'inspecteur, a light touch of scorn in his voice. "Mers-el-Kébir and Dakar."

"The long haul," said Captain Brinckman.

"Okay, the long haul," said l'inspecteur. "What's the plan?"

"Get Captain Brinckman to Algiers," replied le chef.

"Easy enough to do."

"Then point the captain to the American consul general's villa."

"Why? The Americans don't do prisoner escape either," said l'inspecteur. "Algiers is crawling with people who want to get to Gibraltar or England. The Americans can't hazard their precious diplomatic neutrality."

"True. But the Americans can and will courier out the plans in their diplomatic pouch," said le chef. "I have good assurances on that."

"Okay, I can get the captain to Consul General Cole's villa. I know where it is," said l'inspecteur. "But then what do we do with Captain Brinckman?"

"Good question," said le chef. "I was hoping you'd have some thoughts on that."

"There are lots of people trying to get Brits stranded in Algiers to Tangier and then on to Gibraltar."

"I've made it across Occupied France," interjected the captain. "Worked with the Underground. Give me a canteen of water, a map, and a knife, and I can cross the border to Tangier," said Captain Brinckman.

L'inspecteur looked at him and sized him up. "I believe you."

"Your recent wounds, Captain, will not permit you to engage in commando tactics if not antics," said le chef. "Some other way will have to be found."

"Understand," agreed l'inspecteur. "But first, let's get you to Algiers." He looked at the captain who nodded agreement.

He had some ideas. But he would have to do better than last time. The two British officers had been turned in by informers two days after being hidden out near a suburban golf course west of Algiers. The officers were now cooling their heels in a prisoner-of-war camp.

Chapter 17: The White House

Missy LeHand escorted Sumner Welles up to the family quarters on the second floor of the White House and down the hall to the president's bedroom. She had immediately understood Welles's visit was important to the president. LeHand herself lived in a small suite of rooms one floor up; she, more than the First Lady, was mistress to the president's domestic life in the White House.

Roosevelt had asked Welles to come up with some suggestions for a new ambassador to replace William Bullitt at Vichy. Roosevelt was keenly aware of the strategic need to keep the powerful French fleet out of Germany's hands or the entire naval balance of power in the Atlantic would sharply turn against Britain, and ultimately America.

"Is the boss in?" asked Missy of the president's valet.

"Sure is," replied the valet, a large African American who could easily muscle the crippled president around. "He's in bed."

Welles followed LeHand in to find Roosevelt propped up against a wall of pillows and enjoying a breakfast of grapefruit, coffee, cereal, and eggs while he paged through newspapers spread around on the bed. Roosevelt's shoulders were draped with his navy cloak. He looked up, and his face registered curiosity at the unexpected presence of the undersecretary of state. The president knew that Missy wouldn't have brought him up if it were not important.

"You have been thinking about my problem," said Roosevelt. "Have you any ideas?"

"Admiral Leahy," said Welles, giving the name of William D. Leahy, the former chief of naval operations and current governor of Puerto Rico.

Roosevelt's face lit up. The obviousness of the solution that solved so many dilemmas was instantly appealing to the president. "Yes, he has the military background and prestige to form a bond with Marshal Pétain, and he should get along well with senior officers of the French navy."

"Admiral Darlan is the most powerful military officer in Vichy, not only commander of the navy but of the entire military," said Welles. "A good fit."

"Please draft a cable to Leahy and get it off to him," said the president. "Missy, would you please stay behind."

"The cable will go out this morning," said Welles, and he turned and said good-bye to LeHand and departed. Roosevelt watched him leave.

"Missy, get me the telephone," commanded the president. "I'll call Bill down in San Juan and get the show on the road." He leaned back in his pillows and smiled.

Chapter 18: Destination Tangier

Madrid, December 1940. Jacques Dubois stood in the ramshackle waiting room of the airport on the outskirts of Madrid. The building was cold, dreary, and something of a shamble from years of shelling during the Spanish Civil War, a conflict that had ended just the year before with the defeat of the Loyalist forces. Jacques had walked through history when he had checked in at the lobby of the decrepit Hotel Florida the day before. Standing at the battered reception desk, he could imagine the foreign correspondents carousing, drinking, and loving their way through the slow-motion collapse of the Spanish Republic during the long unwinding of the once-noble cause.

Around Jacques were Spanish army officers of Franco's fascist regime returning to the international city of Tangier, the intrigue-filled city that was a mélange of nationalities at the crossroads leading into the Mediterranean. The city had recently been occupied by Spanish troops, supposedly for safekeeping explained the Spanish government.

Jacques had left Robert Murphy in Lisbon after a luxurious trip across the Atlantic on the big Pan American flying boat. Murphy had said that he would catch up with Jacques later, but Murphy had said almost nothing else about Jacques's upcoming assignment in Algiers. He was heading into an adventure, the dimensions of which he could not yet discern.

Jacques stood by a window in a light drizzle, a gray sky overhead, both expectant and anxious. He watched at the trimotor transport airplane, streaked with rust along its boxlike metal fuselage, as it pulled up outside, the engines sputtering to a stop. The double doors leading out from the lobby to the tarmac opened. A loud hailer announced that boarding of the flight "to Tangier" was about to begin. Jacques walked over and joined the queue of officers waiting to board. Some of them looked askance at Jacques's two suitcases and nodded negatively at him. "You'll see," one said. The passengers filed out and climbed up the little boarding stairs into the plane.

Jacques took his seat midway up the right side of the aircraft next to a window just aft of the straight-backed wing.

In a few minutes, the engines wheezed and then caught their ignition in a burst of flame and smoky exhaust. The plane taxied over to the end of the runway. With the brakes on, the pilot revved the engine up, the airframe shook violently, and then the pilot let the brakes go. The plane lumbered down the runway. Jacques looked outside and watched the concrete go by, and then he felt the tail lift off. He waited. Soon there was some more speed from the straining engines, and he could see the right wheel lift off. The wing wobbled, the wheel touched down again, and the airframe shuddered. The plane took a hop, and then the unseen lift grabbed the plane, and it rose into the air. As the plane laboriously pulled away from the ground, the fields raced along below Jacques's window. Like an overfed duck starting on its migration, the plane turned south and headed toward Africa. The Spanish officers looked fatalistically ahead. They knew that every flight to Tangier was like being in a bullfight with fate.

A half hour later, the plane passed over a large city. One of the Spanish officers shouted over the sound of engines to Jacques, "Seville." The officer pointed forward and added, "One more mountain range to pass." He smiled with white teeth and shrugged his shoulders.

Jacques looked out of the window and saw in the falling sunset of the winter afternoon the red-tinted Sierra Morena Mountains ahead. Gray clouds above soon let loose torrents of rain, the bullet-sized drops beating out a tattoo on the metal wings. The plane rose and fell and lurched sideways and back in the turbulence. The rain was replaced with gumdrop-ball-sized hailstones that made a rat-a-tat drumfire on the wings. Jacques's fingers gripped the armrests as the cabin was illuminated in flashes of lightening and peals of thunder seemed to shake the aircraft from the sky. Jacques looked up the aisle and saw the copilot and radio operator frantically pushing the handles of hand pumps to spill excess gas from the tanks. He looked out of the windows and watched the spray of gas as it arched in a colorful rainbow off the wing surfaces. Below the wings he watched the red flare of the exhaust pipes and wondered what would happen if fire met fuel.

The radio operator scurried down the aisle and opened a rear hatch and kicked cases of nonessential freight overboard with his feet. He slid the hatch closed and scurried back down the aisle while flashing an encouraging smile at Jacques. Jacques looked out of the window and saw the ridges of the mountains pass several hundred feet below as the plane struggled for its final feet of altitude. He could pick out the bushes and see goats grazing. Then the nearby peaks fell behind. Soon he saw the Atlantic Ocean with the sun setting in an orange ball on the western horizon. The Spanish officer leaned over and tugged at his sleeve and pointed out of the window to the left and said, "Gibraltar."

Jacques looked at the small sliver of a peninsula just inside the Mediterranean from the narrow Strait of Gibraltar. The smallness of the fabled British fortress struck him. As he looked, the plane flew over the narrow strait with the late afternoon rays of sunlight turning it into a golden portal to the Mediterranean Sea. The Spanish officer pointed forward and said, "Tangier soon."

Jacques felt his fingers loosen on the armrest. A collective relaxation came over the passengers. Soon Jacques felt the plane begin its descent to the aerodrome at Tangier. In thirty minutes the plane was taxiing up to the Moorish-styled terminal building.

Inside the art deco structure, an American consul met Jacques and shook his hand. "Roger Smith, vice-consul. I will take you to the hotel. Tomorrow you will meet Mr. Childs; he is our minister plenipotentiary here in Tangier."

"A plenipotentiary?" said Jacques with a touch of wonder in his voice.

"Yes," replied Smith. "Let me explain. Tangier, which despite the Spanish occupation, is still diplomatically regarded as an international enclave by all the European powers and the United States." Smith explained that J. Rives Childs was the career-consular officer who served as minister to this strategically important quasi-independent city-state.

A uniformed airline employee brought Jacques's two suitcases up and set them down. He was thankful they had not gotten tossed out of the airplane. Jacques gave him a nice tip and said, "Thank you." He picked up the suitcases and said to the consul, "I'll follow." Jacques could see the vice-consul was not in the habit of helping with luggage. Or at least the luggage of lower-ranking employees.

The two men walked outside where a gray government car with driver waited. The driver put the bags in the trunk, and the two men got in the rear seat. The car pulled out onto the highway leading into the city.

Continuing the conversation, Jacques said, "I look forward to meeting the minister. Mr. Murphy briefed me. Said I would receive rudimentary cryptography training here."

"Well, I'm glad you know something. Mr. Childs knows nothing about you except that you are going to be a third secretary at the consulate in Algiers. No one has ever heard of a third secretary at a consulate."

"Neither had I until I was appointed," said Jacques, and he paused, momentarily unsure of his words, and continued, "and assigned to this mission."

"There was only the briefest of cables from the State Department announcing your arrival."

"I believe I'm simply to support a fact-finding mission," said Jacques. "Not very important."

"Fact-finding by whom?"

"I guess I'll find out in Algiers," said Jacques. He'd been warned not to say more than necessary. He had been told that the consular staffs were still in the grip of peacetime thinking and were overburdened with consular duties relating to the massive demand for the limited number of visas available. Thousands of refugees in North Africa vied for the chance to go to America, or anywhere else for that matter.

"Well, you won't find out from Mr. Childs. He's more than a little annoyed, I might say."

"Well, I look forward to the training I'll receive at your legation."

"You're being put up in the El Minzah Palace Hotel; someone in Washington thinks you at least merit first-class lodging."

"I was told my stay here will be brief."

"I should warn you that the hotel is overrun with German and Italian diplomats, some of whom might be Gestapo or OVRA agents." OVRA was Italy's secret police force.

"I know little of interest to them," said Jacques noncommittally.

"Well, they don't know that. And you'll know more about cryptography after your training."

"I'll keep that in strictest confidence."

"There are also many British diplomats and intelligence officers, and they can be just as bothersome. Very nosy."

"Not for me. Not tonight. I'm going straight to bed."

The car pulled up in the circular drive in front of the majestic Moorish-styled El Minzah Palace Hotel. "Here we are," said the consul. The two men got out. The driver opened the trunk and handed the suitcases to Jacques, who picked them up and followed the consul into the lobby of the hotel. The consul inquired at the desk and then turned to Jacques. "Here you are. All set. I'll send a car at nine o'clock tomorrow morning. Mr. Childs is a stickler for appointments being on time."

"I'll be ready," said Jacques. "Thank you for your assistance." The vice-consul turned and without so much as a good-bye handshake left the lobby.

A bellhop came over and said, "Let me show you to your room." He took the bags and started to an elevator.

The Legation

In the morning, the gray government car and driver pulled up in front of the hotel a minute before nine. Jacques walked over and got in and said, "Good morning."

"Good morning, sir" came a crisp reply. "I'll have you at the legation in a jiffy."

The car entered the old part of the city and made its way down a crowded, bustling market street in the middle of the Medina, the old quarter, and pulled up to the side of the crowded street. Roger Smith stood waiting on the sidewalk in a white linen suit and Panama hat. The driver said, "Mr. Smith will show you the rest of the way."

Jacques got out carrying a small dispatch case and approached Smith and said, "Good morning."

"Prompt. Mr. Childs will like that."

"Where is the legation?"

"The chancery is down this alley," said Smith, using the diplomatic term for office. "The driver will take the car around to the residence. That's where the car park is. We'll walk to the legation offices from here." Jacques understood the residence to be the formal quarters of the minister, who was the head of the legation. A legation was one step above a consulate but below an embassy in the diplomatic pecking order.

"Exotic," said Jacques.

"This way."

The pair walked down the crowded alleyway with shop entrances every couple of paces, saleable wares standing on racks outside the shops, other items sitting on temporary wooden shelves. Arab and Berber shopkeepers hovered in long white flowing gowns and wearing round, white Muslim-style headpieces. Shouts came from all corners; smells wafted out from cook shops. The two men came up to a great white-walled Moorish building. "This is the office."

"I see."

"Here's the entrance," said Smith. They walked through the entrance, the doors standing open for business hours. A guard was just inside. "Show the guard your identification each morning, and he'll log you in."

"Yes, sir," said Jacques. He reached into his inside coat pocket and pulled out an identification in a small billfold and presented it to the guard.

"This is Mr. Jacques Dubois," said Smith to the guard. "You can expect him at nine in the morning every day during his stay here."

"Yes, sir," replied the guard.

Smith turned to Jacques with a light smile. "There. Now we'll go to Mr. Childs's office."

Smith turned and walked down the hall, up a stairway, and over to a secretary-receptionist with Jacques following behind. "Mr. Dubois to see Mr. Childs."

The American woman said, "He's expected. Go right in."

The two men entered the spacious office with tall windows overlooking another narrow street with another large Moorish mansion across the street with an American flag flying from a rooftop flagpole. The residence, Jacques presumed.

Mr. Childs stood up and came around and held out his hand. "Nice to meet you, Dubois." He held his hand out. "Take a seat. You, too, Roger." He turned and walked back around the desk and took his seat.

Jacques admired the American flag behind the desk on one side and the flag of the American foreign service on the other side. There was a sense of pride of being part of this, the dignity, the power to do good.

"Short notice on your arrival, Dubois. Didn't say much except that you're in transit to Algiers…to be"—and a look of consternation came over Child's face—"a third secretary at the consulate."

"Yes," said Jacques.

"Hadn't heard of a consulate having a third secretary before," said Childs.

"I believe it's just to support a fact-finding mission," said Jacques.

"You've had consular training?" asked Childs.

"No," said Jacques forthrightly. "I believe I'm supposed to pick up a little cryptography training here in Tangiers." He searched for something else to say. "Transportation to the region came up rather suddenly, and I couldn't stay in Washington for additional training."

"You've diplomatic experience?" asked Childs, furrowing his brow. Something seemed not right here, out of the ordinary.

"Not exactly. Mostly liaison work," said Jacques.

Childs screwed up his face. "I'm not sure what they have planned for you in Algiers, but while you're here, young man—in my jurisdiction—there is going to be no spying or other irregularities. Gentlemen don't spy."

"I'm not a spy, I assure you. If I were, they'd probably have given me cryptography training before I left," said Jacques with a light smile and a small laugh.

"Right," said Childs, visibly relaxing and leaning back in his large stuffed chair. No spies. This time. Rather decent looking young man, he thought. Wonder where the frog accent came from? "Roger will take you downstairs to the message center and introduce you to the cryptography officer." Childs stood up and came around the desk.

Jacques shook hands with Childs, who added, "Ask Roger if you need anything else. And, oh yes, the bar bill at the hotel is on your own account."

"Yes, sir."

Roger and Jacques departed and descended the stairway and then went down another stairway into the basement and entered a large room. Teletypes and coding machines stood like soldiers in formation along the walls. Big flat tables with straight-backed chairs occupied the middle of the room. The cryptography officer came over and held out his hand. "Stanley Turnbull."

"Jacques Dubois," replied Jacques.

"I'll leave you with Stan," said Roger.

"Thank you for your assistance," said Jacques, shaking Roger's hand. Roger turned and departed.

"Right," said Stan. "Over at the tables is where we write out our most secure messages on what are called one-time pads. That's what I've been told to instruct you in."

"Yes, that's my understanding," said Jacques.

"And we'll show you a little about the cryptography machines used for lower-level security messages."

"Fine."

"You'll find message transcription dull and monotonous, I'm afraid," said Stan. "Sort of like consular work in general. Same procedure—over and over again."

"Understand," said Jacques.

"The reason for the one-time pad is that all the messages from Africa go through telegraph services controlled by other powers. Everyone's reading everyone else's mail."

"Spying?" asked Jacques with mock horror. "Despite Mr. Childs's admonition?"

Stan looked askance at Jacques and smiled. "I'm going to like you." The two men laughed.

Chapter 19: Algiers

The French police chief spoke to his two detectives. "I've a tip from Marseilles. Go to the dock and watch the passengers coming off the Spanish steamer. You're looking for a handsome man with a limp. He's a fugitive British officer."

"What do we do with him?" asked one of the detectives.

"Take him to the villa. There's a special cell there for interrogations. Search him for papers—carefully. Then follow the normal procedure for unwanted guests."

"Understand," said the detective. The two men turned and left. They went to the garage and got a police car and driver and explained the mission. They took off for the harbor.

At the harbor, the two detectives stood in the shadows of a freight shed and watched the rusty tramp steamer ease up to the quay. Lines were thrown, and the ship made fast to the quay. They watched the passengers descend the gangway.

"There," said one of the detectives. "It's got to be him."

"You're right," said the other detective. "We'll come up behind him at the end of the quay. It'll be easy to hustle him into the car."

"Got it," said the other detective.

Across the street from the quay at a sidewalk café, l'inspecteur, too, watched the steamer arrive. He saw Captain Brinckman walk down the dock toward the main thoroughfare fronting the harbor. The limp was a dead giveaway, he thought. Then he saw the two detectives. He sighed. Yes, there'd been a leak at Marseilles, a den of double-dealing informants to be sure. Well, we'll see how all this plays out.

At the foot of the dock, the two detectives swept their arms up underneath Brinckman's arms and rushed him into the waiting police car.

"What's all this about," shouted Brinckman, surprised and shocked.

"We want to talk to you," said one of the detectives.

"My papers are all in order," protested Brinckman.

"They all are," said the detective with world-weary insouciance.

"Where am I going?" protested Brinckman.

"To special interrogation," said the detective.

Presently the police car swung into the gates of a large villa and pulled to a stop. The two detectives led Brinckman down a series of steps and into the basement. There was a steel-bared cell in a corner. The basement room was dark. A single covered light shined down on an interrogation table like in a gangster movie.

"Make it easy for yourself," said the detective. "Hand over the papers."

Brinckman, understanding that he'd been betrayed, undid his belt and reached into his pants and pulled out an envelope of papers. He handed them over. The detective thumbed through them and nodded approvingly. Just what they'd been told to expect.

"Anything else?"

"No," said Brinckman.

"Do you have your paybook?" asked the detective.

"Yes," said Brinckman hopelessly, his only connection to his status as a British officer slipping away. He reached into his inside breast pocket and pulled it out. The other detective took it and wrote down the details in a notebook.

Finished writing, the detective handed the paybook back to Brinckman. "Here. You'll need it. The Americans will want to know who you are."

"The Americans?"

"Yes," said the detective. "They're responsible for British officers, particularly wounded ones, who wind up in Algiers."

"Really?" said Brinckman, wondering if this was a trap, an effort to sedate him into cooperation on his own demise.

"Yes," said the detective. "Now let's go. We'll deposit you at the consulate."

The three men left the villa and got in the back seat of the waiting police car. It headed for the American consulate and pulled to a stop out front. There was a long line of nondescript people waiting in a line outside, all hoping to get a visa to leave French Africa. Few would be successful. The detectives got out and walked Brinckman up and through the front door.

"Mr. Taft," said one of the detectives, adding a greeting, "Mrs. Tuyl." The beautiful blond-haired Joan was filling in as receptionist today. The policemen were not surprised to see her.

"This way," she said and led the three men down the hallway. She guessed the man was another British escapee or downed pilot. The three men entered the room as Orray Taft stood to greet them. Joan slipped in behind them and closed the door behind her.

"Captain Brinckman of the British army," said one of the detectives.

"For you," said the other. "He's also recovering from a wound in his leg."

"We can put him in the Glycine clinic," said Taft.

"He has to sign his parole before we can release him to your custody," said the detective, handing over a piece of paper.

Turning to Brinckman, Taft asked, "Do you know what signing the parole means?" Then he added, "The American consulate is guaranteeing your continued presence in Algiers, your promise as an officer not to try to escape."

Brinckman looked rather startled, his expression perplexed. A prisoner's duty was to attempt escape.

"You'd better sign," said a feminine voice coming from behind the captain. He turned and looked at Joan. "Go ahead and sign," she said reassuringly in her best British accent.

Brinckman took the paper and signed. One of the detectives took the paper and said, "He's all yours." The other detective nodded and smiled at Joan as the two policemen departed. For the detectives, a good day's work: their chief had the papers he wanted, and they'd dumped the officer on the Americans. Time for a pastis.

Taft turned to Brinckman. "Sit down and tell me all about it."

Joan took an adjoining chair and put her chin in her palm, gazing at Brinckman expectantly. Brinckman looked at her and then Taft. "It's all right. She'll be important to whatever future you might plan. She's close to the prisoner community doing I do not know what." Yes. She could always be disowned, she knew.

Taft wearily started in with Brinckman. If he could only get away from babysitting these obstreperous young British internees and their constant clamoring to get back into the fight.

Joan thought through the options. The clinic was the best option. Maybe a medical repatriation to Tangier. She smiled—a good plan.

Tangier

Jacques was sitting at a table in coding room laboriously transcribing a dispatch onto the one-time pad and then completing the coded message text next to it. Roger Smith walked into the room, knocking on the open door as he entered.

"Mr. Childs would like to see you," he said to Jacques.

Jacques stood up. "Now?"

"Yes, you better take your things. You won't be back," added Smith in a peremptory fashion.

Jacques turned to Stan and said, "Thank you for the training. I'll be in touch."

"Good luck," said Stan with a friendly smile. Smith scowled—slightly. There were no subordinates in Smith's world, just inferiors. He'd been practicing dismissiveness throughout the snaillike advance of his consular career.

Smith turned for the hallway, and Jacques followed. On the second floor, the two men walked through the open door into Mr. Childs's office. He remained seated and impatiently waved Jacques into an empty chair. Smith took a seat next to him.

"Got a message from Washington. They want you in Algiers PDQ," said Childs with a huff. "Don't understand the urgency." He huffed again. "Well, can't be helped." The huff deflated. He looked at Jacques with curious eyes trying to fathom the young man's importance. "The legation car will take you to Rabat. There you can take a train to Algiers."

"Yes, sir," said Jacques. A sense of relief came over him. He was out of the whirlpool of tedium and back on the odyssey of adventure.

Childs looked up. "You can go now."

Jacques stood up and said, "Thank you for the training." He walked toward the door.

"Mind you," said Childs calling after him. "Pay your own bar bill."

Algiers

Jacques looked out the soot-stained window of the passenger carriage as it rolled down the long verdant valley in the December sunlight toward Algiers, a white cluster of buildings shining in the far distance backed by the azure blue of the Mediterranean. Above, the sky was like a dark-blue dome. Glancing forward, he saw the dirty-brown smoke billowing from the ancient steam locomotive that pulled the derelict carriages along the track. The locomotive burned copious quantities of the low-grade coal because that was all that was available—cheap being a constant in an Algeria cut off from the outside world and its sustaining world trade.

As the train rumbled down the grade along the side of the valley, he could see orchards full of citrus, the bright yellow and orange fruits hanging on the green-leaved limbs. Four growing seasons a year in this natural greenhouse made the area surrounding Algiers a modern Eden, resplendent with the constant fecundity of nature's bounty.

In a few more minutes, he could see the white buildings of Algiers crowding the harbor front and then apartment buildings and houses stepping up the hills to the top of the ridge. Here and there the ridgeline was broken by small valleys in which luxurious villas nestled. The city itself was a modern European city with a Moorish flavor, an exotic mix featuring a blend of art deco and late-nineteenth-century French colonial architecture. Undoubtedly the city's prosperity rested on the incredible agricultural richness of Algeria.

As the train came to a halting stop in the station, there was a cacophony of screeching sounds as rusted steel ground against rusted steel. Jacques stood up and grabbed his suitcases, put on his hat, and moved into the aisle. He followed a couple of Arabs as they herded their goats forward toward the open door at the end of the carriage. He stepped around the poop on the floor. All in all, an interesting journey.

Outside he looked around, and he saw a well-dressed Arab man in a dark suit walk over with a smile of welcome on his face. "I'm Fadi, the driver for the consulate." He held out his hand.

"Pleased to meet you, Fadi," said Jacques as he shook the outstretched hand.

"Let me take your bag, sir," said Fadi. "The car is over there." He nodded toward the street.

At the street was a gray Studebaker touring car. Fadi put the luggage in the trunk and then opened the back door, and Jacques slid into the rear seat. Fadi got in the driver's seat and pulled away into a heavy traffic of a few vehicles and a lot of donkey carts. Jacques looked out of the window and was impressed with the fruits and vegetables stacked in green, purple, and colored piles in the stalls of the market sellers. A true land of plenty.

The car pulled through the gates of the consulate and into a garage. Fadi opened the door, and Jacques alighted. The driver went around and got Jacques's luggage and led him over to a door and into the office. Fadi went up to the attractive blond receptionist and whispered.

"Of course," she said and stood up. She came over to Jacques and held out her hand. "Joan Tuyl. Let me take you to Mr. Taft's office. Follow me." She headed down a hallway, opened a door, and with her hand ushered Jacques inside. She closed the door behind Jacques and returned to the reception area.

Orray Taft stood up and came around from his desk. "Orray Taft, Jr.," he said as he shook Jacques's hand. "Sit down. Enjoy your trip?"

Jacques took a seat. "An interesting journey."

"Mr. Cole, the consul general, received the telegrams from Washington and Tangier. Interesting. Posted as a third secretary?" said Taft with questioning interest. Something was outside the regular about this young man with American diplomatic standing and a flawless French accent.

"Yes, that's what I've been told," said Jacques.

"Well, we're sure underhanded here. Thousands of refugees clamoring for visas. You've had consular training?"

"No."

"That's what we need. Why did they send you?"

"I'm to support a fact-finding mission?"

"Fact-finding? In this backwater?"

"Yes, see what kinds of supplies the French might be interested in buying that we could ship through the British blockage."

"Supplies? Buy?" asked Taft, consternation spreading across his face. "Don't they know there's a war on?"

"The war has resulted in a lot of French blocked currency in American banks. They could use those funds to buy supplies. From American firms. Good business."

"Buy supplies? Good business? Doesn't Washington know what we're up against here?" asked Taft, a red flush spreading across his cheeks. "Why?" Consternation suffused his manner as he shook his head.

"Can't let blocked funds sit idle doing nothing in a bank," said Jacques helpfully.

"So, you're a commercial attaché?" said Taft, turning the question into an accusation.

"Why, yes. That would be a good way of looking at it."

"So, you're going to go around selling stuff?"

"No. I'm too junior. My understanding is a more senior person will actually conduct the negotiations."

"A senior person?"

"Yes, as you well know from your diplomatic experience, it requires years of hard-earned practice to negotiate agreements. Above my pay grade, beyond my background."

"Just what are your instructions?"

"I'm supposed to go over those with Mr. Cole."

"I see," said Taft, now thoroughly at sea. "What do we do with you now?"

Jacques sat quiet.

"I know," exclaimed Taft in a flash. "Let me get Joan. She'll know." He pushed a button on his telephone. Presently there was a knock on the door, and Joan entered.

"Yes, sir?"

"Mr. Dubois has just joined us from Washington. He's going to be doing important commercial work. Do you think you could arrange a room for him at the Hotel Aletti?"

"Yes, no problem," Joan replied. "For how long?"

"Just a few days," said Jacques. "Then I'd like to get something more permanent. An apartment or small house, say."

"Easy to do. There are plenty of nice apartment blocks right in the neighborhood where my mother and I live. They'd be close to the consulate."

"That would be excellent," said Jacques. He turned and looked at Taft with an eyebrow raised seeking his approval.

"Yes, that would do fine," said Taft. "Oh, let's get the formalities out of the way. Can I see your passport?"

"Of course," replied Jacques as he reached into his inside breast pocket. "Here it is." He handed across the brand-new diplomatic passport. Taft picked it up and flipped through it.

"You were born in France?"

"Yes, French father, American mother."

"That doesn't make you an American citizen."

"I was naturalized," said Jacques, stumbling for words, "after the war broke out."

"I see," said Taft as paged through the almost blank pages of the spanking new passport. No past, no tracks. He sighed. "I'll leave you in Joan's capable hands."

Jacques and Joan stood up and walked out of the office. As they walked down the hall, Joan said, "I'll get Fadi, and we'll go over to the Aletti. There's more going on there than might seem. Germans, Italians, French—I'll brief you."

"I look forward to it," said Jacques. "Over a drink?"

"Okay. In the bar at the casino in the hotel—tonight before dinner. Let the Germans and Italians get a good look at you."

Jacques raised his eyebrows but nodded his acceptance. Interesting. She was beautiful.

Casino

Jacques stood up from his chair at a small table in the corner of the casino bar as he saw Joan approach. She was wearing a cream-colored overcoat against the winter chill with a colorful plaid scarf. He stepped forward and helped her out of the coat and set it over a chair. She draped the scarf over it. She was wearing a dark wool sheath and a silk blouse—simply stunning, he thought. He held her chair as she sat down. He sat down across from her.

"Is your room satisfactory?" she asked, blue eyes sparkling underneath the shimmering whiteness of her blond hair, the gloss backlit by a sconce on the wall behind her.

"Yes, quite. I do want to follow up on getting the apartment you suggested."

"Top floor, view of the harbor, just back from Rue Michelet?" she replied, making the question a statement with crisp efficiency.

"Your recommendation?"

"Yes."

"Done."

A waiter came up and looked at Joan. "A Campari on the rocks," she said.

"Same for me," said Jacques.

"Now, about those Germans and Italians," he said.

"Algiers is melting pot of thousands of people fleeing from Europe, from cabinet ministers to actresses to pilots and soldiers. The great topic is how to get away."

"Get away?"

"Algiers is an island surrounded by impassable deserts and a treacherous sea."

"Hard to escape?"

"Very."

"And your interests?"

"How to get information out."

"To whom?"

"Most people think to the British. I used to work at the British consulate."

"And they're not wrong?"

She smiled.

"And your work at the American consulate?" he asked.

"The Americans are the only secure route out for information that"—she hesitated—"I might have."

"So, I'm to be used?"

"No more than necessary."

He smiled. "And the people here in the bar?"

She looked around and said, "Over there a German member of the Armistice Commission. They're all thought to be Gestapo."

Paul A. Myers

"Dangerous?"

"Not yet."

"The Frenchmen?"

"Some are military officers; some are political police."

"Do you know the political police?"

"Most of them. They follow me constantly."

"Really?" asked Jacques incredulously.

"They'll be following you, too."

Jacques absorbed this and asked, "The others?" He looked around the crowded bar to dramatize the sweep of his question.

"Italians. They're handsome and suave. They like to charm French women of either influence or standing, supposedly for information. Mostly they're not successful. But everyone presumes both parties have a good time."

"Do you have a good time?"

"I'm a married woman."

"Oh," said Jacques, and his face fell.

"If you were the true Frenchman you probably are and not a pretend American, that wouldn't bother you," she said with a laugh.

"Right now, I think I need friends," he said thoughtfully.

"I think we have something in common," she said, and reached across the table with her hand and gave his hand a squeeze. "Friends?"

Jacques looked into her eyes and sealed the deal. "Friends." He looked around the lounge and asked, "The blond lady with the German over there?"

"She's a German journalist for *Deutsche Allegemeine Zeitung,* the big Berlin daily."

"Official?"

"She's accredited to the Armistice Commission. That's why she's speaking with the German."

"Sharing information? Or friendship?"

"Information with the Germans. She's good friends with a French navy lieutenant commander at the Winter Palace."

"The French navy?"

"They're the backbone of collaboration in the Vichy regime."

"How so?"

125

"Admiral Darlan is the commander in chief of all military forces in Vichy. He's the one who arranged for General Weygand's exile here to Algiers."

"Why?"

"The Germans wanted him out of Vichy, and the admiral was happy to oblige."

"But they still watch the general?"

"Yes. If there were a coup against the Vichy regime, it would originate in Algiers goes the thinking."

"So, they watch Algiers?"

"Closely."

"Oppressive."

"Yes, but remember, there's lots of mice in Algiers and only one cat."

"Let me take you in to dinner?"

"Yes, I thought you'd never ask. I'm famished," she said with charming forthrightness.

Nineteenth Army Corps

The American consulate car drove in between the twin gates of the army headquarters off Place Bugeaud in Algiers. The Spahi guards recognized the diplomatic plates as Orray Taft got out of the rear seat of the car and started up the steps as their rifles came up to present arms. At the entrance he handed a slip of paper to a supervising sergeant and mumbled, "Military Intelligence."

"The captain is expecting you," said the sergeant crisply. "This way, monsieur." The sergeant led Taft down a long marble-floored corridor to a large wooden door with a frosted glass window. He opened the door and escorted Taft to a desk with a receptionist perched behind. The receptionist, a French woman, said, "This way, the captain is expecting you."

Taft followed the woman into a large office with big windows; a well-tailored French captain came around the desk and shook his hand. The receptionist departed.

"Nice to see you again, Mr. Taft."

"You, too, Captain."

"As you know we routinely question internees as they show up in Algiers."

"Yes."

"Recently we came across these papers, and since you are responsible for British internees, we thought they might be of some interest to you."

"Okay," said Taft noncommittally.

"Yes, now," said the captain. "Here they are. Look them over. They are of no further interest to us."

"Yes?"

"I'll leave you with them. I'm leaving for lunch and will be back later. If I don't see you again, have a good afternoon."

"Thanks," said Taft. The French officer went over to a hat rack and picked up his kepi and put on his overcoat and left. Taft walked around the desk and looked at the papers. Detailed plans in German. He recognized the German general staff format. There were numerous maps of the northern French coast and the south coast of England. Ruler-straight lines crossed the channel demarking traffic lanes from French ports to landing beaches on the south coast of England. Taft marveled at the detailed completeness of the plans. These must have been on Captain Brinckman's person when he was arrested.

Taft swiftly unlocked his attaché case and put the papers inside. He gave the desk a once over to make sure he was not leaving anything behind. Satisfied, he carefully locked the attaché case and walked out of the office.

Passing the receptionist, he said, "Au revoir." Outside he got in the car and said, "Back to consulate. Don't stop for anything."

Chapter 20: Africa

December 18, 1940. The Air France seaplane flew southwest over the Mediterranean, the white-capped waves dancing on the surface of the dark-blue sea. In the distance, the hills surrounding Algiers threw a soft shadow across the white buildings of the city as a golden sun blazed away in the western sky of the vast amphitheater that was the winter sky of the Mediterranean. There it was, thought the passenger—Africa!

Robert Murphy peered out of the window and saw the fabled white city loom into view. He had left Vichy early in the morning for Marseilles where he had caught the seaplane. Originally, he had planned to stay in Vichy only a few days, but days had turned into weeks as his permits were snagged in the bureaucratic morass of shifting bureaucratic power. Pierre Laval had been deposed from his position of power as deputy premier in a bureaucratic coup d'etat and weeks of intrigue followed. He reflected on the whispered meetings in the corridors of Vichy—thankfully behind him—as he watched Algiers come toward him. He understood; he would have to watch his back.

As 1940 approached its end, the new ruling cabal in Vichy aimed to achieve more autonomy for France while scrupulously honoring the Armistice. Many of the ministers had distrusted Prime Minister Pierre Laval, a snaky operator with too many Nazi friends. They despised his craven collaboration toward Germany. Laval's political strategy had been to double down on Germany winning the war. Others were not so sure; Britain was still fighting and receiving significant pledges of aid from the Americans.

In this mix of intrigue, Interior Minister Marcel Peyrouton had suddenly organized a political coup that brought former Third Republic premier Pierre-Étienne Flandin to power underneath the mantle of the Maréchal. The aged Pétain continued as the head of state regally presiding over the still nascent government. In the background, Admiral Darlan consolidated his power over the French military as commander in chief. The only figure of some independence was the delegate general to Africa, General Weygand, who owed much of his independence to his distance from Vichy. Nevertheless, Weygand maintained a strong sense of loyalty to the Maréchal if not to the Vichy politicians. Darlan could not immediately remove Weygand due to Pétain's support; he would have to settle for limiting his influence to Africa.

French politicians all understood that America might eventually join the war, and there were American diplomats in Vichy reminding the French daily of their presence—and the potentiality of a future entry by America into the war. Many top French politicians hoped to carve out a slightly more independent future from Germany while waiting for fate to play the American card—which they felt was sure to come. The last world war had made clear that America was the decisive European power.

The plane made a graceful banking turn and set down in the channel leading into the harbor. The seaplane taxied across the water to a small seaplane terminal. Consul General Felix Cole and the young third secretary, Jacques Dubois, were waiting on the landing to greet him.

The Winter Palace

December 19. The consulate car—a black four-door Studebaker with white sidewall tires—threaded its way through heavy traffic along the Algiers waterfront toward the Winter Palace. Jacques sat in the rear seat with Robert Murphy discussing the coming meeting.

"You just missed General Weygand," said Jacques to Murphy. "He quickly departed for an inspection trip to Dakar once Admiral Darlan established his authority."

"Yes, Weygand will want to explain Darlan's position to the governors in Dakar and Rabat, sensitive places," said Murphy, referring to the capitals of Senegal and Morocco. "Morocco is not French territory, but a protectorate."

"Felix arranged this morning's meeting with *le comte* de Rose," continued Jacques, "who is Weygand's political counselor."

"Yes, Felix filled me in this morning," said Murphy, who had taken up residence in Cole's spacious villa in the heights above Algiers for the duration of his stay.

The limousine pulled up before the entrance to the Winter Palace and a spit-shined Spahi, a white French soldier native to North Africa, came forward and opened the door. Other Spahis snapped their rifles to present arms in salute as Jacques and Murphy walked up the steps and into the foyer. Inside, they walked over to reception where an attractive, dark-haired young woman met them.

"Good morning, gentlemen. You are here to see Monsieur de Rose, I believe?"

"Yes, we are," said Murphy.

"This way," said the young woman, flashing a welcoming smile. She led them upstairs to the second level and past an open door leading into the delegate general's vacant office and down a hall. She rapped lightly on an open door and said, "Monsieur de Rose, your guests are here." She held out her hand, and Murphy and Jacques walked into the office. She silently closed the door behind her and walked over and took a seat in a corner. She opened her pad and sat with pencil poised to take notes.

"You have met our assistant, Madame Rambert?" asked de Rose as he stood and shook Murphy's hand and then Jacques's. Both men said good morning to the young woman and sat down.

"Let me begin," said de Rose. "General Weygand is on an inspection tour and is in Dakar. He believes, as we all do, that both Churchill and de Gaulle were inexcusably rash in their attack on Dakar this past September."

Murphy nodded in agreement; that belief was pervasive in Washington, as he had learned—at the highest level.

"I hope to go to Dakar and visit the general," said Murphy.

"That is being arranged," replied de Rose. "Large efforts are underway to strengthen the defenses of Dakar against future attack."

"Yes, but the American position is to do everything short of war to support the British," said Murphy.

"Understand. And all of us have sympathy for the British cause, but a premature move could easily lead to a German invasion of North Africa. That will help no one."

"Agreed," said Murphy. "It is the American position to preserve French independence in Africa."

"Excellent," said de Rose. "French Africa is the sole, remaining trump France has to play, and it must be played on a carefully and well-timed basis."

"We support that endeavor."

"Our other big complaint is repeated radio announcements from London saying that General Weygand is planning independent action in Africa. That causes great problems for us with the Germans—unnecessary problems."

"I'll look into it, but the British have their own mind on these things."

De Rose nodded. "Then there is the letter Churchill sent to Weygand."

Murphy's interest was sharpened; he looked intently at de Rose.

"He urged Weygand to break away from Vichy and to put himself at the head of a dissident government in Africa with guarantees of British support. Churchill declared that the French fleet and the entire African Empire would follow Weygand."

"For sure, premature," said Murphy.

"Churchill does not understand that Admiral Darlan's fleet is not going to follow any army general," said de Rose.

"Yes," agreed Murphy. "What is the overall objective of the letter?"

"The early collapse of Italy, shatter the Axis, and," de Rose rolled his eyes and said disbelievingly, "lead to the demoralization of Germany."

"Yes, unlikely," said Murphy in measured, diplomatic tones. "How did Weygand respond to the letter?"

Jacques watched the veteran diplomat fish for information like a fly fisherman on a placid stream.

"He forwarded it to Maréchal Pétain in Vichy."

"And?"

"The Maréchal replied that he, too, had received a letter from Churchill."

Murphy's eyebrows shot up. "Extraordinary. Didn't the general provide a comment to you?"

"Yes, he told me that such furtive measures behind Pétain's back were a reflection on both Churchill's intelligence and honor and that it confirmed his distrust in Churchill's judgment."

"Whew," exclaimed Murphy.

"Yes, Britain completely lacks the means to support such an assurance."

"Understand. It creates mischief for no lasting effect." Murphy sat silent for a moment. Churchillian impetuosity could be a problem in this assignment, he realized.

De Rose continued, "The general worries about rash and reckless action coming from London."

Jacques looked at Madame Rambert and saw a flicker of a smile. He sensed her admiration for the general.

"Rest assured, Washington will be fully informed," said Murphy. He could also see that impetuosity on de Gaulle's part would be a problem here. The dislike for the Free French leader in Algiers was plain.

"The British don't understand that their meddling could bring on just what everyone hopes to avoid—a German conquest of French Africa," said de Rose, heat rising in his voice.

Murphy nodded and paused. Then he continued, "I look forward to meeting General Weygand." Jacques could see Murphy was trying to cool things down.

"An Air France plane will take you to Dakar," said de Rose, and he stood up as did Murphy and Jacques. Madame Rambert came over and opened the door, and the two Americans stood and let her go first. They followed her out and down the stairs to the reception area.

Coming up to her desk. Madame Rambert glanced over at an attractive midthirtyish blond woman sitting in the waiting area and said, "I'll be with you in a moment, Madame von Koler." Jacques remembered the woman from the Aletti bar.

Jacques also noticed that Murphy seemed to recognize the woman. The woman flashed a look of recognition at Murphy, who returned a smile—too diplomatically, thought Jacques.

Madame Rambert turned around and faced both Murphy and Jacques. "Pleased to have met you. Be sure to contact me if I can of any assistance."

"Thank you," said Murphy.

"Yes, the pleasure was ours," said Jacques.

The two men turned and walked outside. Jacques noticed that the blond woman stood up and walked over to speak with Madame Rambert. Outside the two men waited as their car came up to the portico. A Spahi guard opened the rear door, and the two men got in. The car took off for the short drive back to the consulate.

Unable to stifle his curiosity, Jacques asked, "You know the blond woman waiting in reception?"

"Yes, Paris 1938. She was in the German press entourage that accompanied Foreign Minister von Ribbentrop to Paris for the Franco-German Accord…the humiliating treaty that Berlin foisted on Paris after Munich."

"Humiliation?"

"A Nazi foreign minister wearing his black party uniform laying a wreath at the tomb of the Unknown Soldier under the Arc de Triomphe. Plenty humiliating."

"I didn't know. I wasn't in France at that time."

"The bitterness of those years is a dividing line running through today's French politics," said Murphy glumly. "The Germans exploit it."

"Yes, their propaganda is effective," said Jacques. "I've heard that there was a correspondent from a big Berlin newspaper here. I guess that's her."

"Yes, and she's one of the best at the propaganda game," said Murphy. He let the subject drop. "We'll leave for Dakar this afternoon."

"Yes, sir."

Dakar

December 20, 1940. Late in the afternoon, the Air France trimotor Dewoitine transport lumbered toward Dakar, the west African provincial capital spread across both sides of a silvery thread of a river that emptied into the spacious harbor ahead.

Murphy could see French warships sitting in the harbor and pointed them out to Jacques sitting next to him.

"That looks like the battleship *Richelieu*. It was damaged in the attack, but it still constitutes a formidable artillery battery for any force trying to take Dakar," said Murphy. Jacques sensed Murphy was well informed.

Dakar was on the bulge of West Africa closest to the Brazilian coast across the South Atlantic, a choke point for merchant ships heading north from South Africa toward Great Britain carrying the empire's bountiful supplies to the besieged mother country. The Royal Navy's ability to keep the sea-lanes open was the difference between staying in the war or capitulation in the face of starvation. Great Britain could not feed itself; merchant shipping was its essential lifeline. Dakar was the great strategic prize south of Gibraltar.

"The State Department reopened the consulate on September 15, just a week before the British and Free French attacked Dakar," said Murphy. "Thomas Watson, the consul, was here for the attack. He provided Washington with a firsthand account." Murphy didn't mention that it was Roosevelt who instructed the State Department to reopen the consulate and that it was Roosevelt who was the most avid reader of Watson's account. Murphy had seen Watson's report laying on Roosevelt's desk the day he met with the president.

"Undoubtedly," said Jacques, "Washington will want to strengthen defenses here...when the time is ripe."

"Exactly," said Murphy. "Casablanca and Dakar are the strategic gems along the Atlantic coast of Africa."

Jacques was getting a clearer idea why he and Murphy were on this mission. The plane began a descent toward an airfield on the outskirts of the African city.

After landing at the airfield, Murphy and Jacques were welcomed by Consul Watson. The three men were driven to the consulate in its limousine.

"I have arranged a dinner at governor general's house with Pierre Boisson, the high commissioner for French West Africa," said Watson.

"Good," said Murphy. "I want to get a close feel for how the French see the coming conflict. And we need a shower. The accommodations at last night's air field were rudimentary, to say the least."

"Know it well," said Watson with a laugh.

The Palace

In the cool of the early evening, the consulate car slowly drove up the red brick drive bordered by palm trees in front of the Palace of the governor general, a building of French colonial grandeur set in a spacious park. The car made a graceful turn on the circular drive and pulled up in front of the columned portico of the large structure, a neoclassical building along the lines of the White House in Washington.

A dark Senegalese soldier came forward and opened the door. The three Americans got out and walked up the steps. Inside, the high commissioner walked forward to greet them, swinging the artificial leg forward that had replaced the leg he lost fighting against the Germans in World War I. Handshakes and introductions were made all around. Boisson pointed toward a dining room, and the men marched inside to a long table resplendent with white linen, polished silverware, and bone-white china. The men took their seats with Boisson at the head of the table.

"Most Frenchmen hope for an eventual British victory," said Boisson.

Murphy was startled. "In Vichy, there is not that level of unanimity of opinion," said Murphy dryly.

"Of course, first came the disgraceful attack against our navy at Mers-el-Kébir by Churchill. He discredited the honor of France when he did not accept the word of our highest leaders. The French fleet would never have been allowed to be used against the British."

"Possibly Churchill moved without proof," said Murphy, "such was the chaos in affairs after the French defeat."

"Then there was the attack here on Dakar. After that, many in the French navy wanted to attack the British."

"There were air raids on Gibraltar," said Murphy.

"Ineffective raids," countered Boisson. "Nevertheless, I am sure upon reflection that the American government will conclude that the French have exercised great self-control and have a basic sympathy with the British cause."

"We want to build upon that understanding," replied Murphy.

Jacques watched with admiration; Murphy always waited for the smallest sliver of common ground and then pounced.

"De Gaulle completely misjudged the situation," continued Boisson. "If de Gaulle had succeeded with his duplicitous scheme I am sure the German High Command would have reacted by occupying all the ports of North Africa."

"That is the German action we want to forestall," said Murphy.

Jacques listened and recalled that Murphy had wondered why the Germans had not already occupied more of French Africa. It was a riddle...and a gifted opportunity.

"London radio inflames the situation," said Boisson in high dudgeon, color in his cheeks.

"Washington is aware of some of the weaknesses in the exile groups in London," soothed Murphy, vaguely alluding to de Gaulle's London committee. "We continue to have diplomatic relations with Vichy, not with any of the committees in London."

Murphy took a sip of wine and leaned back and looked at Boisson. Murphy remembered the distrust Roosevelt had for the Free French in London. Worse for the Free French, Roosevelt had concluded that in addition to being unreliable de Gaulle was putting his personal interests ahead of French and Allied interests. De Gaulle was getting in the way of Roosevelt's grand design for French Africa.

"De Gaulle can never be forgiven for his rashness in creating a situation of Frenchmen killing other Frenchmen," said Boisson, his voice dripping scorn as he downed the remainder of the wine in his glass in a gulp. "He is solely responsible for trying to start a civil war among the French."

"My government," said Murphy, "wishes to stabilize the entire situation in French Africa under French leadership."

"Good," said Boisson. "You meet with General Weygand out at the fort tomorrow morning. You can put your understanding in place at the top. Weygand is independent of mind, but remember, completely loyal to the Maréchal. As we all are."

Paul A. Myers

The men continued chatting through dinner, Murphy discreetly gossiping about what he had seen in Vichy and less discreetly about diplomatic life in Paris before the war.

Military Headquarters

The limousine with the American diplomatic plates carried Murphy and Jacques along the side of the vast crescent-shaped bay of Dakar to the tip of the peninsula where the military headquarters was located. The fortresslike headquarters was strategically perched overlooking the approaches to the bay and its inner harbor. The limousine passed through wrought iron gates with sentries snapping to the salute; they knew the car and had been told to expect it.

Inside the blocklike building, a massive edifice built to withstand nineteenth-century bombardment, Murphy and Jacques were escorted to a conference room where General Weygand and several aides stood waiting for the Americans. Introductions were made and hands shaken. All sat down with General Weygand at the head of the table, the Americans along one side, the French officers along the other.

"I am sorry I was not in Algiers to welcome you," said Weygand.

"We had an informative meeting with comte de Rose," replied Murphy. "And High Commissioner Boisson informed us about the situation here in Dakar yesterday."

"Yes, there is still a lot of disgruntlement with the British attack," he paused and said, "and disgust that de Gaulle was able to put them up to it."

"Well, yes," said Murphy, "the British feel the desperation of their circumstances keenly and are seeking whatever advantage they can find…"

"Yes, but after Mers-el-Kébir and the Dakar attack, I have come to distrust Churchill's judgment. This scheme with de Gaulle was inexcusably rash," said Weygand. "It lacks the long view."

"Yes, Britain is in the grip of short-term events," agreed Murphy.

"During the Battle of France," recalled Weygand, his mind reaching back into the chaos of defeat, "Churchill flew over from London and told us he was waiting for a miracle to save the

137

situation. I am a good Catholic, but in military matters I prefer not to depend upon miracles." The general smiled thinly.

"Neither do we," said Murphy. "And like you, Washington is playing a long game."

"Yes, I understand," said Weygand. "America's great weight will eventually go into the balance that weighs the success or failure of events. The British Empire will never be the same regardless of the outcome of the war. World power has passed to the Americans."

"Probably," agreed Murphy.

"Your trade of the old destroyers for bases in the Caribbean shows Britain's declining power. In the empire's glory days, it would never have given up so much for so little. Some sharp bargaining by your government."

Murphy's face flashed with astonishment; he had never thought of the transaction that way. Jacques looked down the table at the general with curiosity; the general was a strategic thinker, like Jean Monnet, he thought.

"Nevertheless, the American government is going to support Britain with all means short of war," said Murphy.

"We have no disagreement with the American government," said Weygand. "But the time is drawing near when your government should articulate a clearer policy."

Murphy nodded in agreement. Nothing to disagree with in that statement.

"We are ready to believe that Hitler can be defeated," said Weygand and made a sweep with hand to include his aides. "But where are the divisions going to come from?"

Murphy looked at Weygand and said nothing. Weygand's eyes took on a questioning look. It was a puzzle that he had obviously thought much about—where would the forces of victory come from? Defeating Germany would be exceedingly difficult.

Jacques watched silently. He had heard that it would take more than two hundred divisions to defeat Germany in Europe.

Murphy shrugged. A big unknown at this stage in the war. He had never heard a hint in Washington.

"Will the United States provide them?" asked the general. The question hung in the room.

Murphy made a noncommittal answer: "Hard to say."

"Indeed," replied Weygand. The dilemma of the present was clearly set forth. A stillness set in over the conference table to a question with no answer.

"Well, then," said Weygand, "the immediate challenge is to keep the Germans out of French Africa." He nodded at a lieutenant colonel. "My intelligence officer will explain."

"We believe the Germans may move to occupy the entire west coast of French Africa in the spring of 1941 to put a chokehold on British maritime commerce," said the colonel.

"Dakar would make an excellent submarine base," explained another French staff officer.

"From which direction would they come?" asked Murphy.

"Most likely through Spain to Gibraltar and then across the strait," explained the intelligence officer.

Jacques nodded; all the scuttlebutt in Algiers said the same thing. It was obvious, but why were the Germans waiting so long? Why were they, who struck with the suddenness of a lightning bolt, now so uncharacteristically slow?

"Our goal," said Weygand, "is to have our army strong enough to resist any incursion—whether from the Germans or the British. We have one hundred thousand men under arms and another hundred thousand in reserve."

"We need supplies," added a staff officer looking at Murphy.

"We would like to explore the possibility of an agreement where America could provide important civilian supplies," said Murphy.

"Yes, and not to be confused with war material," said Weygand, completing the thought. He rapped his hand on the tabletop. "The British…"

"We could negotiate with the British to get civilian supplies through the British blockade," said Murphy.

"It would be to their benefit," said Weygand. "If they could be made to understand that." He made a disdainful look. "In the Great War…Foch had the same problem of getting the British to understand."

"Maybe we could improve the dialogue," added Murphy.

"There are so many ways we could help the British if, for once, they could learn something of subtlety and did not feel that everything must be shouted from the rooftops," said the general impatiently.

"We have a good dialogue with the British," said Murphy.

"And hold the whip hand," added Weygand with a smile. The Americans had held the whip hand in the First World War, too.

"My aide Jacques," said Murphy, "can survey your major cities while I make my report to Washington next month from our Lisbon legation."

"I will ensure all of our headquarters cooperate," said Weygand. "Let's do this in a low-key fashion."

"My thinking exactly," said Murphy.

"Good," said Weygand. He turned to the staff officer. "Please arrange for Madame Rambert to be in contact for Monsieur Dubois." He turned to Jacques. "You have met Madame Rambert?"

"Yes, we saw her the other day when we met with comte de Rose," said Jacques.

"Good," said Weygand. He looked at Murphy. "I am going to arrange for you to have complete access to the governors and commanders across French Africa and"—he looked at Jacques—"and our staffs."

"One more point, if I may," said Murphy.

Weygand looked at him sharply. "Yes?"

"To get the British to allow the supply ships through their blockade, we must be able to provide assurance that the supplies are not transshipped to Europe or put to some other prohibited purpose."

"Yes, I understand the objection," said Weygand. "What do you propose?"

"I would like to station American diplomatic officials at the ports to supervise the cargoes," said Murphy. Everyone at the table looked at him with keen interest.

"Yes," said Weygand thoughtfully. "We could arrange for such persons to have diplomatic status."

The French staff officer smiled broadly. "Give the Germans on the Armistice Commission something else to spy upon." All the French smiled.

"Yes, a larger American presence in Africa," said Weygand, seeing the strategic aim for the long-term benefit that it was. "Very good, Mr. Murphy." He tilted his head to emphasize the compliment.

The men all stood and shook hands. The Americans went outside and drove back to the consulate.

"You have a larger plan in view?" asked Watson, looking at Murphy.

"It's starting to come into view," said Murphy. "That's what this inspection trip is about." He sat back in the seat and said softly, "Someone in Washington saw the potential."

Jacques sat back and looked out of the window. Maybe this drive across the teeming streets of Dakar was the beginning of something larger for him, too.

Casablanca

Murphy and Jacques sat at a table at the rear of the darkly lit bar in the luxurious hotel overlooking the harbor in Casablanca. They were waiting to meet a German diplomat. Jacques looked around the lounge. There were some businessmen sitting around having a drink before heading home. Behind them a sharp-looking blonde of about thirty was reading a newspaper. A couple of naval officers with some stunningly attractive young women were laughing at another table.

A man in a business suite came in. Murphy whispered to Jacques. "Looks Gestapo. Probably checking the room before Auer gets here."

"They're that careful?"

"Yes, I was surprised to get a telephone call from Herr Auer so quickly after we got here. We're being watched, too," said Murphy.

"Why do you want to meet him?"

"I knew him well in Paris before the war. He was a career diplomat."

"And today's meeting?" asked Jacques.

"We'll soon find out," said Murphy as he stood up. Jacques followed and saw a man of early middle age approach wearing a nice double-breasted business suit, a splash of white in his breast pocket, and a silk tie.

"Nice to see you again, Herr Auer," said Murphy. "My assistant Jacques Dubois. He is our new third secretary in Algiers. Just learning the ropes."

Auer shook each man's hand in turn. He looked at Jacques. "Sounds French."

"My father was French; my mother is American," said Jacques, making sure to get the tenses correct. Jacques could see that Auer caught the tenses.

The three men sat, and a waiter came up.

"Highballs," said Murphy.

"I'll get straight to it, Murphy," said Auer. "What are you doing in Africa?"

"Our consular offices have not been inspected in a long time," explained Murphy.

Auer looked at him with feigned interest and wide-eyed disbelief. "And?"

"We're a nation of businessmen, and we think there might be an opening for the sale of American goods here."

Auer looked at him blankly and blinked like a mole in sunlight.

"Auer, if I may ask, what are you doing here in Casablanca?" asked Murphy, turning the direction of the conversation around. "It's a long way from Paris."

"I'll be more honest with you, Murphy, than you were with me," explained Auer. "I'm here for one purpose only, to convince that prize ass in Berlin, our führer, of the importance of the Mediterranean and of Morocco in particular. Herr Hitler does not seem aware that the area exists. He always looks in every direction except south."

Murphy nodded in appreciation at this insight. Auer's frustration sounded genuine.

Jacques looked across the room and saw another businessman come in, a rumpled heavyset man. The man sat down at a distant corner table and ordered a pastis. French for sure. He got out a newspaper and started to read, unconcerned with what was going on elsewhere in the room.

"I've gotten the Wilhelmstrasse," said Auer, mentioning the German foreign ministry, "to replace the Italians on the

Armistice Commission with Germans. Now we can get the job done properly."

"Yes," said Murphy, his mind inwardly sinking at the expanded German influence. "The American government would like all external parties to respect the Armistice."

"Well, the British didn't at Dakar," said Auer.

"The American government had no knowledge of that attack," said Murphy, adding, "to my knowledge."

"I believe you," said Auer. "It was stupid."

Murphy made a flip of his eyebrows. A lot of people in Africa thought that.

"Do you really think you can get some trade through the British blockade to Morocco?" asked Auer.

"We're going to try," said Murphy. "It would be good for the people of Morocco."

Auer looked inward as if calculating something. It was unlikely he was concerned with what was good for the people of Morocco. He reached some mental conclusion and smiled approvingly as Jacques watched. Possibly an increased American presence in French Africa might draw Berlin's attention to the strategic importance of the western Mediterranean. Jacques watched the German think: maybe this was one more piece on the African chessboard, a more complex game than Jacques had previously imagined.

Auer took a sip of his highball and turned to Murphy. "We had those good years in Paris, you and I."

"Yes," said Murphy. "A fascinating time."

"Dare say, made you the top American diplomat on European affairs."

"Hardly. London, Berlin, Rome—those are the big tickets."

Auer eyed Murphy skeptically. "Roosevelt has rich men to clink champagne glasses in those capitals. But the real players—in your foreign service and ours—toil away in the chanceries. That's why we're so interested in what you're doing here."

"You know as well as I do, Teddy," said Murphy slipping into the familiar, "that I'm as far away from the big negotiations as a diplomat could be. Out here looking at the palm trees."

Auer snorted.

"I'm still just the counselor to the embassy in Vichy, something of a backwater these days," added Murphy.

"Dear me," said Auer in disbelief. He drained his highball, stood up, and held out his hand. "Nice to see you again, Murphy. Thanks for the highball." He turned toward Jacques. "Nice to meet you, too. Third secretary, you say? In a consulate? Surely an interesting position." Auer turned and walked out of the lounge. The French businessman looked up and gave him a bored glance as he walked by.

Outside, Auer walked over to his limousine. The Gestapo-like businessman who had first surveyed the lounge came up and whispered in his ear. Auer nodded and then got in the car.

The German walked back across the street and took up a position next to a market stall reading a newspaper. In a few moments, he watched as the French businessman come out. Then, just as he thought, the sharp-looking blonde came out and walked up to the French businessman. Sûreté, thought the German. He'd been right. He felt the old stirrings. He was attracted to the blonde; beautiful and possibly a little bit dangerous. He put his hand in his pocket and fingered his knife. In time, my lovely. A rendezvous? In time.

The French businessman and the blonde walked away, the Frenchman sensing what was going on behind him. Hours before, he had surveyed the neighborhood before the meeting. He had seen the German come and perform his initial checkout and take his position. The Germans were predictable that way. Then he had gone inside for his pastis providing deep cover for the blonde. Now, out on the street, he barely moved his eyes. Yes, just as he thought. Auer's security was watching to see who else might come out of the cocktail lounge. Maybe the same guy as in Paris. North Africa was becoming more interesting—just as le chef had thought.

Rabat

The gray Studebaker car belonging to the American consulate drove up the cypress-lined drive to the magnificent headquarters of the resident-general of Morocco, the five-star French General Auguste Noguès. Murphy and Jacques looked

Paul A. Myers

at the carefully tended grounds surrounding the building as they approached the portico of the classic Moorish palace that served as headquarters for the French administration. Today, the two Americans were to see Emmanuel Monick, the secretary-general to the resident-general.

As the car approached the palace, Murphy said, "Monsieur Monick has years of experience as a financial diplomat in Washington and London. He's met many of the top leaders including Roosevelt and Churchill."

"Financial sophistication is somewhat rare in diplomatic circles," said Jacques.

Murphy raised an eyebrow at him and hummed.

"Present company excepted," said Jacques.

The car pulled up in front of the portico. A Moroccan of the Berber tribe came down in dress uniform to open the car door wearing a white turban, long flowing white gown cinched with a large black belt, and a beige cape pinned to and falling off the shoulders.

The two men got out and followed the Berber up the steps and into the antechamber. A French staff person in a black business suit met them. "This way, the secretary-general is expecting you." The men walked across the red-tiled floor and down a hallway and through a door into a spacious corner office, large windows overlooking a carefully tended garden. Monick, slick black hair across his head, stood up and walked around the mahogany desk and shook Murphy's hand and then turned toward Jacques.

"My aide, Jacques Dubois, he's our third secretary in the consulate in Algiers," said Murphy.

Jacques shook Monick's hand and noted the sharp Saville Row suit and the British manner of this French high official. Somewhat like Jean Monnet in that regard, thought Jacques.

"My pleasure," said Monick, and he turned and introduced two of his aides. "Now, then, let's get on with it." The men all sat down.

"I have been instructed to examine the feasibility of developing a trade between the United States and French North Africa," said Murphy.

"By whom?" asked Monick.

"By Washington," said Murphy, answering opaquely.

145

"Yes," said Monick. "Such an effort on your part could be quite helpful to our current talks with the British?"

"Talks with the British?" asked Murphy, surprise showing on his face.

"Yes, we, too, have got talks underway with the British Board of Economic Warfare on permitting such things as sugar, tea, and cotton textiles through the British blockade."

"Why?" asked Murphy somewhat surprised at this news.

"We need to get supplies through to keep the Arabs and Berbers from becoming excessively restless. That would destabilize the overall political situation in North Africa."

"Any luck?" asked Murphy. He understood that the British would be the biggest stumbling block to any joint French and American accord.

"The British are of two minds on the issue. One school wants to bring economic ruin to French Africa in the belief that it would help the British war effort."

"What would be the likely impact?" asked Murphy.

"It would play right into Axis hands and offer a pretext for a full-scale German invasion of French Africa."

"Yes, others share that concern. And the other school of thought?" asked Murphy.

"Others want to build up French Africa so that at the decisive moment French Africa can play a vital part in the outcome of the European war."

"That view has a sympathetic understanding in Washington," said Murphy.

"It does?"

"Yes, at high levels," said Murphy evenly.

Jacques watched and could see Monick was assessing at just how high a level. His smile indicated to Jacques that Monick had concluded it was indeed at a high level.

"An initiative from you would provide some leverage for us in our talks with the British," said Monick.

"We share the same overall objective," said Murphy. "I will make Washington aware of your thinking in my report."

Monick smiled with satisfaction.

Murphy explained, "We believe we could put together a program to use French funds held in blocked accounts in New

York to purchase the needed supplies and get them shipped to North Africa. General Weygand supports our proposals."

"Yes, I got a telephone call from one of his aides in Algiers," said Monick. "She said Monsieur Dubois would assist in pulling together a detailed list of desired supplies." Monick turned to Jacques. "You can return to Rabat at any time, and you will get our complete cooperation. Coordinate with Madame Rambert at the Winter Palace."

"I will start in as soon as I get back to Algiers," said Jacques.

Monick nodded and turned back to Murphy. "What are the objections?"

"We expect the British to object to the possible transshipment of civilian supplies to Europe to help their war effort."

"Yes, a reasonable concern," said Monick. "What are your plans?"

"We are going to station American diplomatic personnel in each port to supervise cargoes."

"Diplomatic personnel?"

"Yes, we're going to recruit a specialist group and assign them as vice-consuls with appropriate diplomatic privileges."

"That should work. The Germans will of course accuse them of being spies."

"It will give the Germans something to spy on," said Murphy lightly.

Monick laughed. "Indeed." He reflected for a moment. "Clever...elegant."

Murphy understood the words to be the French seal of approval; he moved to conclude the meeting. "We share the same objective. An effective strategy will come out of our joint efforts."

Monick stood up and came around the desk and walked Murphy and Jacques to the door. One of the aides escorted the two Americans back to their car.

Chapter 21: New Year's

The consulate's sedan threaded its way down the hill from where Felix Cole had his villa, turned on a street running along the base of the hills behind Algiers, and then started up a narrow road flanked by tall trees.

"There are only a couple of villas up here," said Cole to Robert Murphy and Jacques Dubois. "Very private."

"Perfect for tonight's meeting," said Murphy.

"Orray Taft will join us later," said Cole. "He is bringing the young lady who helps out at the consulate that I told you about."

"I look forward to meeting her. She seems to know all the players here in Algiers," said Murphy, "the hidden characters that the consulate doesn't know about."

Cole laughed at the insight and turned to Jacques. "She's a beautiful woman, but Orray has no idea what to do with her. He's dull even for a married man."

Murphy laughed and turned to Jacques. "You tread lightly, young man. A good spy seduces the women on the other side, not his side."

"I'll keep that in mind. Love for country only," said Jacques.

"In that case, I'll never be much of a spy. I'll just keep stamping visas," said Cole with a laugh. "Besides, my wife would never let me...even for my country."

Coming to the crest of the hill, the driver wheeled the car through twin pillars anchoring large iron gates. The car proceeded into a courtyard in front of an old Arab villa, ivy crawling up its stone walls, the roof tiles old and rough. The building was almost hidden behind shrubs and pine trees, the entire property flanked by palm trees standing like sentinels. Cole pulled up next to several other cars.

"This is villa Dar Mahieddine, home of Captain André Beaufre," explained Cole. "He is on the staff of General Weygand. He's the host of tonight's soirée." The three men got out of the car and walked to the front door, and Cole rapped the iron knocker several times.

A maid opened the door and showed them into a large sitting room. Another maid and a butler were setting out refreshments on a long white tablecloth-covered table. The maid at the door went back to arranging flowers around the room. A striking-looking woman in her midthirties supervised the preparations.

Cole escorted Murphy and Jacques over to where two men were standing by a fireplace. A roaring log fire threw an orange light across the polished wood floors of the room. One of the men was a French officer in a resplendent blue-dress uniform while the other was a businessman in a black chalked pinstripe suit. They turned to meet the three American diplomats.

Cole made the introductions: "Captain Beaufre, our host tonight, and Jacques Lemaigre Dubreuil, the head of Huiles Lesieur," he said, motioning toward the businessman while mentioning the large French vegetable-oil manufacturer and distributor. Turning to his associates, Cole introduced them: "Robert Murphy, counselor to our embassy in Vichy, and Jacques Dubois, our new third secretary at the consulate in Algiers. Just in from the States."

The men all shook hands, and Lemaigre Dubreuil said, "Nice to see you again, Bob. Long ways from those cocktail parties in Paris, aren't we?"

"Yes, we sure are," said Murphy. "And your beautiful wife, Simone, she is here in Algiers with you?"

"Why, yes," said Dubreuil nodding with his head across the room. "She and her sister are right over there. Life on the mainland is crumbling."

Murphy gazed at the two women and said, "As striking as I remember them." Murphy turned his head toward the woman supervising the maids. "I presume the other beautiful woman," said Murphy gallantly to Captain Beaufre, "is your charming wife?"

"Quite correct, Mr. Murphy," said Beaufre. "Why don't we go into the library. More private there."

"Yes, an excellent suggestion," said Dubreuil. "Discretion is most advisable in Algiers."

The men walked into the library, and Captain Beaufre closed the large twin doors behind them. Inside, Dubreuil took a seat in a comfortable chair, and Murphy and Jacques sat on a sofa opposite. Cole and Beaufre took up chairs facing across the space.

"What is your mission in Africa, Bob?" asked Dubreuil.

"I'm here collecting political information," said Murphy. "An assessment."

"And your new third secretary?" asked Dubreuil, looking at Jacques with a raised eyebrow.

"He's collecting detailed information on the civilian supplies we might be able to ship through the British blockade."

"I see," said Dubreuil. "We have possibly more ambitious plans. We want to organize a resistance here in French Africa to resume the fight with the Germans." He cast a knowing glance at Captain Beaufre.

"Right now, there is a lot of sympathy in Washington for Weygand's 'against everyone' policy," said Murphy. "For now, keeping the other belligerents out of French Africa is the strategic goal. We do not want to create a pretext for inviting them in."

"That seems to be at variance with British policy," said Dubreuil. "But keeping de Gaulle out has its points."

"We do not want to be premature before any intervention," said Murphy. "Resources must be built up," he said, nailing the big hole in British thinking.

"Yes, timing will be everything," said Dubreuil. "Eventually."

"Preparation, too," added Murphy.

Beaufre entered the conversation: "We are surreptitiously hiding arms to bolster the French army in Africa to be able to withstand invasion from any quarter."

"So we heard," said Murphy. "Later, you might meet with Jacques, who knows something about that subject."

"You do?" asked Beaufre, swinging his gaze toward Jacques like a searchlight. "You're not a visa clerk in training?"

"No. I had a liaison role with the British Purchasing Mission. We worked on reequipping the British divisions after Dunkirk."

"Yes, reequipping the British should be an important priority," said Beaufre thoughtfully, "if Roosevelt can get his plan through Congress."

"The replenishment was completed at the end of last July," said Jacques succinctly.

"Last July?" asked Beaufre in disbelief. "Completed?"

"Thirty shiploads where landed in Britain in July," said Jacques.

"I didn't know," said Beaufre. "Before the destroyer deal?"

"Yes," crisply replied Jacques.

Beaufre looked at Jacques as he rapidly recalculated just what that information meant.

"That's the point I want to make," said Murphy. "When the time comes, we can move more material than you can imagine."

"But the Germans are sinking the ships," said Beaufre. "Now."

"The Americans are launching a ship a day," said Murphy. "Next year, three a day, the year after, five a day."

"That's a lot of tonnage," said the French officer.

"Yes, Washington believes that Germans can only be defeated by the allies achieving significant material superiority," said Murphy.

"What about training...bravery...elan?" asked Beaufre, reciting the French verities of its military tradition.

"The Germans have those qualities in abundance," said Jacques, cutting in. He saw Murphy nod in silent agreement. Beaufre ground his teeth. So true.

Jacques continued, "We are now working on a new reequipment plan that ensures each new British division will be superior to a comparable German division."

"Superior? Division by division?" mumbled Beaufre, chewing over the words. The commonsense of it stood out when you thought about it—if you had the material.

"Let me change subjects," said Murphy. "We have heard at the highest levels on our inspection tour great apprehension that the Germans might invade in the spring."

"Yes, it's possible. But we would be in the defense," said Beaufre. He looked at Jacques and added, "That confers some advantages."

"Yes," agreed Jacques, "but ultimately winning the war means taking the offense, a worldwide offensive that will be much more complicated than 1918."

"Worldwide?" asked Beaufre.

"The Germans will have to be defeated from multiple directions," replied Jacques.

"What does that mean for us here in Algiers?" asked Beaufre, boring in on the young man with all the new answers.

"Reequipping the French divisions in North Africa," said Jacques. "At the right time."

"To the level of the British divisions?" asked Beaufre.

"At least," said Jacques. "Preferably to the new standard the US Army intends to use."

"Yes, I see. Someone in Washington has grand plans for us," said Beaufre with a dawning sense of satisfaction. He turned to Dubreuil. "This goes far beyond our current expectations."

"Yes, whoever commands French Africa will have magnificent vistas for action," said the French businessman. "We would be the base not only for liberating France but also for defeating Germany."

The vastness of the ambition of what he had just heard made Beaufre quiet and thoughtful.

Murphy decided to bring the session to a close. "We must proceed cautiously. America is neutral but is pursuing a policy of aiding Britain with everything short of war. Berlin will not miss the threat we pose."

"And your plans include France?" asked Beaufre.

"We're here for a reason," said Murphy, drawing the conversation to a close.

More Guests

Joan Tuyl looked out of the window of the consulate car, a small Studebaker coupe, as Orray Taft threaded the car up the curving road on a hill above Algiers in the dark shadows of tall trees. Coming to the crest of the hill, he wheeled the car through twin pillars anchoring large iron gates and into a courtyard in front of an old Arab villa. Joan gazed at the ivy crawling up the stone walls and let her eyes sweep across the dense shrubbery and trees surrounding the ancient dwelling. Joan loved its decayed magnificence. Orray pulled up next to the consulate's touring car.

"This is villa Dar Mahieddine, home of Captain André Beaufre. He is on the staff of General Weygand. He's the host of tonight's soirée," said Taft grandly.

"It's a beautiful setting," said Joan as she looked at the palms tress bordering the parking area.

"I want you to meet Robert Murphy. He's the counselor at our embassy in Vichy, and he's touring French Africa, inspecting all the consulates. He's just back from Rabat. He wants to meet people, form some firsthand impressions. You qualify for that—in spades."

"Meet? Why?"

"I'm not quite sure," sputtered Orray.

Joan stifled a growing apprehension, letting it subside into a sigh of resignation; she was involved in too many underground activities to welcome questioning from an outsider. Orray didn't seem to grasp that.

They got out of the car and walked up to the front door, and Orray rapped the iron knocker several times. A maid opened the door and showed them into a large drawing room where about a dozen people congregated in groups chatting.

A French officer came over, Joan admiring his well-presented handsomeness. "Captain Beaufre," he said to them and turned and addressed Joan directly, "So pleased to meet you. I've heard so much about you."

A horrified look came over Joan's face, and she looked beseechingly at Orray.

"Don't worry, Joan," reassured Orray. "Captain Beaufre provides us with what assistance he can with regard to internees and refugees."

Joan took in Captain Beaufre's presence, his thick curly blond hair, striking face, and dashing manner. He appeared like an officer out of a previous century—handsome, debonair, the air of the brave about him.

"I'm involved only in humanitarian activities," said Joan. "My family has been involved in church activities here in Algiers for decades. My father was rector."

"Yes, I understand. We are pleased you render such assistance. So much need, so few resources," said Beaufre. "May I get you a glass of champagne?"

"Yes, thank you," said Joan.

Beaufre walked over to a table and picked up two flutes of champagne and presented them to Orray and Joan. "Let me introduce you to some of the other guests." He ushered Orray and Joan over toward a dark-haired man in a black pinstriped suit speaking with three women.

"The beautiful Simone Lemaigre Dubreuil and her charming sister Christiane Lesieur," said Beaufre.

Joan took in the beautiful young women, stylish waves in their raven-dark hair, the matching pearl necklaces on the two women suggesting a paired gift, a memory from the prewar Paris couture. Joan felt more than a little outclassed in her evening smock. She shook each woman's hand in turn, and they in turn were exquisitely polite to the stunningly blond beauty.

"And Jacques Lemaigre Dubreuil, the head of Huiles Lesieur," said Beaufre.

Dubreuil held out his hand. "Yes, I believe I'm familiar with some of your work at the consulate. I knew Murphy back in Paris," and he nodded at the tall figure in the black suite across the room.

Again, Joan made a sideways glance at Orray. She took a breath and said, "Our charitable work seems to have more interest than funds." She smiled and shook Dubreuil's hand.

"And my wife Sally," said Beaufre as an attractive midthirtyish woman stepped forward and extended her hand.

"So pleased you could join us tonight," said Sally. Joan took in the cool presence, the well-tailored clothes, the simple silver necklace, and the beautiful Moorish bracelets.

"Yes, Orray told me a little about your background on the way up the hill," said Joan.

"We'll try to do something about funds for your charitable work," added Sally. "I appreciate how difficult it must be."

"Thank you," said Joan with a warm smile. A little help for her activities would make the risks of the evening worthwhile.

The group chatted for a few moments, and then Orray broke in and said, "Speaking of Murphy," said Orray, and he gestured toward a tall man in a suit standing over in front of a roaring fire in a stone fireplace, "there's Mr. Murphy. Let me introduce you." The two walked over.

"Mr. Murphy, I would like you to meet Joan Tuyl," said Orray.

"Yes, my pleasure. Felix has told me about you. You help out at the consulate?"

"Yes, I do what I can," said Joan. Damn, she thought, when did I become a center of conversation?

Murphy turned and pulled Jacques into the conversation. "Let me introduce my assistant, Jacques. He's the new third secretary for the consulate. He'll be staying here while I finish my inspection tour."

Jacques held out his hand and smiled. "We meet again."

"Yes, thank you so much for dinner," she said.

Murphy looked askance at Jacques. "You move fast."

Everyone laughed.

"Joan's a married lady," explained Jacques.

"Paris was full of married ladies," said Murphy in a sharp retort.

"Jacques is gallant," said Joan.

"I expect I'll be bogged down in paperwork concerning the supply mission," said Jacques.

"Yes, so preoccupied with Washington busywork I understand you're not going to be able to assist with the consular duties," said Orray with a tinge of sarcasm and disappointment. "Washington doesn't understand our needs."

"That was my experience as a consul in Germany after the last war," said Murphy sympathetically. "Too many consular duties, too little time." He looked understandingly at Orray. "And great need."

Joan added, "Often tragically so." She turned to Orray. "Please don't ever understate the importance of your work. To those it helps, it's a godsend."

Orray brightened. "Thanks."

Murphy stood and directly faced Joan. "I'm interested in what you have to say about Algiers. I'm collecting impressions."

"For your scrapbook?"

"So to speak. Is there much of an expatriate community here?"

"It's small and almost all the English have left. I'm a Dutch national by virtue of marriage."

"Your husband?"

"He went back to Holland. He was a reserve officer. He's there now, but I have no idea doing what. There's almost no mail between there and here, and what there is has to come through Switzerland..."

"And lacks candor."

"Exactly."

"And you're living where?"

"Here in Algiers. My mother has a large apartment, and I and my two boys live with her."

"Hard to get by?"

"Yes, she gets a small stipend through your consulate from the British...and I teach...some...and some work at the consulate."

Orray nodded approvingly. "We couldn't get by without Joan."

"Algiers is a beautiful place," said Joan, "but there's no path from here to anywhere else. For those who come, the road stops."

Murphy nodded at this insight. "Where would they like to go?"

"All to America," said Joan with a light laugh. "After that, Gibraltar...or across French Africa to Casablanca or Dakar. There they can get ships to Lisbon...and from there..."

"Yes, almost anywhere," said Murphy. "One of the things you could do for me, Joan, is show Jacques around Algiers. He's new. Introduce him to any people you think he might find interesting." He looked at her with a friendly and direct stare.

"Yes, I would be pleased to do that," said Joan. Yes, more opportunities for compromising my network.

"Fine," said Murphy.

Orray made a wave. "I promised Joan a look at the harbor from the roof. There's a patio with a spectacular view. It's fetching."

Murphy made a throwaway smile at Orray, a gesture practiced at a thousand diplomatic receptions.

Joan turned and grabbed Orray by the arm and said, "Let's go." Orray was such a safe choice, she thought. The handsome men were always something of a temptation to her.

The two turned and walked across the room and up a staircase and opened a door at the top and walked out.

Outside, Joan exclaimed, "It's beautiful." She stood along the rail and gazed down the hillside and across the residential blocks to the harbor below. Even on New Year's Eve, ships were loading under the arc lights, cargo booms swinging in the darkness, pallet loads swinging in their cargo nets. Stevedores guided the loads down into the holds.

"The villa? It has a history?" asked Joan.

"In some earlier century, it belonged to an Arab corsair," said Orray. "With a pirate's eye, he picked this spot right on the crest of the hill. An excellent view of the harbor and not too far from his ship."

"This would make a wonderful lookout," said Joan. "You would know exactly who was coming into and who was leaving the harbor, even Algiers perhaps."

"Yes, it would," said Orray absently.

Just then Captain Beaufre came up behind them. Joan made a start. She hoped he had not overhead her remark.

"We are all on the same side, or eventually will be," said Beaufre. "Yes, it is a beautiful view. But we better go down. Soon it will be midnight."

They all turned and went through the door and down the stairs. In the drawing room, Beaufre said to Joan, "Let me excuse myself." He turned and walked down a hall and entered another room and closed the door behind him.

Joan walked over and stood next to Murphy, who was heavily engaged with Dubreuil on a discussion of his business interests in Africa. Suddenly the party was interrupted by a man in a dark double-breasted suit and a snap-brim fedora accompanied by several police officers. "I am sorry to interrupt your fine party, but urgent security matters intervene," said the man in the fedora. He waved some of the officers down the hall. "Find them," he ordered.

"Yes, chief," said one of the police officers.

The man in the suit turned to the astonished guests. "I am Captain Achiary of the Special Police."

Orray leaned over to Murphy and whispered, "The political police. They work for Weygand."

"My men will inspect your identity papers," said the police captain, whose full name was André Achiary. Two policemen started to inspect the various guests' identity papers and passports. Murphy remained calm and watched. He could see apprehension in Joan's face and guessed that she also played a hidden role in the intrigues swirling through Algiers. Soon the other policemen returned walking behind Beaufre and two other men in business suits.

"Ah, Captain Beaufre," said Captain Achiary. "And I believe Major Faye and Colonel Lambin."

"What is all this about?" asked Beaufre.

"I am afraid I have arrest warrants for you and the other two officers," said Captain Achiary.

"On whose authority?" asked Beaufre.

"Your superior, General Weygand," said Captain Achiary. "Something about a breach of discipline."

The three military officers stood silent.

"You understand?" asked Captain Achiary, looking at the three men.

"It will be cleared up," said Beaufre.

"Let's hope so," said Captain Achiary agreeably.

Murphy watched, suspecting that there was something of the theater going on with this surprise raid just before New Year's.

Captain Achiary walked over to Joan. "And just what are you doing here, Mrs. Tuyl?"

"She's with me," interjected Orray with more than a little heat.

"Yes," said Captain Achiary, turning to face Orray. "I understand. One of Mrs. Tuyl's many activities here in Algiers is to work for the American consulate." The captain turned back and looked accusingly at Joan and said, "And before that for the British consulate."

"Yes," said Joan with downcast eyes. There had been a rumor that Achiary had some sympathy for resistance activities. Undoubtedly a lie, thought Joan.

"Fine, Mr. Taft," said Captain Achiary. "You may take Mrs. Tuyl home. You're free to go." He turned and faced Murphy and said, "Ah, the counselor from the American embassy. Here to look after consular affairs?" Achiary raised a skeptical eyebrow.

"You understand perfectly," said Murphy with practiced composure.

"Yes, I see, a diplomat," said Achiary. He turned and faced Jacques. "And your new third secretary, I believe, Mr. Jacques Dubois," said Achiary with a dry smile on his face. "Or perhaps it should be Monsieur Dubois?"

"As you wish, *mon capitaine,*" said Jacques, the words cool and even.

Captain Achiary nodded and then turned and addressed the group. "You are all free to go. We are sorry to have disturbed your festivities."

Murphy moved his arms in a wide encompassing arc taking in Jacques and Felix on the one hand and Orray and Joan on the other. "We best be going." They moved toward the front door. Murphy looked over his shoulder and said, "Goodnight, Captain Achiary."

"Goodnight, Mr. Murphy," replied Achiary cheerfully.

Hotel Aletti

The Corsicans stood in their rough-work clothes, wool caps pulled down toward their eyes, and looked down the side street running along the side of the hotel. The undercover police sergeant had given them their instructions. Work over some Italians. Always a pleasure.

The big touring car pulled up to a side entrance. A door from the hotel opened and out came a party of boisterous Italians from the Armistice Commission ready to go to a local restaurant and maybe a little fun afterward.

With a shout, one Corsican hurled another Corsican across the street and into the front of the car. Another threw yet a fourth over toward the automobile and followed with screaming insults. The other Corsicans shoved and threw each other about in a general melee toward the now-startled Italians, who pulled back into a group. Then the Corsicans were upon them. Kicking, screaming, and slugging. Some of the Italians' wallets were pulled out of their pockets. The Corsicans pulled the cash out and threw the wallets on the ground, a maneuver akin to pickpocketing with one's fists. Nothing subtle about the Corsicans tonight.

Soon a police whistle broke through the noise, and two gendarmes came running up the street. The Corsicans took off, leaving several Italians on the ground, battered and bleeding.

The police helped the Italians up and back into the hotel. The touring car quickly pulled away and returned to the garage.

Chapter 22: Lisbon

January 17, 1941. Lisbon. Robert Murphy finished reading the typescript report on his whirlwind inspection tour of French Africa. Yes, he had emphasized succinctly what he wanted to convey to the highest levels in Washington, DC. French possessions in Africa were immense in size with vast potential in the coming war effort. The French administration was skillful but in dire need of supplies to sustain the loyalties of Arab and Berber native populations. If the United States later entered the war, prompt rearming of French military forces in Africa would create an instant and powerful ally at a strategic crossroads of the Mediterranean.

Murphy paged through to the back of the document and reviewed the draft economic agreement one more time. General Weygand had approved the draft. It provided for close supervision of the cargoes by an expanded American diplomatic presence in French Africa. The status of the new American diplomats was not exactly clear, particularly their access to coded communications and the diplomatic pouch. Nevertheless, America's eyes and ears in a territory under Axis supervision would be unprecedented.

Putting the papers in his briefcase, Murphy stood up and went downstairs to the coding center in the basement of the American legation. He handed the documents over to the coding officer and said, "Statement Department. Undersecretary Welles."

Washington, DC

In the Oval Room of the White House, a cozy fire burning in the fireplace, the president sat at his desk reading the report on French Africa received from his special representative, Robert Murphy. Finishing it, he jotted down at the bottom of the report: "I have read this report with great interest, FDR." He turned to Sumner Welles sitting across the desk from him. "Let's move forward with this project. Quietly, indirectly. We may be sneaking up on one of the great opportunities of the war."

161

"Yes, sir, Mr. President," replied Welles. "And the secretary?" Secretary of State Cordell Hull was not in the Roosevelt inner circle.

"Work around him," said Roosevelt with a sly grin. He loved the intrigue of politics that repulsed the less wily.

Welles got up and returned to his office at the State Department. He had a nagging doubt. The president said to proceed quietly, indirectly. He had felt for some time, based on solid evidence, that US diplomatic codes were insecure. Cable traffic from Berlin, Switzerland, and Lisbon was regularly being read by Axis security services; they knew this because a top Nazi economics official in Berlin had told them so. Maintaining timely communications with Murphy in distant Algiers would be difficult.

Algiers

Jacques walked through the streets from the consulate toward Taverne Alsacienne for lunch; the restaurant had been recommended to him by Felix Cole. It was close to the Winter Palace. Jacques was intrigued; it fit in with some plans he had, a place to meet acquaintances in a more relaxed setting. Entering, he asked the maître d' for table out of the way with good light. The diplomatic pouch had brought a letter from Jacqueline postmarked Lisbon. He was anxious to read it.

Seated under a bright light from a wall-mounted sconce, he tore open the letter and started to read the handwritten stationery. She was in Lisbon waiting for a seaplane to take her to London. She had gone to Washington and spoken with Monnet. He told her to go to London and that the imperial capital is where the turn of events would occur. Anne Hare agreed and had wrangled her travel money and an assignment to London. Because of the expense, the news desk wanted her to do some special correspondent work. Jacqueline was in a heaven of expectation about reaching London and this great step up in her journalism career. She wrote:

I'm staying in a small hotel. I'm waiting for my so-called priority to get a seat on one of the planes to England. Lots of

Americans here and every night we gather in the Bar Avenida and swap stories about whose priority had priority. Two other guys in the hotel take me, one of them is Ernie Pyle, the roving correspondent. I don't know if you have read him, but he had an immensely popular travel column where he went around the country writing interesting stories. He went with his wife, always called That Girl. She's still back home.

I asked him about England, and I told him that Anne wanted lots of inside dope from the top-tier people. So she's angling me toward some invitations with the embassy crowd. He said fine; he understood. He enjoyed reading Anne, but he thought the real stories in this war would be with the common people and their struggles with the privation of war and the lives of the regular soldiers and airmen and sailors. Said that's what he'd focus on. I'll keep that in mind and work to sharpen up my interviewing skills. Eventually the war will move on from the society drawing rooms of London to the battlefields, I suppose.

I have to sign off the letter. I got a call from British Overseas Airways. I'm booked for a dawn flight from the marine terminal tomorrow morning. Got to go. Love Jacqueline.

Jacques sat and read through the letter again. He was happy for her and suspected this new trajectory in her career would finish off what was left of their relationship, which had always been friendly if physically intense.

He turned and pulled out a couple of newspapers that had also come in the morning's diplomatic pouch, a weekly event. There were recent copies of the *New York Times Tribune*. He wanted to find out how Harry Hopkins's fact-finding trip to Britain was going. He looked for stories. Here was one about Churchill speaking in Glasgow with Hopkins sitting on the dais. And what the Hell! It was written by our special correspondent; no name, but that would come.

Churchill made a point of introducing Hopkins as the president's special representative. Churchill also made the point that Britain would pay what it could but that it would require far more than that. This was Monnet's point exactly. If Churchill was talking about it, he must have some assurance that Washington will deliver. That's good news, thought Jacques.

The article went on to say that Britain and the Commonwealth were maintaining at present the front line of civilization. Nevertheless, grim and cruel days lay ahead.

Then Jacques saw that Jacqueline had gotten inside dope from informed observers that Germany is expected to strike soon and strike hard, but where the blow will fall is unknown but a matter of intense speculation.

One speculation centered on an offensive east of Bulgaria. East of Bulgaria was the Black Sea. What did that mean? An offensive through Turkey into the Middle East, threatening the British lifeline to India? That was what Dakar had been about: keeping West Africa out of German hands and thus cutting the lifeline from the British Isles to the empire.

Jacques sat back and thought: yes, vulnerabilities everywhere.

Returning to Jacqueline's story, he read that Churchill had made the telling point that Herr Hitler's victories on the continent, as spectacularly successful as they have been, were uncollected winnings as long as Great Britain stayed in the fight.

Turning to Anne Hare's column, he was surprised to see her write about the deployment of German Stuka dive bombers to Sicily, threatening the British lifeline to Malta through the Mediterranean. More vulnerabilities.

Turning to later editions of the *TeeTee*, Jacques found an article on economic warfare that confirmed London wanted a united Anglo-American economic action plan against the Axis. The British wanted to freeze assets of occupied countries and close American ports to ships trading with the enemy in defiance of the British blockade.

Jacques could see that the British plan would scupper Murphy's planned agreement with Weygand to bring nonstrategic supplies to Africa. Acquiescence to the British blockade provision would mean that Britain would control by veto almost all trade with the Eastern Hemisphere. Breathtakingly arrogant, thought Jacques.

Digging into the details of the story, Jacques could see that Secretary of State Cordell Hull was reserving all judgment. Hull was a strong believer in free trade, Jacques knew.

Hull further repeated the "all aid to Britain short of war" policy. Hull said that further decision awaited a full account from Hopkins and his talks in London.

Jacques could see that Murphy would have to overcome vocal British resistance in Washington, but he also knew that Hopkins was one of the behind-the-scenes proponents of Murphy's mission to French Africa, and his own small involvement. Publicly, Hopkins would push aid to Britain hard. Behind the scenes, something else? A wider view?

Jacques took a sip of wine and wondered how high up in Washington came the support for Murphy's mission. From high up in the State Department for sure. He knew that from Sumner Welles's visit to Monnet's house to "volunteer" Jacques for the Murphy mission. It was hard not to believe that somewhere the president's hidden hand was not behind the machinations. Welles was the president's man.

Jacques smiled. Yes, the man sat behind his desk and moved his stamps around in his collection books while he hatched plans of scope and imagination.

He would write a letter to Jacqueline tonight. Keep the friendship warm.

Hotel Aletti

The French police chief, well dressed and polished as a diplomat, walked into the lounge at the hotel. He scanned the room and saw the Italians and walked over. All stood up and shook hands.

"Sit down," said the Italians' leader, Prince Chigi, to the Frenchman.

"Thank you," said Captain Achiary.

"We're upset about the poor security."

"Yes, so many refugees have flooded into Algiers," said Achiary sympathetically.

"To get beat up and robbed by a bunch of Corsicans," said Prince Chigi. "Our own security agent had his wallet stolen."

"Regrettable," said Achiary.

"What are you going to do about it?" asked the prince.

"I can assign one of my detectives to assist your security agent," said Achiary.

"Would you?" asked one of the other Italians, a worried look on his face.

"We owe you security," said the French police chief. "I'll have him here first thing tomorrow morning. We'll arrange twenty-four-hour security."

"We'll see how that goes?" said Prince Chigi. "Otherwise, if we tell Rome, we'll get some bothersome gumshoe they want out of the way. More trouble than he'd be worth."

"This should suit all of our interests," said Achiary as he stood up to leave, smiling inwardly. He would be keeping close tabs on the Italians. "Good night, gentlemen."

Maison Blanche Airfield

Robert Murphy descended the boarding ladder from the Air France trimotor that had just landed from Tangier. Consul General Felix Cole and Jacques waited behind a low fence in front of the small terminal at Maison Blanche aerodrome outside of Algiers.

"Got it," said Murphy, patting his briefcase. "The draft economic agreement has been approved in Washington. It's an accord designed to be signed by myself and General Weygand here in Algiers and then ratified in Vichy and forwarded to Washington."

"What took so long?" asked Cole.

"Our Bureau of Economic Warfare is deeply suspicious of the agreement while the British embassy got word of it through their Bureau of Economic Warfare and is adamantly opposed."

"Why?" asked Cole.

"The British don't seem to realize they have natural allies among the French in Africa," said Murphy.

The three men walked over to the consulate touring car, and Murphy and Cole got in the rear seat while Jacques sat in the front. He turned around and draped himself over the seat so he could speak with Murphy and Cole as the car returned to the consulate.

"Do you have a list of supplies?" asked Murphy looking at Jacques.

"Yes, detailed lists for shipments to Casablanca and Rabat for sure, and Oran if the merchant ships can enter the Mediterranean," replied Jacques.

"Good," said Murphy.

"I have some disquieting news," said Cole. "It goes beyond suspicions in Washington. There are numerous radio broadcasts from London, and even New York, reporting that hundreds of German agents disguised as tourists are descending on Morocco to take over the French administration."

Murphy rolled his eyes. "Okay, I get it." The damned British, first arrogant and now impertinent. He turned to Jacques. "You and I will fly to Rabat tomorrow morning and get to the bottom of this."

"Yes, sir," said Jacques.

Rabat

The consulate Studebaker drove into the courtyard of the magnificent Moorish palace that was the headquarters of the French administration in Morocco. Murphy and Jacques got out and walked up to the entrance.

"Robert Murphy and Jacques Dubois of the American consulate to see General Noguès," said Murphy to the officer at the reception desk. The officer called over another officer and instructed, "Please escort the gentlemen to the resident-General's office."

The two Americans followed the officer down a wide corridor of large dark-red tiles and shining-white plaster walls. Dark mahogany colored beams crossed the ceiling. At a reception area, the officer left the two diplomats with the resident-general's aide. "This way, he's waiting for you."

They entered the large office and General Noguès came around and shook both of their hands and bid them be seated. The aide sat down to one side and got out a notebook to transcribe the conversation.

Coming straight to the point, Murphy said, "News reports indicate you are being flooded with German tourists who are going to take over the French administration."

"Yes, we hear those reports, too," said the French general. "There was one German tourist with a visa issued at the Paris embassy, but he was sent back."

"No Germans?" asked Murphy.

"Some Germans," replied the general. "There are fifty-three additions to the local Armistice Commission as specified by the Armistice Commission in Wiesbaden."

"Are they a source of concern?"

"No, they are mostly clerks and noncommissioned officers. Here, you can look over the list," the general said, pushing over a multipage list of the Germans with complete descriptions. "Our intelligence is on top of the situation."

"They sure are," said Murphy as he quickly read through the pages. "And Consul General Auer in Casablanca?"

"He's not attempted any interference with our control. We know the Arabs and the Berbers; the Germans do not. They know that. You can confirm that with the American consul general in Casablanca."

"Other Germans?"

"Oh, some journalists come through now and again. Propaganda work for their home audience, I believe. The lady is quite nice looking, like one of those German film stars."

"Yes, I knew her in Paris," said Murphy. "Anything else?"

"Those radio broadcasts from London do a lot of harm. If the Germans ever believe them, then maybe they will indeed show up in North Africa. But not as tourists, as soldiers."

"Yes," said Murphy, dismay spreading across his face.

"You are Americans. You have influence. Use it," said the general.

"I'll notify my government," said Murphy. "We'll be heading back to Algiers in the morning."

"You are welcome in Rabat at any time," said Noguès as he stood up to escort the two diplomats out.

Winter Palace

The consulate coup swung into the courtyard in front of the entrance to the Winter Palace. Murphy and Jacques got out of the backseat and walked briskly up the steps to the guard at the door.

"Madame Rambert," said Jacques smoothly. The guard wrote down their names in the register and waved them through. They walked over to the reception area, and Marie came out to meet them.

"This way. He's expecting you," she said as she shook Murphy's hand and then Jacques's hand. She smiled familiarly at him. She started walking up the staircase to the second floor, and Murphy and Jacques followed.

Marie waved them into General Weygand's office, and the general stood to greet them. Marie closed the door behind her and moved over and took a seat at the side of the general's desk. She opened her notepad to take notes.

"Sit down, please," said Weygand. The two diplomats sat down.

"I have a draft agreement and copies with me," said Murphy as he slid two copies across.

"Good," said Weygand. He picked up one and pushed the other over to Marie, who picked it up and started reading. The general read through the pages.

"You mention the need for American cargo inspectors?" asked the general.

"Yes, to monitor the cargoes to make sure none are transshipped to Italy or Germany, or for that matter even metropolitan France."

"Yes, I understand," said the general. "What will their status be?"

"Well, they will be diplomatic personnel, vice-consuls, but we're not sure of their status and rights?"

"I would like to give your government confidence in this matter," said Weygand. "Let's annotate the agreement to permit your vice-consuls to use secret codes and carry locked diplomatic pouches."

"That would be excellent," said Murphy.

"Good," said the general. He turned to Marie and instructed, "Would you please work on some language with Monsieur Dubois and write it in the margin of the agreement?"

"Oui, mon général," said Marie. She walked over to a side table with Jacques, and they whispered phrases as she annotated the two documents. They returned and sat down, and Marie handed the documents to the general.

"Ready to sign?"

"Yes," she said.

Murphy took the two documents and signed and dated each one. Then the general signed each document with a flourish.

"I'll leave for Vichy tomorrow," said Murphy, "to get the agreement ratified and then take it on to Washington."

"Now I want to stress several things," said Weygand gravely. "First, we are all concerned that the Germans might mount an invasion of French Africa this summer. Second, the British are in no better position to support French Africa in 1941 than they were metropolitan France in 1940." The general's face took on a look of pained remembrance about the previous year's terrible defeat.

"Yes, we understand that the British desire that French Africa could rejoin the war against Germany is an illusion," said Murphy. "The means are utterly lacking."

The general nodded in agreement. "We desperately need to use the civilian supplies you arrange to secure the loyalties of the Arab and Berber populations."

"Yes, while I'm getting the agreement through the monkey works in Washington, Jacques will be here working on shipping manifests for the first shiploads," said Murphy.

The general turned and looked at Jacques. "Good. Work closely with Madame Rambert. She has my complete confidence in this matter."

"Yes, sir," said Jacques.

Chapter 23: Lunch—Taverne Alsacienne

February 1941. Far down a corridor on the first floor of the Winter Palace in a small office, Jacques finished speaking with the captain in charge of logistics. The two of them agreed that the first shipment under the Murphy-Weygand Accord should unload at Casablanca.

"Yes, both the German Armistice Commission members and the British spies can see for themselves that the goods are all for civilian consumption," said the French officer.

"Yes, one of our vice-consuls will track the goods to market," said Jacques.

"Both the Germans and the British should have an interest in the French administration maintaining compliant Arab and Berber populations," said the officer. "Why they cause this trouble?"

"So true," said Jacques with a sigh. "Both groups of officials seem to be better at causing trouble than preventing it."

"You Americans are going to find out about the Perfidious English, I'm afraid," said the Frenchman.

"How about the Perfidious Germans?" asked Jacques. "The big black Mercedes outside."

"That is Frau von Koler, the famous German foreign correspondent."

"And who is she seeing?"

"Probably the lieutenant commander."

"Perfidious?"

"Hardly. He arranges interviews and tours for her across North Africa."

"Anything else?"

"The lieutenant commander has a reputation with certain ladies here in Algiers who have a taste for the wild side."

"The wild side for the distinguished lady journalist?"

"She grew up in Berlin in the 1920s, little that a girl or young woman would not have experienced in those years. Some like to travel back…"

"And she has a husband somewhere?"

"In Berlin. A legal official in the Wilhemstrasse," said the officer referring to the German foreign ministry.

"Does he have a taste for the wild side?"

"Hardly. He has a close relationship with his secretary, a matronly hausfrau type. The disorder in 1920s Berlin affected him differently."

"You seem to know a lot."

"Before the war, French intelligence was pretty good. Knew Berlin well."

"Anything else?"

"The lieutenant commander is part of the naval circle around Admiral Darlan. Here to keep an eye on the general."

Jacques took this in and then tossed out a question. "Oh, by the way, what happened to Captain Beaufre? I met him at the New Year's Eve party at which he was arrested."

"Oh, General Weygand recommended some minor discipline here in Algiers, but Vichy insisted on his return. He is now awaiting trial, but he is in comfortable circumstances."

"Comfortable?"

"Yes. With his wife and family."

"Why him?"

"He's quite smart. Vichy knows those are the ones to keep an eye on. But they may have outsmarted themselves. It puts Beaufre close to the top generals in France, some of whom may be wavering."

"An intrigue?" asked Jacques. "I guess I understand."

"Understanding Vichy is difficult. Being defeated is not easy."

"No, I'm sure it isn't," said Jacques as he stood up. "But keeping Germany out of North Africa is a victory."

"General Weygand understands that. General de Gaulle less so."

Jacques said, "I must be on my way." He turned and walked out into the corridor and headed for the front reception area. He hoped to chat with Marie Rambert before leaving, to thank her for her assistance with the logistics arrangements.

As he approached the reception area, he saw Frau von Koler speaking with Marie.

"Meeting with the lieutenant commander?" asked Jacques innocently of the German correspondent.

"Why, yes. Just finished. And you are here meeting with whom?" asked Koler as she tossed her head, throwing some blond locks back behind her ear.

"Oh, someone about arranging the unloading of the civilian supplies that some American businesses are shipping to French Africa,"

Koler looked at him with disbelief but changed the subject and said, "I was just trying to get Marie to agree to go out for lunch with me. Without much luck."

"It would not be appropriate," said Marie.

"If Jacques would join us, then you would have representatives from all sides," said Koler. "Surely that would be above suspicion."

"Yes," said Jacques. "We could all go to Taverne Alsacienne. I was just there the other day. It's actually a short taxi ride from here."

"I have my car," said Koler.

"Marie and I could take a taxi. Very neutral," said Jacques. He turned to Marie. "How about it?"

"Okay, but I have to be at the Red Cross at two o'clock," said Marie.

"Red Cross?" asked Jacques.

"Yes, I'm studying to be a volunteer nurse," replied Marie. "The war."

"And the general?" asked Jacques.

"He is supportive. Everyone must do his or her duty, he says." She would serve.

Jacques smiled and turned to Koler. "We'll meet you there, Frau von Koler."

"Excellent," said Koler. "Please call me Elke."

"Jacques," replied Jacques, happy to establish the mutual informality. He turned to Marie and asked, "Marie?"

She made a weary sigh and said, "Okay." Informality had become an adversary to her well-maintained emotional distance if not isolation.

The three walked outside, and Jacques asked the guard to flag a taxi while Koler got into her long black Mercedes, the uniformed chauffeur holding her door open. The Mercedes sped off.

Taverne Alsacienne

The taxi pulled in front of the restaurant where Frau von Koler stood waiting. Jacques and Marie got out of the taxi and came up to her, and the three went inside.

"Ah, Monsieur Dubois," said the maître d' in recognition. "And with the ladies, today."

"Yes, a table for three," replied Jacques.

"Our pleasure," said the maître d' escorting them to a banquette in a spacious back corner. The two women slid in on one side, and Jacques sat across.

"May I recommend the sea bass today?" said the maître d'.

"Yes, that will be fine for me," said Marie.

"Me too," said Elke.

"Same here," added Jacques. "And some wine."

"Tea for me," said Marie. "I have my Red Cross training."

"My husband, Gerhard," said Elke, "was on foreign-ministry business in Wiesbaden. He said he met with your husband on some economic issues, Marie."

"Yes, Henri would be dealing with economic issues," replied Marie. She turned to Jacques and explained, "Before the war he was banker for Worms & Cie."

"Here in Algiers?" asked Jacques.

"Yes, mostly here. He covered all of French Africa. And there were frequent trips to Paris."

"Did you accompany him to Paris?" asked Elke.

"Sometimes," said Marie. "A chance to go shopping. Real shopping, not wandering through the souks."

"Yes, I was in Paris frequently before the war, too," said Elke, the fondness of the memory softening her expression.

"Doing what?" asked Jacques.

"Among other things I managed the German press coverage of Herr Ribbentrop's state visit to Paris in December 1938."

"I remember the newsreels," said Jacques.

"Did you like them?"

"They were quite effective," said Jacques.

A waiter brought steaming plates of grilled sea bass and heaping piles of green string beans. White wine was poured.

The three tucked in. Jacques turned the conversation to the Armistice Commission and asked, "Your husband Gerhard? Was he satisfied with his work in Wiesbaden?" Marie's head snapped in Elke's direction.

"Yes, quite. Berlin finds the cooperation of the French industrialists in supplying Germany constructive. Not all occupied countries are so cooperative."

"Well, undoubtedly, the price is right," said Jacques.

"The French industrialists understand that only Germany stands between them and Bolshevism," said Elke firmly. She believed.

"What did Gerhard do before the war?" asked Jacques.

"He was a corporate lawyer. We often traveled together to Paris, London, New York."

"New York?"

"You know it?"

"Yes, I did my graduate work there and then worked in banking," said Jacques.

"We probably know some of the same people, the people in the big law firms and investment banks."

"I'm sure we would," replied Jacques, intrigued with the possibilities. He looked at Marie and then ventured, "We might all meet for a drink at the Rainbow Room someday?"

"I will count on that," said Elke. She turned to Marie and explained, "The Rainbow Room is a beautiful supper club at the top of a skyscraper in Manhattan. Dinner and dancing."

"A supper club?" asked Marie in some disbelief. "After the war seems a long way off." Marie looked at the two of them. "Peace?"

"Maybe not so far off," said Elke. "I sense that 1941 is going to be the year that fate turns over the cards one by one. That will determine the course of the war."

"What do you think is the likely outcome?" asked Jacques.

"There will be a negotiated peace between Germany and the Anglo Saxons, Britain and America. Germany can bring Britain to its knees by cutting off the little island in the North Sea—really a weakling country—from its tropical empire. No invasion is necessary."

Jacques nodded. A lot of facts lined up to support Elke's conclusion. He quickly saw that a German submarine base at

Casablanca and an air base at Rabat would cut England off from its Eastern Hemisphere empire.

"I read about German Stuka dive bombers being stationed on Sicily," said Jacques, throwing out a small piece of bait to see what he might reel in.

"Yes," replied Elke, "Germany has to protect its Italian ally from further depredations by the Royal Navy."

Jacques understood. The British had launched a devastating torpedo bomber attack just three months before on the Italian fleet anchored in the Italian port of Taranto near the heel of the Italian boot. Half the Italian capital ships had been sunk or badly damaged.

"I see," said Jacques.

"Do you?" asked Elke. "If the Germans put a cork in the Suez Canal, the eastern Mediterranean becomes a German lake."

"Understand."

"Good."

"And France?" asked Marie, a worried tone to the words coming out, like a mother asking after a missing child.

"Berlin believes France may be an interlocutor with London and Washington," said Elke.

"A go between?" asked Marie.

"Exactly. The Anglo Saxons don't have the power to overcome Germany on the continent. And Russia is never going to side with the capitalist countries, not after their experiences with the British and Americans during their revolution." The British and Americans had strongly backed the Czarist White Armies against the Red Army in the early 1920s.

Again, Elke made good points. Jacques asked, "Just who in France will lead the diplomatic effort?"

"Well, there are many. Of course, that is why Berlin is so accommodating on Mr. Murphy's presence here in Africa. He might be key to establishing the crucial communications links between our countries when the time comes."

"That's what diplomats do," said Jacques.

"Who knows? You might have an important role, Jacques," Elke added.

"No, I'm just doing low-level commercial attaché work. The other stuff is all above my pay grade."

"Yes, one will want to trust such work to the likes of Orray Taft," said Elke, and she laughed.

"He's well meaning," said Marie, coming to the defense of the overworked consular official. "He's overloaded with visa requests and looking after the interests of British prisoners of war."

"Yes, all the unreliable elements scurrying around Europe are looking for the mouse hole out of Algiers," said Elke dismissively.

"Who knows, Elke," said Jacques, "someday you might want to get to the Rainbow Room for that drink, and you'll need a visa. Orray might come in handy."

"Yes," said Elke, momentarily taken aback. "I forgot; one always wants to have American friends at the standby." She smiled warmly at Jacques, a little more warmly than required, thought Marie. Enough of this.

"I must depart for my Red Cross training," said Marie.

"Yes, it's time. I must get back to the office," said Elke. "It has been delightful. We should do it again."

"Enjoyed it," said Jacques. He stood up. "Let me accompany you, Marie."

The two of them walked through the crowded restaurant and outside. He waved at the taxi down the street, which came up. "You are going where?"

"The Hotel St. Georges. The classes are at the naval headquarters."

Jacques opened the door to the taxi, and they both slid inside the rear seat. "What do you think of the lady with all the answers?"

"Answers?" said Marie with a touch of consternation. "Is this not a time to be asking questions?" She turned her head and looked at Jacques with the serious gaze of an experienced diplomat, her manner suddenly taking on a maturity that he had never seen before. He understood General Weygand's reliance on her.

"Good observation," he said, startled by her *savoir-faire*. "We share an outlook, something in common."

She nodded and turned her head straight ahead. "Nevertheless, I remain a married woman. A state we do not have in common."

"We can be friends."

"Perhaps. But only if one doesn't contradict the other." Now she had the haughtiness of a commander in chief.

The taxi came up to the Hotel St. Georges and swung through the gates into the gravel parking area. Jacques got out and held the door as Marie slid out.

"Thank you for lunch," she said. "Au revoir." She turned and entered the hotel without looking back.

Chapter 24: Berlin

The case officer from the decryption section came into the office. "We broke the Americans' current diplomatic code. Here, read this cable." He held the piece of paper across the desk.

"Sit down," said the officer. He scanned the message.

"You're sure it's from Murphy."

"Yes, we intercepted it between Algiers and Lisbon. It is for further transmission from Lisbon to Washington."

"And this header?"

"Yes, for the eyes only of Undersecretary of State Sumner Welles. He seems to be the point of contact for secret diplomacy undertaken on behalf of President Roosevelt. Other cables from other highly placed American diplomats across Europe are similarly routed through Lisbon to Welles in Washington."

"The Americans don't use their ambassadors?"

"Apparently not. There's an entire secret web."

"Yes, this is compromising material. General Weygand is asking President Roosevelt for arms in case the Germans attack the French Empire."

"That could result in Weygand's immediate recall if discovered. Possibly treason."

"A breach of the Armistice for sure." The officer leaned back and thought deeply. "We must be careful how we use this."

"Yes."

"Inform Herr Auer by pouch. Suggest that Frau von Koler keep working the angle about our correspondent in Washington, the one working for the *Deutsche Allegemeine Zeitung*. Make sure the Americans think that he is the source of our information. The stories about him having top-level access in the American State Department are good cover. Their FBI—innocents all—thinks the State Department is a hot bed of spies and isolationists. That'll throw them off track." The German smiled. "The naïve have their uses."

Chapter 25: Murphy in Washington

April 1941. Robert Murphy had enjoyed several days' leave with his wife, a woman of uneven mental health, and his three daughters. The daughters were his three queens and to his personal anguish they were growing up without him, putting on high heels and lipstick, starting to enter the swim of life while their father was far away. He had serious concern that his eldest daughter was carrying too heavy a burden in caring for her fragile mother, a burden that was rightly his. Nevertheless, after several days of domestic recharge, he was upbeat and ready to carry the ball across the finish line, to move the implementation of the Murphy-Weygand Accord from paper to action. Soon, ships sailing with supplies would depart for French North Africa. He entered Old State, the building housing the State Department just up the street from the White House, and went to the undersecretary's office.

"We've got problems," said Sumner Welles as Murphy took a seat.

"Uh huh."

"Yes, Halifax," said Welles, referring to British Ambassador Lord Halifax. "He says that His Majesty's government objects on two grounds. First, British consuls have to be on the ground in North Africa to inspect the cargoes, not American representatives."

"Our inspectors are being specially selected for this task and should be able to document to Britain's satisfaction the safe landings of the cargoes," replied Murphy.

"I believe you, but the British also demand that all French warships anchored in France must be moved to ports beyond possible German control." Welles made a blank look.

"That's a deal killer," replied Murphy. "That's just something conjured up by the British Board of Economic Warfare to kill cooperation."

"Ably assisted by our own State Department's Board of Economic Warfare," added Welles.

"Yes, they're always ready to believe British rumors over our own diplomats' firsthand reports," said Murphy with frustrated disgust.

"But we now have an ally in the British embassy. A young economist just in from London who understands that economic assistance can be a powerful tool to advance allied interests in Africa."

"So, what do I do?"

"Continue your recruitment of special consuls. We'll get you all to Africa," said Welles. "I'll contact you with the final go ahead."

Murphy stood up and with a wan smile said, "Thanks." He turned and departed.

Approval

April 24, 1941. Murphy was escorted into Sumner Welles's office, who stood with a wide smile on his face. "All approved. The agreement is a go."

"What are my instructions?"

"You are to return to Algiers where you'll function as sort of a high commissioner for French Africa."

Murphy's expression fell, and he mumbled, "My wife...my daughters..."

"You have the president's confidence," said Welles gravely.

Murphy bucked up, put on his trademark smile, and asked, "Vichy?"

"As a formality, you'll continue as the counselor of the embassy. But Algiers is your base. You will supervise the new vice-consuls but more importantly, maintain intimate contact with General Weygand."

"Understand."

"Good. Let me invite in our British friend." He reached over and pushed a button on his telephone. Soon the door opened, and a secretary escorted in a well-tailored British diplomat. Murphy and Welles stood. "This is David Eccles, the young British economist I told you about." Murphy and Eccles shook hands, and all sat down.

"There's been a change of attitude in London," said Eccles.

"Spearheaded by Mr. Eccles," added Welles with a broad smile.

181

"One group in London wants to disrupt the Germans at any cost. Making an annoyance in North Africa is their goal."

"Even if it means provoking a German invasion of North Africa?" asked Murphy.

"That's the corner these people don't look around. Rather shortsighted, I would say," coolly responded Eccles.

"Rather," said Murphy drily.

"But others see your supply operation as a tactic to keep North Africa from falling further into German orbit. This opinion has prevailed."

"It's in the British interest," said Murphy.

"Yes," agreed Eccles. "That why we'll also add Dakar to your cooperation sphere. Those of us, how should I say, in the strategic school, want to wish your initiative the best of success. Keeping the French on the sidelines for now is the goal."

Murphy looked at Eccles evenly. "We see the chessboard the same way." The Englishman nodded.

"Good," said Welles. "This view of Africa has quiet support high up here in Washington." Welles summed up, "Let's give it our best go."

Murphy and Eccles stood up and took their leave as Welles's secretary was escorting the next visitor into the busy undersecretary's office.

Foxhall Road

Early May 1941. Blossoms were wafting in the light airs of spring as the taxicab drove through the leafy neighborhoods of west Georgetown to Foxhall Road. Arriving at Jean Monnet's house, the taxi pulled over to the curb, and the driver said, "Here we are, Mac."

Jacques got out while the driver went around to the rear trunk and got out a large suitcase and set it on the sidewalk. Jacques paid the cabbie. "Thank you."

"Thank you, sir," said the cabbie, tipping his fingers to the bill of his cap.

Jacques turned, picked up the suitcase, and walked up to the front door, which opened revealing a smiling Jean Monnet standing in welcome. "Nice to see you again, Jacques."

"You, too, sir," said Jacques. "The State Department people were at a loss why a third secretary from Algiers has been called back to Washington, DC." He wondered, too.

"Well, there's a story behind that," said Monnet.

"I'm all ears," replied Jacques.

"Later," replied Monnet with a smile holding back so much information he wanted to share.

Jacques set down the suitcase, and Monnet's butler approached and looked at Monnet for direction.

"Put it in the front bedroom. He'll be here only for the evening," said Monnet. He turned to Jacques and added, "They're sending you on in the morning." Who "they" were went unexplained. The butler took the suitcase down the hall. Monnet and Jacques walked into the living room where Mrs. Monnet came forward and kissed him on both cheeks.

"So nice to see you again, Jacques," she said. The three sat down.

Monnet launched right in. "Let me tell you what we've been doing here in Washington. Later some friends will join us, and we can talk about what the State and War Departments are doing."

"Great," said Jacques, looking intently at Monnet.

"You remember the combined statement—the balance sheet of needs and production—that we developed at the Anglo-French Purchasing Commission?"

"Yes, that was our blueprint. You said unless the Americans were given production orders, they'd never expand their output."

"And I was right about that. Those early orders from the French government after Munich finally got the American airplane production on the ramp up."

"Yes, but too late for France."

"But not too late for the war," said Monnet, always dismissive of past mistakes in his determination to meet the future demands of the immediate war. "We've expanded the Anglo-French plan into an overall Anglo-American Combined Statement."

"What's your goal?"

"To show that we need to massively expand American war production to defeat both Germany and Japan. We're calling it the Victory Program.'"

"Outproduce by how much?"

"We show the German production in one column and then how much production is required to outproduce them. The Japanese are a lesser problem."

"Outproduce the Germans? Not outfight them?"

"You have to outgun the Germans to defeat them. They're too tough otherwise."

"Their armaments are pretty good."

"Ours will be better, particularly the airplanes."

"Yes, always airplanes."

"They're decisive in this war. They tip the balance."

"When does this new plan go into effect?"

"We're presenting it to Roosevelt in early September."

"When will it be released to the public?"

"Later. At the right time."

"Who decides that?"

"Roosevelt. He has a preternatural sense about such things."

"Who's supporting it?"

"Roosevelt."

"That will do it."

"He's the architect of the coming victory," said Monnet.

"That's the question on everyone's lips in North Africa," said Jacques. "They all want to know when the Americans will enter the battle."

"That's in the hand of events, but probably soon," replied Monnet. "Speaking of the French in Africa. How are they bearing up?" asked Monnet.

"Pretty well, all considered," replied Jacques.

"And the Germans?"

"There are not many in North Africa. They spy but do not have the numbers to do much else."

Just then there was a ring at the front door.

"Our friends are here," said Monnet. They all stood up as the butler ushered Sumner Wells, the undersecretary of state, and John McCloy, the assistant secretary of war, into the room. Jacques stepped forward and shook hands.

"Yes, I believe we met last fall," said Welles.

"Right in this room, I believe," said McCloy. Everyone sat down.

"Well, here he is," said Monnet. "You wanted to speak with him."

"Yes," said Wells. "What we're interested in is the state of the French forces in Africa."

"And the current status of their armaments," added McCloy.

"Fine. Let me summarize," began Jacques in a cool professional manner. "There are about hundred thousand soldiers in various colonial divisions and regiments on active duty. These troops are armed as they were in 1939."

"Which is about the same as in the First World War," said McCloy.

"Yes, the French are slowly getting permission for additional arms from the Germans so they can defend Africa from the British."

"Will they?"

"Yes, anti-British feeling is intense because of Mers-el-Kébir and Dakar. The Germans feel they can trust the French to resist a British invasion."

"Do the French think the British pose a threat?"

"No. General Weygand is dismissive of British power. They worry more about some misguided British provocation leading to a German invasion."

"Yes," said Welles. "Murphy stressed that point in his recent visit."

"The French have hidden substantial arms, including heavy armaments, in the interior away from German eyes," added Jacques.

"The purpose?" asked McCloy.

"To resist a German invasion."

"Will such resistance be successful?"

"That's difficult to gauge," said Jacques. "Depends how many Germans."

"Now, let's talk hypothetical," said McCloy. "If somewhere in the future it was advantageous for the US to occupy North Africa and rearm the French, what would it take?"

"That's the problem I've been working on," replied Jacques. "First, there are another hundred thousand soldiers in the reserve forces. They're not ready to go and would require arms and additional training. Beyond that there is another hundred thousand with some military training."

"So a large rearmament and training program," summed up McCloy.

"The French are ready to go," replied Jacques.

"We're going to send you to Fort Bragg tomorrow to meet with General Devers and his staff of the Ninth Infantry Division. They'll brief you on the type of weaponry we're outfitting our infantry divisions with and which we expect to outfit allied divisions. Commonality will make logistics more efficient—and therefore effective."

"Does it relate to the ten British division project I worked on last fall?"

"I think you'll find we're going well beyond that."

"Really?"

"Yes. The War Department has no illusions about the strength of the German army. They have to be outgunned to be defeated."

"Can I explain that to the French?"

"Indirectly. Explain the extent and amount of weaponry we plan to put into infantry companies, battalions, and regiments."

"And artillery?"

"We going past the old French seventy-fives. All divisions will be equipped with one hundred fives and one hundred fifty-fives."

"Armor?"

"New tanks, more heavily armed..."

"And lots of them," added Monnet.

McCloy smiled. "Yes, lots of them."

"What is the strategic goal?" asked Jacques.

"One year from the start of the rearmament effort, we would like to deploy a ten-division French army alongside other allied armies on the continent of Europe."

"Where?"

McCloy let out a sigh. "A big question. But strong armies in North Africa would be poised to assault Southern France, Sicily, or mainland Italy. Lots of options."

"Which will keep the Germans off balance," added Monnet.

"We hope," said McCloy.

Welles sat and watched the discussion. He smiled inwardly; he could see the president's thinking unfold before his eyes in this Georgetown living room. Welles stood up signaling an end to the meeting.

McCloy arose and said by way of closing, "A War Department car will pick you up here seven o'clock in the morning sharp."

"I'll be ready," said Jacques.

The two cabinet officials departed. Monnet watched them leave and turned to Jacques and said, "Maybe a cognac before bed?"

"Yes," replied Jacques. "This is breathtaking."

"And I've got your lady friend ensconced in London where she can't blab about your work in all the wrong places," said Monnet.

"That has its downsides, I might say," said Jacques with a grin.

"Well, cognac is second best," said Monnet with a laugh.

Fort Bragg

The gray army staff car with the five-point star emblazoned on its side sped down the fresh new macadam roadway through thick pine forests and came to a built-up area of new army barracks. Near a central square with a flagpole, the staff car came to a halt in front of a long single-story, ranch-style building. A sign announced that it was headquarters for the Ninth Infantry Division, and a smaller sign was printed "Jacob Devers, MG, commanding." The driver came around and opened the door, and Jacques stepped out.

"I'll pick you up here whenever I receive a call. Just tell the corporal at the front desk, sir. Those are my instructions," said the sergeant.

"Fine," said Jacques. The sergeant escorted him to the door where a sentry took over and opened the door and escorted Jacques over to a corporal sitting behind a desk.

"Here you are, sir," said the sentry and returned to his post.

"Jacques Dubois to see General Devers," said Jacques.

"Yes, you're expected," said the corporal. Another big shot from Washington. A young big shot, though. The corporal escorted Jacques down a hallway and opened a door to a conference room where several officers were sitting around a long table. The officers politely stood, and one of them pointed Jacques toward a chair, and he took a seat.

"The general will be right with us," said a colonel.

The door opened, and the officers stood bolt upright, and the colonel called, "Attention."

Jacques followed and stood, surprised with the suddenness of the movement.

"Gentlemen," said General Devers evenly. "Please be seated." He came over and held out his hand to Jacques. "General Devers," he said.

"Jacques Dubois," said Jacques.

"Have a seat," said the general and turned and took his place at the head of the table. "Mr. Dubois has been sent down by the War Department to get a detailed briefing on how we're equipping the new American infantry divisions. In particular, the type and number of weapons—machine guns, mortars, artillery, armor support, trucks, tank destroyers."

The officers looked at Jacques with interest.

"Mr. Dubois has a liaison role with French army units…"

"There's or ours?" asked one of the lieutenant colonels.

General Devers laughed. "Eventually ours." He looked at Jacques and asked, "I presume that's the plan?"

"Yes, sir," replied Jacques. "The French officers are expectant at the opportunity to get back in the fight."

"They didn't do so well last time," said another lieutenant colonel.

Jacques relaxed and explained. "Yes, let's talk about last time. The German army massed its armor and struck behind closely coordinated air attacks by their Stuka dive bombers. The massed attack shatters rifle-based infantry defenses. The infantry comes up behind on trucks and mops up."

"Rifle based?" asked one of the lieutenant colonels.

"Antitank weapons have to be right with the infantry to be effective with direct-fire artillery right behind it. Air cover needs to keep the Stukas at bay. The Germans concentrate absolute superiority at the point of attack."

General Devers massaged his chin with his fingers thoughtfully. "If I understand you correctly, you're saying the coming ground war is a big gun fight?"

"Yes, General. You stop the armor or you lose."

"Clear enough," said the general. He looked at the officers. "We need to keep clear in our training that pure rifle-based defense is not good enough. Every action has to be a combined arms effort, echeloned in depth."

"Yes, sir," said the ranking colonel.

One of the lieutenant colonels looked at Jacques. "Do you have any military experience?"

"At another time and in another army I was a *sous lieutenant,*" replied Jacques. The officers chuckled.

"Does the sous lieutenant have any other advice," one of the lieutenant colonels asked playfully.

"The counterattack. The Germans always counterattack—soon, suddenly, when you least expect it."

"Like the last war," said the general, who although not deployed to France had carefully studied the lessons learned.

"They're like hornets," said Jacques.

"Well said, Monsieur Sous Lieutenant," said the general with an engaging smile. "Platoon leader is always the leading edge." He turned to Jacques and said, "I'll leave you with my staff for the remainder of your stay. Stop by my office before you leave." The general stood. The other officers promptly followed as did Jacques. Devers turned and departed.

Rabat

May 16. Robert Murphy read the message at the American consulate in Rabat: "Pending clarification of the situation, all activities on behalf of France and French North Africa are at a standstill."

"Signed by Secretary Hull himself," said the consul general with somewhat smug satisfaction. Having diplomats engage in near-warlike behavior didn't seem proper to him. Could lead to unforeseen complexities.

"Well, I better get over to the resident-general's and explain this firsthand," said Murphy. He stood up.

"I'll have the driver take you over straight away," said the consul general.

"Thanks," said Murphy as he headed for the door.

A half hour later the consulate car dropped Murphy off at the entrance to the great whitewashed Moorish building that was the French headquarters. Murphy went up to the guard desk and showed his credential and an aide took him down the long hallway to Emmanuel Monick's office, the secretary-general to the resident-general.

"Nice to see you again, Robert," said Monick as Murphy entered his office. "Have a seat."

"Thanks, Emmanuel," replied Murphy. "Bad news. Secretary Hull has put a stop on our trade agreement for the time being."

"A stop?" exclaimed Monick with astonishment. "Are you Americans ever going to have an African policy of your own, or do you intend to let London make your policy?"

Murphy laughed. "It's a delay. I'll get it untangled."

"When you were here in January, the British had prestige. Now they have none."

"None?"

"None. They've had serious defeats in Yugoslavia, Greece, Libya, and now Crete looks like a badly misjudged adventure."

"All true," agreed Murphy ruefully.

"The question we ask," said Monick, "is what is the United States going to do? If the United States does intend to act, what is the timetable?"

"I can't be specific, but in time the United States will act, and I think decisively."

"Good. And the current imbroglio?"

"There're rumors that there are sixty thousand Germans massed in Spain waiting to invade Morocco."

"That's a pretty tired rumor," said Monick with a chuckle.

"That's why I'll get it sorted out pretty quickly," said Murphy agreeably.

"And your cargo inspectors?" asked the Frenchman.

"They'll start arriving next month."

"Then we'll be in business."

"Yes, we will," said Murphy. "Finally."

Chapter 26: Algiers

May 1941. At Saturday lunch at British Cottage Hospital, Joan sat next to Captain Brinckman and a host of well-wishers bidding him farewell. His medical evacuation to Tangier had come through. Jacques sat across the table and relaxed in the atmosphere of British bonhomie. Not being an official "frog" in the Britishers' eyes, he was inside their circle of friendship.

"Well, it took a long time, but the board of French doctors finally came through," said Joan.

"Thanks to you," said Jacques. He had admired the way she greased the wheel.

"Yes," said Brinckman. "Never thought I'd look forward to being declared an invalid. Their judgment is probably true. I'm afraid I'll never get back to active service, back to the regiment."

"Well, you've had lots of valuable espionage service here," said Joan.

"Yes, if you like that sort of thing. Me, a Colonel Blimp?"

"If the Americans come…" mused Joan.

"Not if, when," interjected Jacques.

"You really think so?" she asked.

"Yes, just like in the last war. The submarine sinkings…"

"You may be right," added another British officer. Captain Bradford was a captured pilot cooling his heels in Algiers. He sat down at the table. "I think it's time to be getting back into the war," he said enigmatically.

"How?" asked another person.

"Where there's a will there's a way," said Bradford smugly. Jacques noticed the smirk.

"Well, I've got to get back to the consulate," said Jacques. "Good luck on your trip to Tangier." He and several other invalided internees were leaving in the afternoon.

"Thanks, Jacques, catch up with you at some forgotten barricade," said Brinckman, bidding farewell.

Bradford watched Jacques depart, and then he walked over to Joan and planted a kiss on her cheek. "Me, too." Then he whispered, "If I'm not back tonight, take care of my papers."

Startled, Joan looked at him. What did that mean?

Algiers Harbor

The three British men, one carrying a big picnic hamper, another carrying a basket of wine bottles, and third carrying a haversack of supplies, came down to the stout twenty-foot sailboat, the pride of one of their British friends. The men stowed the supplies under the little forecastle, and two of the men got in and unfurled the sails and got ready to hoist. The third untied the lines, gave the boat a push with his foot, and jumped in. They raised the sails and headed for the harbor entrance. They had the drill down.

Coming up to the patrol boat, they heaved to and said, "Just another afternoon sail on the bay." One of them waved a bottle of wine, and all three took big draughts out of their oversized wine glasses.

"You again?" said the Frenchman. The Britishers had been out lollygagging around the bay three Saturdays in a row, drinking wine and having a good time. They weren't much good as sailors.

"Your papers?"

The skipper of the boat handed across three permits. The guard shuffled through them and handed them back. "Fine, Captain Bradford. You know the rules. Be back before dark."

"We'll run out of wine by then," said Bradford with a wave and pulled on the tiller. The little sailboat pulled away.

At the far side of the bay, another patrol boat watched the little sailboat tack haphazardly around the bay as the sun set. Suddenly, dusk fell into darkness as the patrol boat slowly headed back to harbor and Saturday-night dinner. The next day was Sunday, and there would be no duty. The little sailboat fell out of sight and mind.

At the far side of the point, Bradford hauled the sails taut, pulled on the tiller, and in a strong northeast wind set a course for Gibraltar. With luck they'd be there in five days, he'd

Paul A. Myers

reckoned. A sailboat wasn't much different than an airplane, just slower.

Rendezvous at the Villa

As Joan came out of the American consulate late in the afternoon, the inevitable tail from the political police stood across the street in the shade. He motioned at her and walked across the street toward her. A police car slowly drove up the street. She stopped and wondered what this was all about. "Madame Tuyl," said the policeman, "the boss wants to talk to you."

"The boss?"

"Please get in," said the policeman as he held the door open.

"What's all this about?" she asked, trying to keep her voice calm as her heart pounded in her chest.

"There are some concerns," said the policeman as the car pulled up the street and made a turn. Presently the car descended Rue Richelieu to a point close to the harbor and turned through the stone gates and into a parking area next to a large villa.

Not so far away, thought Joan. Torture probably never is.

The policeman opened the door and escorted her out and up the steps onto the veranda. He knocked on the door, and a maid opened it and said, "This way. They're in the drawing room."

Joan entered the foyer, and the policeman followed. The maid pointed them toward the drawing room. Joan walked into the room, and Captain Achiary came forward and offered his hand. "Hello, Madame Tuyl. We meet again."

"Yes," said Joan, somewhat bewildered.

"I believe you know my wife?"

"Yes, we went to lycée together," said Joan. She turned and shook hands. "Simone, nice to see you again."

"You, too," replied the elegant French woman in her early thirties.

"Drink?" asked Achiary.

"Compari," said Joan.

Achiary went over to the sideboard and mixed three drinks and returned and handed one to Joan, one to his wife, and kept one. "Have a seat."

"Thank you."

193

"I suppose you're wondering why I've invited you up here for a drink?"

"That thought had crossed my mind."

Simone smiled. Joan had always been fun, particularly for a rector's daughter.

"Here and there we have common interests. I try to keep tabs on yours but do so from a distance."

"So I've noticed."

"I also have some important interests here in Algiers," said Achiary. "This weekend some of them are coming together, and I want to make sure that you keep your interests away from my interests over the weekend."

"Okay."

"It would be good for your interests," said Achiary with seriousness of tone.

"I want to do what is right for whatever interests I have," said Joan, still not understanding where the conversation was going.

"Let me explain. I watch over the security of the members of the Italian Armistice Commission here in Algiers. There were some unfortunate incidents in the past. The government in Vichy expects me to safeguard the interests of the Italian members."

"No one I know has any issues with the Italians," said Joan. Her and her friends mostly ignored them.

"An Italian general is flying in Saturday evening and will be staying in the Aletti. They've reserved one wing of the hotel."

"Can't imagine that I or any of my friends would interfere."

"Good. Stay away from the Aletti Saturday and Sunday. My security there will be tight."

"Something secret?"

"To the contrary, there will be a welcoming ceremony at the airport. Madame von Koler will have news photographers and newsreel cameramen for the welcoming ceremony. A big show of French, German, and Italian cooperation."

"I'd happily stay away from that."

"Good. Vichy wants nothing to go wrong," said Achiary. He leaned over and said intently, "If it did, it would be bad for me. And that would not be so good for you. The next police chief might not be so understanding."

"I understand," said Joan.

"I'm closing Le Club Saturday night just to make sure there are no troublemakers in the neighborhood."

"Understand."

"Good," said Achiary. "When you're finished with your drink, the detective will take you home."

"I can walk. I don't want to be seen in a police car any more than I have to."

Achiary laughed. "He'll keep an eye on you, and make sure you're safely home."

"Yes, he usually does," said Joan as she finished her drink and set the glass down. She stood up and turned to Simone. "So nice to see you again, Simone."

"Possibly we'll meet again," said Simone hopefully.

Joan smiled and turned, walking out of the room toward the front door.

Le Club

Joan met Curly outside the bar and said, "I need to talk with you."

"About what?" said the undercover operative. "I don't like meeting in the open like this."

"The people watching over me are unlikely to harm you," replied Joan. He escorted Joan inside.

"Over by the windows," said Joan. She looked around the bar. The normal complement. Some pilots, some other officers, a few foreign journalists. Over in the corner, an elegant woman with a couple of attractive younger women sat murmuring among themselves over drinks and looking around. Waiting for someone, surmised Joan.

"Don't believe I've seen them before," said Joan, looking at the women.

"They're new. The young ones are from Marseilles. The older woman has a Parisian accent. They said they're from Rabat," said Curly.

"I've heard—I can't say where and it's not important—about an Italian general coming to Algiers on Saturday evening. Have you heard anything?"

"Well, yes. There's been an honor guard drilling in the plaza in front of nineteenth Army Corps headquarters every morning. And the military band has been practicing the Italian national anthem. It's all for something this weekend. That's all I know."

"It's Saturday evening around sundown. An Italian general is flying in from Tunis."

"So? That happens fairly often."

"It's a big show. Madame von Koler and her news team with photographers and newsreel cameramen will be there. The Vichy government wants this to be a success."

"Yes, demonstrate loyalty and cooperation."

"They're taking over part of one wing of the Aletti," said Joan.

"That's a lot of Italians," agreed Curly. "Do you think they're bringing their own women?"

Joan looked across the room at the French women. "Probably not. Maybe they're already here."

"Yes," said Roger. "Working for themselves…or someone else?"

"Some of both, probably."

"Certainly."

Joan gave a start and sat up straight as the three French pilots came over. Almost boys, thought Joan. The three pilots pulled up chairs and leaned forward.

"We couldn't help but overhear," said one, a lieutenant with two stripes on his epaulette compared to one stripe on the shoulder straps of the other two.

"Overhear what?" asked Curly. For sure this was a place of eavesdropping. Uncomfortable.

"An airplane carrying an Italian general coming to Maison Blanche Saturday night," said the lieutenant.

"Yes, that's the rumor," said Curly guardedly.

"With a lot of Italians," said the officer. "That would be big airplane."

"Large enough for an official party, I suppose," said Curly.

One of the sous lieutenants looked at Joan and nodded over toward the French women. "We're interested in the women."

"You are?" said Joan, sort of unbelieving.

"Yes."

"The local girls aren't good enough?"

"It's not that. They're from Marseilles. They know things..."

Joan rolled her eyes.

"You're too late," interrupted Curly, looking across the room. "Here come the Italians."

They all turned and watched as Prince Chigi and two other polished young Italians walked over and sat down with the women and waved at the bartender for drinks.

"We better be going," said the lieutenant as he stood up and motioned for the others to follow. The three officers quickly left the bar.

Joan and Roger watched out of the corners of their eyes as the older French woman spoke in whispers with the Italians, who were all wolfish interest and wide smiles. The younger French women were effortlessly charming, putting hands over the Italians' hands, squeezing a finger here and there, smiling underneath wide dark eyes and razor-sharp eyebrows like those of the film stars.

"No giggling," said Joan. "Very professional."

"Yes," said Curly. "Look, the older woman has apparently sealed the deal."

Prince Chigi's head was nodding warm agreement. He looked longingly at the young French woman next to him. Business completed, the thirtyish French woman stood up. She smiled at the young women and then the Italians. She murmured, "Saturday night." Then she turned and crossed the bar, high heels sounding on the floor tiles, and headed for the street.

Curly watched her go and turned to Joan. "Come on. Let's take a look down the street."

They walked outside, and Curly glanced down the street. He quickly grabbed Joan and whirled her into a romantic embrace. "They're there," he said conspiratorially. He waltzed her halfway around, and Joan looked over his shoulder and could see a heavyset man in an overcoat and homburg walk up to the French woman and bid hello. The two had a hurried whispered conversation, then smiles crossed their faces, and they turned and walked down the street. After a while Curly let Joan go.

"They seem to be professional associates," said Joan.

"So it seems," said Roger.

"But I don't think they're the local political police or I'd have bumped into them before."

"Neither do I," said Roger. "Possibly mainland, something deep undercover. Watching both the Germans and the Italians."

"Why?"

"Possibly out of habit. The Deuxième Bureau has been watching them for a long time."

"Yes, some national interests are eternal."

"Let me walk you home."

"Thanks."

Maison Blanche Aerodrome

Captain Achiary stood behind the assembled officials from the Winter Palace and nineteenth Army Corps headquarters. Nearby were members of the German Armistice Commission in business suits. To one side was an honor guard of Spahis and regular French troops drawn up in precise ranks. Behind the honor guard was a French military band. In front of the welcoming party was a podium with loud speakers to each side. Behind the podium a red carpet stretched out onto the tarmac of the aerodrome. Nearby was a set of boarding steps. Over to the side, some ground crew lounged around who would service the plane. The Italian plane would presumably stop in front of the red carpet, and the Italian general, the head of the Italian Armistice Commission, would descend the boarding ladder and make a small speech at the podium.

Achiary looked around the aerodrome at the parked planes. He'd checked with security. Yes, all the magnetos had been removed. The fuel tanks had been drained. None of the ducks could fly.

Over to one side was Achiary's favorite German, Frau von Koler. Her journalism activities were an obvious cover; her relationship with the lieutenant commander at the Winter Palace reflecting a love of information, though he did suspect she was a woman who liked the wild side, an aspect for which the lieutenant commander was known for among some women in Algiers. It was Achiary's job to know things like that. The lieutenant commander stood over beyond the official party, a saturnine look on his darkly handsome face.

Frau von Koler was directing the placement of the newsreel cameras, positioning the news photographers for the best shots. The newsreels and the photographs would not only go to Berlin but all over the world through the international German news service, the Deutschland News Bureau and Transocean News Service. The newsreels, the photographs, the news stories, and the live radio broadcast would dramatize the close partnership between Italy and Germany in Africa, the power of their partnership and the support it has from the Vichy government in Africa.

Achiary also knew the show and pomp would go over well in Vichy, which always wanted to dramatize its collaboration with Germany. What better way than to welcome one of the detested Italians?

There was a murmur of airplane engines in the distance. Heads craned to the left and watched the sleek Italian aircraft, a Savoia, descend toward the aerodrome. The plane landed, and ground crew with flashlights guided the plane over to the reception. Other ground crew pushed the boarding ladder forward as someone inside opened the fuselage door.

A group of Italian officials descended the boarding ladder and took up an informal formation next to the official party. Von Koler directed the newsreel cameramen and still photographers in a flurry of movements.

Then the Italian general presented himself in the doorway, flashed a broad smile, all white teeth and shiny-black hair. He looked out and saw that all was ready. He descended the boarding ladder and walked up the red carpet to the podium. He adjusted the microphone and began his speech. After a few words, he would pause, and German and French translators would summarize in their respective languages. Then the general would carry on.

As he watched the general speak, Achiary watched as the ground crew carrying trash sacks went up the boarding ladder and into the plane. Undoubtedly to clean up, he thought.

As the general was concluding his speech, there was a roar from the plane's engines, gray-white smoke belched out of flared exhaust pipes. A foot reached out of the doorway and kicked the boarding ladder back and then an arm pulled the door shut. Achiary could see the outside handle rotate to locked position. Strange.

Everyone stopped. The general turned around and stared, a stunned look on his face. His airplane? It was moving. The plane made a small turn to the left and taxied out on a converging diagonal toward the main runway, picking up speed as it went, and then made a sweeping turn onto the main runway and accelerated down the macadam surface. Suddenly, it lifted off and rose into the western sky, not showing any running lights. Soon the plane was lost in the darkness, the engine sound fading away in the distance.

The crowd stood speechless and gazed toward the now-dark western horizon. Achiary heard Frau von Koler tell the newsreel cameramen and the photographers, "We can still use the pictures. No one has to know about the plane." The Italian general stood there and looked at her speechless. His airplane, his beautiful airplane. Why else even be a general? Colonels could have women, but an airplane?

One of Achiary's detectives hurried up and said to him in a low voice, "The ground crew, they looked like those young pilots that hang out at Le Club."

"The ones that watch Joan Tuyl play chess?"

"Yes, those are the ones."

"Well, she kept her word. She didn't crash the party at the Aletti."

Gibraltar

Captain Brinckman, rested from his stay at the British legation in Tangier, walked down the wide veranda of the Rock Hotel in Gibraltar, a white boxlike structure that looked like a big ocean liner nailed onto the side of a green mountain. From the veranda, he admired the view over the harbor and the warships riding at anchor. Merchant ships unloaded cargo at the wharves.

Nice to be back in a spot of Britannia. The crisp khakis felt good, like being back in the regiment for parade, thought Brinckman. Entering the bar at the far end of the veranda, Brinckman saw a smartly uniformed Captain Bradford regaling several French air-force officers, young pilots, with stories about his derring-do. Brinckman recognized the pilots from Le Club.

"How'd you get here," asked Brinckman as he walked up, perplexity spreading across his face, his gaze turning from Bradford to the pilots and back again.

"I left the same day as you," said Bradford. "By the way, what kept you?" he said insouciantly.

"Formalities, of course. Every border guard for five hundred miles read the papers upside down and all around," replied Brinckman. "But you? How?"

"In a small sailboat. Left that Saturday night. The French wouldn't have missed us until Monday morning. By that time, we were off the Spanish coast, just another fishing smack trolling along the shore."

Brinckman looked at the French pilots. "And you?"

"We arrived last Saturday night, also," replied the senior one, a lieutenant with two stripes on his epaulettes.

"How?"

"In an airplane?"

"Where'd you get the magneto? The gasoline?"

"The Italians graciously filled the tanks before leaving Tunis."

"The magnetos?"

"Everyone thought we were the ground crew."

"I'll be damned," said Brinckman. He turned to Bradford. "Did Joan plan this for you?"

"Well, she did put me in touch with the boat's owner..." said Bradford.

Brinckman turned to the pilots. One of them looked at him and said, "Joan? You mean the nice blond lady at Le Club?"

"Yes, that's the one," said Brinckman. He stood there in an amazement as the bartender handed him a gin and tonic while he put the coincidences together in his head.

Bradford left Brinckman to his thoughts and turned back to his French companions to explain. "And she's a rector's daughter, too."

The officers all laughed.

Café de Paris

Late May 1941. At the Café de Paris on Rue Michelet, Marie sat with Orray Taft at a corner table amid the chatter of the lunchtime crowd. The American consulate was just down the street.

"Yes, I saw Madame Tuyl this morning at Cottage Hospital," said Marie. "As you requested."

"Joan explained the situation to you?" asked Taft.

"Yes, the British officers out at the internee camp are dissatisfied with the French administration," replied Marie.

"Can you do something?" asked the frustrated vice-consul. "The officers hound me constantly."

"Well, Orray, the Americans represent British interests in Algeria, not the Winter Palace. Officially there's no sympathy for the British at all. Unofficially not much more."

Taft gritted his teeth, looked down, and swung his head back and forth with frustration. "Why am stuck with the British prisoner problem? I have endless consular duties dealing with visa requests from the never-ending stream of refugees." He looked up at Marie with almost pleading eyes. "Every packet boat from Marseilles brings more."

"That is another responsibility your government took on," said Marie sympathetically. "I understand your difficulties."

"Could you arrange for some improvements to be made in the camp?"

"I will try," said Marie. "Let me work with the logistics section. They have an understanding with Jacques over the supplies being delivered."

"I would be deeply appreciative," said Orray. "Maybe some of whatever Jacques is doing will be of some good."

Marie looked at him intently, guessing that Orray didn't know the true nature of Jacques's work. Then she did not either, completely, but the interest that General Weygand and the other officers took in Jacques told her it must be important.

"That is why we will do something, but quietly," said Marie. "I will also speak with one of the acquaintances I have in the Red Cross. But I must be careful; Madame Weygand is the head of the Red Cross here in Algiers."

Orray nodded in desultory agreement and looked around the restaurant. "Oops, here comes trouble. Frau von Koler is over there with her Armistice Commission friends. She keeps looking over here. Now she's standing up."

"Maybe she wants to speak with me. I am one of her contacts at the Winter Palace."

"What is it that she wants in Algiers anyway?"

"She does newsreels showcasing the cooperation between the French administration and the Armistice Commission. And news stories for her Berlin newspaper."

"Oh, Jacques just came in," said Taft.

"He must be back from wherever he was," said Marie.

"Yeah, not sure where that was," said Taft, a touch of annoyance with Jacques's special status clouding his expression.

Jacques walked over and said, "Mind if I take a seat?"

"No, go right ahead," said Orray. "It's time for me to get back to the consulate and deal with the afternoon onslaught." Taft stood up and said good-bye to Marie and departed.

Jacques turned to Marie and smiled. "How are you? Long time no see."

"I suppose I could ask where you've been," said Marie. "I'm sure I would be fascinated by your nonanswer."

"I was away working on final shipping arrangements for the initial cargoes. They should be leaving New York soon."

"You went to New York?"

"No, Tangier—and that's only a maybe."

"But not officially."

"Something like that."

"Your friend Elke von Koler is coming over to welcome you back," said Marie with an ironical smile.

"It's mostly professional," said Jacques.

Marie's eyes sparkled at the incompleteness of the word "mostly."

"Hello, Jacques," said Elke as she came up. "Mind if I sit down?"

"Not at all," said Jacques.

"You were away?" said Elke, making the question a statement.

"Yes, arranging the initial shipments of supplies."

"Which are?"

"Cotton goods, tea, and canned goods," said Jacques.

"Yes, for the Arabs and the Berbers," said Elke with a touch of disdain.

"Yes," said Jacques.

"Well, it won't hurt anything. The campaign in the Mediterranean is winding down."

"Winding down?" said Jacques with sudden look of perplexity on his face.

"You saw the German conquest of Crete?" said Elke, referring to the daring German parachute assault on Crete that defeated a larger British force in May. The British withdrawal resulted in significant loss of ships and men. Another rout of British forces in the Middle East.

"Yes," said Jacques evenly.

"The Stukas are on Crete," said Elke with self-satisfied aplomb. "The eastern Mediterranean will be a German lake.

"Is Crete the cork in the Suze Canal?"

"Soon," said Elke cryptically.

Jacques made a quizzical flash of his eyebrows. He didn't know what Elke meant, but he remembered Jacqueline's news story about the Germans doing something east of Bulgaria in 1941. At the time Jacques had thought Jacqueline may have innocently revealed in her news story an inadvertent secret from one of her high-level contacts in London. He wondered if it came from skillful questioning by Jacqueline or pillow talk.

"I read earlier that Germany might do something east of Bulgaria," said Jacques. "Is that the cork for the Canal, too? Or is something brewing with Syria?"

"Syria is safely in the hands of the Vichy French. The French administration there is rock solid. One wishes we could say the same for Algiers." Elke dodged the Bulgaria question, Jacques noticed. Elke looked at Marie.

Marie's eyes flashed with disagreement, but she quickly relaxed and returned a beatific smile to Elke's provocation.

"And the western Mediterranean?" asked Jacques, raising a subject that was of major concern.

"Oh yes, your counselor, Mr. Murphy, has been in Madrid asking about the British rumor that there are sixty thousand German troops in Spain."

Jacques smiled. Elke returned a knowing smile at Jacques. But she was exactly accurate on the source of the rumor. The British had been trying to upset the American apple cart in North Africa all spring. Elke was well informed.

"Those stories all come out of the British embassy in Lisbon. There's nothing to them. You should read my newspaper for accurate news on the world situation," said Elke.

Jacques laughed at the absurdity of reading a Berlin newspaper for accurate information.

"As long as the British hold Gibraltar, the Mediterranean is no one else's lake," said Jacques.

"Gibraltar will be irrelevant."

Jacques's eyes flashed with astonishment. Was French North Africa next up on the Nazi timetable?

"Irrelevant?" asked Jacques, surprise in his voice.

"The American policy of all means of support for Britain short of war will itself come up short," said Elke, smiling at her double entendre.

"Short?"

"It will all be decided before America can enter the war. It won't be like last time," she said referring to America's entry into the First World War almost three years after it had started.

"What's that mean? What's next?"

"Berlin will work through Vichy to open communications channels with Mr. Murphy, so peace talks can begin," Elke pronounced. She looked at him with large eyes. "I sincerely hope for all our sakes something like that can come to pass."

"Mr. Murphy is a man for peace," said Jacques.

"My message will get delivered, won't it?" asked Elke.

"Of course," said Jacques.

"I better return to my table and my guests," said Elke.

"I've enjoyed the conversation," said Jacques.

Marie looked at him. Yes, it had been interesting. She wondered about Jacques. He seemed to be involved in something far larger than supplies, no matter how urgent they were to stability in North Africa. Where had he really been? She couldn't help but be intrigued. And all this interest he has in her?

Headquarters, Political Police

Cosette sat in the office of the police detective who looked at her with interest if not admiration. Attractive, yes. A steely professional? Even more so. He knew she was counterespionage out of Marseilles. Captain Achiary came in and leaned against the wall listening.

Cosette gave a precise rundown. "We understand that the German Armistice Commission chief for Morocco, Theodor Auer, comes to Algiers periodically on business and that he often has an encounter with one of his associates that includes good times with Arab boys."

"You are well informed, Madame," said the detective.

"You have the pimp who arranges these meetings in your pay?"

"Surely."

"Could he do some blackmail. Photos, perhaps?"

"He's exquisitely skilled at those arts, Madame."

"Then the next time Herr Auer visits Algiers, we could arrange for a family photo shoot?"

"Of course," said the police detective. "I understand your connection to counterespionage. This is their operation?"

"Yes."

"Why does counterespionage care?"

"It goes back to Paris before the war."

"Okay. I understand—not my business. The photos will cost a little extra money."

"Tell me how much, and I will arrange payment."

"Fine. Is there anything else?"

"Yes, when the time comes, I'd like the Arab to deliver the photos to me right after the rendezvous. We want to be certain of the originality of the photos and their proximity to the actual event. We don't want to be sold yesterday's news."

"Easy enough, but possibly dangerous."

"I'll be covered."

"Of course," said the detective. "Let me know when Herr Auer is next in Algiers."

"I will," said Cosette, standing up. She smiled at Captain Achiary and left.

Chapter 27: Marine Air Terminal

June 1941. Trim and handsome forty-one-year-old John Knox, wearing a lightweight Brooks Brother suit, walked into the large round first floor of the futuristic art deco building, the LaGuardia Rotunda at New York's Marine Air Terminal. Beside him strode heavyset John Boyd, a widower in his late forties. Behind the two men came stewards with the men's luggage.

"Let's check in," said Boyd in a businesslike tone, and he pointed over to the ticket counter. He turned to the stewards and nodded. They knew where to go. He and Knox walked over to the ticket counter and pulled out their passports and laid them on the white Formica countertop. "Here you go," said Boyd.

"Special passports," said the attractive young woman. "There were two men just like you on the last Clipper with special passports, too."

"Special work," said Knox with a wink. "By special guys."

The woman smiled warmly at him as she wrote out the passport numbers on the tickets, added the passport numbers to the manifest, and handed tickets and passports back. "There you go. Boarding is in an hour. Enjoy your flight."

"Thanks," said Knox, all breeze. The young woman warmed to him like melted butter, Boyd thought. This guy is a real charmer.

"Let's get a farewell drink. Don't know where the next good whiskey might be," said Boyd.

"Good thinking," said Knox. "Distant climes are on the agenda."

The men walked over to the cocktail lounge and took a small table over at the side.

"What were you doing in France before the war?" asked Knox. "Your French is quite good, though the Mississippi accent still comes through here and there," he added with a chuckle.

"I was the manager of Coca-Cola in Marseilles for many years."

"How'd you wind up in Marseilles?"

"I was in the AEF in the First World War and decided to go back. Peacetime in the States was going no-where."

"What's bringing you back now?"

"My wife and I served in the American Field Services when the war broke out in 1939, which eventually left us trapped in southern France. We made it to Spain on a refugee train, but my wife died from the hardships…no medicines…"

"I'm sorry."

"I am, too," said Boyd with downcast eyes. "From Madrid I went on alone to Lisbon and home."

"And now?"

"Maybe finish what my wife and I had started. Finish the journey."

Knox looked at Boyd evenly and said, "I understand. It's about something bigger than just us."

Boyd nodded. "Murphy told me about your background. Groton, Harvard, Oxford," he said as he rattled off the names of the schools Knox had attended.

"I hope he didn't forget Saint-Cyr," said Knox. "That's where I graduated." Saint-Cyr is the military college of France, the French West Point. "Then the French Foreign Legion in Morocco for finishing school. A different set of manners."

"What happened?"

"I was wounded in the Riff War and invalided home," said Knox. "Been knocking around a bit since." Boyd sensed the family money behind the adventurer.

Boyd also felt the same sense of commitment and nodded approvingly. "It'll be a long war. Require lots of commitment."

Knox sighed. "Long? Yes."

Boyd added, "Murphy told me about the other vice-consuls. There's not a cookie pusher among them. Almost all combat guys"

Knox looked at Boyd and said, "Murphy told me the same thing. But you're on to something. Lots of combat experience. Maybe some rough stuff up ahead."

"The German-Italian Armistice Commission is full of OVRA and Gestapo guys," said Boyd, mentioning the Italian and German secret services. "They're mean, and they don't fight fair. Really ugly stories."

Knox drew a breath and said thoughtfully, "They're sending the right guys."

A voice came over the loud hailer. "Pan American Airways Clipper to Lisbon is boarding."

The two men got up and walked out through a passageway onto a long narrow pier projecting out into the water.

"Look at that baby," said Boyd. Tied up at the end of the pier, tail pointing in toward the land, was a huge flying boat with three tail fins jutting straight up off a large tail wing. Crossing the middle of the flying boat was a large main wing on which four engines were mounted.

"That's a lot of tail," said Knox.

"It's a big goose," said Boyd. They continued down the pier and then down a gangway to an open oval-shaped door on the side of the fuselage. Standing next to the door was an attractive young woman wearing starched whites and a wide smile.

"Welcome," the air stewardess said with practiced friendliness.

"My pleasure," said Knox with exaggerated gallantly while giving the attractive young woman a sweeping look of warm interest.

Damn, she almost melted, thought Boyd standing behind him. Bet Knox gets served the first glass of champagne. Whatever it is, this guy has it. This adventure gets more interesting by the minute.

Lisbon

John Boyd looked out of the window of the Clipper and saw the beautiful hillside city of Lisbon pass by the window as it descended toward the Taugus River and gently land with a splash of spray. The plane taxied across the water to the pier jutting out from the air terminal that was upriver from the city. Exiting the plane, the two Americans walked up the pier and were met by an American official.

"Well, well. They're taking pretty good care of you noncareer vice-consuls. When I joined this post, I traveled on a dirty old Portuguese liner."

"Regrettable I'm sure," replied Boyd perfunctorily. "And you are whom?"

"Rhodes, second secretary at the legation."

"The minister sent you?" asked Boyd.

"No, I was directed by a cable from Washington. The minister doesn't involve himself in minutia."

"Of course not," replied John Knox with mock horror at the thought. "I take it we're not staying at the legation?"

"Naw. I've got a hotel for you. If you're lucky, you'll get an airplane to Tangier tomorrow," said Rhodes.

"It sounds as if *you're* lucky we'll get an airplane out of here tomorrow and be out of your hair," sneered Boyd with direct sarcasm in his best slow Mississippi drawl.

"Anyway you want to slice it, Slick," said Rhodes, reacting with mild distaste to the pronounced Mississippi drawl. "I've got a taxi outside."

The three men got into the taxi and proceeded into the city and pulled up to an old hotel on a side street.

"Here you go," said Rhodes getting out and standing on the sidewalk.

"So I see," said Boyd, disgust sweeping across his face.

"It was the best I could do," said Rhodes.

"I'm sure it was," said Boyd. "Has it been fumigated lately?"

"Wouldn't know," replied Rhodes.

"I like the charm," said John Knox, breaking into the conversation while slapping Rhodes on his back.

"Good luck on your mission, whatever it is," said Rhodes, smiling at Knox and then shaking the two men's hands. He got back in the taxi and sped off.

The two men walked inside the hotel, Boyd muttering, "Fucking cookie pusher."

The plane for Tangier took off at first light the following morning.

Tangier

The steady beat of the engines of the old Wibot trimotor airplane did not calm John Boyd as his hands gripped the armrests at each unexpected rattle and shudder of the tired passenger plane, a craft that resembled a flying aluminum toolshed to Boyd's anxious mind. "Are we almost there?"

"That's Tangier ahead," said John Knox, calm and cool.

In ten minutes the plane landed and taxied over to a small terminal building. The passengers including the two Americans got out and walked over to the terminal.

A driver from the legation came over and shook hands. He pointed to a car, clearly identifiable by the red diplomatic license plates, and said, "I'm to take you to the legation."

"Good," said John Boyd.

"To see the minister, Mr. J. Rives Childs," said the driver.

"Excellent," said John Knox breezily. "We missed meeting the minister in Lisbon. Our social calendars didn't overlap."

The driver gave Knox a puzzled look. At the legation, the driver dropped them off at the front portico and pointed toward the door. A marine guard escorted them upstairs into the presence of J. Rives Childs, the minister plenipotentiary, who was standing behind his desk. He shook hands with Knox and Boyd and pointed them toward chairs.

"More of you noncareer consuls," sniffed Childs. "What do they mean to do with you?" he asked with irritation suffusing his voice.

"Something about code training, I believe," said Knox affably.

"Yes, I'll send you down to the coding room in a moment. Excellent chap down there."

"Anything else?" asked Boyd, characteristically direct.

"Yes, you'll be staying at the El Minzah Palace Hotel. Overrun with spies and riffraff," said Childs with disdain.

"I take it the spies are the riffraff," said Knox.

"Quite," said Childs. "Regular foreign-service officers don't spy on one another. It is decidedly against the regulations."

Paul A. Myers

"Possibly the war is interfering with their good manners," said Knox.

"Undoubtedly so," said Childs with a sigh. He looked at Boyd, the shiftier looking of the two new arrivals. "Mind you, when you leave, you pay your own bar bills."

"Just like my country club," said Boyd.

"Ah hem." Childs tried to place the accent. Did they even have country clubs where that drawl came from? Shaking his head, Childs stood and escorted them out to a secretary who took them down to the coding room to begin their training in the use of the one-time pad.

Algiers

The train from Rabat huffed into Algiers under clouds of dirty-brown smoke billowing out of a big black funnel. John Knox looked at John Boyd and said, "Nice to have a train trip after the rigors of code training."

"Never been so happy to pay my bar bill," snorted Boyd.

As the train entered Algiers, Knox stood up from the dusty corner of the aged passenger coach where he had been sitting on his suitcase. He put his suit coat on, patted the rump good naturedly of the goat one of the Arabs was herding toward the door, and said to John Boyd, "We're here. Let's go."

"Nice goat you made friends with," said Boyd.

Out on the broad cement landing, they saw Robert Murphy and another American walk over. Murphy said, "Let me introduce Orray Taft, the senior vice-consul in the consulate."

"Pleased to meet you," said Taft shaking hands.

"Actually," said Murphy, "you merchandise control officers are going to be with me down on the waterfront at the old British consulate."

"Did they leave the picture of the king?" asked Knox.

"Probably," said Murphy looking at Knox a little quizzically. "My car is over here."

Coming up to Murphy's big black Buick, Murphy opened the trunk, and Knox and Boyd stowed their suitcases. The two men got in the rear seat of the big convertible whose roof was down. Taft got in the front passenger side. Murphy pulled away from the train station and started moving through the streets of Algiers; Knox

213

looked around, growing concern on his face. Boyd caught the shift; what had he seen? Knox leaned forward and shouted to Murphy. "We saw all the fields and orchards on our way in from the train window. But the souks are empty. Where is the fruit and produce? I spent three years in Morocco, and I never saw anything like this. It's barren."

"The Germans swept in this spring like locusts. The Armistice set the exchange rate at twenty-to-one. The Germans are buying up everything in sight—with France's money," replied Murphy over his shoulder.

"Economic warfare," said Boyd.

"Exceedingly so," agreed Murphy.

Coming up to the Hotel Aletti, Murphy swung into the entrance drive. "Here we go," he said. "I'll come back later, and we can have dinner together."

Knox and Boyd got out, Murphy opened the trunk, and a bellhop loaded the suitcases onto a dolly and wheeled the luggage into the lobby.

"Just like the Ritz," said Knox with a smile, shifting back to nonchalance. "I'm going to like it here."

Chapter 28: An Earthquake in the East

Sunday, June 22, 1941. The big black Buick roared up the street and swung over to the curb. Jacques walked over and opened the door and jumped into the front seat.

"Good morning," said Murphy, his hands gripping the steering wheel. "Thanks for coming on such short notice."

"I was just getting ready to go down to the consulate," said Jacques. "I heard the news on the radio this morning. Stunning."

"Yes, it changes everything," said the older man.

"And answers a lot of things, too," added Jacques. He had heard the news over the BBC that Germany had invaded Russia on a broad front, from the Baltic to the Black Sea. It was possibly the biggest invasion in history.

Murphy accelerated to the next turn, made a quick right, and in a couple of blocks made a left onto a street winding up the hills overlooking Algiers into the exclusive suburb of El Biar. Murphy came to a stop in front of the closed iron gates of the magnificent villa *Les Oliviers* that was the residence of the delegate general. The villa overlooked the military headquarters of Fort L'Empereur on a hill below. A sergeant came out from a guard kiosk and approached.

"Your papers?" the sergeant asked.

"Here," said Murphy as he showed his diplomatic identification.

"And him?" asked the sergeant making a nod toward Jacques. Jacques pulled out his identification and handed it over.

The sergeant held the identification cards, searched down a clipboard. "Yes, here you are." He handed the identifications back and looked over at the guardhouse and nodded at two tall Senegalese soldiers. The soldiers swung the gates open. The sergeant looked at Murphy and grunted, "Allez." Go.

"Just who are we visiting?" asked Jacques.

"General Weygand," said Murphy.

"He's well guarded," said Jacques. "Does he have a lot of enemies?"

"Oh, some in his own government, some in the German government," said Murphy lightly. He pulled up to a parking area near the front door. As they parked, an officer came up to escort them inside.

"Good afternoon, Mr. Murphy. The general is expecting you," said the young officer.

"Good," said Murphy as he and Jacques walked toward the steps leading into the large villa. They walked through the door and into a large foyer.

"Over here. He's in the drawing room," said the officer, and he escorted them into a spaciously comfortable room with large fans hanging from the ceiling with slowly rotating blades.

The general stood up and walked over, holding out his hand. "Good morning, Mr. Murphy. Thank you for coming so quickly." He held out his hand indicating where the two diplomats could sit.

"Now then," began the general, "last December when we first met, I asked where the Americans were going to get the divisions. Today, I know. The Russians."

"Yes," replied Murphy, "but we did not know it then."

"Understand. It would have seemed farfetched at that time." The general paused and then solemnly said, "This morning's news means Germany will lose the war."

"Yes," said Murphy. "Eventually."

"And Roosevelt?"

"He has instructed me to give you verbal assurances that at a future date the US will provide the French in Africa with military assistance."

"Understand," said Weygand. He looked at Jacques. "Your assistant has thoroughly canvassed our needs here in North Africa."

"That is always the all-important first step."

The general looked intently at Jacques. "You are going to equip us equal to the new British and American divisions, I've been told?"

"Yes," said Jacques with an authoritative tone. "Washington feels that allied infantry and armored divisions should outgun their German adversaries across the board."

"The German tanks are devastating good."

"We'll have better and more of them."

"Yes, numbers."

216

"Artillery?"

"The Americans believe you should never send an infantryman when you can send an artillery shell."

The general nodded in agreement. He remembered the Americans in the last war and their abundant equipment and weapons.

The general looked back at Murphy and asked, "Will the United States become a belligerent?"

"In a sense we already are," replied Murphy.

"Yes," said Weygand thoughtfully. "I had hoped you would remain aloof so that you could use your enormous power to act as an arbiter."

Jacques perked up and looked at the general. The general looked at Jacques and asked, "Does that surprise you?"

"Yes," said Jacques with a laugh. "My German acquaintances hope to be sending peace feelers through Mr. Murphy to Washington."

The general smiled. "The Germans will initially do well in Russia, but it is a vast space—it will suck in their power and devour it."

Murphy was fascinated with the general's assessment, so cool and concise. "You're saying German power will be consumed."

"Yes," replied the general. There was no doubt in his voice.

Jacques looked at Murphy and said, "I understand something of the overall American approach from my time on the Purchasing Commission."

The general quickly looked at Jacques with an expression asking for further elucidation. Jacques looked at him. "The plan is to massively outproduce the combined production of Germany, Italy, and Japan."

"An ambitious strategy," said the general. "Surely sound."

"A strategy that guarantees eventual victory," said Murphy. Now he had some insight into Roosevelt's calm assurance he had seen in his meeting with the president. The same confidence came through in his conversations with Sumner Welles.

"The war goes in an entirely new direction," said the general.

"And no German invasion of North Africa," said Murphy.

"At least for now," said the general. "But they remain close at hand."

"Yes," said Murphy.

"And the Americans?" asked the general.

"I can't say, and I don't know. I'm not sure anyone other than the president knows."

"And he keeps his own counsel," said the general.

"Yes," said Murphy. "He smiles at you with great assurance."

"Ah, to have those means," said the general leaning back in his chair in reflection. He stood up and said, "I better let you gentlemen leave. Messages will be streaming into your consulate." The general escorted the diplomats out to the foyer.

The Consulate

The following day, John Knox walked up Rue Michelet toward the American consulate to meet with Orray Taft, the senior vice-consul. He, John Boyd, and Murphy maintained offices at the now-vacant British consulate right across from the French Admiralty and not too far from the Winter Palace. Their work had nothing to do with regular consular duties, a status much resented by the career-consular officers.

Knox reflected that the German invasion of Russia removed much of the anxiety in North Africa about an imminent German invasion. Less interference was expected from the German and Italian Armistice Commission.

From the point of view of the merchandise control officers, the American consulate was a giant distraction full of people jostling to fill out applications for visas and to meet with regular service vice-consuls for interviews. But he and John Boyd were not exempt from routine duties; they were tasked to take the diplomatic pouch now making the rounds of North Africa when it arrived from Tunis. Knox and Boyd would take the pouch on the next leg of its journey to Rabat. From there, the pouch would go to Tangier, then Lisbon and on to Washington.

Knox walked up to the receptionist and said, "John Knox, I'm one of the new merchandise control officers. I'm here to see Orray Taft."

The receptionist scurried down the hall and returned in a few moments and said, "She'll be with you in a moment."

"She?" he asked, wondering as he looked down the hall.

A slender woman in a nice dress with radiant blond hair and high cheekbones approached him and held out her. "Hi, I'm Joan Tuyl. Orray will see you in a minute."

"Pleased to meet you," said the American holding out his hand. "John Knox."

"Yes, one of the new vice-consuls here to supervise the cargoes from America."

"That's the plan," said Knox laconically.

"Follow me," she said and turned and led him down a long hallway to an office with an open door. Knox followed and watched the hips rhythmically sway; he liked everything he saw. She casually knocked on a door as she walked in and said to the man sitting behind the desk, "Orray, John Knox, one of the new vice-consuls to see you."

"Yes, I met him at the train station," said Taft as he stood up. "That'll be all, Joan."

Knox walked in, and Taft pointed to a chair. Knox sat down and looked over his shoulder and watched Joan walking down the hall. "Who's she?" he asked Taft.

"Oh, she's originally English and worked at the British consulate before Mers-el-Kébir. We hired her when the British left, and she's a great help."

"Originally?"

"Yes, her father was the rector of the Anglican Church here in Algiers. He died. His widow is an artist and lives up on the hill."

"If she's English…"

"She's a Dutch citizen. Her husband is back in Holland. He was a Dutch reserve officer. Poor woman hasn't heard a thing about him in over a year. She lives with her mother and two small boys."

"Very attractive…"

"Yes, but I'd stay away. Every intelligence agency in Algiers keeps close tabs on her. They suspect she's in the local underground helping downed British fliers get to Tangier or Gibraltar."

"Is she?"

"Can't say. I'm a foreign-service officer. We don't spy," said Taft with a puff of self-importance.

"Seems like exactly the type of person I'd like to meet," said Knox glancing back down the now-vacant hallway.

Taft gave Knox a cross-eyed look and changed the subject. "So you're here about the diplomatic pouch?"

"Yes, Boyd and I are to take it to Oran and then Rabat."

"Good. Make yourself useful. This will take another onerous task off the backs of the career personnel." Taft gave him an officious look. "We're swamped with work."

"Glad to help," said Knox genially.

"Here, let's go over the details," said Taft.

The two men talked. Then Knox left. He didn't see Joan Tuyl as he was leaving. He did leave a message.

Le Club

John Knox walked up the street past the Hotel Aletti, turned down a side street, and came up to the bar and restaurant. He walked in, eyes adjusting to the light, and scanned the room. He saw Joan Tuyl wave a hand and stand up. He walked over. Two other men stood up.

"Mr. Knox," she said.

"Please, John," replied Knox.

"Let me introduce Lieutenant Commander Gee Hare of the Royal Navy," said Joan. "He's senior officer of the prisoners of war out in the prisoner-of-war camp. He's receiving medical care at the hospital and is out on his parole."

"Pleased to meet you," said Knox, holding out his hand.

"And Samuel Dashiell, the United Press correspondent here in Algiers."

Knox and Dashiell shook hands, and all sat down. A waiter came up, and Knox said, "Water and ice." Knox reached into his inside coat pocket and pulled out a pint of American whiskey and put it on the table. "Anyone else?"

"Yes," came Dashiell with vigorous nods from Hare and Joan.

"You're one of the new American vice-consuls, aren't you?" said Hare.

"Yes," replied Knox.

"Could we hear about your background, John?" asked Dashiell.

"Sure," replied Knox. "Prep school, then a bit of Harvard," he said in a mocking Boston accent before shifting over to a stiff English accent, "then a bit of Oxford…"

Joan started to laugh, and Dashiell and Hare chuckled at Knox's impromptu performance.

Then shifting to French, Knox continued, "and then Saint-Cyr where I graduated and then went to finishing school with the French Foreign Legion."

The waiter brought back four glasses with ice and a carafe of water, and Knox poured drinks all around.

"Your accent is as good or better than mine," said Joan in open-eyed wonder. "If the Americans are sending men like you, there's hope for the future."

"There's hope for the future," said Knox reaching across the table and patting her hand.

A waiter came up, and they ordered dinner. Knox put some American greenbacks on the table and added, "The good stuff, please." The waiter smiled broadly and nodded.

A few minutes later, a smiling waiter put a steaming dinner with good meat and fresh vegetables on the table. They talked through dinner; Knox recounting adventures fighting in the Riff War in Morocco in the 1920s and then asking about Joan Tuyl's background. She told them about setting up a dairy farm at an oasis on the edge of the Sahara Desert with her husband Gerry. With anguish, she told them about his return to Holland to serve as a reserve officer when the war began.

"Do you hear anything from him?" asked Knox, concerned.

"Not much. A small postcard of twenty-five words through the Red Cross in Switzerland. Little was said," she explained through tear-laden eyes. "You just don't know."

"The occupation across Europe is harsh," said Dashiell.

"Is he in the resistance?" asked Knox.

"I don't know," said Joan, a pleading look on her face.

"If he is," said Hare and let the thought hang. Eventual arrest, torture, and execution awaited members of the underground in occupied Europe.

"I know," said Joan with tears running down her cheeks. "And if I'm caught…I feel the net closing in on me…with luck an agent can only hope to last a certain time…and I'm marked by the Vichy police…so if they catch me and I'm sent back to Holland…the boys…"

"Who wants to send you to Holland?" asked Knox sharply.

"The Dutch consul here in Algiers hints at it," she said. "Rejoin your husband and such."

"What can he do?" asked Knox.

"The Vichy police now know how easy it is to dispose of me. Just repatriate me to Holland."

"Well, we can work on them," said Knox. "We have leverage."

"You do?"

"Yes," said Knox, determination in his voice as he took control of the conversation, "but first we plan to survive because there's much work to be done."

Joan looked at him and asked, "Why?"

"There's a reason I'm here," said Knox.

Joan nodded and took out a handkerchief and dried her eyes. She stood up and looked at Knox. "Can I speak to you outside for a minute?"

"Sure," said Knox, and he stood up and followed her outside.

"I have a network of sorts," said Joan, explaining.

"Yes, Orray tells me you're about to be arrested," said Knox jocularly.

She rolled her eyes. "He may be right. Eventually that happens in a resistance."

"Okay," said Knox seriously.

"I feel I can trust you."

"You can."

"Good. We need to meet so I can share contacts, so if something happens to me…that's why I can't speak in front of the others."

"I'm going to work to make sure that doesn't happen," said Knox reassuringly.

She looked at him. He's interested in me, my well-being, she thought. A sense of assurance flooded over her. "You seem able to take charge," she said.

"I'm not a diplomat."

"I just noticed."

"We better go back in, but we can have lunch soon and start on out partnership," he said.

Every word resonated with her. She looked at him with warm eyes and smiled. Partnership? They walked back in.

Chapter 29: London

July 1941. Claridges Hotel. There was a knock on the door. Jackie rolled over. It had been a late night. "Yes?"

"It's a cable, Miss Smith," said the bellhop.

She got out of bed and put on a dressing gown and opened the door. She took the cablegram and fumbled for some change and tipped the bellhop. "Could you have my breakfast sent up?"

"Yes, ma'am," said the bellhop as he backed out of the room, closing the door behind him.

Jackie went over to the small table and opened the cable and read through it:

JACKIE. IMPORTANT PERSON HEADING LONDON YOUR HOTEL STOP YOU HAVE HAD SCOOPS FROM VIP LAST TIME. KEEP IT UP THIS TIME. WANT INSIDE DOPE ON RUSSIA HOLDING OFF GERMANY. SUPPLIES BIG ISSUE. THE WORLD TURNS ON THE EAST. ANNE.

Jackie put the cable down. There was a knock on the door, and she answered in French, "Entrez." The maid came in with breakfast and a steaming pot of coffee and morning papers. Jackie poured a cup of coffee and leaned back in her chair. She looked at the morning sun streaming through the window. Harry was coming. He had gotten to know her well on his first trip to London. He fed her lots of interesting background stuff and was surprised how quickly it wound up in Anne Hare's column. It all showed up under "Our Correspondent." Hopkins thought it was almost like talking to Roosevelt on the phone. Now, all across breakfast tables in Washington all eyes turned toward Anne Hare's column searching for the subhead, "Our Correspondent." The inside dope from London was riveting.

Jacqueline looked at the cablegram again. Now it was Jackie and Anne. The byline would come soon she was sure. Harry would help her out on that. He had last time. Liked to help young people out, he said. A lot of important men saw him tip special stuff to her. Some inside dope he called it. Ever since they'd fallen all over themselves to ingratiate themselves with the young lady with a pipeline to the top column of the *New York Times Tribune*. She rarely dined alone.

Mayfair

Jackie walked up the steps to the massive front door of the gentlemen's club, the doorframe sandbagged on either side. The building was quite Victorian as was the footman who opened it. Inside she gave her name to the chief steward, who promptly responded, "Yes, the brigadier is in the dining room and expecting you." Women were allowed in the dining room for lunch, one of the not-quite-so necessary changes since the war began, thought the chief steward. A footman led her toward the dining room and over to a table by the window where the brigadier stood up in welcoming courtesy.

"So nice to see you today, Jackie."

"You, too, brigadier."

"Brian, please."

She sat down as the footman held the chair and the brigadier resumed his seat. Wine was poured.

"Wonderful. Brian, it will be...just between us," she said with a touch of conspiracy. "You're rather young for a brigadier?"

"Yes. I was a battalion commander on the retreat to Dunkirk and one thing after another—the Stukas, the artillery," he said in a pained voice of recollection, his eyes taking on a troubled, distant look, "and I wound up officer commanding the brigade. Alex liked me. That's why I'm here in London at ops." Sir Harold Alexander had been his divisional commander.

"And the red hat?" she asked, meaning the coveted badge of flag rank.

"Yes, that's the trend. Younger men," he said. With a wistful air, he added, "I completely skipped over being a colonel. I would have liked to have commanded the regiment, but..."

"I understand," she said sympathetically. "Let me change subjects, New York can't get enough about Russia."

"Yes," said the brigadier. "No one can. Our military attaches feel that the Russians will be able to give ground and draw in

German strength. The further the Germans go, the weaker and more exposed they become."

"What is the crucial determinant of long-term success?"

"Probably the same as for us: supplies from America."

"Decisive?" asked Jackie.

"Absolutely," he said.

"And the winter?"

"Yes, that defeated Napoleon."

"Indeed. What's next?"

"The rumor is someone big from Washington is coming," said the brigadier. "I don't know who."

"I can guess."

"You can? Who?"

"Same as last time."

"Hopkins?"

"You said that. I didn't," replied Jackie with a smile. "How do supplies get to Russia?"

"Devilishly difficult," said the brigadier gravely. "Either up around Norway—and the Germans control the North Cape—or down the South Atlantic and around the African cape and up to Persia. It's a long trip. Ties up scarce shipping."

"The South Atlantic?"

"Yes, down past Dakar and French West Africa. If Vichy were to allow the Germans in…"

"A big difficulty."

"Nearly insuperable," said the brigadier. "London is the center of many worries."

"And they pile up on your desk?"

"Some."

"Thanks for the info," said Jackie. "I'll be in touch with New York on deep background. We must meet regularly. You'll have to keep me informed."

"Yes, it's an entirely new war," he said, crisply summing up. Then he mumbled, "My wife is out in the Midlands with her family…I was wondering…"

Jackie reached her hand across the table and grasped his and gave it a warm squeeze. "We could have dinner together…"

The brigadier's face lit up like a lantern.

Yes, an entirely new type of war, thought Jackie.

Chapter 30: Lunch at Joan's

John Knox walked up a hillside street to the apartment building in front of a steep hill that backed this quarter of Algiers. He knocked on the door, and Joan Tuyl opened it, holding back a rambunctious three-year-old boy with one arm while the five-year-old brother watched from behind her with open-eyed curiosity. This was the new man who would be sharing lunches with them?

"Hi," said Knox as he walked in, holding a big rucksack full of food.

"Welcome," replied Joan. "These are the boys. Derek," and she pushed the five-year-old forward, "and Tony." She held the three-year-old in front of her.

Knox reached into the rucksack and pulled out two tangerines and gave them to the two boys. Derek tore the skin off his and bit part of it off, juice flowing down his chin, while Joan helped Tony to learn to peel his tangerine.

John pulled items of food out of the rucksack and gave them to the cook. He smiled and said, "More tomorrow." The cook smiled at the wonder of it all.

"My mother, Elsie" said Joan, introducing the older lady standing behind her.

"Pleased to meet you," she said. "Having a man around will help with the boys."

"A lot," said Joan with a sense of relief.

"My pleasure," said John, tousling the hair of Derek, who smiled half appreciatively.

"Let me show you around," said Joan. They walked into another room that her mother used as a studio. John admired the paintings hanging on the wall and set on easels, bright sun-drenched landscapes of white houses with russet-colored tile roofs marching up the hillsides of Algiers. Other pictures featured white-sand beaches set against an azure-blue sea. A yearning for the Algiers of before the war suffused the room.

"What's this?" asked John holding up a copy of *The Little Prince.*

"The famous book by Antoine Saint-Exupéry," replied Joan. "I met him at the Hotel Aletti last year, the afternoon of the ultimatum at Mers-el-Kébir. He was a friend of one of the members of the air-force circle."

"How did he react?" asked John.

"He said it was not a game," said Joan. "I learned the next day he was disappointed with the British."

"Yes, that's a wound not likely to be forgotten nor forgiven," replied John. "What do you do with the books?" he asked as he picked up the French edition *Le Petit Prince* sitting next to the English edition.

"I read to the boys, so they'll improve their English," she replied.

"Good," replied John. "Let me read to them while lunch is getting ready."

"Wonderful," she said as she went and called the boys in. "John wants to read to you."

The two boys raced into the room, bundles of enthusiasm, and jumped on the sofa bed and making a place for John between them.

"Which language?" he asked.

"English?" ventured Derek tentatively. "That's what grandma reads to us in."

"English it will be," said John. "You're on your way to being proper little chaps."

"Is that a good thing?" asked Derek.

"The best," replied John.

Chapter 31: A Correspondent in Algiers

August 1941. The old Air France trimotor wobbled in the sky as it began its descent toward Maison Blanche aerodrome like a dark bird coming out of the incandescent western sky. Jacques squinted into the late afternoon sun, a blazing orb just touching the ridgeline behind Algiers. He watched the plane land and taxi over to the small terminal. The ground crew pushed a boarding stair over toward the door, which popped open as soon as the plane rolled to a stop.

Passengers started to descend the ladder. Jacques saw Jacqueline appear in the small doorway and duck her head as she quickly looked out, her eyes darting in a quick sweep, a sense of immense curiosity on her face. He waved, and she waved back, a smile breaking across her face. She hurried across the tarmac and through the open gate into the patio area in front of the terminal. She walked into Jacques's outstretched arms and flung her arms around him and plunged right into a deep welcoming kiss.

"So glad to be here," she exclaimed. "I thought that flight across Spain to Tangier would be my last. Do you do that often?"

"We all do," said Jacques. "We all feel the same way."

"I can't wait to get to your apartment."

"Ah, no. I've got you booked at the Hotel Aletti."

"But I thought…*amour ce soir*…"

"You can come over tonight, but first we want to have a candlelit dinner."

"With real food?"

"Yes."

"You have no idea how little food, good or otherwise, is in England."

"Tonight we'll fix that. Tomorrow, we'll have lunch with Madame Rambert of the Winter Palace."

"What's her role there?"

"She is the confidential secretary to the delegate general, General Weygand."

"Starting at the top?"

"Nothing is too good for my friends."

"What does she do for you?"

"She arranges my visits across North Africa where I meet various officials concerning where to unload the ships coming from America with the relief supplies."

"All humdrum and routine, or so you want me to believe."

"Quite humdrum. All the exciting stuff is done by senior people. You should know that from your experience in Washington," and he looked at her, "and now London."

"Is she humdrum?"

"I would not say so."

"Pretty?"

"Quite."

"Does she accompany you on your visits across North Africa?"

"No," said Jacques, and he let his face sag into disappointment. "She's a married lady."

"Don't recall that stopping you."

"But only when invited."

"Oh, now we're gentlemanly, are we?"

"That counts for a lot in Algiers."

"But not necessarily in war."

"As you've found out?"

"Well, yes. In London…between the air raids…"

"Yes, anyway, Madame Rambert will schedule your interviews with top French officials in Algiers, Oran, Rabat, and Casablanca."

"Top?"

"The very top."

"Good, I've been feeding Anne one small scoop after another. I need to keep it up. Something was going on in London when I left, but I don't know what." She bit her lip; she didn't want to say more.

Winter Palace

The consulate car pulled into the entrance of the Winter Palace and stopped. Jacques held the door as Jacqueline got out, her eyes blinking in the bright summer light as she gazed around at the exquisitely crafted Moorish palace, the well-tended flowerbeds, the beautiful blue mosaics set against the white alabaster walls.

"These are some digs," she said.

Jacques nodded while he spoke to the driver. "Wait here. We'll just be a moment. Then lunch." He turned to Jacqueline. "This way," he said as he guided her up the steps.

After signing in with the guard, they walked into the reception area. Marie came out of the secretarial area with a welcoming smile. She was wearing a light white cotton suit. Her chestnut hair made a pleasing contrast. Her dark eyes sparkled.

Jacques said, "Let me introduce Jacqueline Smith to you, Marie."

Marie held out her hand to Jacqueline. "Jacques has told me so much about you. An exciting life covering the war. You may find North Africa dull in contrast, Miss Smith."

"Please, call me Jackie," said Jacqueline as she shook the outstretched hand.

"Marie," said Marie in quick response. She liked the young American, about her own age, she thought.

"Dull?" repeated Jackie, echoing Marie's statement. "Only in the sense that there's a lot of interest in high places in keeping North Africa out of the war."

Marie's expression brightened with relief. "Pleased to hear that."

Jacques interjected: "I have the consulate car outside to take us to the Taverne Alsacienne."

"Yes," said Marie. "I've been looking forward to it all morning." She headed for the entrance walking beside Jacqueline, complimenting the American on her stylish white dress. They almost looked like sisters, thought Jacques. He idly wondered where this new openness in Marie came from.

The car dropped them off at the restaurant, and they went inside. The maître d' came up, smiled at Jacques, and said, "More ladies today, Monsieur Dubois."

"More ladies?" laughed Jackie. She turned to Marie and loudly whispered, "And I thought he was trapped in Algiers doing dull diplomatic work."

"He does so much dull diplomatic work," said Marie. "I often help him with it."

"Then it's not so dull," replied Jackie.

"We are all interested in Jacques's work," said Marie. "It's important to us."

"This way," said the maître d', and he escorted them to a rear corner booth, and they all took seats. Cool water in a chilled earthenware pitcher was placed on the table; a bottle of chilled white wine quickly followed.

"I have an itinerary prepared for you," said Marie, launching straight into business. "You will meet the admiral in command at Oran, the resident-general at Rabat, and the admiral at Casablanca." She stopped and smiled at Jackie. "We have a lot of admirals in North Africa."

"Because of Admiral Darlan?" asked Jackie.

"Some would say so," said Marie.

Out of his eye, Jacques saw Frau von Koler walk across the room toward them. "Here comes the local Berlin correspondent," said Jacques. "Let's see what she has to say." He stood up.

"By all means," said Jackie, intrigued.

"Elke, how nice of you to come by," said Jacques. "Let me introduce my guest. Jacqueline Smith from New York."

"Jacqueline Smith of the *New York Times Tribune*?" said von Koler.

"Yes," said Jackie reaching out her hand.

"Why don't you join us for a while," said Jacques, and he stepped over and pulled a chair over for Elke.

"Why thank you," she said and sat down. She looked at Jacqueline. "Your last byline was datelined London?"

"Yes, I'm just in via Lisbon."

"And how is London?"

"Indomitable," said Jackie crisply.

"Well, North Africa must seem like a backwater after London?"

"There's a lot of interest in America about the food-relief program to Africa."

"Really?"

"Yes, really."

"And are the indomitable English getting ready to talk peace with Germany once the Reich winds up the Russian campaign?"

"The top people in London think the opposite. They think Russia will hold on and grind Germany down."

"They should read the newspapers."

"They do."

"And what do the Americans in London think?" she smoothly asked, setting up her real question. "Harry Hopkins was in Moscow. What does he think?"

"You'd have to ask him. I haven't had the opportunity."

"But you're the American correspondent in London who seems to have the pipeline to Hopkins," said Elke. "We all read the *TeeTee* avidly."

"I haven't seen Harry…Mr. Hopkins."

"Yes, the papers report he is missing from London and with Mr. Churchill in some undisclosed location."

"I wouldn't know. I've been traveling to Algiers. The flight into Tangier is more than a little exciting."

"Nevertheless, my paper—the *Deutsche Allegemeine Zeitung*— is well informed. Our correspondent in Washington has excellent sources in the State Department, and with Colonel Lindbergh and Senator Wheeler and other sensible Americans who want to keep America out of the European war."

"Yes," interjected Jackie, "great Americans like Senator Wheeler. He said that Roosevelt's Lend-Lease program would plow under every fourth American boy." Disgust colored Jacqueline's face at the widely quoted defeatism of the isolationist senator.

"Well, you can't expect American boys to stand up to German soldiers any better than the French and British and now the Russians have, can you?" asked Elke with ironically raised eyebrows driving home the skepticism.

"You forget 1918 and just who went through the vaunted Hindenburg Line."

"Nevertheless, there is a lot of disgruntlement with Mr. Murphy's mission to North Africa in the State Department and other influential places in America. Sources say that Murphy is trying to get General Weygand to change sides."

Marie's face registered shock, and her face flushed red with anger. "Elke, you know that isn't true. General Weygand is committed to the Armistice and to the Maréchal…as we all are here in North Africa."

"For now," said Elke soothingly. "But for how long? Berlin wonders."

Jackie looked intently at Marie. The intensity of Marie's statement surprised her.

Elke caught Jackie's reaction to Marie. Undoubtedly this would be reported back to London. Good. Elke continued, "When Russia is defeated, Germany hopes to use the American diplomats in Europe to negotiate a peace with Britain. It would be senseless for the two peoples to keep on fighting."

"As I said, most of the people I speak with think Russia will hold on. If Germany can't knock out Russia by winter, then it will lose the war," said Jackie.

"Lose the war? To the British? You must be kidding," said Elke in a haughty voice. "General Rommel may well be in Cairo before the panzers arrive in Moscow. So many fronts, so many opportunities."

"Rommel, of course," exclaimed Jackie. "I saw your newsreels from Cyrenaica of the young general. Was that your idea to put the ski goggles on the visor of his cap?"

Elke beamed. "You're well informed, too."

"The publicity surrounding Rommel is much admired in the ministry of information in London."

Elke smiled in appreciation. "Speaking of newsreels, did you see the newsreels celebrating the first anniversary of the British attack on Mers-el-Kébir that we just did? They're being shown worldwide. That will give you some perspective on French opinion in Africa."

"Yes, in Lisbon on my layover while coming here."

"It is unlikely the French in North Africa will forget that British perfidy anytime soon," said Elke with sweeping self-assurance.

A pained look came over Marie's face. So true. She looked at Jacques. He returned her bleak stare and shrugged his soldiers.

"Nevertheless, the Americans are committed to British victory," said Jackie with cold assurance.

"I am told on good authority that American support will ultimately hang in the balance while Germany advances across Russia. Our correspondent in Washington is well informed on American opinion. No sensible American will commit all the way with the British while Russia is reeling toward defeat."

Marie's shoulders sagged. German striking power was awesome. The Russian retreat was like a door to a dark cellar in which lurked indescribable horrors for occupied Europe.

Jackie put her shoulders back and led with her self-assurance. "I haven't been in Washington lately, so I wouldn't know what the so-called sensible people think," she said. "Maybe your correspondent does." Disbelief dripped from Jackie's voice.

Marie liked Jackie's insouciance. Few got the better of Elke von Koler, but she had. These Americans were buoyantly self-confident.

Jacques stood up signaling an end to the encounter. "Elke, don't let us keep you from your luncheon guests." He pulled her chair back as she stood up.

Elke smiled sweetly at Jacques. "You're always so thoughtful, Jacques. But yes, I must be going." She turned and held out her hand to Jackie. "So nice to have met you. Thank you for the compliments on the newsreels."

"*Enchanteé*," said Jackie in a warm voice as she politely stood up in good-bye. She would get a cable off to Anne Hare right away. This would also be a tale for the brigadier.

Hotel Aletti

In the dimly lit cocktail lounge of the Hotel Aletti, Jacques and Jacqueline sat at a corner table with a candle in a red glass bowl throwing a soft light. Soon Jacques spotted John Knox and Joan Tuyl coming across the room, and he stood up. He shook John's hand as he came up and said, "Let me introduce my friend Jacqueline."

"Our pleasure," said John Knox.

"Joan Tuyl," said Joan holding out her hand.

"Jackie," said Jacqueline as she reached her hand out and shook it.

Joan sat down as Knox held her chair. The others followed.

"Now then," said John. "Have you heard the news?"

"News? No," said Jacques.

"Roosevelt and Churchill met at sea somewhere off the coast of North America with their chiefs of staff," said John.

"So that's what was going on," said Jackie surprised. "Was Hopkins with them?"

"Yes," replied Knox. "He came over from Britain with Churchill and then went over to Roosevelt's cruiser to give the president a complete briefing."

"What was the purpose of the meeting?" asked Jacques.

"To exchange views on the war," said John, reciting the news story.

"Are the Americans going to join the war?" asked Joan.

"Roosevelt says that America is no closer to war," said Knox.

Jacques nodded, but his face looked puzzled. He muttered, "How do you meet with Churchill and discuss the war without getting closer to it?"

"What did they agree upon? Was there a communiqué?" asked Jackie, voracious for information.

"Yes, the two leaders agreed on eight points of what the world should be like when the war is over," said John.

"Over?" asked Joan, confusion on her face. "First, it has to start for the Americans."

"War aims? Now?" asked Jackie, mulling the information over.

"Yeah, probably preliminaries," said Knox. "But I think we're closer to the big game starting."

"Anything more about Hopkins?" asked Jackie. "What did the story say about his Russia trip?"

"News reports say he told Roosevelt that Russia would hold on and eventually prevail," said John.

"Prevail?" said Jackie, using the question to lead into a statement. "Jacques's friend Frau von Koler thinks victory will be in the bag this fall for the Germans."

"Well, that's obviously the German hope," said John.

"Besides Hopkins, who else was there?" asked Jacques, changing the line of thought.

"Well, General…"

"I don't mean military, I mean civilian," interrupted Jacques.

"Averell Harriman, the Lend-Lease administrator," said John. "And Sumner Welles, the undersecretary…"

"Harriman will be arranging the Lend-Lease for Russia," said Jacques. "Welles probably drafted the communiqué."

"Yeah, that's probably true," said John. "But the generals…"

"Roosevelt and the top civilians run the war," said Jacques firmly.

"Then what were the generals and admirals for?" asked Joan, somewhat confused.

"To disguise the reality of just who makes up the American high command," said Jacques, the shape of that high command now coming clearly into his view. He'd met most of them in Jean Monnet's living room.

"You mean Roosevelt keeps the strategy in his hands?" asked John.

"I'd bet my paycheck on that," said Jacques, trying to sound American. "You and the other vice-consuls aren't here because of some general."

"Agreed," said John, remembering the confusion at the War Department. "And the State Department sure wasn't keen on it either. So who was it?"

"People at the top?" said Jacques.

"The same people who sent you here as third secretary, Jacques?" asked Jackie.

"No, I'm just an errand boy."

"Who used to work for Jean Monnet," replied Jackie. "The economic field marshal."

"I was just crunching numbers, the same as when I worked for his bank," said Jacques with a touch of heat to shut off further conversation. Understanding registered in John's eyes. More to the third secretary than he thought. But then he had suspected that all along.

"What about the Germans here on the Armistice Commission?" asked Joan. "Are they going to cause us trouble? Will the Germans invade North Africa to preempt any American involvement?"

"Probably not," said John. "All German eyes are on Russia. That is where the war will be won or lost."

"Roosevelt knows that," said Jacques. "I can feel it."

"Sounds to me like Harry made the biggest call of his career," said Jackie. "So far."

"Do you know Hopkins?" asked John.

"We both had rooms in Claridges. He promised me the inside dope on his Russia trip when he got back. But the newspapers announced his return," and then she stammered, "but he never showed up at the hotel."

"And you started to wonder?" asked John.

"We all did. But we couldn't speculate in our stories. The censors. When the correspondents found out Churchill had left London, they all assumed a meeting with Roosevelt—somewhere—was in the cards. It had been rumored all spring. You just can't write about it."

"The Russia invasion would make that meeting urgent," said John.

"And Harriman will have to divide the Lend-Lease loaves between both the British and the Russians now," said Jacques.

"But it's the Russians that will kill Germans," said John, his military experience speaking. "And the hard truth is a lot of Germans have to be killed before there will be a victory, the victory necessary to establish those war aims."

Jacques could see it. Roosevelt shifting the public gaze far out to the future while he maneuvered adroitly in the foreground.

Harbor Office

The consulate car brought Jacqueline down to the vice-consuls' office on the harbor quay. The driver got out and walked around and opened the rear door. Jacqueline got out, and the driver pointed her over toward the front door.

A security guard opened the door—she was expected—and Jacqueline walked in. Simone Hardy, Murphy's secretary, stood up and said, "Good morning, Miss Smith. This way." She led Jacqueline down a hall and through an open door where Jacques was sitting at a table scanning a pile of newspaper clippings.

"Hi, Jackie, sit down," said Jacques casually. "I've got newspaper clippings just in this morning."

Jackie pulled up a chair to the other side of the worktable. "Let me see."

"Here." He pushed some clippings across the table. He'd marked some with a red pencil.

"Oh, good. Here's a nice quote from a London editor," said Jackie. "The United States is on to the peace before she is even in the war," she read. "Well, it's a natural complaint, but it ignores the enormous implication of an Anglo-American agreement on war aims."

"Do you know him?"

"Probably," said Jackie. "There are so many."

"Busy girl," said Jacques with a laugh.

"Do you think the meeting was a war council, Jacques?"

"Not likely. America is still neutral."

"That fig leaf is wearing thin."

"The communiqué coming out of the meeting is about an eight-point statement about the peace aims to come out of the war," said Jacques. "Roosevelt's keeping everyone's eyes on the forward picture." Keep the public focused on the prospect of peace, not the inevitability of the war.

"What else?"

"Roosevelt emphasized the need for allies inside Europe, otherwise the democratic war cannot be won. He's making a promise of future independence to millions of people."

"Is that a core principle?"

"It is for Roosevelt. He always stresses future self-determination."

"Everywhere?"

"Everywhere."

"That principle will not rest easy in London; it is very much the capital of an empire," said Jackie.

"Yes, India. Churchill bitterly resisted independence for the Subcontinent during the 1930s."

"And Russia?" asked Jackie. "That's a wild card."

"Yes," agreed Jacques. Changing subjects, he said, "We have your itinerary to plan."

A pained look came over Jacqueline's face. "I got a telegram from Anne this morning. She wants me back in London PDQ."

"Well, that shouldn't be a problem," said Jacques. "We can get you a flight to Rabat, and you can have an interview tomorrow morning with the resident-general, General Noguès, before driving on to Tangier."

Jackie's eyes brightened. "That would be great…I'd stay tonight, but…"

"Understand. Let me make a few telephone calls while you go back to the hotel and pack, and I'll have you on your way."

The two stood up and walked out to the reception area.

Chapter 32: Taverne Alsacienne

September 1941. John Knox walked up the street to the Taverne Alsacienne and through the front door. The maître d' came over and whispered, "She's upstairs in the private dining room you requested." Knox said thank you and walked over to the stairwell and up the stairs. He walked down the hall and knocked on a door as he opened it. Joan Tuyl stood up from a chair near the window. She was wearing a bright summer silk dress and a radiant smile, blond hair shining in the twilight.

"So secret," she said. "Or do you have designs on me?" as she glanced around the room and its long divan so easily used for discreet liaisons.

"Secret for a reason, designs yes," said Knox with a smile. "But not tonight and surely not here."

She walked up and held her hands out to him, and he grasped them and leaned over and kissed her on the cheek. "We do have a future together."

"A future?" she said hesitantly. "I've hardly dared to think that far."

Knox held her chair as she sat down. He sat down across the small table and reached into the ice bucket and poured some chilled white wine in the glasses.

"Yes, a future. The Russians will grind the Germans down. The Americans will eventually come in. That's what the meeting with Churchill last month was all about."

"And?"

"There will be victory."

"For those who live to see it. But so many of us aren't going to make it."

"You're the mother of two boys. You need to survive."

"But my work."

"I'm going to help so I can keep an eye on you."

"But I can't compromise your work."

"You're my work," said Knox, and he reached across and held her hand in his. He looked at her sternly. "And besides, this is bigger than you."

"Bigger?"

"What's coming will be much bigger."

"You know?"

"I know we're just the first."

"I appreciate your concern, John. And my boys love you, and lord knows they need a father...but I'm a married woman..."

"With a husband far away...at best."

She sighed. "I know. I've not heard anything from him in months..."

"That's the worst. No knowing."

She looked at him seriously. "I don't do disloyalty well."

"Loyalty is written all over you. That's the big quality that has nourished my love for you, this sense of something being bigger than you."

"Yes, and marriage is about loyalty. If he's in the resistance...how cannot I not keep solidarity?"

"When you commit to action, you become part of the sacrifice. That's always the deal in war," said Knox.

"Not much of a deal in Holland," she said, disappointment with the cruel fate that befell her husband in her voice.

"If he's in the resistance, he eventually gets caught...I'm afraid that's the fate," said John.

She started to cry. "I know...but I'm not brave enough to face it."

John patted her hand. She looked at him through tear-streaked eyes and said, "If he comes back?"

"I guess I go home," said John. "Not the first time."

"I'd hate to do that to you...I need to get comfortable with this, John...I need time."

"You have time...I want to keep you safe...no matter what you decide."

She looked at him, the light coming into her eyes. She sighed. "I need time." She looked left and right, confusion on her face. "Yes, I need time."

"I understand."

"I know you do," she said and, with a faint smile, continued, "but I think you know the answer, don't you?"

"Yes," he said. He held up his wine glass. "To the future."

"The future," said Joan as she clinked the glass. She looked thoughtful for a moment. "When you have a future, then you start to be afraid of losing it. I've just felt so much has been lost already…"

"Your boys."

"I always thought if the worst came—and I was almost sure it would—then my mother would see to them." The forlorn look on her face betrayed her uneasiness with that thought. The tears came again. She put her glass down and reached for the napkin and dabbed the tears off her cheek. She looked up and smiled. The future had come sooner than she thought, maybe sooner than she would have liked. But John Knox was a pretty good future, she thought.

There was a knock on the door, and John said, "Entrez."

A cart was wheeled in with sumptuous dinners heaped on each plate and a bowl of steaming cut green beans on the side.

"I haven't seen anything like this since before the war," she exclaimed. She looked at him. "Algeria used to be the Garden of Eden to the world, abundance everywhere."

"And now les Boches."

"Yes, but tonight let's forget about defeating them." She ravenously eyed the food. One of things John liked about her was she was always hungry.

"My thoughts exactly," said John, and he raised his glass again.

She clinked her glass again and said, "I hope my guilt doesn't dampen my affection for you." She smiled—with some ease and increasing warmth.

Headquarters, Political Police

The telephone rang. The police detective picked it up. "Telephone call from Casablanca" came the voice out of the earpiece. "Yes, I'll take it." A woman's voice came on the line. He recognized the sound of the attractive counterespionage agent Cosette.

"Yes?"

He listened and repeated the message, "This weekend. Probably Friday night after a reception." He wrote down the particulars. "I'll arrange it." He hung up. He went and shared the information with Captain Achiary.

Morocco

Rabat. September. Robert Murphy was escorted into the office of the senior police official in the Palace of the resident-general in Rabat. He took the proffered chair and looked across the broad desk to the uniformed police general.

"General Noguès wanted me to share this information about your vice-consuls. We intercepted the report from the Germans."

"The Germans already have an opinion?"

"Yes, Consul General Auer in Casablanca has reported to Berlin."

"Fine, I've known Auer for a long time. What does Teddy have to say?"

"I'll let you read the intercept," said the police general as he slipped the paper across the desk.

Murphy picked it up and read:

The vice-consuls whom Murphy directs represent a perfect picture of the mixture of races and characteristics in that wild conglomeration called the United States of America.

Murphy looked up and said, "Yes, I can see it's addressed to the highest levels in Berlin." He continued reading:

We can only congratulate ourselves on the selection of this group of enemy agents who will give us no trouble. In view of the fact that they are totally lacking in method, organization, and discipline, the danger presented by their arrival in North Africa may be considered as nil. It would be merely a waste of paper to describe their personal idiosyncrasies and characteristics.

Murphy put the paper down and said, "Thanks for sharing. But our vice-consuls are here to do what we said they were here to do—supervise cargoes arriving under the Trade Agreement."

"Well, the Germans will believe that for now," said the police general.

Murphy stood up. "Well, I'm off for the corner office. Keep General Noguès on side," he said cheerily referring to the resident-general, the biggest fence sitter in North Africa.

Chapter 33: Kiev Falls

Hotel Aletti. Friday afternoon, September 13. The phone rang in one of the suites reserved for visiting members of the German Armistice Commission. A middle-aged German walked over and picked it up.

"Yes?" He listened to the voice coming down the line.

"Not to worry. Everything is arranged. I have my own security man with me." The man listened some more. "The apartment is secure."

Another question came down the line about his security man. "Yes, thorough if a tad extreme." He then said with furrowed brow, "What do you mean, one of us?"

The German listened with growing impatience. "No. He's a hetero. But, you know, like so many of them, kind of obsessive, even sick." He listened some more.

"He was in the trenches in 1918. Just a boy. The French artillery knocked him a little cuckoo."

He listened some more. A problem?

"No. Gives him an edge."

"No. The Arab checks out. I've used him before. You'll like the boy."

"Yes. See you tonight."

The Villa

Friday evening. In the twilight shadow of the entrance to a vacant villa in the El Biar quarter of Algiers, the agent stood in the warm air cupping a cigarette as he passed his time. The big black homburg was pushed down on his head, throwing a shadow over his face. The bulky trench coat accentuated his hefty presence while obscuring his profile. He calmly drew on his cigarette; he had been doing this business for years. First in Paris, now in North Africa. The new identification he'd picked up from le chef in Marseilles worked fine all over North Africa. So Hervé it was. He thought about the two Germans he was tailing. An intricate web had been spun. He was sure that the Germans would show up at the rendezvous. They liked what they liked—a lot.

Hervé craned his neck around the corner to peer across the cobble-stoned street at the two large wooden doors of the coach entrance to the luxurious two-story villa, a *grand maison* nestled into the side of a hill overlooking Algiers. He knew this was the residence of Elke von Koler, the important German foreign correspondent. He had seen her peek out from behind the curtains in an upstairs room—presumably her bedroom—when he first took position. Possibly she saw him. Nothing unusual, he thought. The French political police normally kept a careful eye on her.

Looking back across the street, he knew that behind the large doors facing the street was an interior courtyard. When opened, the portal could accommodate the entrance of automobiles. At the right side, a smaller door through the wall allowed people to enter the courtyard.

The man scanned the few windows on the second story that were visible from the street. The upstairs rooms were dark. Earlier, he had heard the sound of jazz music drift out from the drawing room bordering the courtyard. A cocktail party was underway. The agent knew it would be a while before the guests would start leaving. He unobtrusively snuffed his cigarette.

He reviewed his plans. Most likely the two guests he was interested in would be among the last to leave. He would catch up with them near the apartment down the hill. He also wanted to understand just who—one man in particular—was in the neighborhood. A third man.

He also needed to know exactly where Cosette was. He had to stay between her and the third man. He had seen him in Casablanca and didn't like the look of him.

Would there be a rendezvous after the cocktail party? He was pretty sure that would happen. With these two, the *soirée privée* was always at the finish of an evening's entertainment. Do enough stake-outs and you know life, particularly its all-too-human underside.

Another thought nagged at him. The American was across the street, too. Not really an American; a one-time French national on an American diplomatic passport working as a third secretary at the consul general's office. Rare to find a foreign national holding diplomatic status. And as le chef frequently observed, rare always asks the question why? He, l'inspecteur, had also learned that during the years in Paris, those years when he learned to read the streets. Except for that one lapse that night in Paris.

What was the third German up to?

Praise from Berlin

In a corner of the drawing room in the villa, an important-looking German member of the Armistice Commission, Theodor Auer, was engaged in whispered conversations with two impeccably dressed Germans, one a major in one of the security services and the head of Oran station, and the other his young and beautifully presented assistant.

"What did you learn in Berlin?" asked Auer.

"Your correspondent," and the German nodded across the room toward Elke von Koler, "has been successful at feeding the international correspondents, mostly the Americans, the information German intelligence feels supports the isolationist forces in America, particularly those of Colonel Lindberg and Senator Wheeler."

"How do you know that?" asked Auer.

"There was a long story quoting Koler in the *New York Times Tribune* after the successful Crete operations," said the major. "The Americans understand that the British position in Egypt is fragile. The story was sourced to unnamed individuals in Algiers."

"Algiers?"

"Yes, Berlin cross-referenced the story to Koler's report on her lunch with the American correspondent Jacqueline Smith. Furthermore, Koler's comments reinforce what the American diplomats are reporting back to the State Department about Britain."

"A double coup?"

"Yes."

"Subterfuge? The Americans aren't suspicious?"

"No. The Americans don't suspect that the Black Chamber is reading their diplomatic cables."

"They don't know we're reading their cable traffic?" asked Auer, smelling a rat.

"They haven't made a move to change any of their codes," said the major. "They're transparent as day to us."

Jazz

The guitar riffs from Django Reinhardt came out of the drawing room as Jacques entered the foyer and handed his coat and hat to the *bonne,* a maid pertly dressed in a black dress with white pinafore. The music came from a modern record player in the corner. Jacques knew the music well. Jazz captured his imagination as a student in Paris, an infatuation that became an obsession in New York during graduate studies.

Looking around the room, he saw his hostess. He walked over to the attractive blonde, ravishing in her shimmering white-satin evening dress, her foot gently tapping to the rhythm as she listened intently to the conversation of her guests, silently pleased with her selection of music. Jacques knew the gift that he had in his hands would be well received.

"Madame von Koler," he said with no click of the heels but with a slight bow.

"Please, Elke," she responded. "We've been at least acquaintances for some time now, Jacques. Tonight will be a night of friendship." That he already understood.

"A small gift," said Jacques as he handed over a square box tied with a ribbon. "Toward tonight's friendship."

"Oh, how thoughtful," she said. "May I open it?"

"By all means."

She tore off the wrapping paper and found inside the box a half-dozen seventy-eight rpm records. She quickly scrutinized the records one by one. "Oh my goodness, Duke Ellington with Ivie Anderson." She looked at Jacques with bright luminous eyes and said, "I shall treasure them. You know my weak spot—or one of them at least," she added with a mischievous look.

"Yes, I know," he said. "The music has been a constant with you."

"As with you. Well, ever since my time in New York," she replied. "It becomes like a craving. So vibrantly American."

Another guest—a French naval officer, a commander—and his wife came up. Jacques stepped back.

"We'll talk later," she said, serious intent in her voice. "About other things than the war." There had been hints from her over the past several weeks that she had things to say.

"Elke, my wife Valérie," said the naval officer by way of introduction to the hostess. "Frau Elke von Koler, my dear. She's the correspondent here in Algiers for *Deutsche Allegemeine Zeitung.*"

"Enchanteé," said the French woman, holding out her hand.

"Madame de Roussillon. Such a pleasure to meet you."

"Please, call me Valérie."

"Your husband," and Elke nodded, "is so kind to help the lieutenant commander arrange interviews for me with important people in the headquarters and prefectures in Algiers and across North Africa. If there were no interviews, there would be nothing to write, no events to film."

"Yes, we've been blessed," said Valérie. "So far the war hardly touches North Africa."

"Yes, the Gaullist adventurers are bogged down on the wrong side of the Sahara Desert," said Elke. The Free French were struggling to hold on to the oasis at Koufra in southern Libya.

"Our goal," said Commander de Roussillon, "is to keep both the Free French and the British out of North Africa." He looked across the room at Jacques and said nothing. The Americans were an enigma. Elke noticed and made a mental shrug. The American presence in North Africa was an intriguing angle, an opportunity for her on many levels. The Vichy French government under Maréchal Pétain maintained diplomatic relations with the Americans even though Germany was now almost at war with them out in the Atlantic Ocean. This was still one of the few places in the world where Germans could mix with Americans. From experience, she liked Americans. New York was one of her favorite cities.

"Marcel says that our loyalty to the legitimate French government must be complete," said Valérie, mentioning her husband. "Our loyalty to Admiral Darlan, of course, is absolute."

"And Maréchal Pétain," her husband quickly added.

"Well, I cannot help but applaud and agree," said Elke with a smile. She and her German associates had been impressed with the iron-tight loyalty of French naval officers to Admiral Darlan, who had said that he had not created a French fleet to give it to the British—whom he despised. His great-grandfather had been killed at Trafalgar.

"And your husband is in Berlin?" inquired Valérie, barely able to contain her curiosity. The other wives gossiped about the slinky German foreign correspondent who spent so much time at the various headquarters in Algiers—the Winter Palace, the Prefecture, and the naval headquarters among them—and with their husbands. She seemed to know everyone who was anyone in Algiers. Even the Americans.

"Yes, my husband. He is at the Wilhelmstrasse. Legal department," said Elke, mentioning the German foreign ministry. She always stressed the legal aspect to emphasize the dry paperwork nature of his duties, all of which was true. He had been a lawyer specializing in American business affairs before the war, a career that often took the couple to New York in those years.

Another couple came up, the man a prominent official in the Prefecture.

"Ah, Etienne, you made it," exclaimed Elke. "And this is your charming wife?"

"Yes, Monica," said the man, a *sous-préfet* in Algiers. Introductions were made, and the French official quickly complimented Elke. "Madame von Koler, we watch with amazement as the German army enters Russia." He paused. "Eventually someone had to confront Bolshevism in its lair."

"This is the campaign that will bring peace to Europe," said Elke. "Vanquish the Bolshevik threat."

"How so?" asked the official's wife eagerly. "We so want it."

Elke turned and directly engaged Monica. "France will play a big role. Victory on the eastern front will call forth requests to Maréchal Pétain to intercede with Washington to start peace talks with Great Britain on ending the war."

"With Churchill?" said the French official disbelievingly.

"No, with the government that succeeds him. The fall of Moscow will topple the Churchill government in London."

The French commander smiled approvingly. "Yes, put the English war criminal in the Tower. The massacre of French sailors at Mers-el-Kébir cries for justice."

"Yes, and ending the Bolshevik menace from Russia will be a great blessing to Europe," said the French official, the small conversational circle nodding in agreement. Jacques listened with intent interest; this was why he was here. He looked over at a table where champagne was being served, excused himself and walked over, letting the conversation about Russia recede behind him.

At the table, a second bonne was pouring flutes of champagne for guests.

"Bonjour, mademoiselle," said Jacques.

"Bonjour, monsieur," said the maid as she handed Jacques a glass of the light-golden liquid.

He walked unobtrusively over to the fireplace, quite unlit in the autumn climate, and stood in the shadow to one side. Nearby, several Germans in business suits were chatting among themselves. Jacques could overhear references to Joachim von Ribbentrop, the German foreign minister. "You're close to him, Theodor. What does he think?" one of the Germans asked. He recognized Theodor Auer from lunch the previous winter standing in the middle of the Germans.

"I can't speak for the foreign minister. But I know the führer has been blind to the Mediterranean and Africa. With the fall of Crete, all forces should have been concentrated on General Rommel's push into Egypt. We could have knocked Britain out of the Middle East. No Middle East and India becomes a pawn shop jewel."

"Yes, I see the strategic opportunity missed," said one of the Germans with a furrowed brow.

"Missed?" said Auer with scorn. "A couple of German divisions and we could have Casablanca and Dakar. We could shut off the South Atlantic."

"The South Atlantic?" another German asked.

"Yes, the South Atlantic. That's how the Americans move supplies to the Russians."

"We could have shut that off? Take Moscow by shutting down the South Atlantic?"

"Exactly," said Auer heatedly. "Who's going to stop you? General de Gaulle?" he said with contempt in his voice.

"But would Vichy cooperate?"

"Cooperate? Are you forgetting June 1940. Hold a pistol to the Frenchman's head, and he'll sign any paper put in front of him."

From the first group, Jacques saw Auer break away and head over toward him. The German held out his hand and said, "Theodor Auer, German consul general in Casablanca. We met at lunch with Mr. Murphy in Casablanca last winter."

"Yes, good memory. I'm Jacques Dubois, third secretary at the American consul general's office." Jacques held out his hand.

"I did not get a much of a chance to talk with you at the lunch. Bob Murphy and his diplomatic work were foremost on my mind," said Auer with easy familiarity. "I knew Bob well in Paris before the war. America was quite neutral then," he said with a laugh.

"We still are."

"In legal theory but not in practice. Your ships out on the Atlantic…"

"Here, we still share the same interests," interrupted Jacques. "To keep French North Africa out of the war."

"Possibly we can continue to share that interest," said the German as he sipped his champagne and looked appraisingly at Jacques, sizing him up. "And now you have your vice-consuls from America supervising the Murphy-Weygand shipments."

"Yes," said Jacques.

"Maintaining your neutrality?" asked Auer with a wry smile.

"Yes, we're trying to get relief supplies to the civilian population of North Africa. That's crucial to keeping North Africa neutral."

"Yes, keep the Muslims eating. How noble." The dry cynicism came easily to the German.

"A matter of common interest," said Jacques. "To the French, to the Americans, to the Germans."

"Your concern for German interests is touching," said Auer. "But as you can see, Germany has new interests with the invasion of Russia."

"Yes, but France has interests, too. So many food exports are now going to metropolitan France," said Jacques, replying with a straight fact. The German purchasing agents were like locusts buying up the crops in North Africa to feed their armies in Russia. The German administration was mismanaging the agricultural economies of eastern Europe beyond anyone's imagining.

"The people in Europe have to eat, too," said the German.

"And live. Our government is still trying to get Red Cross supplies into Marseilles for French children. Tinned milk for the infants."

"Yes, the children," said the German with a tinge of irony.

"Soon, it will be approaching Christmas," added Jacques with a touch of insistence.

"You speak French like a native."

"My father was French; my mother is American."

"You're quite a friend of Frau von Koler?" said the German, making the question a statement. He arched an inquisitive eyebrow.

"An acquaintance, I should say. I met her soon after I arrived here last December."

"You arrived well before the other control officers?"

"I'm not a control officer. Third secretary, a lowly diplomatic clerk, I should say. Answering inquiries from journalists such as Frau von Koler. She is interested in what goes on in French North Africa."

"Yes, undoubtedly her readers in Berlin are quite interested."

"So more bureaucratic routine for me," said Jacques. "Press relations."

"Yes, so many reports going to Washington, so much coding to do."

"I wouldn't know. I have no cipher training. All my reports go back to Washington by diplomatic pouch—mostly by slow boat, I think."

"Nevertheless, there are few lowly clerks in Algiers. Everyone is here for a reason."

"The control officers generate a lot of reports."

"And you are of course of some assistance to Frau von Koler?"

"Where possible, I arrange interviews for her with American diplomats…about the food shipments reaching North Africa."

"Yes, but I should like to tell you—so you can share with Mister Murphy who can share with your State Department—that the best way to keep North Africa at peace is to keep the British out…and that adventurer General de Gaulle and his brigands, too. Look what they did in Syria."

"Our diplomatic corps deals with the Vichy French, not the others," said Jacques with sincerity in his voice.

"Good. I realize the British are your allies…"

"Last time I heard we were still neutral," said Jacques. "But we do have to coordinate with them so that the ships coming from America can be allowed past the British blockade…"

"Understand."

"Now your ally Italy…sometimes troublesome…" Jacques let the words hang.

Auer stammered. "Italy?"

"Difficulties with an ally, *mein herr?*"

"Always…in war," said the German. Again, he mumbled, "Italy…"

Jacques laughed.

"You laugh easily for a lowly diplomatic clerk," said the German.

"You have to admit North Africa is a three-penny opera."

"Well, let me wish you a good evening," said the German. "If you're ever in Casablanca again, you can stop by and spy on me over lunch. We can meet for a discreet meal—just you, me, and the Deuxième Bureau."

Jacques laughed again and said, "*Auf wiedersehen.*" The German walked back to his group.

Jacques continued standing by the fireplace and looked over to the windows where a dandyish man with an Austrian accent was regaling several French gentlemen and ladies with stories about the Foreign Legion. The man was something of a fixer and was doing a roaring business getting paperwork approved at the Prefecture for shipments of agricultural products to metropolitan France. Rumor was he could get you authentic French documents from sources in

Morocco allowing transit to either Spain or Portugal—for a hefty price. Jacques walked over and joined the group.

"Hello, Jacques," one of them said as he came up. Gerald Renoit was a senior official at the Prefecture supervising trade to Marseilles. He was formally dressed in black pants and dinner jacket with a black tie crowning his white shirtfront. The other men were similarly dressed. The wives were all in luxuriant floor-length evening gowns over trim ladylike figures, not a matronly one in the bunch observed Jacques. "Franz has been regaling us about tales of dessert fortresses and beautiful white women kept in harems," said the man from the Prefecture.

"Rescued by the Legion," added Franz solemnly. The women twittered at this tale while glancing at Jacques with laughing eyes. "Let me go keep my German in practice with those who supervise us," said Franz. He turned and walked over toward the German group and was heartily welcomed with handshakes all around.

"So, you're keeping a sharp eye on the American imports, are you, Jacques?" asked one of the men.

"No, the control officers will. I just go around to the ports and collect routine reports that go back to the State Department."

"You seem to know a lot of army and naval officers."

"Yes, liaison work. We want our ships to get into port and quickly unload and clear the area. It is getting increasingly dangerous."

"Just more dull routine," said Gerald with a laugh.

"Exactly," said Jacques with a smile.

Across the room, Frau von Koler broke free of the naval officers and their wives and walked over to the record player and stacked the new records from Jacques on the changer and set the arm. As the first sounds of the Duke Ellington classic *Solitude* filled the room, she walked over and held Jacques by the arm and announced to the group: "We owe this new music to Jacques. From America."

"Yes, the music is wonderful," said one of the wives, rocking her shoulders with the rhythm.

"So now I know why Jacques is here tonight. He's in charge of smuggled records. I knew there was an ulterior motive to his presence here in Algiers," said Gerald. "Cultural propaganda from America."

Frau von Koler stood up on tiptoe and whispered in Jacques's ear loud enough for the others to hear, "We'll listen to the last one together…later…"

"Oh la la," said Gerald as the wives watched with fascination. Jacques was darkly handsome and charming. They also knew that Frau von Koler's good friend at the Winter Palace, the lieutenant commander and assistant chief of staff, was not here tonight. Once a month he visited his wife in Toulon.

The maid circulated around the room with a tray of champagne flutes, signaling a last round and the end of the soirée. Jacques took a glass as did the others. He held his out in a toast. "Thanks to Elke for a lovely party."

The others chanted, "*Santé*," and took their sips.

Soon the maid was handing out coats to the men and wraps to the women. Frau von Koler stood by the door and thanked people for coming. Jacques stood by the maid. He watched Herr Auer depart with some of the other Germans. He was quickly followed by the Austrian Franz. There had been rumors, Jacques knew. But not his business.

Presently, one of the maids came up to Frau von Koler. "Anything else, Madame?"

"No, thank you very much, Ernestine. That will be all for the night."

The maids departed to return to their rooms behind the kitchen.

Frau von Koler came up and held Jacques by the arm. "Let's listen to the last Ellington record?"

"By all means," said Jacques. "*Stormy Weather* seems not to have played yet this evening."

"I was saving it just for us," said Elke in a whisper.

"I was hoping."

"Good. I want to make fond memories tonight." She walked over and pulled a record out of its brown slipcover and put it on the changer. She clicked the lever, and the changer dropped the platter onto the turntable, and the arm came out and placed the needle on the edge of the record. Soon the sultry sound filled the room. Again, she walked over and wrapped herself on Jacques's arm. "I asked you to keep the evening free for me?"

"I have."

"Good. This way." She held his hand and led him down the hall and up the staircase to the second floor. She opened the door to the master bedroom and led him in. She walked over and closed the heavy curtains. She lit a candle on the mantle above a small fireplace. "There's champagne in a bucket over on the side table."

Jacques went over and pulled the bottle out and popped the cork, muffling the sound with a towel around the top. He poured two glasses and turned around. Elke had hung her evening dress over the back of a chair and stood in satin and silk lingerie, a brassiere over small breasts, a garter belt around a slender waist, the small silk panties over girlish hips. Silk stockings completed an ensemble meant to excite if not kill. Jacques handed her a glass of champagne.

"You like?"

"Very much so."

"Just in case we never make that rendezvous at the Rainbow Room."

"Maybe we will."

"I promised I wouldn't talk about the war, but my husband told me of evil things in the east, in Poland, when I met him in Rome last month. There is disquiet in certain circles in Berlin below the pomp of all the victories." There was an emptiness in Elke's voice that Jacques had not heard before.

"Maybe we're survivors," he said.

"We can hope," she said as she set her glass down. She began to undo her brassier. "Come to bed."

"I will. One moment." He walked over and snuffed out the candle and then went over to the curtains. He opened them slightly and gazed out across the street. Yes, just as he thought, they were being watched. Then movement. He saw the man leave, the unmistakable trench coat, the scarf, the big homburg hat. He recognized the shadow if not the man.

"What do you see?" she asked from the bed.

"We're being watched. The local Gestapo…"

"*Non, mon cher.* The Gestapo left a half hour ago with his boyfriend."

Paul A. Myers

Jacques laughed. Elke would know. "Probably French then."

"They're all very interested in me. Aren't you?"

He turned and hung his clothes over the back of the chair and slid into the spacious bed next to Elke. "Very much so."

In the Shadows

Across the street, the heavyset man watched the guests leave. Herr Auer left in a touring car with several other guests all speaking German. Later, the Austrian named Franz got into a taxicab that came up at his beckon. The man watched the cab bump along the street and make a turn to the right. Probably heading to the apartment, he thought. Good. The plant, a young Arab, was there. Cosette had assured him the Arab would get the job done.

The man took one last look across the street and scanned the upper windows. A faint light came out of one of the rooms. Then it went dark. The American had never left. Interesting. Was he staying? That would be a new development. He stepped out into the street and turned down the hill. There was more work to do this evening.

Chapter 34: Dark Rendezvous

A couple of blocks back from the Hotel Aletti, there was an old apartment building back up a dingy street. The German looked at the crumbling edifice, the peeling shutters, and wondered why the boss had to have his trysts in such nondescript places. Did the seediness add an extra thrill? He much preferred the casino in Casablanca. A gifted cheater, he had soaked more than one wealthy Jew out of his travel money. They didn't understand that paying off the croupier was child's play. But what he really liked was women. When you got to do with them what you liked. Maybe tonight. He smiled.

Then he returned to the present. Men were just business. Best to be done quickly. He remembered that providing security for Herr Auer was a trip back to the basics. If there were any French security men involved, well, he'd handled them before. He decided to start his routine. The German walked the surrounding streets, and at each turn he came closer to the old apartment building as if working his way through a maze to the center box.

On one side street, there was a nondescript zinc bar, a disheveled barman behind. He looked in and saw in a corner a reward for his practiced curiosity. The woman was too good looking, too well dressed for the neighborhood, even if this was her profession. Difference always raised questions in his mind. He made a mental note. She was probably the brains behind the scheme. But she didn't look like an assassin. Was there one? Or was this just a photo expedition? A little light blackmail. The French were so behind the times.

The German went back and carefully examined the apartment building for entrances and exits. Yes, probably there—the rear fire escape. He found a place in a dark shadow and watched the fire escape. He heard a car stop on the next street. A door slammed. Good-byes were made. But the man didn't start walking toward the Hotel Aletti. He was coming up the street toward the apartment building. He recognized Auer.

Paul A. Myers

Where was Franz? Soon she heard the taxi come from the other direction. Franz got out about a block away and walked toward the apartment building.

The German watched carefully. There, coming over a nearby wall, came a slithering, wraith-like presence. An Arab. With what looked like an empty satchel. If there were cameras, they were probably already in place. The Arab went up the fire escape with experienced ease.

After the Arab was in the building, the German carefully stepped out and searched around the building looking for anything else out of the ordinary. Then he went back toward the bistro to double-check. If she were an assassin, she'd want to be close to the building to confirm the kill. But if it were just photos or maybe home movies, then she would wait here. Plenty of time to catch up with her later, he thought. He snorted. Nice looking. She might be fun. He didn't really get enough of that in his new assignment. Told not to make waves. He fingered the knife in his pocket, the sharp blade giving him a thrill of excitement.

The German came up to the bistro and peeked through the window. The blonde was still there. He pursed his lips, now he really felt the tingle of excitement.

The German turned around into the shadows and then went back to the apartment building and took his place in the shadows. If he heard shouts from inside—trouble—he'd rush the place. But he didn't think so tonight. This was just like last time except then the Arab had already been in the apartment, and there was no stunning looker down at the bistro. He waited. A long time. Finally, there was movement on the fire escape. The Arab was coming down. With the satchel.

The Frenchman

The heavyset French agent walked to a side street near the bistro. He was sure that with Auer there would be a security agent around somewhere, probably Gestapo. The man stood in the shadows and watched the bistro. He saw the Arab coming. He looked behind him. There, a block back. A shadow moved. The Frenchmen stayed deep in his own shadow, barely peering over the top of a trash box. Yes, he'd been right. Probably Mr. Casablanca.

261

The shadow moved. Was that a knife in his right hand? Entirely unnecessary for a job like this. Unless something else was on the shadow's mind. Uneasiness filled the Frenchman's stomach. He reached into his trench coat and moved his knife from its customary inside pocket to an easily accessible outside pocket.

The Arab went in the bistro. The shadow didn't move. The Frenchman then looked the other way down the street toward the Aletti for a likely spot to cross. He'd have to make do. He moved down a side street and circled around, his plan crystallizing in his head.

He got across the street in a blind spot past the next corner. Then he worked his way back up the street closer to a spot near the bistro. He got as close to the bistro as he could. If he could see a shadow, maybe the shadow could see a shadow. On the other hand, it was too risky to wait for Cosette near the Aletti.

He didn't know when the German might strike. If the German had in mind what the Frenchman feared, the first dark alley would do. On the other hand, the German wouldn't try to kill her right away; he'd take his time. And he had to recover the film first—there would be some conversation. The Frenchman could rush him. But from this spot, as long as he heard Cosette's footsteps, he knew she was all right. The Frenchman positioned himself in the alley and waited. A thought nagged at him, had he lost half a step since those years in Paris. Maybe he should simply use his automatic on this one...

He heard the heels come out of the bistro and down the sidewalk. A wave of relief came over him. As long as he heard the heels...Cosette would be heading toward him. He could see the lights of the Aletti down the street. They would backlight the German if all went to plan. Possibly dim the German's night vision a little. A bonus.

Cosette walked by. The Frenchman's heart skipped a beat. Knife to the ready. He heard a rustle on the sidewalk. A shadow slunk past hugging the wall. The Frenchman stepped forward and called out, "*Was ist das?*" The German whirled, the knife in his right hand flashing silver as the head tried to figure out where the voice came from in the blackness. The Frenchman's blade went up under the German's sternum before he grasped the suddenness of the attack coming.

The German slumped to the sidewalk, his knife laying on the sidewalk next to his open and outstretched hand, blood pumping out through the chest wound from a heart pumping its last beats. The Frenchman watched. Soon the blood quit gushing and slowed to a trickle. The Frenchman didn't touch a thing.

The Frenchman stepped back and looked everything over. The political police could blame it on the Corsicans. He looked up the sidewalk and saw Cosette approach the Aletti. He quickly moved down the sidewalk to catch up with her.

"I was wondering where you were?" she said as he approached, a touch of concern in her voice.

"Making sure there were no loose ends," he said.

"Were there?"

"Not now," he said in a tone of grave finality.

The film arrived in Marseilles several days later.

Headquarters: Political Police

Theodor Auer sat at the conference table with Captain Achiary sitting just across.

"I appreciate that you could come in on such short notice," said the French police captain.

"Yes, it's about my security aide," said Auer, repeating the message he had received that morning over the telephone at his hotel room. Possibly a troubling development after an evening of pleasurable and edgy sensuality. Usually Hans was as reliable as a good clock.

"Yes, he was found last night several blocks from the Hotel Aletti, a bad section of town."

"And?" Auer was all steely determination.

"This," said Achiary as he pushed large glossy photos across the table of the German splayed out on the sidewalk in a puddle of blood. "An unfortunate ending."

Auer took the photo and turned it around and looked at it carefully. Then he looked through the other photos coming across the table one after another as if being shuffled off the top of a card deck at a *chemin de fer* table at the casino. His eyes registered every significant detail. "Yes," said Auer in conclusion. He looked at Achiary and subtly moved to turn the tables. "What do you think happened?"

"Possibly Corsicans. They have been a problem. The Italian members of the Armistice Commission had an unfortunate experience. Possibly the German members might want to coordinate outside evening activities with our liaison officer at the Commission offices at the Aletti."

"Duly noted," said Auer succinctly. He looked at Achiary with a riveting gaze.

"Like I said, possibly Corsicans," said Achiary.

"Corsicans wouldn't leave the knife behind," said Auer, stating clearly a rather obvious fact and shredding Achiary's premise.

Achiary smiled and nodded. Auer was everything he had been told. Highly professional. "Yes…"

Auer kept a steady gaze on Achiary.

"Let me assure you, we—the Algerian police—had nothing to do with this unfortunate episode," said Achiary with evident sincerity.

"I believe you," said Auer with cold condescension. "None of you are that good." He nodded at the photo of the assassinated corpse of what had once been a very good Gestapo thug.

Achiary nodded again with a wan smile. "As you wish." He stood up signaling an end to the interview.

"Thank you for informing me," said Auer as he stood up.

Achiary watched Auer leave and reflected on the interview. Sarcasm aside, Auer had been correct that the taking down of the German had been exceptionally professional. That fact raised the question of just who had done it. Achiary smiled. He was sure Auer had the same question in his mind. No good answer came to the police captain's mind. A French intelligence agent would have probably just used a pistol. Who would risk a knife fight with such a formidable Gestapo agent? He knew that the beautiful French counterintelligence agent had been running a blackmail operation. In addition to the Arab doing the photos, had she had a second Arab for security, a very special Arab? Some of them liked knife work.

Chapter 35: The Shipping Business

October 1941. John Knox walked out the front entrance of the Hotel Aletti in the dawn twilight and turned down the street walking toward the harbor. At the waterfront he turned left and started a slow walk along the boulevard until he came up to a zinc bar and went inside. At one end of the bar were Arab stevedores taking coffee and at the other end French dockworkers taking either coffee or a vin rosé. Knox walked in and ordered a café au lait and looked around.

A Frenchman, a stevedore supervisor, came over and put his coffee down next to Knox's. He looked at Knox and said, "I've got news. The Italian ship at the quay is loading phosphates, but the bill of lading says foodstuffs for Marseilles."

"Are you sure?"

The Frenchman nodded down the bar, and an Arab stevedore came over. The Frenchman asked, "The cargo?"

The Arab reached in his pocket and brought out a small flake-like slab of phosphate. "Here."

"How much?" asked Knox.

"Three days to load," said the Arab in French. "A lot."

"Where's it going?"

The Frenchman said, "The bill of lading says Marseilles. The crew talks incessantly about the whores in Genoa. Go figure."

"Got it," said Knox. He gulped down his coffee and nodded at the bartender to pay. Knox pulled out some bills and pushed one over to the bartender and slipped another bill to his left and second to his right. "Thanks gentlemen. I'll see what I can do."

Lunch with Joan

In the afternoon, as usual, John Knox went to Joan Tuyl's for lunch. Arriving, he brought some fresh vegetables and some fruit and handed them to the family's maid and cook.

The two boys started yelling, "John's here."

Joan and her mother came out from the studio with relieved smiles. The boys were raring to go. John got down on the rug and

265

roughhoused with them to their great delight, a daily highlight of their war-constrained days.

"John, what would I do without you?" said Joan with great satisfaction.

"We're partners, remember," said Knox. "We're in this together."

Mrs. Fry looked at this exchange with beatific understanding. The boys needed a father; she suspected her daughter needed a husband.

The five of them sat down to a lunch long on green beans and light on meat and with what passed for decent bread from a region that was once the breadbasket of the entire Mediterranean. Now the harvests were stripped by German agents buying up all the foodstuffs in sight. The buying went on and on.

After lunch, John said, "Joan, let's take a walk. Go to the park."

"Sure," she said. She looked at her two sons. "Come on boys, we're going to the park."

"Oh, goody," they chimed in unison.

They walked outside and down the street to Parc de Galland. They went over and sat down at a park bench where a lot of other mothers were looking after their rambunctious offspring playing on the grass.

John casually said, "The Italian ship down on the waterfront is loaded with phosphates. Probably bound for Genoa and quick train ride to German munitions factories over the Alps."

"Are you going to sink it?" she asked mischievously.

"Yes, if you can help me?"

"What do you want me to do?"

"Just get a message to your network. It needs to go by radio. The pouch is too slow."

"Maybe I can do that."

"Good."

They watched the boys play and eventually went back to Joan's flat.

Night Rendezvous

Late in the afternoon, Joan Tuyl walked out of her flat and strolled a couple of blocks over. She came to an apartment building on the side of the hill and went in and spoke to the Italian janitor. "I'm here to pay the rent." The organization had long ago decided the janitor could not be trusted.

The elderly lady nodded at the stairway. Joan walked over and up the stairs, past the second floor where the landlord lived and then trudged up to the ninth floor where Curly resided. She knocked on the door, and Madame Escoute opened it and gave Joan a bored look. "He's in the study."

Joan walked into the study, and Curly stood up. After a hearty greeting and kissed cheeks, they walked over to a corner, and Curly whispered, "What's up?"

"John wants a message radioed."

"Yes?"

"The Italian ship in the harbor has been loading phosphates and a lot of it. The crew says the ship's going to Genoa. The bill of lading says foodstuffs for Marseilles."

"I'll get it to Rygor."

"Good. I've got to go."

"Understand."

Morning Walks

John Knox took his customary early-morning walk along the waterfront. The Italian ship had left its berth and was tied up across the harbor, possibly waiting for departure. Knox walked into the zinc bar and ordered up a coffee. He looked inquiringly at the Frenchman. He just shrugged. Knox understood.

The following morning Knox repeated the walk. The Italian ship was now tied to a landing along the seawall close to the harbor entrance. He walked into the zinc bar again and ordered a coffee. He looked at the Frenchman and got another shrug. Knox smiled. The master of the Italian ship—the mouse—could sense the presence of the cat—a British submarine—outside the harbor.

On the third morning, Knox walked to the harbor and was rewarded with the sight of the stern of the Italian ship disappearing around the sea wall and big black plumes of smoke coming out of the stack. The ship was going to make a run for it.

Knox picked up his step and quickly marched down the harbor front, past the old British consulate offices where he and Murphy had their offices, to the French Admiralty building. He showed his identification to the guard in the lobby who already knew the American well from his frequent visits. Knox said, "Harbormaster."

"Upstairs," said the guard.

Knox hurried up four flights of stairs and walked through the glass doors into a wide glass-enclosed area that looked like a control tower at an aerodrome. He went up to the uniformed official of the port police. "Good morning."

"Good morning, Mr. Knox. What are you going to bother us with today?"

"That ship steaming out of the harbor. It's carrying phosphates to Italy. You shouldn't let it sail."

"Mr. Knox," said the official pulling out a carbon copy of a bill of lading. "The bill of lading clearly shows the ship is carrying foodstuffs for Marseilles."

Knox looked out of the window. "Sure looks like it's shaping a course for Italy."

"The bill of lading says Marseilles."

"Are you sure?"

"You doubt the bill of lading?"

"Always."

"Mr. Knox, you should worry about your cargoes, not other people's."

"Don't want there to be any violations of international law."

"Nor do we." The expression on the port policeman's face said these discussions with Knox were getting increasingly tedious.

Knox walked over to the window and looked out and watched the heavily laden ship set its course to the northeast toward Italy. "Sure looks like Genoa."

"Marseilles," said the bored official, wiping his brow with exasperation.

"Really," said Knox. He looked out at the ship as it passed the three-mile boundary line and entered the open sea. He waited and watched. Ten minutes later he saw the flash, the big plume of dirty-brown smoke from a mighty explosion rising up from the ship. Then the back of the ship broke, and the bow pointed up into the sky, the round stern heaving up into the air.

The French official came up and stood next to Knox with openmouthed astonishment and watched the ship come apart just as the muffled sound of the explosion reached the building and rattled the windows.

A siren went off outside, and men raced across the dock and down to a red fire-rescue boat to head out to the sinking ship.

Knox turned to the French policeman and said, "Looks like Genoa to me." He walked out of the office, descended the stairs, and walked back to the Hotel Aletti to get dressed for work.

Rue Michelet

John Knox walked into the little bistro across the street from the American consulate in his shirtsleeves and wearing his trademark butterfly tie. At the bar he ordered a vin rosé and said good morning to various regulars crowded along the bar taking a morning drink before a day's work. At this end of the bar, English was spoken; at the other end, Arabic where employees of the streetcar lines gathered. All were gossiping about the day's events.

Knox looked up at the ever-present portrait of Maréchal Pétain on the wall, winked, tossed back his rosé, and then turned and departed. He walked across the street and into the American consulate to check in with Joan before going down to the waterfront where he and Murphy maintained offices. Inside he waved at the receptionist and went into a small office down the hall where Joan was sifting through visa applications.

"Good morning," said John with a glint in his eye.

"You look like you swallowed the canary," she said, tossing her blond hair and letting her blue eyes sparkle.

"Your message got through."

"It did? How do you know?"

"The proof is in the pudding."

Joan looked at him quizzically.

"The Italian ship with the phosphates was torpedoed in international waters just outside the harbor at daybreak this morning. Trying to make a run for it to Italy."

"We did something!"

"You bet. I'll meet you here tonight, and we'll go out to dinner."

She looked at him. "I'd like that."

"I better head to work," he said as he looked around furtively, "before someone puts me to work processing visa applications."

Café de Paris

John Knox met Joan outside the consulate, and they walked across Rue Michelet and up the street to the shaded outside *terrasse* of the Café de Paris and took chairs at a table overlooking the broad avenue, one of the most beautiful in this jewel of a city of the French Empire.

"A perfect setting," said John as he whispered an order to the waiter who returned with a bottle of champagne, an ice bucket, and two flutes. The waiter opened the bottle and poured the flutes full, the bubbles making columns in the tall, narrow glasses.

"Our partnership's first success," said John, lifting up his glass and clinking with Joan.

"Yes," she said. "The message got through."

"Your network..."

Joan hurriedly put up her hand. "Say no more."

"Got it," said John.

"The effort paid off," said Joan, giving silent thanks to Rygor and the network of Polish agents working underground in Algiers. She relaxed.

"Now," said John, looking directly at Joan, "to our relationship."

"Us?"

"Us," said John resolutely. "This is more than about sinking some ships; it's about launching our relationship."

Just then Joan looked at the sharply suited man walking across the terrasse toward them. "Captain Achiary of the political police is walking over."

Achiary came up to the table and stopped. He looked at John and then at Joan.

"John," said Joan, "I'd like you to meet Captain André Achiary of the political police."

John stood up and held out his hand. "I've heard a lot about you."

"Well, yes," said Achiary making a bow with his head, "and this afternoon I've been hearing more about you than I care. My good friend Theodor Auer has been on to me from Casablanca by telephone."

"Diplomatic, I presume," said John.

"Quite so. He says that he understands your mission to supervise the cargoes under the Weygand-Murphy agreement."

"Good."

"But with regard to cargoes, he is concerned that you are even more interested in sinking his."

"No, I was simply concerned about the bills of lading being properly completed. Bureaucratic correctness."

"Yes, well, sometimes all details are not exactly correct. My Auer is influential in Vichy, and I would not like for Vichy's concerns to disturb our many well-worked-out arrangements here in Algiers."

"Sometimes war brings difficulties."

"That is why we try to keep the war and its troubles away from the sunny shores of Algiers." Achiary smiled. "Could I suggest more discretion in your activities."

"We will," said Joan, interrupting and making her statement with great earnestness.

"Ah, champagne," said Achiary. "You are celebrating something?"

"Yes," said John. "Our new relationship."

"May I be the first to congratulate you," said Achiary, making a small bow from the waist. "A match made in heaven," and he paused and smiled, "or on the devil's own chessboard." He made a beatific smile and turned and departed.

John sat back down. "Doesn't seem so bad a chap."

"He's not," said Joan. "Are you serious about our new relationship?"

"Totally," he said. He reached across the table and held both her hands. "Tonight?"

"Mother is going to give the boys breakfast."

"Good." He squeezed her hands.

"And Gerry…"

"I sincerely hope he makes it back. You know that."

"I know," she said, a tear rolling down her cheek. "But I might not let you go."

"Some fortune-teller far down the road will turn that card."

John refilled the flutes, and they lifted them in salute. "To us."

Joan felt that she had come alive under the spell of this fascinating man's love.

Chapter 36: The Winter Palace

Mid-November 1941. Jacques Lemaigre Dubreuil followed Marie Rambert up the stairs of the Winter Palace to the office of General Weygand. She held her hand out, and he walked through the door. She closed the door and went back to her desk.

Inside, General Weygand stood to greet his visitor. "Please sit down."

Dubreuil sat down.

"What can I do for you?" asked Weygand.

"The time for action may be now," said Dubreuil.

"This is hardly the time for any action," said Weygand contradicting him.

"The current policy by Vichy of collaborating with Germany assumes a German victory," countered Dubreuil. "Collaboration is a necessary policy only if the Germans win."

"Well, for now doing nothing is the right policy for North Africa," countered Weygand. "And it will continue to be the right policy as long as Germany has the ability to invade North Africa."

"But the Vichy policy is now linked to a terrible political mistake. The Germans are going to lose," argued Dubreuil.

"Yes, you and I know that, but that hardly changes the present," said the general.

"There is an opportunity. It may be time to try to broker a settlement between Britain and Germany," insisted Dubreuil, "thereby winning the peace through diplomacy and restoring France's position as a great power."

"I am hardly a foreign minister," said Weygand standing up, signaling an end to the interview. "I appreciate the sincerity of your interest in France, M. Dubreuil."

"Thank you," said Dubreuil as he stood up and walked toward the office door.

"We must remain loyal to the Maréchal," said Weygand. "He is our best hope."

Dubreuil nodded in halfhearted agreement. "For now," he mumbled.

Marie came up and escorted Dubreuil down the stairs and out of the building.

Vichy, France

Saturday, November 16, 1941. In the cold sunlight, the soldiers fired their blank shots into the gray wintry sky, a final salute to General Léon Huntziger, the Vichy defense minister who had been killed in a recent airplane crash. The tricolor-draped casket was lowered into the grave. The German ambassador, Otto Abetz, and his aide, General Vogl, stood in silent respect. They had just arrived from Paris. At the head of the grave stood Maréchal Philippe Pétain and Admiral François Darlan. Afterward the men returned to the finely appointed Hotel du Parc in the spa town of Vichy and met in a conference room.

"Our agenda from last May's Protocols of Paris is stalled," said Abetz with some vehemence.

Maréchal Pétain watched with stony silence and looked toward Admiral Darlan, the deputy premier and effective head of government, for a reply.

"We need to see some prospects of a more generous peace from Germany that we can show to the French people," said Darlan.

"That can only come after the defeat of the Allies," replied Abetz.

Pétain moved to speak. "Dear ambassador, we have done much already against England, and I am prepared to acknowledge Hitler publicly as the leader of Europe."

Darlan quickly followed. "Let me reintroduce you to all the things we have done against England." General Vogl was amazed at the depth and intensity of Darlan's hatred for the British. The general was a careful student of the Vichy French and their shifting loyalties. Darlan finished by saying that possibly a joint French-German action against British African colonies could be mounted.

"And Weygand?" asked Abetz. Weygand was the true purpose of his trip to Vichy; Berlin despised the French general.

"We will remove him," said Darlan, who considered Weygand a rival, not an ally. Pétain sat in silence.

"He's been talking to the Americans. We know that," said Abetz. "So, Monsieur le Admiral, the question becomes when?"

"Soon," replied Darlan.

"Not good enough. If he is not removed now, I can't guarantee food supplies for the civil population in France this winter," said Abetz, his dark threat infused with a sense of menace.

"We will recall the general to Vichy Monday morning," said Darlan. Pétain sat silent. Weygand was now beyond his protection, the Maréchal understood.

"Good," said Abetz. "When that is completed, we can move on to other items on the agenda."

The four men stood up, and Abetz turned and headed for the door followed by General Vogl.

Return to Paris

As the long black Mercedes sped up the deserted roads of central France toward Paris, General Vogl turned to Abetz and said, "The one constant with the Vichy French is their implacable hatred of the British."

"Yes, General," replied Abetz, "but if it were just the British, we would have won the war long ago. It is the Americans who are our adversaries in Vichy. All those vice-consuls in North Africa are there for a reason."

Weygand Recall

Monday, November 18, 1941. Jacques walked into the American consulate, and Joan Tuyl hurried up to him and said, "I got a call from the Winter Palace, and a male voice said that there was an urgent supply problem and that Madame Rambert is waiting for you in the upstairs office."

"Anything else?" asked Jacques.

"They also wanted Mr. Murphy, but he's out at an undisclosed appointment and can't be reached. He'll be back later this morning."

"Understand," said Jacques as he quickly ran through the events that created this call for help. The rumors circulating in Vichy about General Weygand's recall must be true.

"I'll head right over."

The taxi dropped Jacques off at the entrance to the courtyard, and Jacques checked in with the guard. Waved through, he walked across the courtyard, a light breeze ruffling the palm fronds high above him. He took the steps two at a time and hurried past the Spahi guard sharply turned out in his billowy-khaki trousers and sky-blue kepi. Marie was waiting for him in the reception area.

"Upstairs," she said and turned and started up the narrow staircase leading to the suite of offices serving the delegate general. Jacques followed, and at the top she said, "Over here." They walked over to a large closed door, and she knocked. A voice said come in. They entered.

Jacques saw General Weygand standing behind his desk while his aide-de-camp stood nearby. The general motioned them into vacant chairs. They sat down.

"I have been recalled to Vichy," said the general. "I leave this afternoon."

"We're sorry to hear that," said Jacques. "Why now?"

"The Nazis threaten to occupy all of France and let the French population starve by letting the German army plunder the land," said the general.

Undoubtedly to feed their armies in Russia, thought Jacques.

"The order is signed by Maréchal Pétain," said the general. "He would only do that under enormous pressure."

"Yes, that's what our embassy believes," said Jacques.

The general picked up an envelope and gave it to Jacques, who reached forward and took it. "Please give this to Mr. Murphy. It's my political testament, and I intend to read it to Maréchal Pétain."

"I'll take special care," said Jacques.

"In the memorandum, I explain that I came to Africa at a time when Britain had established it could withstand the German air attacks. This greatly increased the strategic value of French Africa, the only part of Europe not under direct Axis control. Then in early 1941, we signed the economic accord with the United States. That further increased the strategic value of French Africa, giving the French government at least one trump card in the general diplomatic game." The general stopped and looked directly at Jacques and Marie.

"You and Marie have been assiduous in your efforts to advance this vital effort."

"Thank you," said Jacques.

"Monsieur," said Marie softly.

"Despite opposition from the British and the Germans, the accord has conferred an important advantage on France as events have evolved during 1941. France, particularly in Africa, is stronger at every point. And we have maintained a cordial relationship with the United States."

"Yes," said Jacques.

"I did this for France. Opening Africa to Germany would mean in the last analysis giving Germany a unique opportunity to continue the war for ten years and to impose its will on France without possibility of reaction."

Again, looking directly at Jacques and Marie, the general said, "Continue I beg of you to favor the supply program. Nothing has changed. The collaboration in Africa does not depend upon one man but rather on the vast organization that has been created since 1940."

"I will stress each and every point to Mr. Murphy," said Jacques.

The general stood up. "It's time to depart for the aerodrome." He moved around the desk and shook Jacques's hand and then embraced Marie and kissed her on each cheek. "You have been steadfast for France," said the general, looking at her as he held her by the shoulders. "Keep to your duty." He turned and headed for the door followed by his two aides. Jacques and Marie followed.

At the base of the stairs, the general stopped as Robert Murphy hurried across the tile floors, explaining, "The consulate just informed me."

"Thank you for coming," said the general. "Your aide Jacques has my written memorandum for you. I want to stress that what you and I have accomplished this past year does not depend upon just one man. You must continue the work we have started."

"I agree completely," said Murphy.

"Please ensure your government understands that," said the general.

"There is complete understanding at the top," said Murphy.

"As there is in my government. Maréchal Pétain understands the importance of what we have done. It is others that lack understanding."

Chapter 37: Family Dinner

Late November 1941. The taxi climbed the narrow twisting streets of one of the wealthy suburbs nestled in the western hills overlooking the city of Algiers. The taxi carrying Jacques was heading toward the villa owned by Marie Rambert's family. Jacques knew they were wealthy *grand colons* whose prominence came from agricultural interests stretching across Algeria. A thriving export business down in the port was doing a roaring business. Boatloads of agricultural products had been leaving Algiers daily for Marseilles since midyear to feed the voracious German war economy in its march into Russia. Money was flowing back into the bank branches of Algiers with every returning ship. In an occupation devastating to most of the French on the mainland, some in North Africa were doing quite well.

He had been a little surprised last Wednesday afternoon when Madame Sauveterre had invited him to Sunday dinner. He had been attending weekly piano jazz performances put on by Marie's younger sister Madeleine in the lounge at the officers' club for the past month. Madeleine had studied piano at a conservatory in Paris until the Germans overran the city in June 1940. She had eventually made her way back to Algiers that summer. She had picked up a taste for jazz while in Paris in addition to her classical training.

The taxi came up to a spacious villa situated on a beautiful lawn with tall narrow palm trees bordering the property. The taxi pulled into the drive. Jacques got out and paid the driver. The taxi turned around and gingerly poked its way back down the steep twisting lane. Jacques walked over through an open portico and up to a large Moorish wooden door. He rapped the brass knocker several times, and a maid in a black dress and white pinafore opened the door. "This way, monsieur."

Jacques walked in and handed the maid his hat and scarf. He looked at the wall of the foyer where a large picture of Maréchal Pétain stared straight at him. Above the portrait hung a finely carved crucifixion in dark wood. A small light shined down from above. *The two agonies*, thought Jacques. The twin deities were found in all the houses of the *colons* of French Africa, like good-luck charms to ward off evil tidings from a distant and evil war.

Marie stood waiting to greet him. Today, her thick dark hair shined luminously in the light. She wore a simple black dress with a red rose pinned above the soft turn of her left breast. She was lightly made up, and Jacques thought he had never seen her so beautiful. At the Winter Palace, she always presented a professionally restrained demeanor consistent with working for the highest governing officials in Algeria.

"Bonjour, Marie," he said to the hostess as he took off his overcoat and handed it to the maid. "How are you today?"

"Fine," she said. "This way. The family is in the drawing room."

Jacques followed Marie into the drawing room. As they entered, Marie's father and mother stood up, and her sister Madeleine turned from the piano where she was playing and smiled.

"Nice to see you again, Jacques," said the father as he walked over and shook Jacques's hand.

"You, too, Monsieur Sauveterre," said Jacques. He turned and handed a small gift to Madame Sauveterre. "Madame, once again you present the elegance of your family."

"How gallant. Thank you, Jacques."

Jacques turned to Marie's younger sister and said, "You're playing that classical piece quite well, Madeleine." Monsieur Sauveterre walked around the room pouring thick red wine in everyone's glass.

"Thank you, Jacques. I learned that during the day at the conservatory," she said. "And in the evening..." She strummed the keys and a riff of jazz music floated into the room.

"Is that a hint, Madeleine?" asked Jacques.

"I just thought maybe you had something fresh from the States for me," she said. "The diplomatic pouch was in Friday, I heard."

Jacques reached into his jacket pocket and pulled out a folded piece of sheet music. "Here's a jazz score—I'll play it for you in a moment—but I have something even better," he said and opened his satchel and pulled out a couple of new jazz records, big shiny-black seventy-eights in brown-paper sleeves, and handed them over.

Madeleine jumped up and took the records over to a gramophone and put one on the turntable. Soon swing music from Artie Shaw filled the room.

"Oh, *Begin the Beguine*," she said with enthusiasm. "It will be such a hit down at the officers' club. They hear it on the radio from London, but no one has it here in Algiers." She returned and sat down at the piano. She quickly captured on the keyboard the tune she heard coming from the gramophone.

"You're quick, Madeleine. Let me sit down, and I'll show you some other tunes from my repertoire."

"Would you?" said Madeleine enthusiastically.

Jacques sat down next to Madeleine and put his hands up on the keyboard and then let his fingers smoothly glide over the keyboard. He played one of the smooth melodies of one of the more avant-garde pieces he'd picked up in New York.

"Where'd you learn these?" asked Madeleine.

"In the jazz clubs lining fifty-eighth Street in New York. That was back when I was working for the Anglo-French Purchasing Mission before someone decided I'd make a nice clerk in Algiers."

Marie came over and stood by the piano and watched Jacques's hands move up and down the keyboard.

Madeleine quickly picked up the tune and repeated it on the keyboard. "How's that?" she asked.

"You have the gift."

"I'll have a lot of new songs to play this week," said Madeleine as she and Jacques stood up.

"Yes," said Madame Sauveterre agreeably. Turning to Jacques, she added, "She's been like a caged bird here in Algiers since coming back from Paris."

"So the caged bird gets set loose to play at the officers' club at the Hotel St. Georges," said Madeleine gaily. The hotel was a stately presence on a hill overlooking Algiers where the naval command was elegantly ensconced. "I go up the hill right after my ambulance training at the Red Cross on Tuesdays and Thursdays."

"Ambulance training?" asked Jacques.

"Yes, I'm learning how to drive an ambulance."

"Well, let's hope you don't ever need to serve in a real war," said Jacques. "What are the times of your performances?"

"Teatime," said Madeleine. "I'm not trusted down there in the evenings."

"Of course not—they're all French officers," said Marie, and she winked at her mother, "at least until you're engaged. Too often, the officers like to pick the flowers before they're properly put in the vase."

"You make it sound like taking the veil," said Madeleine. "Paris wasn't like that—at all."

"Well, yes. But that's over," replied Marie. She turned reflective and said, "Adult relationships involve adult commitments—there are vows involved. Those young officers interested in you are hardly looking for commitment."

"Even if they were, I might not be interested in them," said Madeleine with some heat. "I'm not signing up for a husband not of my choosing…just for respectability's sake."

"We were talking about music," said Jacques, verbally stepping between the two sparring sisters.

Madeleine's expression relaxed. "Yes, I do like to play jazz, Jacques. It's so much more fun with an audience. I appreciate everything you share with me."

"Now she's trying to sweep Jacques off his feet," said Marie with a laugh.

"I would never interfere with my sister's interests," said Madeleine tartly.

"He's here as a guest of our entire family," corrected Marie, putting on a severe expression. Madeleine looked at her with sisterly disbelief.

"I'm so pleased to hear that, Madeleine," said Jacques quickly, again interjecting himself between the two sisters. He explained to Madeleine. "Marie has always been one of the most reliable of friends I have here in Algiers." He looked at Marie sympathetically. "Everyone else thinks I'm a diplomat able to do magic favors…or that I am up to nefarious deeds…"

"Like spying on the Germans," said Madeleine, suddenly letting an eager look spread across her face.

"No, I'm afraid not," said Jacques. "Not that it stops them from spying on little lowly me."

"The Germans?" asked Madeleine, thrilled that she knew someone deserving of this special attention.

"Yes, and the Italians and the French," said Jacques.

"Why?"

"I'm not sure. America's not in the war."

"Yet," said Marie pointedly. "The Germans are not so sure about that. They've read about the Roosevelt-Churchill meeting on the battleships in August."

"But entrance into the war may be a long time coming," said Jacques. "The political resistance in America is intense."

"Yes, Frau von Koler made that point last August at that lunch with your friend Jacqueline."

"Well, Jacqueline was just in from London…so she sees things the British way."

"And she is now where?" asked Marie.

Jacques detected a touch of jealous concern and was secretly pleased. "Back in London…leastwise from what I read in the *New York Times Tribune*." Jacques shrugged his shoulders. "Jacqueline and I were great friends in New York. But now our paths have diverged. She's embarked on a completely different arc of life from what we had in New York. Then, we were really just two kids starting out."

"Well, she seemed to enjoy being in the middle of the war—or at least in the middle of all the important men running it," said Marie. Her voice dropped, and she added, "I hope it passes us by here in Algiers."

"We all do," said Jacques. "But it is unlikely to play out that way."

Monsieur Sauveterre interrupted and said, "We don't want to talk about the war today. The recall of General Weygand is almost more than our minds can bear."

"Yes, I agree," said Madame Sauveterre. "We all must trust that the Maréchal will keep the war away from our shores." She muttered about the British and the Gaullists.

"Now a dreadful uncertainty sets in. Like the chaotic feebleness of the Third Republic," said Monsieur Sauveterre. His face took on a look of disgust as he remembered the last French government and its collapse in defeat. For Monsieur Sauveterre and the other *grands colons*, the military command in Africa had become the incarnation of the spirit of the Maréchal, the living hope that loyalty to the aged Maréchal would see France through the shoals of this cruelest of new wars.

"Yes, we all await to see what happens," said Marie. She looked at her father with sympathetic understanding. The hard-fought victory of the Great War when he had been young had turned to ashes in the 1940 defeat.

The maid came to the entrance and announced that dinner was ready. The group filed into the long dining room. Monsieur Sauveterre pointed Jacques to a chair next to him, and Marie took the chair next to Jacques. Madeleine sat across; Madame Sauveterre at the other end.

Monsieur Sauveterre bowed his head and recited a short prayer, finishing up with "and for those not with us today."

Jacques understood. A reference to Marie's husband, Henri Rambert, serving at Armistice Commission in Germany.

Madame Sauveterre looked at her eldest daughter with some concern; she did not understand her daughter's relationship with her husband. She had of course heard rumors…always about him…never about her, thank God. They were good Catholics. Scandals with husbands were a commonplace in France, but with a daughter…mortifying.

Jacques watched Madame Sauveterre's face cloud over at the allusion to her daughter's absent husband and guessed at her concerns.

They continued chatting about Algiers through the dinner. After dessert, the maid came in and poured black coffee, a drink still easily obtained in Algiers.

Coffee

Jacques looked at Marie over his coffee cup. "Maybe we could drink it outside on the terrace in the garden?"

"Yes, I would like that," replied Marie, wanting to engage further this man she found so compellingly fascinating. She had looked forward to this dinner for days, a tingle in her expectation that surprised and pleased her. She turned to her parents and sister. "Please excuse us."

All warmly agreed, and Jacques and Marie stood up and walked outside and through a spacious walled garden to a small patio up on the hill. It was pleasant outside, and the two of them stood sipping their coffee and looking out across the harbor to the dark-blue sea beyond, a golden glow of the late-afternoon sun on the hills surrounding Algiers.

"Your sister is right, Marie," said Jacques, breaking the silence. "You do interest me."

"But I'm a married woman," said Marie, and she looked off across the distance, down at the harbor and then out over the dark-indigo sea beyond. Well-traveled friends told her it was one of the most beautiful views in the world.

"Or a grass widow," said Jacques.

"I don't know," she said, suddenly giving in. "Henri and I grew apart…even before the war."

"You can't let the past trap your future."

"Past? It's a marriage. There are obligations…before God…in a church…"

"To keep living…that is the only answer as the tragedies of war sweep through life."

"And the vows…"

"I would never stand before a woman and her vows…but vows end sometimes…"

"When? How?" she asked with the pained anguish of a woman who was missing the other half of her marital relationship. But Jacques had long ago concluded that for Marie it had been an incomplete relationship, not one that a young woman would welcome. He sensed the missing emotional bond. There was an empty space in her life.

"Sometimes commitments get left to languish…by distance if nothing else…wars do that," said Jacques sympathetically. Henri Rambert had been absent on his diplomatic duties for a long time.

"Do you tell all the waiting wives that?" she asked, an icy disdain rising in her voice. Jacques had a certain reputation, and she knew he had not just been studying economics in New York. Jacqueline's visit to Algiers in August proved that. But Marie's eyes betrayed her; they were sparkling with expectation.

"There weren't many waiting wives in American when I left."

"There will be," said Marie, and her face fell, bleakness engulfing her expression. "You can feel the war approach America…just like last time."

"I know…"

"Yes, the waiting women, another the unspoken casualty of war…"

"Of our times."

She turned and stood facing him, holding her cup in front of her, prim and insistent. "Yes, possibly it's over…if it ever truly began…sometimes I wish he would just tell me…for sure…but a little part of me…" He could sense that her marriage was a dark cloud on her horizon.

Jacques stood silent.

"And you?" she asked, a questioning tone now animating her presence. She looked at him directly.

"I'm here."

"Any assurances from you that I won't be…how do you say…be widowed a second time?" she asked as she raised an ironical eyebrow.

"Your family," he said and nodded toward the house, "is like my family…maybe having a Sunday dinner just like this…"

"In America? Like your dead French father and American mother?"

"No," said Jacques, his face flushed with momentary confusion; he had briefly forgotten his cover identity about a dead French father and a live American mother and let his memory flashed back to his actual parents—both resolutely French—living somewhere in Occupied France. "Somewhere else…together…" He smiled at her. "Sometimes I get the story backward…"

"Yes, no one in Algiers believes you are who you say you are. Should I?"

"But there is a great truth behind it…I am like you…"

"Like me…standing in the winter sun contemplating the breaking of vows?"

"No, not like that at all."

She stood there looking at him. "I do want to believe you," she said with a long sigh.

"Good," he said, taking charge of the conversation. "Maybe we can go together to next Sunday night's dinner at the Hotel Aletti. Have some fun?"

"Dinner at the Aletti?"

"Yes, the staff at the consulate is getting together. A lot of the vice-consuls from the other consulates are in Algiers sharing notes. We could enjoy ourselves together among friendly faces."

She looked at him, a conflicted expression on her face. "It might confirm more of a relationship between us than people might think proper?"

"I would like to deepen that relationship, at least privately. Proper or not."

"But going together? That would be a public confirmation. They all think there's something between us already...Frau von Koler winks at me when she mentions your name. They don't believe you're been just taking one of the general's secretaries out to lunch to spy on troop strength."

"They also know you would never tell me anything secret," he reassured.

"That's worse," she said. "They will assume there's something else."

"Well, going to a party at the Hotel Aletti is neither one nor the other."

"Let me think about it."

"Okay."

"I have a duty of discretion to my position," said Marie, coming back with another consideration.

"Everyone knows I already see the officials at the Winter Palace frequently. My job is to stay in touch with them," said Jacques. "And then there's the matter of the supplies."

"Yes. I have been asked to help you compile a list of civilian supplies for the native population. Nevertheless, half the headquarters now thinks I'm some sort of a spy," said Marie.

"The civilian supplies are real. It's genuine diplomatic business."

"Yes, first the supplies—the camel's nose in the tent—and then all the French think that someday the Americans will come and save us."

"The Americans probably will…someday…until that day comes we watch and talk…so I appreciate being able to speak with the necessary officials."

"Yes, I understand. But now they're all Admiral Darlan's men," said Marie. That had not always been true, leastwise before the most recent shakeup.

"Some of the generals are more open."

"But not really relevant. Admiral Darlan is the number-two man in Vichy."

"Yes," said Jacques with a sigh. "He is the premier who holds all the civil and military power in Vichy…"

"Yes, on behalf of the aged Maréchal…the Maréchal is now more spirit than substance…a face staring out of ten thousand portraits across France," said Marie with a sad fall in her voice.

"I have to communicate with whoever has position," said Jacques.

"I sometimes wonder what it is you—and all the other visitors—really want to know when you visit the Winter Palace?" asked Marie. "I've never asked anyone what all the maneuvering is about…all the big secrets at the Winter Palace are hidden from me; they're whispered secrets kept behind closed doors."

"Well, for the American diplomats, to start with, they want to know what trade-offs Darlan is making to keep the Germans at bay?" said Jacques. "Can he keep the Germans out of French North Africa?"

Marie nodded in understanding. "I understand keeping the Germans out." Then she added, "There's more…isn't there?"

"Yes, a lot of people think Darlan can eventually be induced to switch sides. But only when the time is ripe."

"Switch sides?" asked Marie, consternation spreading across her face. "Admiral Darlan hates the British. He'd never side with them…not after Mers-el-Kébir," she said. "Most people here think it is the Armistice that keeps the Germans away from our shores. Surely not the British and Gaullists meddling in our affairs. No French leader would plunge France back into the war lightly."

"But almost all the French will be willing to switch over to the Americans—someday."

"Someday. But only if you can protect us from the Germans," Marie countered. "Otherwise we'd wind up like Poland...or worse...there's two million French soldiers in German POW camps...you can't put two million men's lives to risk."

"No, but when the time comes..."

"So, we all watch the admirals and wait," said Marie.

"Speaking of the admirals," said Jacques lightly, "you know what they say about the French admirals?"

"No, tell me," she replied.

"They can be found everywhere but at sea." The two of them laughed at the joke, a riposte to the bitter politics of Vichy and the French fleet mostly rusting away at its moorings in Toulon and the harbors of Africa.

"We can watch together."

"Watching doesn't mean I know anything," said Marie. "The inner sanctums of the Winter Palace don't confide in me." She looked at Jacques with a softened expression. "I'll try to open the doors you want."

"You never know," said Jacques. "Someday one of those open doors will lead to something better."

"I hope so," said Marie with a sigh.

"While we wait..."

"Yes, Mata Hari understands."

"Understands what?"

"A rendezvous at Hotel Aletti next Sunday night...a first step in the descent into La Boheme."

"It's a dinner, not a rendezvous."

"It isn't?"

"Come on. We'll have a good time. The vice-consuls are a boisterous group. I'll see you home at a proper hour."

She let that assurance go by, somewhat untested, he thought to his surprise.

"Your apartment is nearby, isn't it?" she asked.

"Yes," replied Jacques.

"I'll have my father's driver drop me off."

"Drop you off? At my apartment?"

"Yes, see how the bachelor diplomat lives."

"Okay." He shrugged.

"What time?" she asked, her eyes brightening.

"Oh, eight or so," he said.

She stood a little straighter and turned and looked Jacques straight in the eye. "Yes, I'd love to go to the party at the Aletti with you."

"I would, too," he said. He felt a movement in their relationship.

She caught the sincerity in his voice and looked off into the distance, the deep indigo of the sea beyond the harbor holding her attention. She reached out and took his hand in hers and squeezed it. She kept hold of his hand and turned and guided them down the path back to the house. They walked hand in hand in the falling light of dusk.

"Yes," she murmured to herself. There was a lightness in her step.

Jacques looked at her. He was more than pleased with acceptance of his invitation. Notwithstanding her husband in Germany—a spectral presence that he felt might never come back into her life—he sensed that Marie was the partner with whom to face the coming storm, a storm he was sure in coming. When the tempest sets loose its fury, the right person becomes a transcendental question. He looked forward to the following Sunday with keen expectation. Sometimes destiny is a crooked road, he thought.

Murphy Responds

The official French limousine from the Winter Palace pulled up in front of the former British consulate where Robert Murphy and the merchandise control officers maintained offices. The driver opened the rear door, and Marie Rambert alighted and walked in and spoke to Simone Hardy, Murphy's longtime secretary. "I need to see Mr. Murphy."

Hardy stood up and said, "This way." She led Marie down the hall to a spacious office where Murphy was busy with papers.

"Good morning," said Murphy standing up, somewhat surprised. "What can I do for you this morning?" He pointed to a chair, and Marie sat down.

"I have been asked to deliver this message," said Marie gravely. She reached into her handbag and pulled out an envelope and slid it across the desk to Murphy.

Murphy took the envelope and opened and read the handwritten message from General Weygand.

Continue I beg of you to favor the supply program. As the Maréchal told Admiral Leahy, nothing is changed in French policy by my departure. My messenger will tell you how much I count on the maintenance between our two countries of the union necessary for the near future of the world.

He looked at Marie and asked, "Do you know its contents?"

"Word for word," replied Marie. "I memorized it in case something happened to the document."

"Yes, I will forward it directly to the State Department."

"Thank you."

"I can see the general reposed a high level of trust in you. Let's chat a few moments so I can get some sense about the changes going on in the Winter Palace."

Marie spoke about Admiral Fenard taking General Weygand's place. "He occupies the same suite of offices, and everything looks the same. But he has no military command."

"A figurehead?"

"He's Admiral Darlan's man. That's something different."

"Yes, Darlan now holds the military commands—all of them—at Vichy," said Murphy thoughtfully.

"You would understand that better than me," replied Marie modestly.

Murphy smiled. The two continued to talk about changes in the Winter Palace. Then Marie departed.

Murphy pulled over a pad of paper and headed it "For the Eyes of Undersecretary Welles Only." It was time to appeal directly to the man in the White House about the urgency of preserving the Murphy-Weygand Pact. Too many little people were stepping on the big plan.

Chapter 38: Committee of Five

Early December 1941. The car wound its way up the roadway in the dark toward the villas of El Biar high above Algiers and then swung through the open gate and up the tree-lined carriageway to the villa Dar Mahieddine. The car pulled into a dark space under some trees. Three men got out of the car and walked over to the door and knocked. A maid opened the door and said, "They're in the library."

The men walked through the foyer and across the drawing room to the library. Inside, Jacques Lemaigre Dubreuil and his aide Jean Rigault stood up. The five men shook hands all around. "Have a seat," said Dubreuil, "and let me get right to the heart of the matter."

The men sat down.

"We have a post-Weygand problem; let's call it the high-command problem," said Dubreuil. "There's no French leader with the prestige and Africa-wide authority to lead French Africa into the Allied camp."

"No indispensable man, no white horse," added Rigault, a gifted journalist and propagandist.

"But there may be an indispensable man in German detention who if he could escape…Captain Beaufre is on the mainland, and he assures me he is working this angle," added Dubreuil. "The general's name must remain secret; its revelation would be a death sentence."

"Ah, a white horse at least," said Rigault. The men all laughed.

"So our goal—and by that I mean us, the Committee of Five—must be to keep our first goal of the liberation of French Africa clearly in mind," said Dubreuil.

"What is the next step?" asked Colonel Jean Van Hecke.

"I am going to meet with the American diplomat Murphy Friday night here at Dar Mahieddine," said Dubreuil.

"What are you going to offer him?" asked Jacques Tarbé, a French career diplomat and assistant secretary-general in what

292

had been Weygand's Winter Palace. He had understood Murphy and his supply accord with Africa. What the Americans had wanted in return had always remained opaque.

"A provisional government in North Africa with immediate recognition by the United States government," replied Dubreuil.

"That will bring the German army right in," said Lieutenant Henri d'Astier de la Vigerie.

"That is why the Americans must immediately send three divisions to North Africa and at least four warships to Bizerte to keep the Germans and Italians out of Tunisia," countered Dubreuil with the crispness of a general staff officer. He turned to Tarbé and asked, "You worked with Murphy on the Murphy-Weygand agreement. What do you think?"

"The Americans are neutral. Murphy will never go beyond his instructions. So for now expect a tepid response," answered Tarbé. "But longer term you are planting a seed that may bear fruit."

"Good enough," concluded Dubreuil. He turned to Lieutenant d'Astier. "Will we have support in Oran?"

"Some," said the young lieutenant. "There is a social group of mainland French, some of whom are pro-Allies, among whom the American vice-consuls circulate socially. I have a source who helps out two afternoons a week in their consular office in the Grand Hotel, a married woman above suspicion who has taken a fancy to one of the Americans." D'Astier smirked. "The office is between the consuls' bedrooms." The men all laughed.

"Ingrid, my source, tells me that the two Americans have pouched to Washington complete details and maps of all French military units and installations around Oran."

"Yes, the Americans will know how to get here when the time comes," added Colonel Hecke.

"Okay, what you're telling me is that an immediate landing by three American divisions could be done," said Dubreuil. "The intelligence groundwork is complete. That will be good to know when I speak with Murphy." Dubreuil smiled at the results of the meeting. "Our group should be at the center of a new provisional government...possibly with our own general at its head."

Algiers Waterfront

The touring car descended Rue Michelet and went past the Hotel Aletti and turned along the quay. The chauffeur pulled over about a block away from a large white steamship tied to the quay. Madame Sauveterre spoke to the chauffer. "This will be fine, Pierre. Please wait here. We shan't be long." The chauffer got out and walked around and opened the door, and Madame Sauveterre, Madeleine, and Marie slid out and stood on the street, straightening dresses and squaring their hats.

"Quite a crowd today," said Madame Sauveterre. "Remarkable. Many of them are Moslem."

"Yes, the people of Algiers hold Madame Weygand in high regard for her Red Cross work for all the people of Algiers," said Marie.

"It's a shame she has to go back to the mainland," added Madeleine.

"Vichy trusts no Weygand in Algeria," said Marie with a laugh.

The chauffeur handed each of the ladies a large bouquet of flowers from the rear boot.

"Let's be off," said Madame Sauveterre, nodding toward the large crowd of women gathered on the quay below the steamship A canvas-lined gangway led from the quay up to the promenade deck where white-suited merchant marine officers stood waiting. An official limousine pulled up with French flags flying from the front fenders.

A large crowd of women started to clap and cheer as Madame Weygand got out of the limousine. Women surged forward and threw bouquets of flowers in her path from the limousine to the gangway and on to the gangway itself. Madame Weygand walked several meters up the gangway, stopped, and turned. She waved and addressed the crowd: "Thanks so much for this marvelous sendoff. My husband, the general, will be greatly heartened by this show of goodwill." She waved and ended her speech. "Vive la France."

The crowd chanted "Vive la France" and then broke into the *Marseillaise* as Madame Weygand walked up the gangway, shook hands with the captain and his officers, and was escorted to her cabin.

Dar Mahieddine

Friday night, December 5, 1941. Robert Murphy swung his big Buick between the stone pillars leading into Dar Mahieddine and parked. He knocked on the front door, and the maid escorted him to the library where Jacques Lemaigre Dubreuil stood to receive him. The two men sat down in front of a warm fire.

"The Committee of Five has been busy," said Dubreuil as an opening remark. "We are ready to move on a plan to establish a provisional government in Africa separate and independent from Vichy."

"Whoa," said Murphy. "Let's not get ahead of ourselves here."

"What is the American policy?" asked Dubreuil.

"It is under discussion in Washington right now," replied Murphy.

"Where is it today?"

"Right now, the general policy is to assist all those who offer resistance to Axis aggression."

"With regard to Vichy?"

"Vichy is neither a resistant nor a German ally. The US is at peace with Vichy and maintains diplomatic relations."

"So your current policy?"

"To work with the existing Vichy establishment in Africa to resist German demands, to prevent any extension of Axis control in North Africa."

"So a holding game?"

"That's a fair characterization," replied Murphy.

"Longer term?"

"To prevail against Nazi Germany."

"And France's role?"

"Eventually, a large role," said Murphy. "I can't say more now. Diplomats must stay within the scope of their instructions." He stood up.

Dubreuil arose and escorted Murphy to the front door, saying as parting words, "And conspirators must dream big thoughts and think far into the future, the golden thoughts of destiny."

Murphy smiled. A good place to leave it. He walked out to his car.

Chapter 39: Party at the Hotel Aletti

Sunday, December 7, 1941. The limousine glided down the curving boulevard, descending from the heights above Algiers toward a residential district of tall apartment buildings marching up the hill from the harbor just off Rue Michelet. Marie leaned forward and said to the chauffeur, "Rue Saint Saens."

"Oui, Madame."

Marie leaned back into the plush rear seat with her hands folded on her lap and looked out of the window. She had looked forward to this evening all week. Yesterday she had laid out on her bed the black silk stockings, the black dress purchased in Paris before the war, a cream-colored silk blouse with a high collar, and the black wool Bolero jacket with the silver buttons on the front—a flash of elegance against the blackness of the overall outfit. She had a wide-brimmed black hat rakishly upswept on one side while curving down over her ear and cheek on the other—a femme fatale in the best Hollywood film star style. A narrow hatband of rainbow-colored silk clearly signaled she was not in mourning, but possibly on some other kind of adventure.

Her mother had looked at her with concern. "This does not look like the attire for a holiday party?" she said. Her expression said something was deadly serious here.

Marie's sister had looked at her with longing envy. Madeleine understood.

As she sat in the rear of the limousine, everything perfectly in place, there was that sense of tingling that had been with her all week, a feeling of fingers crawling spiderlike down her belly. She had welcomed the feeling; it was like opening one's eyes after too restful a sleep. Too much had been walled up behind a façade of rectitude for too long, she thought.

Last month when Jacques had first mentioned going to the party at the Hotel Aletti, she had been hesitant, unsure of almost everything in her once ordered world. Then the letter from Henri came from Wiesbaden saying he would not be back for the holidays. She had not expected him to return, but the tone had been curt and hurtful. She still had feelings. And then the departure of the general stood her world on its head. All had changed. Whatever the new future was, it had arrived.

Last Sunday when Jacques was over for dinner, she was rather surprised with herself how quickly she had said yes to his importuning. To go to a late evening party with a gentleman not her husband, and to contemplate not even returning home at all, was a momentous change in the manners that had ruled her life, maybe for too long she thought.

Down deep, she had also seen the unspoken question coming for a long time, a necessary conclusion to a chain of weekly luncheons to an increasingly handsome man. She had thought about her answer for a long time, often late at night with the prospect of a more intimate relationship pulling back the layers of her manners, unbarring her deeper imagination. Now the time was at hand.

The limousine turned off the avenue and threaded its way up a narrow street among the tall Belle Époque apartment buildings of a downtown residential quarter. The automobile pulled over to the curb, and the chauffeur got out and walked around and opened the rear door. "Here it is, madame. The door is on the right."

Marie stepped out onto the sidewalk. She turned around and picked up her handbag and a large wicker basket from the rear seat. "Thank you, Pierre. That will be all. I may spend the night with a friend."

She walked over and entered the apartment building and rang a bell. The concierge opened her door and came out into the entranceway. The chauffeur watched and then made a wave and started up the street. The concierge had been told to expect a lady. "The ascenseur is just over there," she said.

"Thank you."

The concierge turned on a hall light, and Marie walked over toward the small cage elevator and opened the door. "Fifth floor," said the concierge as Marie got in the elevator. The concierge closed the folding door, and Marie pushed the button marked five. Top floor.

As the elevator creaked to a stop, Marie got out and walked over to the door on the right and knocked. Jacques opened it

Paul A. Myers

wearing formal black pants with a black stripe running down the leg and a white shirtfront. "Entrez," he said warmly. Marie walked in. "What do you have here?" asked Jacques, eyeing the basket.

"Oh, some wine, some cheese, some olives, some bread. In case we get hungry later."

"Later?" he asked with a touch of puzzlement on his face.

"Yes, later," she crisply replied.

Jacques smiled and took the basket and set it on a chair; he helped Marie out of her dark fur coat and took her scarf and hat. She walked into the little drawing room as Jacques took the basket into the kitchen. She walked over to the window. "Nice view of the harbor," she said. She turned around and smiled. "I like it."

"I'm glad."

"If we could leave a little early tonight..."

"Of course," said Jacques. "No one will miss us."

"Everyone will miss us, monsieur," she said with a raised eyebrow. "Are you sure you're a spy?"

"A diplomat."

"I'm told they're the same thing."

"Not quite. But possibly I'll be able to point out some real spies tonight."

"Frau von Koler?"

"Yes, but some of her friends even more so."

"You've met them?"

"Yes, most recently at her soirée in September, the one you ducked."

"Too many of the wrong people," she said. "And I'm not sure I approve...she's something of a vamp...even for Algiers."

"Well, I've not done much more than promise Elke a drink in the Rainbow Room at Rockefeller Center in New York after the war."

"You promised?"

"I think that's a signal she wants a special arrangement with the Americans."

"Or with you," she said, suspicion in her voice. "Why?"

"She has visited America several times with her husband. He's a lawyer and visited New York on business. She likes New York."

"So you'll just buy her a drink at the Rainbow Room?"

"Yes."

299

"And your newspaper lady friend, Jacqueline? Does she get another drink, too, at the Rainbow Room?"

"She's already had hers."

"So many lady friends."

"I like women."

"Yes, one by one, I gather."

"That's how you find the right one." He smiled at her warmly. "You can come and chaperone?"

"I'm a French woman…we don't chaperone men…the futility of such an effort…"

"Well, right now in Algiers…"

"May I remind you she's quite German."

"She's my canary in the German coal mine."

"Coal mine?"

"Yes, the Germans here in Algiers are all watching what is starting to look like a German retreat from Moscow. The winter is setting in."

"They know the story of Napoleon?"

"All too well."

"And Elke?"

"She'll trade information when the time comes."

"And you, what do you trade? A little bird seed for the canary?" The eyebrow arched upward.

"Papers—visas and such—in exchange for what we want to know."

She made a deep sigh. "I so want to trust you."

"You should. I keep treaties. Very diplomatic."

She laughed, and then she looked out of the window toward the lights in the harbor where cranes were lowering agricultural produce onto ships, even on Sunday night. "When the war's over…" she said absently as if talking about a distant, unattainable dream.

"It will be some day."

She turned abruptly and faced him. "Will I be with you?"

"I want to make that happen…"

She looked at him with bright eyes. Then she reached out and put her arms around him and pulled him tight against her as she turned her face up into his. He lowered his face, and the two kissed warmly and deeply. After a while she pushed away. "We better go to the dinner…it starts at ten this evening…before…we get too involved…"

"Yes." She could see he, too, was thinking of what would come later. He walked over and got her fur coat and held it out as she put one arm and then other into the sleeves.

"Thank you." She pulled on her gloves and put on her hat and scarf. She picked up her handbag. "Ready," she said. The couple—now a couple—departed and walked through the cool evening streets to the brightly lit hotel.

Hotel Aletti

There was knock on the suite in the German occupied wing of the hotel. Theodor Auer went over and opened the door. "Oh, Major Beck. Come in."

"I am back from Berlin."

"And what are the glad tidings there?" asked Auer with weary sarcasm.

"Things are not going well on the Eastern Front."

"As I long suspected," said Auer. "The strategic masterstroke last June would have been to hit the British in Egypt and knock them out of the war."

"Hitler only has eyes for the east," said the major.

"Yes, the east," said Auer wearily. "First the horrible mud in the autumn, and now the winter."

"It's worse than that," said Beck. "It's the coldest winter on record since Napoleon's disastrous foray in 1812."

"God looks out for the Communists. That's rich," said Auer with a bitter laugh and shrugged his shoulders.

"The Americans are now supplying the Russians," said Beck. "Who would have thought the arch-capitalists would be in alliance with the Bolsheviks?"

Auer nodded wearily. "I've underestimated the Americans. They're becoming more than just a nuisance in North Africa." Auer screwed up his face as he thought about the dilemma posed by the Americans. "Nothing I can do about them now." Had the French sent him a warning by taking out Hans? He couldn't quite believe it had just been an Arab. A message to watch your step, all laid out in a puddle of blood on a sidewalk in Algiers.

Hotel Foyer

Captain Achiary left the reception desk where he had been lounging and walked over to the French couple walking through the front entrance.

"Cosette," said Achiary. "We meet again."

"Yes," replied Cosette. "At the police headquarters, I believe?"

"Yes," said Achiary, and he turned and looked directly at Hervé. "Monsieur?"

"Hervé," said the Frenchman.

"And your identification is of course perfect?" asked Achiary.

"Right you are," said Hervé.

"Are you planning on leaving Algiers soon?" asked Achiary.

"This very night. As soon as we finish dinner," said Hervé.

"I wish you a pleasant trip," said Achiary. "It was a pleasure meeting you, Cosette. Your professionalism is astonishing. We who are just provincials." He courteously turned to Hervé to bid adieu. "Monsieur."

Hervé smiled.

Achiary saluted and turned toward the entrance. As he walked out, he put the pieces together. As he had thought— probably not an Arab. He walked over to a waiting police car and got in. Algiers, always interesting.

The Casino

In the casino of the Hotel Aletti, John Knox and Joan Tuyl arrived early, and John went to the baccarat table while Joan went to the roulette wheel. John Boyd and Simone Hardy stood at the back of the room and watched. At the baccarat table, the French players backed away in anticipation of another face-off between the cool American and Prince Chigi, the handsome front man of the Armistice Commission. The croupier looked at the two men and said, "*Messieurs, encore?*"

The croupier announced grandly to the room, *"Chemin der fer."*

The croupier cut the deck and looked at John and announced, "Banker." John Knox would hold the banker position for the first round, then it wound pass to the prince. Both men pushed bundles of franc notes out on to the table.

The French men placed side bets among themselves while the French women pointed at the two men, captivated by the confrontation. Frau von Koler whispered to the German escorting her, "Boys will be boys."

The German nodded gravely and said, "It's not the prince's money."

The croupier dealt the cards from the carousel and placed them before the two men. He looked at the prince. The prince signaled for another card. The croupier slid it across with his baccarat pallet. The prince stood pat.

All eyes switched to Knox. He nodded for a card, looked at it, and stood pat. The croupier flipped the cards of the prince with his pallet. There was a murmur. Good hand. The croupier flipped the cards of Knox. The crowd gasped—better. The pile of franc notes slid over to Knox's side of the table.

The play flowed back and forth, Knox winning four to every three for the prince. The franc notes piled up in front of the American. Finally, the Italian signaled enough and with a white-toothed smiled said, "Again the American has the luck."

John Boyd turned to Simone and said, "Let's go over and watch Joan. See if she has any of John's luck tonight." They walked over to the roulette table where Joan stood counting her chips. She pushed a small stack out onto the table and said, *"vingt-sept en plein,"* or taking the last dozen, a favorite wager. Theodor Auer came up beside Joan and took an opposite bet. He placed double the number of chips on top of Joan's and gallantly said, "Madame."

"Encore, monsieur, ce soir?" asked Joan. *"Deutschland über alles?"*

"Bien sûr," said the German. Of course.

The other players stood back as the contest began, one of the French women whispering to the lady on her left, "The beauty and the beast." The lady made a small appreciative laugh.

Slowly the results went Joan's way, and the stacks of chips in front of her mounted impressively. Soon, Herr Auer put up his hands in mock surrender. "Again, the luck is with the beautiful lady."

"And not with Germany," said Joan with a barbed twist.

"My misfortune is hardly my country's," said the German diplomat.

"To French North Africa's continued peace," said John Knox coming up behind Joan and speaking to Auer.

"Yes, peace," said Auer. He hoped for it more than the American knew. The news from Berlin about the campaign in Russia taking a grave turn still rankled. A new level of anxiety had been added to his life.

John Boyd and Simone came up and said to Knox and an exceedingly pleased Joan, "Let's go into the dining room. Everyone's there." He looked at the Germans and added, "They'll be along—after they pow wow."

The Lobby

Leaving the casino, Frau von Koler walked into the hotel lobby looking for a powder room. She saw the burly Frenchman come in with the rather-stunning French lady. Koler thought she knew the woman from Rabat and Casablanca. At the time Koler had guessed she was using the young women to collect intelligence. Now, she guessed that the Frenchman with her was the cover. His bulky shape seemed familiar. Had he been the man across from her villa the night of the soirée in September? Yes, maybe, but she paused. Something else in the resemblance nagged at her. Yes, it was the two of them together. She remembered now—Paris 1938. She walked over and held out her hand to the somewhat startled Frenchman.

"Frau von Koler," she said by way of introduction. "Elke to my friends."

"Hervé," said the Frenchman and turned to his escort and introduced her: "Cosette." Koler smiled to herself—of course no last names. He wasn't going to show her his identification.

"Delighted," said Koler. She shook Cosette's hand and said, "Casablanca?"

"Perhaps," replied Cosette with a fetching smile that conveyed a well-practiced nothing.

Koler turned to Hervé. "Of course, I remember our last meeting now."

"Remember?" asked Hervé, astonishment on his face.

"Paris, December 1938. I saw you at the Hotel Crillon when Foreign Minister von Ribbentrop made his state visit to cement the understandings reached at Munich."

"Well, yes…"

"You were working at the concierge desk," said Koler. She turned and smiled at Cosette and added, "You were working at reception."

"Well, security…for the distinguished guests…"

"Security?" exclaimed Koler in loud disbelief followed by a sarcastic laugh. "The Hotel Crillon normally keeps the girls and boys out, the ones trading in paid up joy. But that night the hotel was opening up the back doors to let them in."

Hervé simply sat and looked at Koler, his eyes twinkling. Cosette smirked.

"Anyway, I have something more recent to communicate. From Berlin."

"You do?" asked Hervé, intrigued.

"Photos of Herr Auer arrived in Berlin in October. Berlin wants me to tell my French intelligence friends that this is all a wasted effort. Berlin knows all about Herr Auer. They have dossiers full of compromising photos about him from across Europe."

"So?" asked Hervé.

"In 1938," replied Koler, "Berlin knew all about Auer and the monsignor and the circle in Paris around the cardinal. That was his job."

"Yes, he pursues it with zest."

"He's well protected by Foreign Minister von Ribbentrop. Family. You should know that."

"We do," said the Frenchmen.'

"You do?" asked Koler, momentarily startled. "Which? The family or the photographs?"

"Both."

"Then why the photos here in Algiers?"

"We're just closing out the file."

"Closing out?"

"Yes, we've closed our file on Auer's scandalous doings. You may tell Herr Auer that, Frau von Koler"

"I will."

"Oh, and there is little interest in the cardinal," added the Frenchman.

"You mean for now," said Koler.

"Of course not, the German authorities will not disturb the Catholics while they're...preoccupied...with the Jews."

"No," said Koler, a touch of regret in her voice.

"A lot of people know what is going on in the east..." said Hervé in a melancholy voice.

"It's not my doing," said Koler, trying to put distance between herself and any acknowledgment of the darkest side of Nazism.

"So, no, the cardinal is not an issue," said Hervé.

Quickly seeing an opportunity to change the conversation, Koler said, "Well, you know what they say about the cardinal?" Her eyes twinkled.

"The cardinal? No?" said Hervé, caught off guard by the change in direction.

"If the cardinal gets sacked, who will Admiral Darlan pick as his replacement?"

"Admiral Darlan?" asked Cosette, puzzled at the question.

"Yes, Vichy must approve a new cardinal," said Hervé knowingly. "Nevertheless, a riddle." He looked at Koler with interest. Cosette leaned in to hear the answer.

"A vice admiral or a rear admiral?" said Koler.

Cosette roared with laughter, and Hervé guffawed.

"Enjoy your dinner," said Koler, and she turned and continued toward the ladies' room.

Dinner

A few seconds later, Jacques escorted Marie through the front doors and walked across the lobby of the Hotel Aletti to the cloakroom. The two of them checked their overcoats, scarves, and hats and then walked up to the entrance to the dining room. The maître d' escorted them over to a long table filled with boisterous Americans and several ladies including the now-radiant Joan Tuyl flush with gambling winnings and seated with her constant friend, John Knox. Jacques looked across the room and saw another long table set for dinner but for which the guests had not yet arrived.

"Where are the Germans?" asked Jacques.

"In the casino counting up their losses," chuckled Knox. "It's now the second game in Algiers they're losing at."

"Yes, one more thing for them to explain to Berlin," said Jacques.

"Enough," said Joan, and she turned to Marie. "So nice to see you, Marie. Dinner with Jacques? Is this a first?"

"She wasn't available for lunch tomorrow," said Jacques jokingly.

"Yes, and she always goes back to work after lunch," said Joan.

"Your spies tell you that?" asked Jacques.

"Gossip does," replied Joan and batted an eyelash. "But dinner? Tonight?"

"I believe we're both neutral," said Marie coolly, trying to put an end to what could become a public speculation about something deeply personal. "My family has had Jacques chez nous for Sunday dinner. He's just returning the favor."

Joan's eyes blazed with delighted understanding, and she turned to Knox and whispered in his ear. He laughed.

There was a bustle and a dozen Germans entered the dining room and went over to the far table and took seats. A couple of well-tended young women, hair still short, rounded out the cast. Now that General Weygand was gone, fraternizing with the Germans came back into fashion.

Herr Auer caught Jacques's attention from across the room, and he raised his champagne glass and said, "*Salut.*"

Jacques lifted his glass in return and said, "Salut."

"Friends?" asked Knox, looking at Jacques accusingly.

"Mr. Murphy and Herr Auer are on good terms going back to their days when they were both diplomats in Paris in the 1930s," replied Jacques.

"Nevertheless, friends? Fraternizing with the enemy?" asked John Boyd, boring in on Jacques.

Divided Loyalties

"I had lunch with him once in Casablanca, with Mr. Murphy. Sometimes talking with the Germans yields information," said Jacques. "Anyway, I've been asked to keep in touch with anyone who might talk. Herr Auer talks. He has our interest."

Knox nodded. The conversation quickly veered back to gossip and chat. Marie watched as another couple, speaking good French to the waiter, came into the dining room and sat at a small corner table along the far wall. She had seen them speaking with Frau von Koler just as she and Jacques had entered the hotel. Who were they?

Frau von Koler and Auer

Elke von Koler returned from the ladies' room and walked across the dining room and sat down next to Auer. She leaned over and whispered in Auer's ear. His face perked up and turned serious. He looked across the dining room to where Hervé and Cosette had just taken seats. A momentary look of concern came over his face.

"What did you say, Elke?"

"They were at the Hotel Crillon in Paris in 1938. They're French security agents."

"At the Hotel Crillon?" said Auer in a dawning realization. "Security or counterespionage?"

"Counterespionage. She spent the night with a foreign-affairs aide from the chancellery. I don't know what the Frenchman was doing."

Auer looked long and carefully at the Frenchman. Yes, maybe, he thought. "Tell me what he said again?"

"I told him Berlin didn't care about the photos. That you were an open book to them."

"Yes, I understand that," said Auer.

"He said they understood."

"The French understood?" asked Auer, looking at Elke incredulously. "Then what was all that about?" he said half to himself, perplexity spread across his face.

Auer did not explain to Koler what "that" was. When told about the photos last month, he knew where they had come from

308

and that the French were involved. A bothersome concern. Plus the incident had had an unsettling cost, the loss of a good agent, a fact that he never shared with the other Germans. But the "why" behind these photos had eluded him—until now.

"He said they were closing the file, whatever that means," said Koler.

Auer looked at the ceiling. "Closing the file?"

"Yes. Closing the file."

Auer collected himself and looked across the room at the Frenchman and Frenchwoman, his eyes narrowing.

"What is this about, Theodor?" asked Koler. "Some sort of mystery?"

"Yes. A whodunit," said Auer. Again he looked up at the ceiling and mumbled, "Someone once tried to tell me it was the Corsicans."

"The Corsicans? What do they have to do with anything?"

"Nothing or everything," said Auer. He again looked up at the ceiling and mumbled, "I knew the Corsicans would have never have left the knife behind."

"The knife? What are you talking about, Theodor?" She gave him a concerned look.

"Nothing that you would understand," said Auer coming back to eye level and speaking to Elke dismissively. He looked again at the Frenchman. He knew in October when he heard about the photos being in Berlin that the French had been involved. Possibly they had used an Arab blackmail ring, and one of them took out Hans when he got too close. That would explain what happened—maybe. But not the why behind it. He'd never been convinced it was simple blackmail. Auer scratched his chin thoughtfully and collected his thoughts. "Maybe it was him," he mused.

"Him?" mumbled Koler, now quite puzzled.

Auer looked at Koler with a distracted air, his mind far away. "I have tried to understand who would have been so good as willing to risk the encounter. First I thought an Arab…"

"An Arab?" asked Koler, her confusing growing.

Auer looked back across the room at Hervé. "Now I understand."

"Understand what?"

Auer turned back to Koler and asked peremptorily, "You said, 'closing the file.'"

309

"Yes, that's what he said."

Looking up at the ceiling, Auer pondered, "Does that file ever close?" He would have to watch his back for a long time to come. He understood that now.

She looked at him with consternation and decided to say nothing. Must be some Gestapo thing, she thought. Those were good things to leave alone.

Marie and Jacques

Marie watched the conversation between Koler and Auer from across the room. She nudged Jacques and said, "Herr Auer seems to have understood something."

"Yes, so it appears," said Jacques. He idly wondered what.

Looking across the room at the French couple, she asked, "Do you know the Frenchman?"

Jacques turned slightly and recognized the profile of the man who he thought was the counterespionage agent. Interesting that he was so public with his presence tonight.

"Yes, he's some sort of French agent."

"And the lady?"

"I saw her once in Casablanca in a dining room when I had lunch with Murphy and Herr Auer on one of my visits; at that time Auer was head of the Armistice Commission in Morocco."

"What does it mean?"

"Maybe she was watching Auer. I thought she was spying on some French officers. The Frenchman was there, too."

"Spying? Why are they here tonight?"

"I don't know. Maybe they're sending a message to the Germans."

"Why?"

"Herr Auer is not all that he seems."

"You know that?"

"Yes."

"Are you going to share with me?"

"He's a spy...and other things."

Paul A. Myers

A Radio Bulletin

There was a bustle, and the maître d' came across the room and went up to a shelf where a large radio was placed. He turned on the device, and as it warmed up, he turned to the seated guests and said, "Messieurs, Mesdames, an important news broadcast." He turned back and fine-tuned the receiving dial and then turned up the volume. Through the sputtering and static soon blared a voice in French.

"This is Radio Algiers. An important bulletin. News reports from America say that Japanese planes attacked the American fleet at Pearl Harbor this morning. Heavy loss of life, many ships sunk."

"Pearl Harbor?" asked Marie. "What's that? A place?" She looked with darting eyes at Jacques.

"It's a big navy base in Hawaii," replied Jacques as he tried to take in the news, grasp its world-shattering significance.

"Near Tahiti...out in the Pacific Ocean?" asked Marie, consternation spreading across her face as she contemplated the big blue space on the far side of the globe.

"Yes."

"Why start a war there?" she asked.

"Good question," replied Jacques. "I always thought it would start in the Atlantic with the American navy going after the German U-boats."

"Yes, help the British," said Marie with dawning understanding. "I thought the Japanese were Germany's friends. Is this going to help Germany?"

"Probably not," said Jacques as he looked across the room at the hurried and worried conversations between the Germans. He could catch sounds of "Americans" and "Russians" scattered among the German conversations. This shock now on top of the bad news coming from Russia was rocking their confidence. Auer said something about a "two-front war" and scowled at the looming perpetual nightmare of German foreign-military policy.

Looking around the table, Jacques could see the American vice-consuls smile and clap one another on the back. "We're in it now," said Boyd.

Then the Americans would look across the room at the Germans triumphantly. "Their turn is coming," Knox said.

311

Joan Tuyl's eyes were as bright as headlights, her head bobbing with the excitement of it all.

Jacques silently thought that, yes, everything changes.

"Maybe we should go now," said Marie to Jacques behind a cupped palm.

"Good idea," said Jacques. He stood up, and Marie followed. He looked across the room to where Koler was looking at him with questioning eyes. The beautiful correspondent held up her hand and winkled her fingers at him like a child. He held up his hand and winkled his fingers back.

"What's that all about?" demanded Marie.

"Au revoir," said Jacques.

"Yes," said Marie, "it will never be the same again. Frau von Koler has always understood that."

He placed his arm behind Marie's back and escorted her across the room. He glanced at the burly Frenchman and the attractive French woman and flashed an impersonal smile. The Frenchwoman made an appraising glance at Marie and seemed suitably impressed.

Hervé and Cosette

Cosette watched Marie walk past with something akin to professional admiration and leaned over and whispered to Hervé, "I promise you something better tonight, *mon petit.*"

Hervé smiled; his new friendship with Cosette was blossoming beyond his hopes. Cosette looked across the room. "Herr Auer does not seem too concerned with us?"

"As Frau von Koler said, he's related to von Ribbentrop, the German foreign minister. Not easy to get to," said Hervé.

"I got to Ribbentrop once in Paris. Back when he was selling champagne."

Hervé laughed.

"Is that all that protects Auer?" asked Cosette. "Ribbentrop?"

"No. The Americans, too," said Hervé. He nodded in their direction. "They are coming. Probably by taking over North Africa first."

"Invade?"

"Probably not. They're hoping for an open-door invitation from the French military in North Africa."

"When?"

"No one knows. But that's Herr Auer's job. To give Berlin advance notice of when the Americans are coming. He's good. Berlin knows that."

"How?"

"Well, he put that French woman in the American's bed in Casablanca."

"Yes, he bumped my girl out," said Cosette with a certain professional admiration. "Are there others?"

"Probably. We'll find out over time."

"And the Frenchman—he is French—who just left?"

"He has an American diplomatic passport. The woman he's with tonight works for Admiral Fenard at the Winter Palace. She was close to Weygand."

"So he's spying on the French?"

"Sort of. Maybe a deeper game. The woman is married. Her husband is a French diplomat on the Armistice Commission in Wiesbaden, Germany."

"So the Americans are interested in how France is getting along with Germany?"

"Perhaps."

"You said he was also close to Frau von Koler."

"Frau von Koler's husband is in Berlin and is a high official in the foreign ministry. The American spent the night with her in September while we were taking family photos of Herr Auer."

"So another source deep inside Germany."

"Yes."

"So young to be playing such a sophisticated game," she said with a certain wonder in her voice.

"Yes. He spends a lot of time with the French military, supplies, and such, but maybe Berlin is his real interest."

Cosette and Hervé watched Jacques and Marie walk toward the cloakroom. Jacques handed a slip to the young woman behind the counter, who promptly returned with their overcoats, scarves, and hats. The couple put the overcoats on and headed toward the door. Behind them, guests scurried about in the lobby in a mad hatter's frenzy, all sensing that their world had been stood upside down by the news coming from half a world away.

Hervé and Cosette took final sips of their drinks and stood up. Hervé looked at Auer, caught his eye, and made a slight nod and turned. He and Cosette went to the cloakroom. "We'll be in Oran tomorrow," he said. "The *Ville de Oran* sails for Marseilles in the evening."

"Good, we'll be home the next day," said Cosette, a pleasant expectation in her voice.

John Knox and Joan Tuyl

"What does it mean, John?" asked Joan.

"It means we're in," said John. "We'll play this diplomatic game for a while, and then the rough stuff starts."

"You relish it, don't you?" she said.

"Yes, that's why we're here."

John Boyd broke in and shoved his left arm forward like pointing a rifle and with his right hand mimicked the motion of locking and loading a Springfield 1903 rifle.

"What are you?" asked Joan with some confusion, looking at the middle-aged Boyd.

"American Expeditionary Force in the last war," said Boyd with steely determination. "It'll be good to get back to the shooting."

She looked at the two men and took strength from their determination and their assurance. She looked at the Germans. She saw uncertainty in every face. The Russians? Now the Americans? Was a repeat of 1918 in their future?

Dinner Party

Far up a curving road bordered by Eucalyptus trees, past the other villas, was the entrance to another villa nestled back in the inky blackness, one small light at the front. Several limousines were parked in front under the trees, Murphy's big black Buick among them. Inside toward the rear was a brightly lit dining room. Le comte François de Rose sat at one end. At the other end was Bob Murphy. La comtesse de Polignanc was seated to Murphy's left and just across was la princesse de Marie de Ligne. A maid was serving coffee; a butler topping off snifters with cognac.

Murphy and the two ladies were exchanging reminisces about the gay social life of the café society in Paris before the war, the soirees and cocktail parties.

A telephone rang in another room, and the butler went to answer it. He came back shortly and whispered in le comte's ear.

"Really," said le comte, truly surprised. "A radio bulletin?" He got up and walked to the sideboard where a large radio sat. He turned it on and static crackled from the speaker. The guests stopped talking and watched. Le comte turned the dial, and a news announcer's voice filled the room. Le comte turned and faced his guests, saying nothing, but intently listening to the voice coming out of the wooden box.

"There has been an attack by Japanese aircraft on the American naval base at Pearl Harbor in Hawaii" came the words from the announcer. "Many ships have been lost, the loss of life heavy."

Then the bulletin began to repeat itself. Le comte turned the volume down and asked, "Bob, what does it mean?"

"Yes, Bob, please tell us. Hawaii is near Los Angeles, isn't it?" asked la princesse.

"Where did the airplanes come from?" asked la comtesse.

Murphy collected his thoughts. "Good questions, all."

"Is it war?" asked le comte.

"Yes, this brings America into the war. I didn't think it would start in the Pacific but rather with the Germans in the Atlantic." He looked at la princesse and explained the geography half a globe away. "Hawaii is way out in the Pacific Ocean halfway between Los Angeles and Japan." He turned to la comtesse and said, "Most likely the airplanes came from aircraft carriers."

"Will Germany come in?" asked le comte.

"That is an excellent question. Germany is pledged to come to Japan's aid under the Tri-Partite Pact. So most likely yes."

"What does that mean for us in North Africa?" asked le comte.

"I can't say for sure or speak for my government," said Murphy.

"But you could give us some guesses, Bob?" said la comtesse. "This is not a time to be shy."

"The US would have a strong interest in maintaining the neutrality of French Africa."

"For how long?" asked the comte.

Murphy made a grin. "Until Washington is ready to move."

"Where will they move first?"

"A lot of talk about building up on Great Britain and attacking across the Channel."

"Yes," said le comte thoughtfully. "But going to North Africa first and then attacking through the South of France or Italy would make more sense." He sensed the hidden strategy.

"There are people in Washington who understand that," said Murphy with a grin.

The dinner guests continued with involved discussion late into the evening.

Dawn

In the darkness the following morning, a gray twilight peeked around the edges of the heavy drapes in Jacques's bedroom. He awoke with Marie running her fingers over his chest and kissing him on the shoulder; she was as wide awake as a vixen on the prowl.

"You carried me away," she murmured. "Then you were fun."

"Your enthusiasm is contagious," he said. But not unexpected, he thought; he had sensed the Latin fire smoldering for months.

"Not like a wedding night. Everything nervous, new, unexpected—and love so uncertain."

"Love adds pleasure."

"New love...I understand the frisson..."

"Of a new lover..."

"I don't think I want to make new lovers a habit," she said uncertainly, her self-satisfaction with Jacques nevertheless evident. He was deeply pleased.

"Yes, you want to make a life...a real life is made with a partner...not frisson," she added in revelatory tone.

She got out of bed and pulled a big robe off the chair and put it on against the cold chill in the room. She opened the drapes and watched the first rays of the sunrise hit the waters beyond the harbor. She gazed at the sight. "So the war begins for the Americans?" she asked.

"Yes."

"Will you have to leave Algiers?"

"I don't think so. At least not soon. I have work here."

"And what of the French in Africa? We can't fight. We have nothing to fight with. You know that."

"Yes. That's why the Americans want to keep the French out of the war for now."

"Is that why they don't support de Gaulle?"

"Mostly. They also don't trust him."

"And us—you and I?"

"We can be together where we can. In each other's hearts when we can't."

"And the war?"

"It has to start before it can end."

"Yes, I see that now."

"Remember," said Jacques.

"What?"

"You're the right one. Now come back to bed."

"Yes. The right one," she said, her voice filled with the assurance of newly discovered love.

END

Afterword

French counterespionage (from *The Hunt for Nazi Spies* by Simon Kitson). An excerpt:

Paul Paillole, the head of *Travaux Ruraux* (rural works, or TR) is probably the best known figure of wartime French counterespionage…The service's headquarters were located in Marseille and known under the codename Cambronne. (pp 44-45)

Henri Navarre of the Deuxième Bureau in Algiers has written about this sort of incident in his memoirs. He described the case of an active member of the German commission with a penchant for young Arab boys. To blackmail him into cooling his spying zeal, the secret services recruited a young Arab and took compromising photographs.

The target of one such maneuver was Theodor Auer, leader of the Gestapo in Morocco and thorn in the side of counterespionage services. Born in 1899 in Cologne, Germany, Auer studied law before becoming a diplomat. In October of 1940, he was sent to Morocco to head the German economic office. In reality he was a spy, whose efficiency deeply irritated the French authorities. In April of 1941, the BMS in Morocco expressed the wish to use Auer's homosexuality against him: "In Algiers, 'Teddy' Auer met one of his old friends, Franz Duschnitz, an Austrian Jew, a former member of the French foreign legion and a notorious homosexual. Auer boasted to his 'friend' that he was the head of the Gestapo in Morocco and could obtain transit and residence permits for him thanks to his influence with the local police in Morocco." (p.113)

Theodor Auer (from *Diplomat Among Warriors* by Robert Murphy). An excerpt:

When I arrived in Casablanca early in January, I was dismayed an hour after arrival to receive a telephone call from a German career diplomat, Theodor Auer, whom I had known before the war when he was counselor of the German Embassy in Paris. He wanted to see me urgently, but I did not reciprocate this desire. I had rather liked Auer in Paris, but I did not want him poking into my affairs. However, the French authorities said it might be useful to meet Auer because, since his recent appointment as consul general in Casablanca, it was rumored that he was forerunner of a German group which was to replace the Italians who had been allowed to staff the Armistice Commission in Morocco, to see that the armistice terms were being observed. When we did get together for a drink at my hotel, I regretted that I had not seen Auer sooner and oftener because he proved as eager to talk as General von Studnitz had been during his first day in Paris... (p 78)

[Later} Auer barely escaped a trap we had set to capture him, and it might have fared better for him if he had not. He and his group failed to give Berlin any warning of the Allied troop landings in November 1942 and such gross incompetence was not lightly forgiven by the Auswaertiges Amt [foreign ministry]. He was cashiered by Ribbentrop and captured by the Russians in Berlin. I respected him as an intelligent diplomat. (p. 79)

Robert Murphy held ambassadorial rank in numerous assignments over the remainder of his diplomatic career, retiring in 1959 as Undersecretary of State, the foreign service's highest career post.

Joan Tuyl (from *How Long Till Dawn* by Joan Fry Knox). An excerpt:

"I shall never forget the evening after the American Consulate had news of Pearl Harbor. We all agreed that it had only been a question of time before America came into the war, but there is no doubt the tension had been nerve-wracking. When the whole staff had got through discussing everything at Felix Cole's villa in voices that could be heard far and wide, they picked me up on their way down to dinner at the Aletti.

"Sixteen excited and bellicose Americans and I were given a large corner table next to the German Commission. We drank to America's entry into the war, and to the confusion of our enemies.

The enemies looked a little uncomfortable here, having a well-founded fear that if they did get embroiled in a public scrap, their punishment would be an assignment of duty on the Russian Front. We became more and more riotous, sending back the measly portions served to us and demanding as big or bigger portions than those being served to the Germans beside us…Incidents would certainly have occurred, had not the Germans packed up and left us in possession of the "field" of the dining room. (p. 67)"

Note: John Knox and Joan Tuyl were married in Algiers on April 28, 1943. Knox was then an American lieutenant colonel serving on the staff rearming the French army in North Africa. (p. 170) Joan's first husband Gerry Tuyl had been arrested on March 18, 1942 in Holland and was eventually executed in a mass shooting on July 20, 1943.

Rearming the *Armée d'Afrique*

The Americans rearmed 11 French divisions, consisting of two Free French divisions and nine from the Army of Africa. In late 1943, two Army of Africa divisions (the 2nd Moroccan Infantry and the 3rd Algerian Infantry) were sent to Italy as a French corps under General Alphonse Juin. This was followed by two more Army of Africa divisions and the 1st Free French division. The French corps established itself as the premier infantry combat force in Italy primarily due to their mountain fighting prowess and exceptional tenacity in combat (even better than the Germans). The Army of Africa divisions typically comprised two-thirds Magrebi soldiers (Muslim) and one-third European.

Later, the other Free French division, the 2nd Armored under General Philippe Leclerc, was sent to England from Morocco to participate in the Normandy invasion, the liberation of Paris, and eternal fame.

The French divisions were withdrawn from Italy in July 1944 and were combined with additional French divisions completing training in North Africa into the First French Army. This army landed on the south coast of France on August 15, 1944 under the command of French General Jean de Lattre de

Tassigny. The French force eventually totaled 10 divisions and fought side-by-side with the US Seventh Army under the overall command of the US Sixth Army Group commanded by General Jacob Devers. The Sixth Army Group spearheaded the Riviera to Rhine campaign and put the first Allied troops on the Rhine River with both the US Seventh Army and the French First Army arriving on the river between November 13 and 23, 1944, a little over three months after having landed on the Mediterranean coast. This was one of the most successful Allied land campaigns anywhere in the Mediterranean or European theaters during World War II. On the March 1945 War Department promotion list, Devers was promoted the senior four-star general in the European Theater second only to five-star General of the Army Dwight D. Eisenhower and ahead of such other well-known generals as Carl Spaatz and Omar Bradley.

Franklin D. Roosevelt

Roosevelt was the strategic mastermind and forceful champion behind what became known as Operation Torch, the combined British and American invasion of North Africa in November 1942 only eleven months after Pearl Harbor. Roosevelt kept the strategic leadership of not only the American military but the entire western Allied alliance firmly in his hands for the rest of the war. Roosevelt set the strategy of starting with an indirect attack in North Africa followed with a direct attack from Britain at Normandy in 1944. Winston Churchill actively worked at undermining both strategic approaches from 1943 onwards with ill-considered schemes which Roosevelt tactfully but firmly turned away. British historian Nigel Hamilton's first two volumes of a planned trilogy on Roosevelt's war-time global leadership provide riveting reading and make clear that Roosevelt stood alone on the summit of world leadership in the 1940s as the sole architect of the world-wide, war-winning strategy.

Selected Sources

Atkinson, Rick. *An Army at Dawn: The War in North Africa, 1942-43*. New York. Holt, 2007.

Clayton, Anthony. *General Maxime Weygand, 1867-1965: Fortune and Misfortune*. New York. Indiana University Press, 2015.

Cook, Don. *Charles de Gaulle: A Biography*. New York. Perigee Books, 1983.

Crawley, Aidan. *De Gaulle*. New York. HarperCollins Distribution Services, 1969.

de Gaulle, Charles. *War Memoirs: The Call to Honor*. New York. Viking. 1955.

Fenby, Jonathan. *The General: Charles De Gaulle and the France He Saved*. New York. Skyhorse Publishing.

Gosset, Renée. *Conspiracy in Algiers 1943-43: The inside story of the intrigues that paved the way for the American landings in North Africa*. New York. The Nation, 1945.

Hamilton, Nigel. *The Mantle of Command: FDR at War, 1941-1942*. New York. Mariner Books, 2014.

Hastings, Max. *The Secret War: Spies, Ciphers, and Guerrillas, 1939-45*. New York. Harper, 2016.

Hoisington, Jr, William A. *The Assassination of Jacques Lemaigre Dubreuil*. New York. Routledge, 2005.

Horne, Alistair. *To Lose a Battle: France 1940*. New York. Penguin, 2007.

Kitson, Simon. *The Hunt for Nazi Spies: Fighting Espionage in Vichy France*. Chicago and London, The University of Chicago Press, 2008.

Knox, Daphne Joan Fry (Tuyl). *How Long Till Dawn: Memoirs of one of the Charter Members and Original Founders of the Resistance Movement in Algiers and a Member of OSS during World War II*. Outskirts Press, Denver, 2014.

Monnet, Jean. *Memoirs*. New York. Third Millennium, 2015.

Murphy, Robert. *Diplomat Among Warriors*. New York. Doubleday & Company, Inc. 1964.

Paxton, Robert O. *Vichy France: Old Guard and New Order 1940-1944*. New York. Columbia University Press, 1972, 2001.

Schiff, Stacy. *Saint-Exupery: A Biography*. New York. Knopf, 2011.

Spears, Sir Edward. *Assignment to Catastrophe: Volume II, The Fall of France June 1940*. London. William Heinemann Ltd, 1954.

Vaughan, Hal. *FDR's 12 Apostles: The Spies Who Paved the Way for the Invasion of North Africa*. New York. Lyons Press, 2006.

Wells, Sherrill Brown. *Jean Monnet: Unconventional Statesman*. London. Lynne Rienner Publishers, 2011.

New York Times archives, 1939-42. Numerous news articles.

CreateSpace—Copy edit. Excellent service.

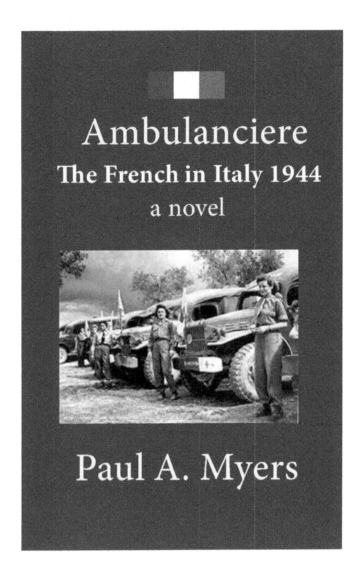

Ambulanciere
The French in Italy 1944
a novel

Paul A. Myers

Madeleine Sauveterre enlists in the French *Armée d'Afrique* in
early 1943 to drive ambulances. After hard training—"your
ambulance is your rifle"—she is promoted and leads a section of

ambulances in the big push against the Germans and Italians in Tunisia as part of the Allied victory in May 1943.

After Tunisia, she is assigned to the 3rd Algerian Infantry division, and a new romance with an infantry officer in a rifle regiment blooms. The 3rd Algerians are deployed to Italy in December 1943. Arduous duty follows as the Algerians make a heartbreaking but victorious assault on the strategic high ground of Belvedere north of Cassino. In the spring, leaving winter mud behind, Mado, now promoted lieutenant, leads the ambulances of the first medical evacuation company through the Liri Valley behind the leading infantry regiments of the 3rd Algerians as the French clear the high ground southeast of Rome in May 1944. She celebrates the liberation of Rome with newfound friends.

The French chase the Germans north, taking Sienna. The French army celebrates Bastille Day in Sienna with a big parade and celebrations, a fitting capstone before moving south and redeploying for the invasion of the South of France in August 1944.

The novel will be released in 2019.

Made in the USA
Las Vegas, NV
08 February 2021